A Jay of Italy

by

Bernard Capes

Double 9
BOOKS

A Jay of Italy
by Bernard Capes

Copyright © 2024

All Rights reserved.

ISBN: 978-93-62209-50-4

Published by

DOUBLE 9 BOOKS
2/13-B, Ansari Road
Daryaganj, New Delhi – 110002
info@double9books.com
www.double9books.com
Tel. 011-40042856

ABOUT THE AUTHOR

Bernard Capes an English novelist and journalist, is most known for his contributions to the subgenres of mystery, horror, and historical fiction. He began his writing career as a journalist and went on to compose plays, short stories, and novels. Capes was known for his ability to compose dramatic and frightening stories, as well as his flowing writing style. His literature frequently mixed historical settings with mystery, horror, and supernatural elements. Capes was an expert at evoking a sense of time and place in his writing, with a keen eye for detail. Although Capes worked in a number of genres, he is best known for his contributions to supernatural literature. His short stories had a devoted readership and were frequently published in the time's major publications. His writing was praised for its innovative subjects, well-developed characters, and ability to create a haunting, tense atmosphere. Bernard Capes' unique blend of mystery, horror, and historical fiction had a huge impact on the literary world, despite the fact that he was not as well-known as some of his contemporaries. Fans of the genre continue to praise his work, which proves his ability to tell intriguing and scary stories that leave an impression on readers.

CONTENTS

CHAPTER I

On a hot morning, in the year 1476 of poignant memory, there drew up before an osteria on the Milan road a fair cavalcade of travellers. These were Messer Carlo Lanti and his inamorata, together with a suite of tentmen, pages, falconers, bed-carriers, and other personnel of a migratory lord on his way from the cooling hills to the Indian summer of the plains. The chief of the little party, halting in advance of his fellows, lifted his plumed scarlet biretta with one strong young hand, and with the other, his reins hanging loose, ran a cluster of swarthy fingers through his black hair.

'O little host!' he boomed, blaspheming—for all good Catholics, conscious of their exclusive caste, swore by God prescriptively—'O little host, by the thirst of Christ's passion, wine!'

'He will bring you hyssop—by the token, he will,' murmured the lady, who sat her white palfrey languidly beside him. She was a slumberous, ivory-faced creature warm and insolent and lazy; and the little bells of her bridle tinkled sleepily, as her horse pawed, gently rocking her.

The cavalier grunted ferociously. 'Let me see him!' and, bonneting himself again, sat with right arm akimbo, glaring for a response to his cry. He looked on first acquaintance a bully and profligate—which he was; but, for his times, with some redeeming features. His thigh, in its close violet hose, and the long blade which hung at it seemed somehow in a common accord of steel and muscle. His jaw was underhung, his brows were very thick and black, but the eyes beneath were good-humored, and he had a great dimple in his cheek.

A murmur of voices came from the inn, but no answer whatever to the demand. The building, glaring white as a rock rolled into the plains from the great mountains to the north, had a little bush of juniper thrust out on a staff above its door. It looked like a dry tongue protruded in derision, and awoke the demon in Messer Lanti. He turned to a Page:—'Ercole!' he roared, pointing; 'set a light there, and give these hinds a lesson!'

The lady laughed, and, stirring a little, watched the page curiously. But the boy had scarcely reached the ground when the landlord appeared bowing at the door. The cavalier fumed.

'Ciacco—hog!' he thundered: 'did you not hear us call?'

'Illustrious, no.'

'Where were your ears? Nailed to the pillory?'

'Nay, Magnificent, but to the utterances of the little Parablist of San Zeno.'

'O hog! now by the Mass, I say, they had been better pricked to thy business. O ciacco, I tell thee thy Parablist was like, in another moment, to have addressed thee out of a burning bush. What! I would drink, swine! And, harkee, somewhere from those deep vats of thine the perfume of an old wine of Cana rises to my nostrils. I say no more. Despatch!'

The landlord, abasing himself outwardly, took solace of a private curse as he turned into the shadow of his porch—

'These skipjacks of the Sforzas! limbs of a country churl!'

Something lithe and gripping sprang upon his back as he muttered, making him roar out; and the chirrup of a great cricket shrilled in his ear—

'Biting limbs! clawing, hooking, scoring limbs! ha-ha, hee-hee, ho-bir-r-r-r!'

Boniface, sweating with panic, wriggled to shake off his incubus. It clung to him toe and claw. Slewing his gross head, he saw, squatted upon his shoulders, a manikin in green livery, a monstrous grasshopper in seeming.

'Messer Fool,' he gurgled—'dear my lord's most honoured jester!' (he was essaying all the time to stagger with his burden out of earshot)—'prithee spare to damn a poor fellow for a hasty word under provocation! Prithee, sweet Messer Fool!'

The little creature, sitting him as a frog a pike, hooked its small talons into the corners of his eyes.

'Provocation!' it laughed, rocking—'provocation by his grandness to a guts! If I fail to baste thee on a spit for it, call me not Cicada!'

'Mercy!' implored the landlord, staggering and groping.

'Nothing for nothing. At what price, tunbelly?'

The landlord clutched in his blindness at the post of a descending stair.

'The best in my house.'

'What best, paunch?'

'Milan cheese—boiled bacon. Ah, dear Messer Cicada, there is a fat cold capon, for which I will go fasting to thee.'

'And what wine, beast?'

'What thou wilt, indeed.'

The jester spurred him with a vicious heel.

'Away, then! Sink, submerge, titubate, and evanish into thy crystal vaults!'

'Alas, I cannot see!'

The rider shifted his clutch to the fat jowls of his victim, who thereupon, with a groan, descended a rude flight of steps at a run, and brought up with his burden in a cool grotto. Here were casks and stoppered jars innumerable; shelves of deep blue flasks; lolling amphoræ, and festoons of cobwebs drunk with must. Cicada leapt with one spring to a barrel, on which he squatted, rather now like a green frog than a grasshopper. His face, lean and leathery, looked as if dipped in a tan-pit; his eyes were as aspish as his tongue; he was a stunted, grotesque little creature, all vice and whipcord.

'Despatch!' he shrilled. 'Thy wit is less a desert than my throat.'

'Anon!' mumbled the landlord, and hurried for a flask. 'Let thy tongue roll on that,' he said, 'and call me grateful. As to the capon, prithee, for my bones' sake, let me serve thy masters first.'

The jester had already the flask at his mouth. The wine sank into him as into hot sand.

'Go,' he said, stopping a moment, and bubbling—'go, and damn thy capon; I ask no grosser aliment than this.'

The landlord, bustling in a restored confidence, filled a great bottle from a remote jar, and armed with it and some vessels of twisted glass, mounted to daylight once more. Messer Lanti, scowling in the sun, cursed him for a laggard.

'Magnificent!' pleaded the man, 'the sweetest wine, like the sweetest meat, is near the bone.'

'Deep in the ribs of the cellars, meanest, O, ciacco?'

He took a long draught, and turned to his lady.

'Trust the rogue, Beatrice; it is, indeed, near the marrow of deliciousness.'

She sipped of her glass delicately, and nodded. The cavalier held out his for more.

'Malvasia, hog?'

'Malvasia, most honoured; trod out by the white feet of prettiest contadina, and much favoured, by the token, of the Abbot of San Zeno yonder.'

Messer Lanti looked up with a new good-humour. The party was halted in a great flat basin among hills, on one of the lowest of which, remote and austere, sparkled the high, white towers of a monastery.

'There,' he said, signifying the spot to his companion with a grin; 'hast heard of Giuseppe della Grande, Beatrice, the *father* of his people?'

'And not least of our own little Parablist, Madonna,' put in the landlord, with a salutation.

'Plague, man!' cried Lanti; 'who the devil is this Parablist you keep throwing at us?'

'They call him Bernardo Bembo, my lord. He was dropped and bred among the monks—some by-blow of a star, they say, in the year of the great fall. He was found at the feet of Mary's statue; and, certes, he is gifted like an angel. He mouths parables as it were prick-songs, and is esteemed among all for a saint.'

'A fair saint, i'faith, to be carousing in a tavern.'

'O my lord! he but lies here an hour from the sun, on his way, this very morning, to Milan, whither he vouches he has had a call. And for his carousing, spring water is it all, and the saints to pay, as I know to my cost.'

'He should have stopped at the rill, methinks.'

'He will stop at nothing,' protested the landlord humbly; 'nay, not even the rebuking by his parables of our most illustrious lord, the Duke Galeazzo himself.'

Lanti guffawed.

'Thou talkest treason, dog. What is to rebuke there?'

'What indeed, Magnificent? Set a saint, *I* say, to catch a saint.'

The other laughed louder.

'The right sort of saint for that, I trow, from Giuseppe's loins.'

'Nay, good my lord, the Lord Abbot himself is no less a saint.'

'What!' roared Lanti, 'saints all around! This is the right hagiolatry, where I need never despair of a niche for myself. I too am the son of my father, dear Messer Ciacco, as this Parablist is, I'll protest, of your Abbot, whose piety is an old story. What! you don't recognise a family likeness?'

The landlord abased himself between deference and roguery.

'It is not for me to say, Magnificent. I am no expert to prove the common authorship of this picture and the other.'

He lowered his eyes with a demure leer. Honest Lanti, bending to rally him, chuckled loudly, and then, rising, brought his whip with a boisterous smack across his shoulders. The landlord jumped and winced.

'Spoken like a discreet son of the Church!' cried the cavalier.

He breathed out his chest, drained his glass, still laughing into it, and, handing it down, settled himself in his saddle.

'And so,' he said, 'this saintly whelp of a saint is on his way to rebuke the lord of Sforza?'

'With deference, my lord, like a younger Nathan. So he hath been miscalled—I speak nothing from myself. The young man hath lived all his days among visions and voices; and at the last, it seems, they've spelled him out Galeazzo—though what the devil the need is there? as your Magnificence says. But perhaps they made a mistake in the spelling. The blessed Fathers themselves teach us that the best holiness lacks education.'

Madonna laughed out a little. 'This is a very good fool!' she murmured, and yawned.

'I don't know about that,' said Lanti, answering the landlord, and wagging his sage head. 'I'm not the most pious of men myself. But tell us, sirrah, how travels his innocence?'

'On foot, my lord, like a prophet's.'

'"Twill the sooner lie prone.' He turned to my lady. 'Wouldst like to add him to Cicada and thy monkey, and carry him along with us?'

'Nay,' she said pettishly, 'I have enough of monstrosities. Will you keep me in the sun all day?'

'Well,' said Lanti, gathering his reins, 'it puzzles me only how the Abbot could part thus with his discretion.'

'Nay, Illustrious,' answered the landlord, 'he was in a grievous pet, 'tis stated. But, there! prophecy will no more be denied than love. A' must out or kill. And so he had to let Messer Bembo go his gaits with a letter only to this monastery and that, in providence of a sanctuary, and one even, 'tis whispered, to the good Duchess Bona herself. But here, by the token, he comes.'

He bowed deferentially, backing apart. Messer Lanti stared, and gave a profound whistle.

'O, indeed!' he muttered, showing his strong teeth, 'this Giuseppe propagates the faith very prettily!'

Madam Beatrice was staring too. She expressed no further impatience to be gone for the moment. A young man, followed by some kitchen company adoring and obsequious, had come out by the door, and stood regarding her quietly. She had expected some apparition of austerity, some lean, neurotic friar, wasting between dogmatism and sensuality. And instead she saw an angel of the breed that wrestled with Jacob.

He was so much a child in appearance, with such an aspect of wonder and prettiness, that the first motion of her heart towards him was like the leap of motherhood. Then she laughed, with a little dye come to her cheek, and eyed him over the screen of feathers she held in her hand.

He advanced into the sunlight.

'Greeting, sweet Madonna,' he said, in his grave young voice, 'and fair as your face be your way!' and he was offering to pass her.

She could only stare, the bold jade, at a loss for an answer. The soft umber eyes of the youth looked into hers. They were round and velvety as a rabbit's, with high, clean-pencilled brows over. His nose was short and pretty broad at the bridge, and his mouth was a little mouth, pouting as a child's, something combative, and with lips like tinted wax. Like a girl's his jaw was round and beardless, and his hair a golden fleece, cut square at the neck, and its ends brittle as if they had been singed in fire. His doublet and hose were of palest pink; his bonnet, shoes, and mantlet of cypress-green velvet. Rose-coloured ribbons, knotted into silver buckles, adorned his feet; and over his shoulder, pendent from a strand of the same hue, was slung a fair lute. He could not have passed, by his looks, his sixteenth summer.

Lanti pushed rudely forward.

'A moment, saint troubadour, a moment!' he cried. 'It will please us, hearing of your mission, to have a taste of your quality.'

The youth, looking at him a little, swung his lute forward and smiled.

'What would you have, gracious sir?' he said.

'What? Why, prophesy us our case in parable.'

'I know not your name nor calling.'

'A pretty prophet, forsooth. But I will enlighten thee. I am Carlo Lanti, gentleman of the Duke, and this fair lady the wife of him we call the Count of Casa Caprona.'

The boy frowned a little, then nodded and touched the strings. And all in a moment he was improvising the strangest ditty, a sort of cantefable between prose and song:—

'A lord of little else possessed a jewel,
Of his small state incomparably the crown.
But he, going on a journey once,
To his wife committed it, saying,
"This trust with you I pledge till my return;
See, by your love, that I redeem my trust."
But she, when he was gone, thinking "he will not know,"
Procured its exact fellow in green glass,
And sold her lord's gem to one who bid her fair;
Then, conscience-haunted, wasted all those gains
Secretly, without enjoyment, lest he should hear and wonder.
But he returning, she gave him the bauble,
And, deceived, he commended her; and, shortly after, dying,
Left her that precious jewel for all dower,
Bequeathing elsewhere the residue of his estate.
Now, was not this lady very well served,
Inheriting the whole value, as she had appraised it,
Of her lord's dearest possession?
Gentles, Dishonour is a poor estate.'

Half-chaunting, half-talking, to an accompaniment of soft-touched chords, he ended with a little shrug of abandonment, and dropped the lute from his fingers. His voice had been small and low, but pure; the sweet thrum of the strings had lifted it to rhapsody. Messer Lanti scratched his head.

'Well, if that is a parable!' he puzzled. 'But supposing it aims at our case, why—Casa Caprona is neither poor nor dead; and as to a jewel——'

He looked at Madam Beatrice, who was frowning and biting her lip.

'Why heed the peevish stuff?' she said. 'Will you come? I am sick to be moving.'

Carlo was suddenly illuminated.

'O, to be sure, of course!' he ejaculated—'the jewel——'

'Hold your tongue!' cried the lady sharply.

The honest blockhead went into a roar of laughter.

'He has touched thee, he has touched thee! And these are his means to convert the Duke! By Saint Ambrose, 'twill be a game to watch! I swear he shall go with us.'

'Not with my consent,' cried madam.

Carlo, chuckling tormentingly, looked at her, then doffed his cap mockingly to the boy.

'Sweet Messer Bembo,' he said, 'I take your lesson much to heart, and pray you gratefully—as we are both for Milan, I understand—to give us the honour of your company thither. I am in good standing with the Duke, I say, and you would lose nothing by having a friend at court. Those half-boots'—he glanced at the pretty pumps—'could as ill afford the penalties of the road as your innocence its dangers.'

'I have no more fear than my divine Master,' said the boy boldly, 'in carrying His gospel of love.'

'Well for you,' said Carlo, with a grin of approval for his spirit; 'but a gospel that goes in silken doublet and lovelocks is like to be struck dumb before it is uttered.'

'As to my condition, sir,' said the boy, 'I dress as for a feast, our Master having prepared the board. Are we not redeemed and invited? We walk in joy since the Resurrection, and Limbo is emptied of its gloom. The kingdom of man shall be love, and the government thereof. Preach heresy in rags. 'Twas the Lord Abbot equipped me thus, my own stout heart prevailing. "Well, they will encounter an angel walking by the road," quoth he, "and, if they doubt, show 'em thy white shoulder-knobs, little Bernardino, and they will see the wings sprouting underneath like the teeth in a baby's gums."'

He was evidently, if sage or lunatic, an amazing child. The rough libertine was quite captivated by him.

'Well, you will come with us, Bernardino?' said he; 'for with a cracked skull it might go hard with you to prove your shoulder-blades.'

'I will come, lord, to reap the harvest where I have sowed the grain.'

He looked with a serene severity at the countess.

'Shalt take thee pillion, Beatrice,' shouted Lanti. 'Up, pretty troubadour, and recount her more parables by the way.'

'May I die but he shall not,' cried the girl.

'He shall, I say.'

'I will bite, and rake him with my nails.'

'The more fool you, to spoil a saint! Reproofs come not often in such a guise as this. Up, Bernardino, and parable her into submission!'

She made a show of resisting, in the midst of which Bembo won to his place deftly on the fore-saddle. At the moment of his success, the fool Cicada sprang from the tavern door, and, lurching with wild, glazed eyes, leapt, hooting, upon the crupper of the beast, almost bringing it upon its haunches. With an oath Lanti brought down his whip with such fury that the fool rolled in the dust.

'Drunken dog!' he roared, and would have ridden over the writhing body, had not Bembo backed the white palfrey to prevent him.

'Thou strik'st the livery, not the man!' he cried. 'Hast never thyself been drunk, and without the excuse of this poor fool to make a trade of folly?'

Messer Lanti glared, then in a moment laughed. The battered grasshopper took advantage of the diversion to rise and slink to the rear. The next moment the whole cavalcade was in motion.

CHAPTER II

They travelled on till sundown through the green plains; and, for one good hour dating from their start, not a word would Madam Beatrice utter. Then she gave out—Messer Carlo being a distance in advance—but with no grace at all.

'You are an ill horseman, Saint. I am near jogged from my seat.'

'Put thine arms about me.'

'Nay, I am not holy enough.'

She was silent again, for five minutes.

'Your lute bangs my nose.'

He shifted it. She held her peace during two minutes.

'Who taught you to play it, Saint?'

'It was one of the fathers. What would it profit you to know which?'

'Nothing at all. I trow he was a good master to that and your gospel.'

'My gospel?'

'Ay, of love. He has made you worldly-wise for a saint. Hast ever before been beyond thy walls?'

'Of course.'

'And studied this and that? Experience, methinks is the right nurse for such a creed. What made you accuse me of dishonour?'

'I did not.'

'Nay, is that to be a saint?'

'Whom the shoe fits, let her wear it.'

'Bernardo! *Where got you the shoe?*'

'Does it fit, I say?'

'I fear me 'twas in some bagnio.'

'Where you had dropped it? For shame!'

A rather long pause.

'I will not be angry—just yet. Where got you the shoe, I say? An eavesdropper is well equipped for a prophet.'

'I am no eavesdropper.'

'Who enlightened you?'

'Your cicisbeo.'

'Under that title?'

'Nay; it is not the devil's policy to call himself devil.'

A shorter pause.

'But you had heard of me?'

'Nothing escapes the Church's hearing. Besides, Messer Lanti's summer lodge is within call, one may say of San Zeno.'

'You are daring. Dost know in what high favour he stands with the Duke?'

'Else how could he have compassed Uriah's dismissal to the wars?'

Silence, and then a sigh.

'Whom do you mean by Uriah?'

'Thy lord, the Count of Casa Caprona.'

'He is a soldier, and an old man.'

'Didst covenant with his age in thy marriage vows?'

'Bernardino, I am very sleepy.'

'Sleep, then, and forget thyself, and awake, another.'

She sighed, and put her arms softly about him and her cheek against his shoulder. Messer Lanti, falling back, saw her thus, with closed eyes; and laughed, and then frowned, and cried boisterously—

'Hast converted her, Parablist? Art a saint indeed?'

He spurred forward again, with a discontented look, and madam opened her eyes.

'What gossips are thine old monks, Bernardino; and what hypocrites, denouncing the licence they example!'

'I know not what you mean.'

'Are they all saints, then, in San Zeno?'

'That is for Rome to say. It is a good law which lays down this wine of sanctity to mature. In a hundred years we shall know what stood the test.'

'Ah me! And I am but seventeen. Will you speak for your Abbot?'

'Ay, like a dear son.'

'Is he your father, Bernardo?'

'Is he not the father of us all?'

'Maybe. But 'tis of Benjamin I ask. Now, he is a strange father, methinks, to bid his Benjamin, thus apparelled, on a wild goose chase.'

'He could not discount the voices.'

'What voices?'

The boy lifted his face and eyes to the heavens, and lowered them again with no answer but a sigh of rapture.

'So? And did the voices bid thee wear a velvet mantlet and roses to thy shoes?' whispered the girl, with a tiny chuckle.

'They said, "Not in cockle shells, but a plume, goes the Pilgrim of Love,"' answered Bembo. 'As I am and have been, God finds me fitting in His sight.'

'And the Father Abbot, I wot?'

'Yes: "Since," says he, "Christ bequeathed His Kingdom to beauty."'

'And you have inherited it? I think I will be your subject, Bernardo.'

'I hope so, Madonna.'

He spoke perfectly gravely, and made her a little courtly gesture backwards.

'Well,' said she, 'had *I* been Father Abbot, I had put this pet of my fancy in a cage.'

'You know not of what you speak,' he answered seriously. 'God works great ends with little instruments. The puny bee is yet the very fairy midwife of the forests, I should have broke my heart had he denied me.'

'It would have saved others, alack!'

'What do you mean?'

'Nothing at all. Will you sing me another parable, Bernardo?'

'Ay, Madonna; and on what subject? The woman taken in adultery?'

'If you like; and whom Christ forgave.'

'*And He said: "Go, and sin no more"*'

She began to weep softly.

'It is shocking to be so abused for a little thing. I would you were back with your monks.'

He sighed.

'Ah!' she murmured, still weeping, 'that this bee had been content to remain a pander to his flowers! To dup hell's door with a reed! You know not to what you have engaged yourself, my poor boy.'

'To Christ, His service of Love,' he said simply.

'Go back, go back!' she cried in pain. 'There are ten thousand sophisters to interpret that word according to their lusts. Convert Galeazzo? Convert the brimstone lake from burning! Dost know the manner of man he is?'

'Else why am I here?'

'Ay, but his moods, his passions, his nameless, shameless deeds? He hath no pity but for his desires; no mercy but through his caprices. To cross him is to taste the rack, the fire, the living burial. He is possessed. Some believe him Caligula reincarnate—an atavism of that dreadful stock. And dost think to quench that furnace with a parable? Unless, indeed—Go back, little Bembo, and waste thy passion for reform on thy monks.'

'Madonna,' he said, 'I obey the voices. I shall not be let to perish, since Christ died to save His world to loveliness.'

It was the early rapture of the renaissance, penetrating like an April song into these newly reclaimed lands. The wind blew from Florence, and all the peaceful vales, so long trodden into a bloody mire, were awakening to the ecstasy of the *Promise*. That men interpreted according to their lights—lights burning fast and passionate in most places, but in a few quiet and holy. The breed of German bandits, of foreign mercenaries, was swept away. Gone was the whole warring race of the Visconti, and in its place the peasant Sforza had set a guard about the land of his fierce adoption, that he might till and graft and prosper in peace. Italy had asserted itself the inheritance of its children, the Court of God's Vicegerent, the chosen land of Love's gospel. That, too, men interpreted according to their lights. 'We are all the vineyard of Rome,' said the little Parablist. Alas! he thought Rome the Holy of Holies, and his father a saint. But his father, who adored him, had committed him, with his blessing, to this mad romance! Such were the paradoxes of the Gospel of Love.

Beatrice spoke no more, and they rode on in silence. About evening they came into a pleasant dell, where there was a level sward among rocks; and a little stream, running down a stairway of stones, dropped laughing, like a child going to bed, into the quiet of a rushy pool. Great chestnuts clothed the slopes, and made a mantle, powdered with stars, to the setting sun. It was a very nest for love.

Messer Lanti, halting, commanded the green tents to be pitched on the grass. Then, with a stormy scowl and a mockery of courtesy, he came to dismount his lady.

'Now,' says he, as he got her aside, 'if I do not show thy saint to be a petticoat, my hug of thee is like to prove a bear's.'

'What!' she said, amazed: 'Bernardo?'

He ground his teeth.

'I do not mark his pink cheeks for nothing.'

'Well, an he be,' she retorted coldly, 'I am liker, than if he be not, to lose my gallant.'

'That depends,' he growled, 'upon whom your fickleship honours with that title'; and he strode away, calling roughly to Bembo, 'Art for a bath, saint, before supper?'

'Why, gladly, Carlo,' said the boy, 'so we may be private.'

They went down to the pool together, and stripped and entered. Lanti saw a Ganymede, and was not pleased thereat. He came to supper in a very bad humour, which no innocent artifice of his guest could allay. The kill that day of their falcons—partridges, served in their own feathers, and stuffed with artichokes and truffles—was tough; the pears and peaches were sour; the confetti savourless and of stale design. He rated his cook, cursed his servitors, and drank more than he ate. When the disagreeable meal was ended, he strode ruffling away, saying he desired his own sole company, which it were well that all should respect. Bembo saw him go, with a sigh and a smile.

'Good, honest soul,' quoth he, 'that already wakes to the reckoning!'

Madam misunderstood him, and pressed a little closer, with a happy echo of his sigh. Her eyes were soft with wine and passion. She had no precedent for doubting her influence on the moment she chose to make her own.

'The reckoning!' she murmured. 'But I am wax in thy hands, pretty saint. Shalt confess me, and take what toll thou wilt of my sins?'

Her hand settled light as a bird on his.

'Sing to me, Bernardino,' she whispered wooingly, 'sith the cloud is gone from our moon, and I am in the will to love.'

He shot one little startled glance her way; then slowly slung round his lute, and, touching the strings pensively, melted into the following reproach: —

'Speak low! What do you ask, false love? Speak low!
Sin cannot speak too low.
The night-wind stealing to thy bosom,
The dead star, dropping like a blossom,
Less voiceless be than thou!

Low, lower yet, false love, if to confess
What guilt, what shameful need?
God, who can hear the budding grass,
And flake kiss flake in the snowy pass,
Your secret else will heed.

Ah! thou art silent, not from love, but fear,
And true love knows no fear.
Creeping, soft-footed, in the dust,
It is not love, but conscious lust,
Which dreads that God shall hear.'

He rose swiftly beside her, while she sat, dumbly biting a lock of her own hair. The frown of outraged passion was in her eyes. What had the fool dared in rejecting her!

To touch the perfumed essence of sin with a rebuke which was like a caress—that, *pace* his monks, was Bernardo's rendering of the Gospel; and who shall say that, in its girlish tenderness, its earnest emotionalism, it was not the most dangerous method of all? Not every adulterous woman is fit to meet the gentle fate of Christ's. It is not always well to doctor too much kindness with more. Surfeit, surely, is not safely cured, unless by a God, with sugar-plums.

'For shame!' he said quietly; 'for shame! Christ weeps for thee!'

She looked up with a frozen, insolent smile.

'Yet there is no tear in all the night, prophet.'

He raised his hand. A star trailed down the sky, and disappeared behind the trees. It startled her for a moment, and in that moment he was gone, striding into the moonlight. She saw a sword gleam in the shadow of the tent.

'Carlo!' she hissed; 'Carlo! follow and kill him!'

Messer Lanti came out of his ambush, sheathing his blade. His teeth grinned in the white glow. He sauntered up to her, and stood looking down, hand on hip.

'Not for all the bona-robas in the world,' he said, and struck his hilt lightly. 'This I dedicate to his service from this day. Let who crosses my little saint beware it.'

He burst out laughing, not fierce, but low.

'Thou art well served in thy confessor, woman. Wert never dealt a fitter penance.'

It was significant enough that he had no word but mockery for her discomfiture. He might have spitted the seduced on a point of gallantry; for the siren, she was sacred through her calling.

In the meanwhile Bernardo had left the green, had passed the low, roistering camp pitched at a respectful distance beyond, and had thrown himself upon his knees in the wide fields.

'Sweet Jesus,' he prayed, 'O justify Thy Kingdom before Thy servant! Already my young footsteps are warned of the bitter pass to come. Be Thou with me in the rocky ways, lest I faint and slip before my time.'

He remained long minutes beseeching, while the moon, anchored in a little stream of clouds, seemed to his excited imagination the very boat which awaited the coming of One who should walk the waters. He stretched out his arms to it.

'Lord save me,' he cried, 'or I sink!'

He heard a snuffle at his back, and looked round and up to find the fool Cicada regarding him glassily.

'Sink!' stuttered the creature, swaying where he stood. 'Lord save me too! I am under already—drowned in Malmsey!'

Bembo rose to his feet with a happy sigh. '*Exultate Deo adjutori nostro!*' he murmured, 'I am answered.'

His clear, serene young brow confronted the fuddled wrinkles of the other's like an angel's.

'Cicada mio,' he said endearingly; 'judge if God is dull of hearing, when, on the echo of my cry, here is one holding out his hand to me!'

The Fool, staring stupidly, lifted his own lean right paw, and squinted to focus his gaze on it.

'Meaning me?—meaning this?' he said.

Bembo nodded.

'A return, with interest, on the little service I was able to render thee this morning. O, I am grateful, Cicada!'

The Fool, utterly bemused, squatted him down on the grass in a sudden inspiration, and so brought his wits to anchor. Bernardo fell on his knees beside him.

'What moved you to come and save me?' he said softly. 'What moved you?'

Cicada, disciplined to seize the worst occasion with an epigram, made a desperate effort to concentrate his parts on the present one.

'The wine in my head,' he mumbled, waggling that sage member. ''Tis the wet-nurse to all valour. I walked but out of the furnace a furlong to cool myself, and lo! I am a hero without knowing it.'

He looked up dimly, his face working and twitching in the moonlight.

'Recount, expound, and enucleate,' said he. 'From what has the Fool saved the Parablist?'

'From the deep waters,' said Bembo, 'into which he had entered, magnifying his height.'

The Fool fell a-chuckling.

'There was a hunter once,' said he, 'that thought he would sound his horn to a hymn, and behold! he was chasing the deer before he had fingered the first stops. Expound me the parable, Parablist. Thou preachest universal goodwill, they say?'

'Ay, do I.'

'Thou shalt be confuted with thine own text.'

'How, dear Fool?'

'Why, shall not every wife be kind to her friend's husband?'

'Ay, if she would be unkind to her own.'

The Fool scratched his head, his hood thrown back.

'And so, in thy wisdom, thou step'st into a puddle, and lo! it is over thy ears. Will you come out, good Signor Goodwill, and ride home in a baby's pannier?'

Bembo caught one of the wrinkled hands in his soft palms.

'Dear Cicada,' he said, 'are there not tears in your heart the whiles you mock? Do you not love me, Cicada, as one you have saved from death?'

Some sort of emotion startled the harsh features of the Fool.

'What better love could I show,' he muttered, 'than to warn thee back from the toils that stretch for thy wings?'

'Ah, to warn me, to warn me, Cicada!' cried the boy, 'but not home to the nest. How shall he ever fly that fears to quit it? Be rather like my mother, Cicada, and advise these my simple wings.'

The Fool caught his breath in a sudden gasp—

'Thy mother! I!'

A spasm of pain seemed to cross his face. He laughed wildly.

'An Angel out of a Fool! That were a worthy parent to hold divinity in leading-strings.'

'Zitto, Cicca mio!' said Bembo sweetly, pressing a finger to his lips. 'Do I not know what wit goes to the acting of folly—what experience, what observation? If thou wouldst lend these all to my help and aid!'

'In what?'

'In this propaganda to govern men by love.'

'Thou playest, a child, with the cross-bow.'

'I know it. I have been warned; direct thou my hand.'

'I!' exclaimed the Fool once more in a startled cry. And suddenly, wonder of wonders! he was grovelling at the other's knees, pawing them, weeping and moaning, hiding his face in the grass.

'What saint is this?' he cried, 'what saint that claims the Fool to his guide?'

'Alas!' said the boy, 'no saint, but a child of the human God.'

'And He mated with Folly,' cried Cicada, 'and Folly is to direct the bolt!'

He sat up, beating his brow in an ecstasy, then all in a moment forbore, and was as calm as death.

'So be it,' he said. 'Be thou the divine fool, and I thy mother.'

With a quick movement Bembo caught the Fool's cheeks between his palms.

'Ay, mother,' said he, with a little choking laugh, 'but see that thy hand on mine be steady, lest the quarrel fly wide or rebound upon ourselves.'

It was the true mark indeed to which the cunning rascal had all this time been sighting his bow. He watched anxiously now for the tokens of a hit.

The Fool sat very still awhile.

'Speak clearer,' he muttered; then of a sudden: 'What wouldst ask of me?'

'Ah! dear,' sighed Bembo; 'only that thou wouldst justify thyself of this new compact of ours.'

'I am clean—as thou readest love. Who but God would consort with Folly? The Fool is cursed to virginity.'

'Cicada, dear, but there is no Chastity without Temperance.'

The Fool tore himself away, and slunk crouching back upon the grass.

'I renounce thy God!' he chattered hoarsely, 'that would have me false to my love, my mistress, my one friend! Who has borne me through these passes, stood by me in pain and madness, dulled the bitter tooth of shame while it tore my entrails? Cure wantonness in women, gluttony in wolves, before you ask me to be dastard to my dear.'

'Alas!' cried Bembo, 'then am I lost indeed!'

A long pause followed, till in a moment the Fool had flung himself once more upon his face.

'Lay not this thing on me,' he cried, clutching at the grass; 'lay it not! It is to tear my last hope by the roots, to banish me from the kingdom of dreams, to bury me in the everlasting ice! I will follow thee in all else, humbly and adoringly; I will try to vindicate this love which has stooped from heaven to a clown; I will perish in thy service—only waste not my paradise in the moment of its realisation.'

Bembo stooped, kneeling, and laid one hand softly on his shoulder.

'Poor Cicada,' he said, 'poor Cicada! Alas! I am a child where I had hoped a man, and my head sinks beneath the waters. Tired am I, and fain to go rest my head in a lap that erst invited me. Return thou to thy bottle, as I to my love.'

The Fool, trailing himself up on his knees, caught his hands in a wild, convulsive clutch.

'Fiend or angel!' he cried, 'thou shall not!—The woman!—The skirts of the scarlet woman! Go rest thyself—not there—but in peace. From this moment I abjure it—dost hear, I abjure it? I kill my love for love's sake. O! O!'

And he fell writhing, like a wounded snake, on the grass.

'*Salve, sancta parens!*' said Bembo, lifting up his hands fervently to the queen of night. The pious rogue was quite happy in his stratagem, since it had won him his first convert to cleanness.

CHAPTER III

The lady of Casa Caprona had flown her tassel-gentle and missed her quarry. Outwardly she seemed little disturbed by her failure—as insolent as indolent—an imperious serenity in a velvet frame. The occasion which had given, which was still giving, Carlo a tough thought or two to digest, she had already, on the morning following her discomfiture, assimilated, apparently without a pang. 'The which doth demonstrate,' thought Cicada, as he took covert and venomous note of her, 'a signal point of difference between the sexes. In self-indulgent wickedness there may be little to distinguish man from woman. In the reaction from it, there is this: The man is subject to qualms of conscience; the woman is not. She may be disenchanted, surfeited, aggrieved against fate or circumstance; she is not offended with herself. Remorse never yet spoiled her sleep, unless where she desired and doubted it on her account in another. What she hath done she hath done; and what she hath failed to do slumbers for her among the unrealities—among things unborn—seeds in the womb of Romance, which, though she be the first subject for it, she understands as little as she does beauty. From the outset hath she been manoeuvring to confuse the Nature in man by using its distorted image in herself to lure him. Out upon her crimps and lacings! *He* would be dressing and thinking to-day like an Arcadian shepherd, an she had not warped his poor vision with her sorcery! She wears the vestments of ugliness, and its worship is her religion.'

It must be admitted that he offered himself a cross illustration to his own text. The desperate concession wrung from him last night in a moment of vinous exaltation, had found his sober morning senses under a mountain of depression. He was bitterly aggrieved against fate; yet the only quarrel he had with himself was for that mad vow of temperance, not for the vice which had exacted it of him. The tongue in his head was like a heater in an iron. Tantalus draughts lipped and bubbled against his palate. The parched soil of his heart, he felt, would never again blossom in little lonely oases—never again know the solace of dreams aloof from the world. His traffic being by no means with heaven, God, he supposed, had sent an angel to convert it. And he had succumbed through the angel's calling him—mother!

He struck his hollow breast with a wild laugh. He groaned over the memory of that emotional folly. He damned himself, his trade, his employer, his aching head—everything and every one, in short, but the author of his misery. Him he could not curse—not more than if that preposterous relationship between them had been real. Neither did he once dream of violating his word to him, since it had been given—absurd thought—to his child.

He was none the less savage against circumstance—vicious, desperate, insolent with his master, as cross all over as a Good Friday bun. Messer Lanti, himself in a curiously sober mood, indulged his most acrid sallies with a good-humoured tolerance which, contemptuously oblivious as it was of any late smart of his own inflicting, was harder than the blow itself in its implication of a fault overlooked.

'Rally, Cicca!' said he, as they were preparing to horse; 'look'st as sour as a green crab. What! if we are to ride with Folly, give us a fool's text for the journey, man.'

Cicada dwelt a moment on his stirrup, looking round banefully.

'And who to illustrate it, lord?'

'Why, thy lord, if thou wilt,' said Carlo. 'He will be no curmudgeon in a bid for laughter.'

The Fool gained his mule's saddle, and digging heels into the beast's flanks, drove forward. Lanti, with a whoop, spurred alongside of him. Cicada slowed to a stop.

'Hast overtaken Folly, master?' said he, with a leer. 'I knew you would not be long.'

Carlo scratched his head. The Fool turned and rode back; so did the other. By the brook-side little Bembo was preparing to mount a steed with which he had been accommodated, since the lady had peremptorily declined to ride pillion to him again. Cicada referred to him with a gesture.

'For us,' he said, 'we are two fools in a leash, sith Sanctity, stopping where he was, is at the goal before us.'

Lanti grumbled: 'O, if this is a text!' and beat his wits desperately.

'A text, sirrah!' he roared, 'a text for the journey.'

'I will rhyme it you,' said the Fool imperturbably, pointing his bauble at Madam Beatrice, who at the moment stepped from the green tent:—

'Nothing is gained to start apace,

After another hath won the race.

Shall you and I be jogging, master?'

Lanti raised his whip furiously. Cicada, slipping from his mule, dodged behind Bembo.

'Save me!' he squealed, 'save me! I am sound. It is folly to give a sound man a tonic.'

Carlo burst into a vexed laugh.

'Well,' said he, 'go to. I think I am in a rare mood for charity.'

The little party breakfasted on cups of clear water from the spring, and, in the fresh of the morning, folded its tents and started leisurely on the final stages of its journey. Madonna, lazy-lidded, sat her palfrey like a vine-goddess. Her bosom rose and fell in absolute tranquillity. She bestirred herself only, when Bembo rode near, to lavish ostentatious fondness on her Carlo, a regard which her Carlo repaid with a like ostentation of attention towards his little saint. It was an open conspiracy of souls, bared to one another, to justify their nakedness before heaven; only the woman carried off her shame with an air. Bernardo she ignored loftily; but her heart was busy, under all its calm exterior, with a poisonous point of vengeance.

Presently, the sun striking hot, she dismounted and withdrew into her litter, a miniature long waggon, drawn on rude wheels by a yoke of sleepy oxen, and having an embroidered tilt opening to the side. A groom, walking there in attendance, led her palfrey by the bridle. Lanti and his guest, with the Fool for company, rode a distance ahead. The young nobleman was thoughtful and silent; yet it was obvious that he, with the others, felt the relief of that secession. Bernardo broke into a bright laugh, and rallied Cicada on his glumness.

'Why should I be merry,' said the jester, with a sour face, 'when I was invited to a feast, and threatened with a cudgelling for attending?'

Bernardo looked at him lovingly. He thought this was some allusion to his self-enforced abstinence.

'Dear Cicca,' said he, 'the feast was not worth the reckoning.'

'O, was it not!' cried Cicada with a hoarse crow. 'But I spoke of my lord's brains, which, by the token, are the right flap-doodle.'

He put Bembo between himself and Lanti.

'Judge between us,' he cried, 'judge between us, Messer Parablist. He offered to serve himself up to me, and, when I had no more than opened my mouth, was already at my ribs.'

Carlo, on the further side, laughed loud.

'It is always the same here,' grumbled the Fool. 'They will have our stings drawn like snakes' before they will sport with us. They love not in this Italy the joke which tells against themselves—of that a poor motley must ware. It muzzles him, muzzles him—drives the poison down and in; and you wonder at the bile in my face!'

He fell back, having uttered his snarl, with politic suddenness, and posted to the rear of the litter. The moment he was away, Bembo turned upon his host with a kindling look of affection.

'I am glad to have thee alone one moment,' said he. 'O Carlo, dear! the base bright metal so to seduce thine eyes. Are they not opened?'

Now the tale of madam's discomfiture at her amoroso's hands the night before had not been long in reaching the boy's ears. She had not deigned, equally in confessing her predilections as her shame, to utter them out of the common hearing. Modesty in intrigue was a paradox; and, in any case, one could undress without emotion in the presence of one's dogs.

So Cicada, putting two and two together, had gathered the whole story, and given this spiritual bantling of his a hint as to his wise policy thereon, scarce a sentence of which had he uttered before he was casting down his eyes and mumbling inarticulate under the piercing gaze of an honesty which would have been even less effective had it spoken. Then had he slunk away, blessing all beatitudes whose innocence entailed such responsibilities on their worshippers; and, as a result, here was Master Truth taking his own course with the problem.

Messer Lanti's eyes opened indeed to hear truth so fearless; but he made an acrid face.

'On my soul!' he muttered, glistening, and stopped, and his brow was shadowed a moment under a devil's wing. Then suddenly, with an oath, he clapped spurs to his horse, and galloped a furlong, and, circling, came back at a trot, and falling again alongside, put a quite gentle hand on the boy's bridle arm.

'Dear, pretty Messer Truth,' said he, 'I pray you, on my sincerity, turn your horse's head. Whither, think you, are you making?'

'Why, for heaven, I hope, Carlo,' said the boy with a smile.

'Milan is not the gate to it,' answered the rough voice, quite entreatingly. 'Go back, I advise you. You will break your heart on the stones. Why, look here: dost think I am so concerned to have this intrigue proved the common stuff of passion? I care not the feather in thy cap, Bernardino. Nay, I am the better for it, sith it opens the way to a change. And so with ten thousand others. There is the measure of your task. Now, will you go back?'

'No, by my faith!'

Lanti growled, and grunted, and smacked his thigh.

'Then I cannot help thee: and yet I will help thee. Saint Ambrose! To remodel the world to goodwill, statecraft and all, on the lisp of a red mouth! Wilt be the fashion for just a year and a day, shouldering us, every one, poor gallants, to the wall? Why should I love thee for that? and I love thee nevertheless. There thou goest in a silken doublet, to whip all hell with a lute-string; and I—I had shown less temerity horsed and armoured, and with a whole roaring crusade at my back.'

Bembo smiled very kindly.

'Christ's love was all *His* sword and buckler,' said he.

'And He was crucified,' said Carlo grimly.

'And died a virgin,' answered the boy, 'that He might make for ever chaste Love His heir.'

'Well,' grumbled Lanti, 'there reigns an impostor these fourteen hundred years or so in His place, that's all. I hope the right heir may prove his title. 'Tis a long tenure to dispossess. Methinks men have forgotten.'

'Yes, they have forgotten,' said the boy; and he began to sing so sweetly as he rode, that the other, after a grunt or two, sunk into a mere grudging rapture of listening.

In the meantime, sombre and taciturn, the Fool rode in the rear. Before him hulked the great shoulders, stoppered with the little round head, of Narcisso, the groom who led Madonna's palfrey. Cicada, regarding this beauty, snarled out a laugh to himself. 'Sure never,' he thought, 'was parental fondness worse bestowed than in nicknaming such a satyr.' The creature's small, bony jaw, like a pike's, underhung, black-tufted, viciousness incarnate; his pursed, overlapping brow, with the dirty specks of eyes set fixedly in the under-hollows—in all, the mean smallness of his features, contrasted with the slouching, fleshly bulk below, suggested one of those antediluvian monsters, whose huge bodies and little mouths and throttles give one a sense of disproportion that is almost like an indecency. Nevertheless, Narcisso was madam's chosen attendant at her curtain side, where occasionally Cicada would detect some movement, or the shadow of one, which convinced him that the two were in stealthy communication. Indeed, he had posted himself where he was, with no other purpose than to watch for such a sign.

Once he saw the hem of the curtain lift ever so slightly, and Narcisso at the same instant respond, with a secret movement of his hand, towards the place. Something glittered momentarily, and was extinguished. Cicada stretched himself in his saddle, and began to whistle.

Presently he pushed ahead once more and joined his master. Opening with some jest, he led him away, and they fell into an amble together. Afterwards it was apparent to some of Messer Lanti's following that, as the morning advanced, their lord's brow darkened from its early rude frankness, and began to exhibit certain tokens of a wakening devil with which they had plenty of reason to be familiar. Perhaps he wanted his dinner. Perhaps the near-approaching termination of his summer idyll—for they were long now in the great Lombardy plain, and the towers of Milan were growing, low and small, out of the horizon—was depressing him. Anyhow, his first condescension was all gone by noon, when they halted, a league short of the city, to rest and dine at the 'Angel and Tower,' a prosperous inn of the suburbs set among mellowing vineyards.

Of all the company Bernardo was perhaps the only one unconscious of the threatening atmosphere. Wonderful thoughts were kindling in him at the near prospect of this, the goal to all his hopes and ambitions. Milan! It was Milan at last—the capital of his promised estate of love. Blue and small, swimming far away in the sun mists of the plains, he felt that he could clasp it all in his arms, and carry it to the foot of the Throne. His eyes brightened with clear tears: this salvage of the dark, dead ages reclaimed to God! '*Domine!*' he exclaimed in ecstasy, clasping his hands: '*Emitte lucem tuam et veritatem tuam!* O Lord, touch mine eyes, that they may penetrate even where Thy light shineth like a glow-worm in deep mosses!'

Carlo roughly shouted him to their meal. His heart was throbbing with an emotional rapture as he obeyed. The table was served in a trellised alley, under hanging stalactites of grapes. Beatrice flagged on a bench at the end of the board, her shoulders sunk into a bower all crushed of sunshine and green shadows. It was the vine-goddess come home, soft, sensual, making a lust of fatigue. Her lids were half-closed; her teeth showed in a small, indolent smile; light, reflected from the purple clusters, slept on the warm ivory of her skin. Bernardo, coming opposite her, stood transfixed before a vision of such utter animal loveliness. His breath seemed to mount quicker as he gazed. Carlo drummed on the board, where he sat hunched over it. Looking from one to the other, he puffed out a little ironic laugh.

'Wonderest what is passing there, boy?' said he. 'Wilt never know. Not a hair would she turn though, like Althea, she were to find herself in child with a firebrand.'

Bernardo lowered his eyes with a blush.

'Nay,' said he, 'my thoughts of Madonna were more tempered. I coveted only her beauty for heaven.'

'Anon, Messer, anon!' cried the other banteringly: 'be not so free with my property. I hold her yet about the waist, seest, with a silver fetter? If there be a prior claim to mine——'

'Ay, Chastity's,' put in the boy.

Lanti hooted.

'Tempt her, if thou wilt, with such a suitor. She will follow him as she would the hangman. Wilt throw off thy belt, Beatrice? I gave a thousand scudi for it. See what Chastity here will offer thee in its room.'

'I will answer, if I may examine it,' said Bembo gravely. 'Will you tell her to unclasp it, Carlo, and let me look? I see it is all hinged of antique coins. There was a Father at San Zeno collected such things.'

'What, ladies' girdles!'

'Now, Carlo! you know I mean the coins. Methinks I recognise a text in one of them.'

Beatrice shrugged her shoulders, with a little yawn expressive of intolerable boredom.

'Well,' quoth Lanti impatiently, 'let him see it, you and he shall parable us for grace to meat, while these laggard dogs'—he looked over his shoulder, growling for his dinner.

Beatrice unclasped the cincture without a word, and flung it indifferently across the table. She had lain as impassive throughout her own discussing by the others as a slave being negotiated in a market. Not a tremor of her eyelids had acknowledged either her lord's rudeness or Bembo's provisional compliment.

The boy took up the belt and examined it. He was conscious of a sweet perfume that had come into his hands with the trinket. His lips were parted a little, his cheeks flushed. Presently he put it down softly, and looked across at Beatrice.

'It is what I thought,' said he—'the coin, I mean—a denarius of Tiberius, in the thirty-first year of Our Lord Shall I tell you what it says to me, Madonna?'

She did not take the trouble to answer.

'Yes,' roared Carlo.

Bembo slung his lute to the front, and began coaxing forth one of those odd, shy accompaniments of his, into which, a moment later, his voice melted:—

'When Tiberius was Emperor,
For thirty silver pieces bearing his image
Did Judas betray his Lord;
Then, himself betrayed to blood-guilt, cast them ringing
On the flags of the Temple, and maddened forth and died.
But the Jew elders eyed askance
The sleek, round coins, accurst and yet no whit
Depreciated as currency,
And ogling them and each other, were silent, till one spoke:
"Ill come; well sped. We need a place to bury the dead.
Let the Potter take these, and in return
Change us his field, o'er which we long have haggled.
So shall this outlay bring us two-fold profit,
Yet leave us conscience-clean before the Lord."

Thus, gentles dear, was bought "The Field of Blood";
And thus the wicked, damned price returned
Into the veins of traffic, there to circulate
And poison where it ran.
One piece found Hope, and changed was for Despair;
And Charity one led to hoard for self;
And one reached Faith, and Faith became a whore.
But, most of all, what had betrayed Love sore,
Sweet Love was used to betray for evermore.'

His voice broke on a long-drawn wailing chord. A little silence succeeded. Then, like one spent, he took up the belt and offered it to Beatrice.

'O Madonna!' he said, 'it is a denarius of the Cæsar that betrayed Love. Take back thy wages.'

She dragged down a spray of vine-leaves, and fanned herself furiously with it, making no other response.

'So! I am Judas!' cried Carlo; and began to bite his moustache, mouthing and glowering.

'Love!' he sputtered, 'love! Is there no love in nature? You talk of the human God, you——'

Beatrice broke in scornfully:—

'It is the world-wisdom of the monastery. He shall sing you love only by the Litany. His queen shall be a virgin immaculate, and her bosom a shrine for the white lambs of chastity to fold in. A fine proselyte for passion's understanding! I would not be so converted for all Palestine.'

Carlo laughed, with some fierce recovery to good-humour.

'Hearest her, Bernardo? Thou shalt not prevail there, unless by convincing that thou speak'st from experience.'

Bembo had sunk down upon the bench, where, resting languidly, he still fingered the strings of his lute. Now suddenly, steadfastly, he looked across at the girl, and began to sing again:—

> 'Love kept me an hour
> From all hours that pass;
> In her breast, like a flower,
> She stored it, sweet, fragrant,
> Of all time the vagrant,
> Alas, and alas!
>
> Of all time the flower,
> Of all hours that pass,
> For me was that hour,
> When I cared claim it,
> And kiss it and shame it,
> Alas, and alas!
>
> I dared not, sweet hour—
> I let thee go pass;
> And heaven is my dower.
> My crown is stars seven:
> I am a saint in heaven,
> Alas, and alas!'

He never took his eyes, while he sang, off the wondering face opposite him. It was strangely transformed by the end—flesh startled out of ivory—the face of a wakened Galatea. Narcisso coming at the moment to place the first dishes of the meal before the company, she sat up, her hands to her bosom, with a quick, agitated movement.

'It is well,' she said. 'I am thy convert, saint in heaven!' She lifted the dish before her, and held it out with a nervous smile. 'Let us exchange pledges, by the token. Give me thy meat, and take mine.'

Carlo, watching and listening, knitted his brow in a sudden frown, and his hand stole down to his belt.

'Give me thy dish,' said Beatrice, almost with entreaty.

Bernardo laughed. With the finish of his madrigal he had pushed his lute, in a hurry of pink shame, to his shoulder.

'Nay, Madonna,' he protested. 'Like the simplest doctor, I but spoke my qualifications. Feeling is half-way to curing, and the best recommended physician is he who hath practised on himself. I ask no reward but thy forbearance.'

'Give it me,' she still said. She was on her feet. She kissed the rim of the dish. 'Wilt thou refuse now? Bid him to, Carlo.'

'Not I,' said Lanti. 'Hath not, no more than myself, been whipped into the classics for nothing? *Quod ali cibus est aliis fuat acre venenum.* We know what that means, he and I.'

She seemed to turn very pale.

'Nay,' said Bernardo, jumping up, 'if Madonna condescends?' and the exchange was made, and the men fell to.

In a moment or two Lanti looked up.

'What ails thee, Beatrice?'

'I am not hungry.'

The word had scarcely left her lips before, leaping to his feet, and sprawling across the table, he had snatched the untasted dish from under her hands, turned, and dashed it with its contents full in the face of Narcisso, who waited, with others, behind. Fouled, bleeding, half-stunned, the man crashed down in a heap, and in the same instant his master was upon him, poniard in hand.

'Confess, wretch, before I kill thee!' he roared. 'It was meant for my guest! Thou wouldst have poisoned him.'

'Mercy!' shrieked the creature, through his filthy mask. 'O lord, mercy!'

The girl, risen in her place, stood panting as if she had been running. She had voice no more than to gasp across, 'Bernardo! For the love of God! Bernardo!' and that was all.

'No mercy, beast!' thundered Carlo. 'Down with thee to hell unshriven!'

His strenuous lifted arm was caught in a baby grasp.

'Carlo! forbear! The right is mine! Give me the knife! Nay, I am the stronger!'

With the blood-lust halted in him for one moment, the powerful creature turned upon his puny assailant with a roar:—

'The stronger! Thou!'

Nevertheless he rose, though he held the reptile crushed under his foot, while the company, landlord and all, stood huddled aghast. His breast was heaving like the pulse of a volcano.

'The knife!' he gurgled hoarsely; 'well, the right is thine, as thou sayest. Take it—under with thee, dog!—and drive in.'

Bembo seized and flung the dagger into the thick of the vines; then threw himself on his knees, and, with all his strength, tore the heavy foot from its victim.

'Narcisso,' he said, 'is it true? wouldst have slain Love! Ah, fool, not to know that Love is immortal!'

'Now, Christ in heaven,' roared Carlo, 'if that shall save him!'

Bernardo rose, and sprang, and cast himself upon his breast, writhing his limbs about him.

'Fly!' he shrieked, 'fly! while I hold him!' Then to Lanti: 'Ah, dear, do not hurt me, who owe thee so much!'

The fallen scoundrel was quick to the opportunity. He rose and fled, bloody and bemired, from the arbour. Madonna, seeing him escape, sunk, with a fainting sigh, upon her bench.

Carlo mouthed after his vanishing prey; yet he was tender with his burden.

'Love!' he groaned: 'Thou ow'st me? Not this—so damned to folly! There, let go. He was but the tool—and, for the rest——'

He glowered round.

'Hush!' said Bembo. 'It is but the fruits of her teaching. Blame not thy pupil, Carlo.'

'*My* pupil!'

'Is she Christ's—or art thou? Love gives life, Carlo; and all life is God's, since Christ redeemed it.'

'What then?'

'Why, is not thine honour thy life?'

'I would die at least to prove it.'

'Alas! and thou hast dishonoured love, which is life, which is God's. Wouldst eat thy cake and have it, great schoolboy?'

'Pish! Art beyond me.'

'Why, if love is life, and life is honour—ergo, love is honour.'

'Is it? I dare say.'

'But thou must know it.'

'I know nothing but that thou hast balked my vengeance; and with that, and having exercised thy jaw, let us go back to dinner.'

'*Domine, emitte tuam lucem!*' sighed Bembo.

CHAPTER IV

Galeazzo Maria Sforza, third Duke of Milan of his line, was very characteristically engaged in a very characteristic room of his resplendent castello of the Porta Giovia, which dominated the whole city from the northeast. This room, buried like a captivating lust in the heart of the Rocca, or inner citadel of the castello, swarmed with those deft procurers to the great, panders between Art and emotion, who are satisfied, by contributing, each his share, to the glorification of a sensual despotism, to partake a rediffused flavour of its sum. They were poets, painters, and musicians, sculptors and learned doctors, and every one, despite his independent calling, a sycophant. Before the power, central and paramount, which alone in their particular orbit could amass within itself the total of their lesser lights, they prostrated themselves as before a God. It is so in all ages of man. He will contribute, of choice, to the prosperous charity; he will lay his gifts at the opulent shrine. The worldling, says Shakespeare, makes his testament of more to much. *'Ah! c'est le plus grand roi du monde!'* once cried Madame de Sévigné of Louis XIV., who had danced with her. 'He is the finest gentleman I have ever seen!' cried Johnson enthusiastically at a later date, after an interview with Farmer George; and though—perhaps because—the stout old Colossus was as independent as reason itself, he spoke the general moral. Professors were here, too, who did not blush to proclaim the exalted scion of Condottieri, the blood-lusting monster, the infernal atavism of Caligula, for the first gentleman in Italy, or to prostitute their erudition in his service.

It was Madonna Beatrice who had drawn that analogy, and there was plenty of justification for it; as also, it must be said, plenty of more immediate precedent for the abominations of this Galeazzo. If, like the grand-matricidal Roman, he had poisoned his mother, the Visconti, his predecessors, with their atrocious blood-profanations and exaltations of bastardy, were responsible for the conditions which had made so dreadful an act conceivable. If, emulating Caligula's treatment of frail vestals, he had buried alive some too-accommodating virgin of the cloister, whom he had first debauched, he could quote the Visconti precedent of carnality indulged till it became a very ecstasy of fiend-possession. Between old Rome and modern Milan, indeed, there was little to prefer. Caligula used to throw spectators in the theatres to the beasts, having first torn out the tongues of his victims, lest his ears should be offended by their articulate appeals. Bernabo Visconti and his brother, with whom he shared the duchy, agreed upon an edict subjecting State criminals to a scale of tortures which was calculated to culminate in death in not less than forty days. Giovanni Maria and Filippo Maria, last of the accursed race, organised man-hunts in the streets of their capitals, and fed their hounds on human flesh.

To starve his victims to death, and, when they complained (it was an age of practical jokes), to stuff their mouths with filth, was a pet sport with Galeazzo. Once, for a wretch who had killed a hare, a crime unpardonable, he procured a death of laughable, unspeakable torment by forcing him to devour the animal, bones and fur and all.

It is enough. They were all madmen, in fact, moral abortions of that 'breeding-in' of demi-gods which sows the world with chimeras. It is not good for any man to be subject to no government but his own, and least of all when a vicious heredity has imposed a sickness on his reason. Blood affinities on the near side of incest, power unquestioned, unbridled self-indulgences—these are no progenitors of temperance and liberality. Amongst savages, generations of inter-marryings will but refine exquisitely on savagery; and the despots of this era were little more than the last expressions of a decadent barbarism. Galeazzo, and such as Galeazzo, were, it is true, to project the long shadows of their lusts and cruelties over the times forthcoming; yet it is as certain that with him the limits of the worst were reached, and hereafter peoples and rulers were to grow to some common accord of participation in the enlightenments of their ages.

One might have fancied in him, in his apparent reachings to foreclose on such a state, to appropriate to himself not its moral but its material accessories, some uneasy premonition of the truth. He stood on the line of partition, his sympathies with the past, his greed for the opulent future, and, hesitating, was presently to drop between. That paradox of the lusts of savagery and the lusts of intellect hobnobbing in the individual, which characterised so many of his contemporaries, cried aloud in him. He was superstitious and a sceptic. Like Malatesta of Rimini—who could enshrine beneath the shadow of one glorious church the bones of a favourite mistress and those of an admired heathen philosopher which he had brought expressly from Greece for the purpose—he would make a compromise between Paganism and Christianity. He worshipped God and the devil, as if his arrogance halted at nothing short of reconciling two equal but antagonistic powers. He surrounded himself with monks and infidels; acclaimed impartially an illuminated psalter or a painting for a bagnio, a Roman canticle or a hymn to the Paphian Venus; sobbed in the soft throbbings of a lute, and went sobbing to witness a captive's torturing; conceived himself an enlightened patron of the arts, and, in a mad caprice, ordered his craftsmen, under penalty of instant death, to paint and hang with portraits of the ducal family in a single night a hall of the castello. He groped and grovelled in bestiality; founded a library and peopled a university with erudition; encouraged profligacy and printing; was covetous and lavish, and splendid as the clusters of diamonds on a Jewess's unclean fingers. His palaces swarmed with cutthroats and physicians, philosophers and empirics, pimps and theologians, heaven-commissioned artists and pope-commissioned agents for indulgences, who would sell one absolution beforehand for the foulest excesses in lust or violence. His crowded halls were the very stage of the ante-renaissance, where the priest, the poisoner, the romantic hero and the sordid villain, the flaunting doxy and the white dove of innocence, rubbed shoulders with the scene-painter and conductor in a disordered rehearsal of the melodrama to come. And so we alight on him in this Rocca, sinister and lonely, the protagonist of the piece to which he was in a little to supply the most tragic dénouement.

He lay sunk back in pillows on a couch set in an alcove high and apart. One long, jewelled hand caressed the head of a boarhound. Judged by the swift code of his times, he was already mature, a sage of thirty-one. His eyes were small and deep-seated under gloomy thatches, his forehead narrow and receding, his cheeks ravenous, his nose was hooked. But in contrast with this pinched hunger of feature were the bagging chin and sensual neck, as well as the grossness of the body, which attenuated into feeble legs. One could not look on him and gather from crown to foot the assurance of a single generous youthful impulse. The curse of an inherited despotism had wrinkled him from his birth.

An effeminate luxury, which was presently to make Milan a byword among the austerer principalities, spoke in his dress. His short-skirted tunic, puff-shouldered, and pinched and pleated at the waist within a gem-encrusted girdle, was of Damascene silk, rose-coloured and lined with costliest fur. His hose were of white satin; his slippers, of crimson velvet, sparkled with rosettes of diamonds and rubies. On his head he wore a cap of maintenance, also of red velvet, and sewn with pearls; and a short jewelled dagger hung at his waist.

By his side, a very foil to his magnificence, stood one in a sad-coloured cloak. This was Lascaris, a Greek professor, whom he had invited to Milan for his learning, and used, like Pharaoh, to expound him his dreams. For he was subject to evil dreams, was this Galeazzo—hauntings and visions which wrought in him that state that he would become a very madman if so little as the shadow of an opposition crossed his imagination. And even now such a mood was working in him, as he lounged darkly conning the life of the hall from his eyrie.

That was a deep, semi-domed alcove, approached from the main chamber by a short avenue of square-sided pillars, and roofed with a mosaic of ultramarine and gold, into which were wrought the arms of the Sforzas and Viscontis, the lilies of France and the red cross of Savoy. Entablatures of white marble carved into bas-reliefs filled the inter-columniations of this approach; while the pillars themselves, of dark green panels inlaid on white, were sprayed and flowered with exquisite mouldings in gold. The capitals, blossoming crowns of gilt foliage and marble faces, supported a white cornice, which at the alcove's mouth ran down into twin fluted shafts, between which rose a shallow flight of steps to a sort of dais or shrine within. And thence, from a carved marble bench, Galeazzo looked down on the soft surging motley of the throng in the hall below.

Every sound there was instinctively subdued to the occasion: the laughter of girls, the thrum of lutes, the ring of steel and rustle of silk. Not so much as a misdirected glance, even, would venture to appropriate to the company's cynic merriment the figure of a solitary captive, who stood bound and guarded at the foot of the dais. Yet it was plain that this captive felt the enforced forbearance, and mocked it with a bitterer cynicism than its own.

He was a small, ill-formed, harsh-featured man, very soberly dressed, and with a cropped head—a feature sufficiently disdainful of the bushed and elaborately waved locks of those by whom he was surrounded. Lean-throated and short-sighted, his face was a face to scorn falsehood without loving truth, a face the mouthpiece of dead languages for dead languages' sake, a face the contemner of the present just because it was the present and alive. As he stood, loweringly phlegmatic as any caged hate, his peering eyes and snarling lip would occasionally lift themselves together, not towards the glittering lord of destinies on the dais, but towards his henchman, the Greek, who would answer the challenge with a stare of serene and opulent contempt. And so a long interval of silence held them opposed.

Suddenly the Duke stirred from his black reverie, his lips sputtering little inarticulate blasphemies. His knee peevishly dismissing the hound, he gripped an arm of the bench, and turning gloomily on Lascaris, uttered the one impatient word, 'Well?'

The Greek, temporising for the moment, inclined his smooth, black-bearded face, so that the oily essence on his hair, which was foppishly crimped and snooded, was wafted to the Sforza nostrils, offending their delicacy. Galeazzo, momentarily repelled, rallied to a harsher frown, and demanded: 'The fruit, man, the fruit of all this meditation? Jesu! it should be rotten-ripe by its smell!'

Lascaris expanded his chest, unoffended, and, caressing his beard, answered impassively:—

'Thou questionest of this vision, Theosutos? I answer, How many changes can be rung on a carillon of eight bells? By such measure shalt thou imagine, an thou canst, the changes possible to the myriad of particles that go to the composition of a single human eye. Now, in the unthinkable dispersements and readjustments of Infinity, shall it not sometimes happen that two particles, or two thousand particles, or two billion particles, out of the sum of particles which were that eye, shall chance together again, and recover, because of that meeting, some very ancient, very remote impression which they once absorbed in common? These, Theosutos, be the ghosts, haphazard, indefinable, visible to one and unseen of all the rest, which make the solitary seer; these be the lonely hauntings of the ages— dust blown over desolate places, to commingle a moment at some cross roads, and weave a phantom wreath of memory, and so again be cast and scattered among the cycles. Thy vision is but a shadow of old dead years.'

An ill-repressed stutter of laughter from the prisoner at the foot of the steps greeted the finish of this exegesis. Lascaris flushed scarcely perceptibly. The Duke took no more notice of man or sound than he would have of a whimpering dog. Once or twice he stammered an oath, gnawing his finger, and frowning up, and down, and up again at the Greek. Finally he broke out, in a fury:—

'Now, by the Host, thou consolest me—now, by the Host! To reconcile to this spectre by arguing it perpetual! To——'

Grinding his teeth, he clipped his long fingers on the bench arm, as if he were about to spring. Lascaris forestalled him with a placid word:—

'Not perpetual. The mood invokes these shadows, as the mood shall lay them.'

Galeazzo snarled.

'The mood! What mood, fool? You shift and shift. God! it will be the mood of the mood next. Hast thou no master-key to all? Go to, then!'

He sank back into his cushions, glooming and panting. The sleek olive mask of the face near him yielded no sign of perturbation.

Gradually a very deadly expression came to usurp in the Duke's eyes that blinder madness of desperation. An indolent smile relaxed his features. He yawned, it was because, the soul horror being temporarily withdrawn, the incontinent devil was supplanting in him the tempestuous one. He rolled lazily about, addressing his creature once more:—

'You doctors—all the same! Big words to little cures. Treat a State's constitution or a man's—'tis the word's the thing. Ye woo not the truth, but her raiment. Hear'st me? I had a tutor once, a crabbed fellow called Montano.'

He yawned again. The prisoner below (Cola Montano himself) gasped slightly, and shot one stealthy glance his way. Lascaris sniggered.

'Surely, lord,' he said, 'we need no reminding while the man himself keeps his tongue.'

A half-suppressed snarl broke from the prisoner. Galeazzo, hunched on his cushions, stared vacantly before him.

'Ah!' he said, 'he could talk. I remember him, a midwife to the wind—as ye all be—as ye all be. What of the fellow?'

Lascaris wondered.

'Little, in truth, Magnificence, save in so far as your Magnificence was pleased to introduce his name.'

'Did I? I had forgot. What was the connection? Empty words, was it not, and vainglory and presumption?'

'And discontent. Add it thereto, Illustrious.'

'Discontent? Of what? The man prospers, I understand, on his school of all the virtues. Discontent? Why, hath he not risen to that independence of power that he dares lampoon his prince? Discontent?'

'Like Alexander, thou standest in his light, Theosutos.'

'Discontent?'

'Ay, that he should be twitted with having schooled a despot.'

'Why, true; he taught me how to score a lesson with a scourge. My shoulders could tell.'

'Gods! did he dare?'

'He dared. 'Twas a fellow of Roman mettle.'

'He would dare more now.'

'What?'

'A republic, so they say.'

'Ah! he should be the man for visions—a seer, an exorcist.'

'Short-sighted for a seer, Illustrious. The man cannot see the length of his own nose.'

'Yet may he see far. I would he were here.'

The prisoner, wrought at last beyond self-control, turned on the Greek and squirted a little shriek of venom—

'Yet through and through thee, thou loathsome, envious pimp!'

Then he whipped upon the other—

'And why not a republic, Galeazzo? Thy father Francesco was a republican at heart, else had he never given his son's leading-strings into my hands. There was a confederacy dreamed of in his day—Genoa, Milan, and Venice; Florence, Sienna, and Bologna. One rampart to the rolling Alps, one wall on which barbarian hordes might burst and waste themselves in foam. Northwards, a baffled sea; south, all Italy a tranquil haven, a watered garden, where knowledge with all its flowers should find space, and breathing-space to grow. Dost thou love Italy? Then why not a republic, Galeazzo?'

The Duke, as utterly impassive as if he were deaf, turned musingly to Lascaris.

'I heard one talk once,' said he, 'of a confederacy of republics, as who should say, An army all serfs. Words! The tails must obey the heads. Every ox knows it.'

'Saving the frog-ox,' giggled the Greek, 'who bursts himself in emulation.'

'Ah!' murmured the Duke, 'the frog-ox: see us tickle his self-puffery.'

He feigned to catch sight all at once of Montano. His eyes opened wide in astonishment: he held out his hands.

'What!' he cried, 'the man of visions! the very man! Come hither, old friend. I was but now speaking of thee.'

His guards permitting him, Montano sullenly mounted the steps, and stood facing the tyrant. His arms hung very plainly fettered before him; but the other never took his languid, smiling eyes from his face.

'Galeazzo,' said the scholar, harsh and quick, 'I did not write the epigrams; but no matter. You seek to make an example; I submit myself. It is the despot's part to lay hands on order and sobriety. Despatch, then. Thou wilt serve my ends better than thine own. Every blow to freedom is a link gone from thy mail.'

The Duke listened to him as if in bland wonder.

'Epigrams! An example!' he exclaimed. 'O, surely there is some mistake here.'

The thick brows of the prisoner contracted over his leaden eyes. He set his teeth, breathing between them. Galeazzo appealed to Lascaris:—

'Know'st aught of this?'

The Greek shook his head ineffably, licking his lips.

'No,' said Galeazzo, 'nor is it conceivable that my old friend and reprover should condescend to that meaner scourge. Jesu! for one of his learning and condition to incur the fate of the common lampooner. Why, I mind me how one was invited to a ragout minced of his own tongue.'

'Yes, Illustrious.'

'And another to having his couplets scored in steel on the soles of his feet.'

'Yes, Illustrious.'

'And yet another to boiling eggs under his arm-pits, since he was clever at hatching those winged epigrams'—he turned smoothly again to the tutor—'but not clever, as thou art, at reforming constitutions.'

He fell back, with a sleek and hateful smile; then, sighing suddenly, advanced his body again.

'I am troubled, Montano, I am troubled, and, since you chance to be here——'

He yielded the explanation to Lascaris.

'I weary of relating. Tell him of my symptoms, thou'—and he sunk once more into his cushions.

The Greek diagnosed, his shifty eyes refusing to encounter the hard inquisition of the other's:—

'His Magnificence is of late ever conscious of a face behind him, mournful and threatening. And still, if he turns to challenge it, it is behind him; and still behind, maddening him with a thought of something he can never overtake.'

Galeazzo fixed his burning eyes on the prisoner, as if, through all his mockery, the hunger of a hopeless hope betrayed his soul.

'Canst *thou* strike it away,' he whispered hoarsely, 'or at least tell me what it is?'

Montano growled:—

'Ghosts, and dead years, and eye-particles! This trash of pseudo-science—a saltimbanco braying in a doctor's skin! Less licence, Galeazzo, and more exercise—'tis all contained in that. This vision is but a swimming blot of bile.'

He was really half-deceived, half-convinced. The Duke seemed to listen reassured, then slowly rose, and, with an ingratiatory smile, patted his erst tutor's shoulder.

'Old honest friend,' he said, 'and ever true to the Roman in thee! Thou hast spoken as one might expect. Bile, is it—bile? and little wonder in this upset of constitutions. Ebbene! we will take instant means to throw it off.'

He made a sign to the chief of the guard below.

'Andrea!'

Lascaris slunk back with a little gloating smile. The officer brought up his men about Montano. The Duke murmured softly:—

'Take good Messer Cola, and—' he paused a little, gazing winningly into his captive's surprised, splenetic face—'and have him soundly flogged before the gate-house—to the bone, Andrea, tell Messer Jacopo.'

Before the luring treachery of this stroke the prisoner stood for one moment shocked, aghast. The next, as the guard seized him, he broke into a storm of vituperations and blasphemies, calling upon all the gods of Rome to protect him from a monster. Andrea crushed his mailed hand down on his writhing lips; he was dragged away struggling and screaming. As he disappeared Galeazzo descended mincingly to the hall, bent on pursuing the show. A cloud of courtiers, male and female flocked, like rooks following a plough, in his wake. As he left the citadel and was crossing the outer ward, two ladies—one a young woman in her late twenties; the other a slim, pale girl of thirteen—broke from a group of attendants, and came, wreathed in one embrace, to accost him. The elder, looking in his face with a certain questioning anxiety, spoke him with a propitiatory smile and sigh:—

'Galeazino, O thou little sweetest burden on my heart!'

The endearment was really an inquiry, a warning; for there was a foreboding madness in his eyes. He made as if he would have struck her from his path. Her child companion caught his wrist with a merry cry:—

'My little father, whither sportest thou without thy women?'

He changed the direction of his hand and flipped the younger's cheek.

'Come, then, chuck,' said he. 'There is a frolic toward that will speed an idle hour.'

She caught up her skirts and followed him, as did the other, but less closely.

The gatehouse commanded from its battlements an open panorama of the town as far as the piazza of the duomo. Immediately to its front, in a bare extended space, stood the whipping-post, a stout beam set on end on a stage and furnished with hooks and chains. Already on the ground beside this (by preconcerted arrangement indeed) was a certain functionary, much respected of Milan. This was Messer Jacopo, the high court executioner—one, by virtue of his dealings in blood, almost on an equality with the master herald himself. Immobile and voiceless, he stood there like a model in an armoury. A short shirt of mail, and over it a scarlet jerkin with a plain dagger at the waist; hose of sober grey; a bonnet and shoes of black velvet, the first adorned with a red quill, the second with red rosettes; gorget and steel gauntlets—such was the whole of Messer Jacopo, save for the wooden, inessential detail of his face and its fixed eyes of glass. There was something painfully human, by contrast, in his understrappers, two or three of whom stood at hand in leathern aprons—men of a rich, moist physique and greasy palms, and jocund, slaughter-house expression. These were on bantering terms with the mob, with all that loose raff of the neighbourhood, which had come streaming and pushing and chattering to witness the sport. It was not often that the rats of the quarter Giovia had a master of philosophy to desert.

They had not long to wait. Almost simultaneously a little surging group appeared at the gates, and a throng of gay heads above the ramparts. The jostle and delighted whisper went among the crowd. What proportion would the scourging of a prince's tutor bear to the punishment it avenged? It surely would not be allowed to lose by procrastination. They craned their necks to catch an early sight of the victim. One of the assistants whipped experimentally through his fingers a thick, cruel thong of bullock-hide. It clacked a dry tongue.

'Be quiet, thirsty one,' he cried boisterously. 'In a moment thou shalt drink thyself to a sop.'

Up on the ramparts the ladies, with bright, inquisitive eyes, stood by their lord. The girl Catherine, petted love-child of her father, hugged confidingly to his arm.

'Padre mio,' she said, 'how sweet the world looks from here! I could fancy we were all Lazaruses, laughing down on that wicked Dives!'

CHAPTER V

Messer Lanti and his party entered Milan, in a very subdued mood, by the Gate of Saint Mark. It had been with an emotion beyond words that Bembo had found himself approaching the walls of this fair city of his dreams. The prosperous contado, watered in every direction by broad dykes; the clustering vines and saintly-hued olive gardens; the busy peasantry; the richness of the very wayside shrines, had all appeared to speak a content and holiness with which the perverse passions of men were at such bitter variance. The discrepancy confounded, as it was presently upon a fuller experience to inspire, him. Here in one land, incessantly jostling and reacting on one another, were a devotional and a sensuous fervour, both exhibiting a lust of beauty at fever-heat; were a gross superstition and an excellent reason; were a powerful priestcraft and a jeering scepticism—all drawing from the forehead of a Papacy, which, latterly pledged to the most unscrupulous temporal self-aggrandisement, was reverenced for the vicarship of a poor and celibate Christ. Issuing, equipped with an artless conventual purpose, from the cool groves of his cloister, he found a land dyed in blood and the blue of heaven, festering under God's sun, and rejoicing in the colour schemes of its sores. On what principle could he study to sweeten this paradox of a constitution, where health was enamoured of disease? '*Deus meus, in te confido,*' he prayed, with hands clasped fervently upon his breast; '*Non erubescam, neque irrideant me inimici mei*! O Lord, give me the vision to find and show to others a path through this beautiful wilderness!'

As the long walls of the town, broken at intervals into turrets, broadened before him, violet against a deep, cloudless sky, his ecstasy but increased— he held out his arms.

'O thou,' he murmured, 'that I have hungered for, looking down on thee from the mountain of myrrh! Until the day break and the shadows flee away!'

A little later, in a deep angle of the enceinte, they came upon a gruesome sight. This was no less than the Montmartre of Milan—a great stone gallows with dangling chains, and tenanted—faugh! A cloud of winged creatures rose as they approached, and scattered, dropping fragments. It was the common repast, stuff of rogues and pilferers—nothing especial. The ground was trodden underneath, and Bembo shrieked to see two white, stiff feet sticking from it. Lanti followed the direction of his hand, and exclaimed with a moody shrug:—

'An assassin, Saint—nothing more. We plant them like that, head down.'

'Alive?'

'O, of course!'

Bembo cried out: 'These are not sons of God, but of Belial!' and passed on, with his head drooping. Carlo turned to Beatrice, where she rode behind, and, without a word, pointed significantly to the horrible vision. She laughed, and went by unmoved.

In a little after they had all entered by the gate, and the city was before them. Bembo, kindled against his will, rose in his saddle and uttered an exclamation of delight. Before his eyes was spread a white town with blue water and upstanding cypresses—wedges of midnight in midday. There were terraces and broad flagged walks, and palaces and spacious loggias—fair glooms of marble shaken in the spray of fountains. From its cold, shadowless bridges to the heaped drift of the duomo in its midst, there seemed no slur, but those dark cypresses, on all its candid purity. It looked like a city flushed under a veil of hoar frost, the glare of its streets and markets and gardens subdued to one softest harmony of opal.

Yet in quick contrast with this chill, sweet austerity, glowed the burning life of it. In the distance, like travelling sparks in wood ashes; nearer, flashing from roof or balcony in harlequin spots of light; nearest of all, a very baggage-rout of figures, fantastic, chameleonic, an endless mutation and interflowing of blues, and crimsons, and purples—tirelessly that life circulated, the hot arterial blood which gave their tender hue to those encompassing veins of marble.

It was on this drift of souls going by him, gay and light, it seemed, as blown petals, that Bernardo gazed with the most loving fondness. He pictured them all, eager, passionate, ardent, moving about the business of the Nature-God, propagating His Gospel of sweetness, adapting to imperishable works the endlessly varying arabesques of woods, and starry meadows, and running clouds and waters—epitomising His System. He admired these works, their beauty, their stability, their triumphant achievement; though, in truth, his soul of souls could conceive no achievement for man so ideal as a world of glorious gardens and little abodes. But the sun was once more in his heart, and heaven in his eyes.

The swallows stooped in the streets to welcome him: 'Hail, little priest of the cloistered hills!' The scent of flowers offered itself the incense to his ritual; the fountains leapt more merrily for his coming. 'Love! love!' sang the birds under the great eaves; 'He will woo this cruel world to harmlessness. Where men shall lead with charity, all animals shall follow. The good fruits ripen to be eaten; it is their love, their lust to be consumed in joy. What lamb ever gave its throat to the knife? The violet flowers the thicker the more its blossoms are ravished. What new limb ever budded on a maimed beast?'

'Ah! the secret,' sang Bembo's soul—'the secret, or the secret grievance, of the cosmos will yield itself only to love. Useless to try to wrench forth its confession by torture. Let retaliation spell love, for once and for ever, and to the infinite sorrows of life will appear at last their returned Redeemer.'

His heart was full as they rode by the narrow streets. His eyes and ears were tranced with colour, the murmur of happy voices, the clash of melodious bells. He could not think of that late vision of horror but as a dream. These blithe souls, in all their moods and worships such true apostles of his gay, sweet God! They could not love or practise harshness but as a deterrent from things unnameable. The very absence of sightseers from that pit of scowling death proved it.

And then, in a moment, they had debouched upon an open place overlooked by a massive fortress, and in its midst, the cynosure of hundreds of gloating eyes, was a human thing under the flail—a voice moaning from the midst of a red jelly.

His heart sunk under a very avalanche. He uttered a cry so loud as to attract the attention of the spectators nearest.

'Who is it? What hath he done?' he roared of one. 'Trampled on the Host? Defiled a virgin of the mother? Murdered a priest?'

The face puckered and grinned.

'Worse, Messer Cavalier. He once whipped the Duke when his tutor.'

Bembo's whole little body braced itself to the spring.

'Tutor!' he cried: 'is that, then, Cola Montano?'

The gross eye winked—

'What is left of it.'

He was answered with a leap and rush. The mob at that point staggered, and bellowed, and fell away from the hoofs of a furious assailant. Carlo, pre-admonished, was already on the boy's flank. 'Stop, little lunatic!' he shouted, sweating and spurring to intervene. He had no concern for the feet he trampled or the ribs he bruised. He stooped and snatched at the struggling horse's bridle. 'It is the Duke's vengeance!' he panted. 'See him there above! Art mad?'

A face, flushed as the face of Him who scourged the hucksters from the temple, was turned upon him.

'Art thou? Strike for retaliation by love, or get behind!'

'Know'st nothing of his deserts,' cried Carlo. 'Be advised!'

'By love,' cried the boy. 'He is worthy of it—a good man—I carry a letter to him from my father. Fall back, I say.'

He drove in his heels, and the horse plunged and started, tearing the rein from Lanti's grasp. It was true that Bembo bore this letter, among others, in his pouch. The Abbot of San Zeno was so long out of the world as to have miscalculated the durations of court favour. Cola had been an influence in *his* time.

'Devil take him!' growled Carlo; but he followed, scowling and slashing, in his wake. The mob, authorised of its worst humour, took his truculence ill. That reduced him to a very devilish sobriety. He began to strike with an eye to details, 'blazing' his passage through the throng. The method justified itself in the opening out of a human lane, at the end of which he saw Bembo spring upon the stage.

The executioner was cutting deliberately, monotonously on, and as monotonously the voice went moaning. Messer Jacopo, standing at iron ease beside, took no thought, it seemed, of anything—least of all of interference with the Duke's will. It must have been, therefore, no less than an amazing shock to that functionary to find himself all in an instant stung and staggered by a bolt from the blue. He may have been, like some phlegmatic serpent, conscious of a hornet winging his way; but that the insect should have had it in its mind to pounce on *him*!

He found himself and his voice in one metallic clang:—

'Seize him, men!'

Carlo panted up, and Jacopo recognised him on the moment.

'Messer Lanti! Death of the Cross! Is this the Duke's order?'

'Christ's, old fool!' gasped the cavalier. 'Touch him, I say, and die. I neither know nor care.'

His great chest was heaving; he whipped out his sword, and stood glaring and at bay. Bembo had thrown himself between the upraised thong and its quivering victim. He, too, faced the stricken mob.

'Christ is coming! Christ is coming!' he shrieked. 'Prepare ye all to answer to Him for this!'

A dead silence fell. Some turned their faces in terror. Here and there a woman cried out. In the midst, Messer Jacopo raised his eyes to the battlements, and saw a white hand lifted against the blue. He shrugged round grumpily on his fellows.

'Unbind him,' he said; and the whip was lowered.

The poor body sunk beside the post. Bembo knelt, with a sob of pity, to whisper to it—

'Courage, sad heart! He comes indeed.'

The livid and suffering face was twisted to view its deliverer.

'Escape, then,' the blue lips muttered, 'while there is time.'

Bembo cried out: 'O, thou mistakest who I mean!'

The face dropped again.

'Never. Christ or Galeazzo—it is all one.'

A hand was laid on the boy's shoulder. He looked up to find himself captive to one of the Duke's guard. A grim little troop, steel-bonneted and armed with halberts, surrounded the stage. Messer Lanti, dismounted, had already committed himself to the inevitable. He addressed himself, with a laugh, to his friend:—

'Very well acquitted, little Saint,' said he—'of all but the reckoning.'

Bembo lingered a moment, pointing down to the bleeding and shattered body.

'"And there passed by a certain priest,"' he cried, '"and likewise a Levite; but a Samaritan had compassion on him,"' and he bowed his head, and went down with the soldiers.

Now, because of his beauty, or of the fear or of the pity he had wrought in some of his hearers, for whatever reason a woman or two of the people was emboldened to come and ask the healing of that wounded thing; and they took it away, undeterred of the executioners, and carried it to their quarters. And in the meanwhile, Bembo and his comrade were brought before the Duke.

Galeazzo had descended from the battlements, and sat in a little room of the gatehouse, with only a few, including his wife and child, to attend him. And his brow was wrinkled, and the lust of fury, beyond dissembling, in his veins. He took no notice of Lanti—though generally well enough disposed to the bully—but glared, even with some amazement in his rage, on the boy.

'Who art thou?' he thundered at length.

'Bernardo Bembo.'

The clear voice was like the call of a bird's through tempest.

'Whence comest thou?'

'From San Zeno in the hills.'

'What seek'st thou here?'

'Thy cure.'

The Duke started, and seemed actually to crouch for a moment. Then, while all held their breath in fear, of a sudden he fell back, and gripped a hand to his heart, and muttered, staring: 'The face!'

He closed his eyes, and passed a tremulous hand across his brow before he looked again; and lo! when he did so, the madness was past.

'Child,' he said hoarsely, almost whispered, 'what said'st thou? Come nearer: let me look at thee.'

He rose himself, with the word, stiffly, like an old man, and stood before the boy, and gazing hungrily for a little into the solemn eyes, dropped his own as if abashed—half-blinded. In the background, Bona, his wife, and the child Catherine clung together in a silence of fear and wonder.

'Ah, I am haunted!' shuddered the tyrant. 'Who told thee that? It is a face, child, a face—there—in the dead watches of the night—behind me— and by day, always the same, a damned clinging bur on my soul—not to be shaken off—always behind me!'

He gave a little jerk and motion of repugnance, as if he were trying to throw something off. Carlo struck in: 'Lord, let him sing to thee! I say no more.'

The deep, gloomy eyes of the Duke were lifted one instant to the strange seraph-gaze fixed silently upon him; then, making an acquiescent motion with his hand, he turned, and sat himself down again as if exhausted, and hid his brow under his palm.

Now the boy, never looking away, slung forward his lute, and like one that charms a serpent, began softly to finger the strings. And Galeazzo's head, in very truth like an adder's, swung to the rhythm; and as the chords rose piercing, he clutched his brow, and as they melted and sobbed away, so did he sink and moan. And then, suddenly, into that wild symphony drew the voice, as a spray of sweetbriar is drawn into a wheel; and all around caught their breath to listen:—

'Two children, a boy and girl, were playing between wood and meadow.

They pledged their faith, each to the other, with rosy lips on lips,

He to protect, she to trust—always together for ever and ever.

A storm rose: the dragon of the thunder roared and hissed,

Probing the earth with its keen tongue.

How she cowered, the pretty, fearful thing!

Yet adored her little love to see him dare

That tree-cleaving monster with his sword of lath.

And in the end, because she trusted in her love, her love prevailed,

And drove the roaring terror from the woods.

She never felt such faith, nor he such pride of virtue in his strength.

Then shone out the rainbow,

And he bethought him of the jewelled cup hid at its foot.

"Stay here," quoth he, new boldened by his triumph,

"And I'll fetch it ye."

But she cried to him: "Nay, leveling, take me too!

We were to be aye together: O leave me not behind!"

But he was already on his way.

And still, as he pursued, the rainbow fled before,

And the voice of his playmate, faint and fainter, followed in his wake:

"O leave me not behind!"

Then grew he wild and desperate, clutching at that mirage, the unattainable,

The lustrous cup that was to bring him happiness in its possession.

And the voice blew ghostly in his wake, mingling with rain and the whirl of dead leaves:

"Leave me not behind!"

But now the fire of unfulfilment seared his brain,

And often he staggered in the slough,

Or fell and cut himself on rocks.

And so, pushing on half-blindly,

Knew not at last from the dead rainbow the *ignis fatuus*,
The false witch-light that danced upon his path,
Leading him to destruction. Until, lo!
With a flash and laugh it was not,
And he awoke to a mid-horror of darkness—
Night in the infernal swamps—
Blind, crawling, desolate; and for ever in his heart
The weeping shadow of a voice, "O leave me not behind!"
Then at that, like one amazed, he turned,
And cried in agony: "Innocenza, my lost Innocence,
Where art thou? O, little playmate, follow to my call!"
And there answered him only from the gates of the sunset a
heart-broken sigh.'

He ended to a deep silence, and, while all stood stricken between tears and expectancy, moved to within a pace of the Duke.

'O prince!' he cried, 'haunted of that Innocence! Turn back, turn back, and find in thy lost playmate's face the ghost that now eludes thee!'

Carlo gave a little gasp, and his hand shivered down to his sword-hilt. He must die for his Saint, if provoked to that martyrdom; but he would take a desperate pledge or two of the sacrifice with him. One of the women, the younger, watching him, knew what was in his mind, and breathed a little scornfully. The other's eyes were set in a sort of rapture upon the singer's face. A minute may have passed, holding them all thus suspended, when suddenly Galeazzo rose, and, throwing himself at Bembo's feet, broke into a passion of sobs and moans.

'Margherita, my little playmate, that liest under the daisies. O, I will be good, sweet—I will be good again for thy sake.'

CHAPTER VI

Many a head in the palace, though accustomed witness of strange things, tossed on its pillow that night in sleepless review of a scene which had been as amazing in its singularity as it was potential in its promise. What were to be the first-fruits of that cataclysmic revulsion of feeling in a nature so habitually frozen from all tenderness? If no more than a shy snowdrop or two of reason, mercy, justice, pushing their way up through a savage soil, the result would be marvel enough. Yet there seemed somehow in the atmosphere an earnest of that and better. The hearts of all trod on tiptoe, fearful of waking their souls to disenchantment—agitated, exultant; wooing them to convalescence from an ancient sickness. The spring of a joyous hope was rising voiceless somewhere in the thick of those drear corridors. The f[oe]tid air, wafted through a healing spray, came charged with an unwonted sweetness. Whence had he risen, the lovely singing-boy, spirit of change, harbinger of a new humanity? Whither had he gone? To the Duke's quarters—that was all they knew. They had seen him carried off, persuaded, fondled, revered by that very despot whom he had dared divinely to rebuke, and the doors had clanged and the dream passed. To what phase of its development, confirming or disillusioning, would they reopen? The answer to them was at least a respite; and that was an answer sufficient and satisfying to lives that obtained on a succession of respites. Alas! as there is no logic in tyranny, so can there be none in those who endure it.

The earliest ratification of the promise was to witness in the figure of the Duke coming radiant from his rooms in company with the stranger himself, his left arm fondly passed about the boy's neck, his eyes full of admiration and flattery. He felt no more discomfort, it appeared, than had Madam Beatrice on a certain occasion, in the thought of his late self-exposure before his creatures. Such shamelessness is the final condition of autocracy. He had slept well, untormented of his vision. As is the case with neurotics, a confident diagnosis of his disease had proved the shortest means to its cure. Clever the doctor, too, who could make such a patient's treatment jump with his caprices; and with an inspired intuition Bernardo had so manoeuvred to reconcile the two. A whim much indulged may become a habit, and he was determined to encourage to the top of its bent this whim of reformation in the Duke. No ungrateful physicking of a soured bile for him; no uncomfortable philosophy of organic atoms recombined. He just restored to him that long-lost toy of innocence, trusting that the imagination of the man would find ever novel resources for play in that of which the invention of the child had soon tired. So for the present, and until virtue in his patient should have become a second nature, was he resolved wisely to eschew all reference to the intermediate state, and only by example and analogy to win him to consciousness and repentance of the enormities by which it had been stained. A very profound little missionary, to be sure.

The Duke, leaning on his arm as he strolled, had a smile and a word for many. The only visible token of his familiar self which he revealed was the arbitrariness with which he exacted from all a fitting deference towards his protégé. This, however, none, not the greatest, was inclined to withhold, especially on such a morning. Soft-footed cardinals, princes of the blood, nobles and jingling captains, vied with one another in obsequious attentions to our little neophyte of love. The reasons, apart from superstitious reverence, were plentiful: his sweetness, his beauty, his gifts of song—all warm recommendations to a sensuous sociality; the whispered romance of his origin, no less a patent in its eyes because it turned on a title doubly bastard; finally, and most cogently, no doubt, his political potentialities as a favourite *in posse*.

This last reason above any other may have accounted for the extraordinary complaisance shown him by Messer Ludovico, the Duke's third younger brother, at present at court, who was otherwise of a rather inward and withdrawing nature. He, this brother, had come from Pavia, riding the final stage that morning, and though he had only gathered by report the story of the last twelve hours, thought it worth his while to go and ingratiate himself with the stranger. He found him in the great hall of the castello, awaiting the trial of certain causes, which, as coming immediately under the ducal jurisdiction, it was Galeazzo's sport often to preside over in person. Here he saw the boy, standing at his brother's shoulder by the judgment-seat—the comeliest figure, between Cupid and angel, he had ever beheld; frank, sweet, child-eyed—in every feature and quality, it would seem, the antithesis of himself. Messer Ludovico came up arm in arm, very condescendingly, with his excellency the Ser Simonetta, Secretary of State, a gentleman whom he was always at pains to flatter, since he intended by and by to destroy him. Not that he had any personal spite against this minister, however much he might suspect him of misrepresenting his motives and character to the Duchess Bona, his sister-in-law, to whom he, Ludovico, was in reality, he assured himself, quite attached. His policy, on the contrary, was always a passionless one; and the point here was simply that the man, in his humble opinion, affected too much reason and temperance for a despotic government.

As he approached the tribune he uncapped, a thought on the near side of self-abasement, to his brother, whose cavalier acknowledgment of the salute halted him, however, affable and smiling, on the lowest step of the dais. He was studious, while there, to inform with the right touch of pleasant condescension (at least while Galeazzo's regard was fixed on him) his attitude towards Simonetta, lest the ever-suspicious mind of the tyrant should discover in it some sign of a corruptive intimacy. With heirs-possibly-presumptive in Milan, sufficient for the day's life must be the sleepless diplomacy thereof; and better than any man Ludovico knew on what small juggleries of the moment the continuance of his depended. His complexion being of a swarthiness to have earned him the surname of The Moor, he had acquired a habit of drooping his lids in company, lest the contrastive effect of white eyeballs moving in a dark, motionless face should betray him to the subjects of those covert side-long glances by which he was wont to observe unobserved. Even to his shoulders, which were slightly rounded by nature, he managed, when in his brother's presence, to give the suggestion of a self-deprecatory hump, as though the slight burden of State which they already endured were too much for them. His voice was low-toned; his expression generally of a soft and rather apologetic benignity. His manner towards all was calculated on a graduated scale of propitiation. Paying every disputant the compliment of deferring outwardly to his opinions, he would not whip so little as a swineherd without apologising for the inconvenience to which he was putting him. His dress was rich, but while always conceived on the subdominant note, so to speak, as implying the higher ducal standard, was in excellent taste, a quality which he could afford to indulge with impunity, since it excited no suspicion but of his simplicity in Galeazzo's crude mind. In point of fact Messer Ludovico was a born connoisseur, and, equally in his choice of men, methods, and tools, a first exemplar of the faculty of selection.

Presently, seeing the Duke's gaze withdrawn from him, he spoke to Messer Simonetta more intimately, but still out of the twisted corner of his mouth, while his eyes remained slewed under their lids towards the throne:—

'Indeed, my lord, indeed yes; 'tis a veritable Castalidis, fresh from Parnassus and the spring. Tell me, now—'tis no uncommon choice of my brother to favour a fair boy—what differentiates this case from many?'

The secretary, long caged in office, and worn and toothless from friction on its bars, had yet his ideals of Government, personal as well as political.

'Your Highness,' said he, in his hoarse, thin voice, 'what differentiates sacramental wine from Malvasia?'

'Why,' answered Ludovico, 'perhaps a degree or two of headiness.'

'Nay,' said the secretary, 'is it not rather a degree or two of holiness?'

'Ebbene!' said the other, 'I stand excellently corrected. (Your servant, Messer Tassino,' he said, in parenthesis, to a pert and confident young exquisite, who held himself arrogantly forward of the group of spectators. The jay responded to the attention with a condescending nod. Ludovico readdressed himself to the secretary.) 'How neatly you put things! It is a degree or two, as you say—between the intoxication of the spirit and the intoxication of the senses. And is this pretty stranger sacramental wine, and hath Heaven vouchsafed us the Grael without the Quest? It is a sign of its high favour, Messer Slmonetta, of which I hope and trust we shall prove ourselves worthy.'

'And I hope so, Highness,' said the grave secretary.

'Hush!' whispered Ludovico. 'The court opens.'

There was a little stir and buzz among the spectators who, thronging the hall, left a semi-circle of clear space about the dais; and into this, at the moment, a fellow in a ragged gabardine was haled by a guard of city officers. The Duke, seated above, stroked his chin with a glance at the prisoner of sinister relish, which, on the thought, he smoothed, with a little apologetic cough, into an expression of mild benignancy. Messer Lanti, planted near at hand amid a very parterre of nobles, envoys, ecclesiastics, bedizened *chères amies* and great officers of the court who supported their lord on the dais, sniggered under his breath till his huge shoulders shook.

The Jew was charged with a very heinous offence—sweating coins, no less. He was voluble and nasal over his innocence, until one of the officers flicked him bloodily on the mouth with his mailed hand.

'Nay,' said Bembo, shrinking; 'that is to give the poor man a dumb advocate, methinks.'

The Duke applauded—eliciting some louder applause from Ludovico— and forbade the fellow sternly to strike again without orders. A sudden sigh and movement seemed to ripple the congregated faces and to subside. The prisoner, however, was convicted, on sound enough evidence, and stood sullen and desperate to hear his sentence. Galeazzo eyed him covetously a moment; then turning to a clerk of the court who knelt beside him with his tablets ready, bade that obsequious functionary proclaim the penalty which by statute obtained against all coiners or defacers of the ducal image. It was bad enough—breaking on the wheel—to pass without deadlier revision; yet to such, and to the high will or caprice of his lord, Master Scrivener humbly submitted it.

Then, to the dumfoundering of all, did his Magnificence appeal, with a smile, to the little Parablist at his shoulder:—

'Mi' amico; thou hearest? What say'st?'

'Lord,' answered Bernardo, in the soft, clear young voice that all might hear like a bird's song in the stillness after rain, 'this wretch hath defaced thy graven image.'

'It is true.'

'What if, in a more impious mood, he had dared to raise his hand against thyself?'

'Ha! He would be made to die—not pleasantly.'

'Is to be broken on the wheel pleasant?'

'Well, the dog shall hang.'

'Still for so little? Why, were he Cain he could pay no higher. Valuest thy life, then, at a pinch of gold dust? This is to put a premium on regicide.'

The Duke bit his lip, and frowned, and laughed vexedly.

'How now, Bernardino?'

'Lord, I am young—a child, and without comparative experience. I pray thee put this rogue aside, while we consider.'

Galeazzo waved his hand, and the Jew, staring and stumbling, was removed. Another, a creature gaunt and wolfish, took his place. What had he done? He had trodden on a hare in her form, and, half-killing, had despatched her. Why? asked Bembo. To still her telltale cries, intimated the wretched creature. Galeazzo's eyes gleamed; but still he called upon Heaven to sentence. In such a case? Men glanced at one another half terrified. Any portent, even of good, is fearful in its rising. Bembo turned to the kneeling clerk.

'Come, Master Scrivener! A little offence, in any case, and with humanity to condone it.'

The frightened servant shook his head, with a glance at his master. He murmured the worst he dared—that the law exacted the extremest penalty from the unauthorised killer of game. Bembo stared a moment incredulous, then pounced in mock fury at the prisoner:—

'Wretch! what didst thou with this hare?'

The hind had to be goaded to an answer.

'Master, I ate it.'

'What!' cried the other—'a monster, to devour thy prince's flesh!'

'God knows I did not!'

'Nay, God is nothing to the law, which says you did. Else why should it draw no distinction between the crimes of harecide and regicide? Thou hast eaten of thy prince.'

'Well, if I have I have.'

'Thou art anthropophagous.'

'Mercy!'

'No shame to thee—a lover of thy kind' (the Saint chuckled). 'And no cannibal neither, since we have made game of thy prince.' He chuckled again, and turned merrily on the Duke. 'Is the hare to be prince, or the prince hare? And yet, in either case, O Galeazzo, I see no way for thee out of this thy loving subject's belly!'

The tyrant, half captivated, half furious, started forward.

'Give him,' he roared—and stopped. 'Give him,' he repeated, 'a kick on his breach and send him flying. Nay!' he snarled, 'even that were too much honour. Give him a scudo with which to buy an emetic.'

Bembo smiled and sighed: 'I begin to see daylight'; and Ludovico, after laughing enjoyingly over his brother's pleasantry, exclaimed audibly to Simonetta: 'This is the very wedding of human wit and divine. I seem to see the air full of laughing cherubs having my brother's features.'

Now there brake into the arena one clad like an artificer in a leathern apron; a sinewy figure, but eloquent, in his groping hands and bandaged face, of some sudden blight of ruin seizing prime. And he cried out in a great voice:—

'A boon, lord Duke, a boon! I am one Lupo, an armourer, and thou seest me!'

'Certes,' said the Duke. 'Art big enough.'

'O lord!' cried the shattered thing, 'let me see justice as plain with these blinded eyes.'

'Well, on whom?'

'Lord, on him that took me sleeping, and struck me for ever from the rolls of daylight, sith I had cursed him for the ruin of my daughter.'

Galeazzo shrugged his shoulders.

'This thine assailant—is he noble?'

'Master, as titles go.'

'Wert a fool, then, to presume. He were like else to have made it good to thee. Now, an eye for—' but he checked himself in the midst of the enormous blasphemy.

'Judge thou, my guardian angel,' he murmured meekly.

'What!' answered the boy, with a burning face, 'needs *this* revision by Heaven?' And he cried terribly: 'Master armourer, summon thy transgressor!'

For a moment the man seemed to shrink.

'Nay,' cried the Saint, 'thou need'st not. I see the hand of God come forth and write upon a forehead.' His eyes sparkled, as if in actual inspiration. 'Tassino!' he cried, in a ringing voice.

('He heard me address him,' thought Ludovico, curious and watchful.)

At the utterance of that name, the whole nerve of the audience seemed to leap and fall like a candle-flame. Galeazzo himself started, and his lids lifted, and his mouth creased a moment to a little malevolent grin. For why? This Tassino, while too indifferent a skipjack for his jealousy, was yet the squire amoroso, the lover *comme il faut* to his own correct Duchess, Madam Bona.

A minute's ticking silence was ended by the stir and pert laugh of the challenged himself, as he left the ring of spectators and sauntered into the arena. It was a little showy upstart, to be sure, as ebulliently curled and groomed as her Grace's lap-dog, and sharing, indeed, with Messer Tinopino the whole present caprice of their mistress's spoiling. His own base origin and inherent vulgarity, moreover, seeming to associate him with the ducal brutishness (an assumption which Galeazzo rather favoured than resented), confirmed in him a self-confidence which had early come to see no bounds to its own viciousness or effrontery.

Now he cocked one arm akimbo, and stared with insufferable insolence on the pronouncer of his name.

'Know'st me, Prophet?' bawled he. 'Not more than I thee, methinks. Wert well coached in this same inspiration.'

'Well, indeed,' answered Bembo. 'Thou hast said it. It was God spake in mine ear.'

Tassino laughed scornfully. It was a study to see these young wits opposed, the one such plated goods, the other so silver pure.

'In the name of this lying carle,' he cried, 'what spake He?'

'He said,' said Bembo quietly, '"Let the false swearer remember Ananias!"'

Then in a moment he was all ruffled and combative, like a young eagle.

'Answer!' he roared. 'Didst thou this thing?'

Now, a woman-petted, cake-fed belswagger is too much of an anomaly for the test of nerves. Tassino, shouted at, gave an hysteric jump which brought him to the very brink of tears. He was really an ill-bred little coward, made arrogant by spoiling. He had the greatest pity and tenderness for himself, and to any sense of his being lost would always respond with a lump in his throat. Now he suddenly realised his position, alone and baited before all—no petticoat to fly to, no sympathy to expect from a converted tyrant, none from a mob which, habitually the butt to his viciousness, would rejoice in his discomfiture. Actually the little beast began to whimper.

'Darest thou!' he cried, stamping.

'Didst thou this thing?' repeated Bernardo.

'It is no business of thine.'

'Didst thou this thing?'

'An oaf's word against— —'

'Didst thou this thing?'

'Lord Duke!' appealed Tassino.

'Didst thou this thing?'

The victim fairly burst into tears.

'If I say no——'

'Die, Ananias!' shouted the Duke. His eyes gleamed maniacally. He half rose in his chair. He seemed as if furious to foreclose on a dénouement his superstition had already anticipated. Tassino fell upon his knees.

'I did it!' he screamed.

The Duke sank back, his lips twitching and grinning. Then he glanced covertly at Bembo, and rubbed his hands together, with a motion part gloating, part deprecatory. The Ser Ludovico's eyes, shaded under his palm, were very busy, to and fro. Bembo stood like frowning marble.

'The law, Master Scrivener?' said he quietly.

The kneeling clerk murmured from a dry throat—

'Holy sir, it takes no cognisance of these accidents. The condescensions of the great compensate them.'

The Parablist, his lips pressed together, nodded gravely twice or thrice.

'I see,' he said; 'a condescension which ruins two lives.'

He addressed himself, with a deadly sweetness, to the Duke.

'I prithee, who standest for God's vicegerent, call up the Jew to sentence.'

Jehoshaphat was produced, and placed beside the blubbered, resentful young popinjay. The Saint addressed him:—

'Wretch, thou art convicted of the crime of defacing the Duke's image; and he at thine elbow of defacing God's image. Shall man dare the awful impiety to pronounce the greater guilt thine? Yet, if it merits death and mutilation, what for this other?'

He paused, and a stir went through the dead stillness of the hall. Then Bembo addressed one of the tipstaves with ineffable civility:—

'Good officer, this rogue hath sweated coins, say'st?'

'Ay, your worship,' answered the man; 'a hundred gold ducats, if a lire. Shook 'em in a leathern bag, a' did, like so much rusted harness.'

Bembo nodded.

'They are forfeit, by the token; and he shall labour to provide other hundred, with cost of metal and stamping.'

Jehoshaphat, secure of his limbs, shrieked derisive—

'God of Ishril! O, yes! O, to be sure! I can bleed moneys!'

'Nay,' said the Saint, 'but sweat them. Go!'

The coiner was dragged away blaspheming. He would have preferred a moderate dose of the rack; but the standard set by his sentence elicited a murmur of popular approval. From all, that is to say, but Tassino, who saw his own fate looming big by comparison. He rose and looked about him desperately, as if he contemplated bolting. The spectators edged together. He whinnied. Suddenly the stranger's voice swooped upon him like a hawk:—

'Man's image shall be restored; restore thou God's.'

The little wretch screamed in a sudden access of passion:—

'I don't know what you mean! Leave me alone. It was his own fault, I say. Why did he insult me?'

'Restore thou this image of God his sight,' said Bembo quietly.

'You know I cannot!'

'Thou canst not? Then an eye for an eye, as it was spoken. Take ye this wicked thing, good officers, and blind him even as he blinded the poor armourer.'

A vibrant sound went up from the spectators, and died. Messer Ludovico veiled his sight, and, it might be said, his laughter. Tassino was seen struggling and crying in the half-fearful clutch of his gaolers.

'Thou darest not! Dogs! Let me go, I say. What! would ye brave Madonna? Lord Duke, lord Duke, help me!'

'To repentance, my poor Tassino,' cried Galeazzo, leaning lustfully forward. 'I trow thy part on earth is closed.'

The little monster could not believe it. This instant fall from the heights! He was flaccid with terror as he fell screeching on his knees.

'Mercy, good stranger! Mercy, dear lord saint! The terror! the torture! I could not suffer them and live. O, let me live, I pray thee!—anywhere, anyhow, and I will do all; make whatever restitution you impose.'

As he prayed and wept and grovelled, the Saint looked down with icy pity on his abasement.

'Restitution, Tassino!' he cried, 'for that murthered vision, for that ruined virtue? Wouldst thou even in thine impiousness arrogate to thyself such divine prerogatives? Yet, in respect of that reason with which true justice doth hedge her reprisals, the Duke's mercy shall still allot thee an alternative. Sith thou canst not restore his honour or his eyes to poor Lupo, thou shalt take his shame to wife, and in her seek to renew that image of God which thou hast defaced. Do this, and only doing it, know thyself spared.'

A silence of stupefaction fell upon the court. What would Bona say to this arbitrary disposal of her pet, made husband to a common gipsy he had debauched? True, the sentence, by virtue of its ethical completeness, seemed an inspiration. But it was a disappointment too. None doubted but that the popinjay would subscribe to the present letter in order to evade the practice of it by and by. Already the paltry soul of the creature was struggling from its submersion, gasping, and blinking wickedly to see how it could retort upon its judge and deliverer. It had been better to have trodden it under for once and for good—better for the moral of the lesson, as for all who foresaw some hope for themselves in the crushing of an insufferable petty tyranny. Galeazzo himself frowned and bit his nails. He would have lusted to see heaven pluck off this vulgar burr for him. Only his brother, sleek and smiling, applauded the verdict. He had a far-seeing vision, had Ludovico, and perhaps already it was alotting a more telling rôle to the little aristocrat of San Zeno than had ever been played by the cockney parvenu down in the arena.

Suddenly the Duke was on his feet, fierce and glaring.

'Answer, dog!' he roared; 'acceptest thou the condition?'

Tassino started and sobbed.

'Yes, yes. I accept. I will marry her.'

The Duke took a costly chain from his own neck, and hung it about the shoulders of the Parablist.

'Wear this,' he said, 'in earnest of our love and duty.'

Then he turned upon the mob.

'These judgments stand, and all that shall be spoken hereafter by our dear monitor and proctor. It is our will. Make way, gentlemen.'

He took Bernardo's arm and descended the steps. A cloud of courtiers hovered near, acclaiming the boy Saint and Daniel. Messer Ludovico saluted him with fervour. He foresaw the millennium in this association of piety with greatness. Galeazzo sneered.

'Remember that three spoils company, brother,' said he. 'Keep thou thine own confessor, and leave me mine.'

It was then only that Bernardo learned the rank of his accoster.

'Alas! sweet lord,' said he, 'is piety such a stranger here that ye must entertain him like a king?'

The Duke laughed loudly and drew him on. He was extravagant in his attentions to him—eager, voluble, feverish. He would point out to him the lavish decorations of his house—marbles, sculptures, paintings, the rising fabric of a new era—and ask his opinion on all. A word from the child at that period would have floored a cardinal or a scaffolding, have clothed Aphrodite in a cassock, have made a *fête champêtre* of all Milan, or darkened its walls with mourning. Messer Lanti, following in their wake, was amazed, and dubious, and savage in turns. Earlier in the day the Duke had had from him the whole story of his connection with the Parablist, up to the moment of their interference in Montano's punishment.

'*Meschino me!*' he had said, greatly laughing over that episode; 'yet I cannot but be glad that the old code beat itself out on his back. 'Twas a reptile well served—a venomous, ungrateful beast. A mercy if it has broken his fang.'

That remained to be seen; and in the meantime Carlo, the old auxiliary in debauch, was taken again into full favour. He accepted the condescension with reserve. The oddest new attachment had come to supplant in him some ancient devotions that were the furthest from devout. He found himself in a very queer mood, between irritable and gentle. He had never before felt this inclination to hit hard for virtue, and it bewildered his honest head. But it made him a dangerous watchdog.

By and by the Duke carried his protégé into the Duchess's privy garden. There was a necessary economy of ornamental ground about the castello, though the most was made of what could be spared. In a nest of green alleys, and falling terraces, and rose-wreathed arches, they came upon the two ladies whom Bembo had already seen, themselves as pretty, graceful flowers as any in the borders. The young Catherine sat upon a fountain edge, fanning herself with a great leaf, and talking to a flushed, down-looking page, who, it seemed likely, had brought news from the court of a recent scandal and its sequel. Her shrewd, pretty face took curious stock of the new comers. She was a pale slip of a girl, lithe, bosomless, the green plum of womanhood. Her thin, plain dress was green, fitting her like a sheath its blade of corn, and she wore on her sleek fair head a cap of green velvet banded with a scroll of beaten gold. A child she was, yet already for two years betrothed to a Pope's nephew. His presents on the occasion had included a camera of green velvet, sewn with pearls as thick as daisies in grass. It seemed natural to associate her with spring verdure, so sweet and fair she was; yet never, surely, worked a more politic little brain under its cap of innocence.

Hard by, on one of the walks, a woman and a child of seven played at ball. These were Bona, and her little son Gian-Galeazzo. As the other was spring, so was she summer, ripe in figure and mellowed in the passion of motherhood. Her eyes burned with the caress and entreaty of it—appealed in loveliness to the fathers of her desires. Her beauty, her stateliness, the very milk of her were all sweet lures to increase. She loved babies, not men—saw them most lusty, perhaps, in the glossy eyes of fools, the breeding-grounds of Cupids. She was always a mother before a wife.

The Duke led Bernardo to her side. Pale as ivory, she bent and embraced her boy, and dismissed him to the fountain; then rose to face the ordeal.

'Hail, judgments of Solomon!' she said, with a smile that quivered a little. 'O believe me, sir, thy fame has run before!'

'Which was the reason thou dismissedst Gian,' said Galeazzo, 'in fears that Solomon would propose to halve him?'

He did not doubt her, or wing his shaft with anything but brutality. It was his coward way, and, having asserted it, he strolled off, grinning and whistling, to the fountain.

Bona shivered and drew herself up. Her robe was all of daffodil, with a writhed golden hem to it that looked like a long flicker of flame. On her forehead, between wings of auburn hair, burned a great emerald. She seemed to Bernardo the loveliest, most gracious thing, a vision personified of fruitfulness, the golden angel of maternity, warm, fragrant, kind-bosomed. He met the gaze of her eyes with wonderment, but no fear.

'Sweet Madonna,' he said, 'hail me nothing, I pray thee, but the clear herald of our Christ—His mouthpiece and recorder. We may all be played upon for truth, so we be pure of heart.'

'And that art thou? No guile? No duplicity? No self-interest?'

He marvelled. She looked at him earnestly.

'Bernardo, didst know this Tassino was my servant?'

'Nay, I knew it not.'

'Wouldst have spared him hadst thou known?'

'How could I spare him the truth?'

'But its shame, its punishment?'

'Greater shame could no man have than to debauch innocence. His punishment was his redemption.'

'Ah! I defend him not. Yet, bethink thee, she may have been the temptress?'

'He should have loathed, not loved her, then.'

'Madreperla, mother-of-pearl,' cried Catherine, with a little shriek of laughter, from the fountain; 'come and help me! I have caught a butterfly in my hand, and my father wishes to take it from me and kill it!'

CHAPTER VII

Bernardo wrote to the Abbot of San Zeno:—

'MOST DEAR AND HONOURED FATHER,—Many words from me would but dilute the wonder of my narrative. Also thou lovest brevity in all things but God's praise. Know, then, how I have surpassed expectation in the early propagation of our creed, which is by Love to banish Law, that old engine of necessarianism. [*Here follows a brief recapitulation of the events which had landed him, a little sweet oracle of light, in the dark old castello of Milanl.*] Man' (he goes on) 'is of all creatures the most susceptible to his environments. Thou shalt induce him but to feed on the olive branches of Peace in order that he may take their colour. O sorrow, then, on the false appetites which have warped his nature! on the beastly doctrines which, Satan-engendered, have led him half to believe there is no wrong or right, but only necessity! Is there no such thing as discord in music, at which even a dog will howl? Harmony is God—so plain. Yet there is a learned doctor here, one Lascaris who disputeth this. My father, I do not think that learned doctors seek so much the intrinsic truth of things as to impress their followers with their perspicacity in the pursuit. John led James over-the-way by a "short cut" of three miles, and James thought John a very clever fellow. Pray for me!...

'I will speak first of the Duchess, to whom I delivered your letter. She is a most sweet lady, with eyes, so kind and loving were they, they made me think of those soft stars which light the flocks to fold. She asked me did I remember my mother? "That is a strange question," quoth I, "to a foundling." "Ah!" said she, "poor child! I had forgot how thou fell'st, a star, into Mary's lap. I would have taken care, for my part, not so to tumble out of heaven." "Nay," I said, "but if thou, a mother there, hadst let slip thy baby first?" "What," she said, looking at me so strange and wistful, "did she follow, then?" My father, thou know'st my fancies. "I cannot tell," I said. "Sometimes, in a dream, the dim, sad shadow of a woman's face seems to hang over me lying on that altar." She held out her arms to me, then withdrew them, and she was weeping. "We are all wicked," she cried; "there is no heart, nor faith, nor virtue, in any of us!" and she ran away lamenting. Now, was not that strange? for she is in truth a lady of great virtue, a pure wife and mother, and to me most sweet-forgiving for an ill-favour I was forced to do her upon one of her servants. But not women nor men know their own hearts. They wear the devil's livery for fashion's sake, when he introduces it on a pretty sister or young gentleman, and so believe themselves bound to his service. But it is as easy as talking to make virtue the mode. Thou shalt see.

'Does not the beautiful Duomo itself stand in their midst, the fairest earnest of their true piety? Could intrinsic baseness conceive this ethereal fabric, or, year by year, graft it with sprigs of new loveliness? There is that in them yet like a little child that stretches out its arms to the sky.

'I have, besides the greatest, two converts, or half-converts, already, my dear Carlo and his Fool. The former is a great bull gallant, whom a spark will set roaring and a kiss allay. I love him greatly, and he bellows and prances, and swearing "I will not" follows to the pipe of peace. Alas! if I could woo him from a great wrong! It will happen, when men see honour whole, and not partisanly. In the meantime I have every reason to be charitable to that lady Beatrice, sith she holds herself my mortal enemy. And indeed I excuse her for myself, but not for the honest soul she keeps in thrall. My father, is it not a strange paradox, that holding the senses such a rich possession and life so cheap? Here is one would prolong the body's pleasure to eternity, yet at any moment will risk its destruction for a spite. Nathless she is warm, loamy soil for the bearing of our right lily of love, and some day shall be fruitful in cleanliness.

'Now the Fool—poor Fool! I have won to temperance, and so Carlo growleth, "A murrain on thee, spoil-sport! What want I with a sober Fool? Take him, thou, to be valet to thy temperance!" by which gibe he seeks to cover a gracious act. And, lo! I have a Fool for servant, a most notable Fool and auxiliary, who, having sworn himself to abstinence, would unplug and sink to the bottomless abyss every floating hogshead. In sooth the good soul is my shadow, and so they call him. "Well," says he, "so be it. But what sort of fool art thou, to cast a fool for shadow?" "Why, look," says I, for it was sunset on the grass—"at least not so great a fool as thou." "That may well be," says he, "for you do not serve Messer Bembo." So caustic is he—a biting love; yet, as is proper between a man and his shadow, equal attached to me as I to him. And so, talking of his gift to me, brings me to the greater gifts of the Duke.

'O my father! How can I speak my gratitude to heaven and thy teaching, which brought me so swiftly, so wonderfully, to prevail with that dread man! I think evil is like the false opal, which needs but the first touch of pure light to shatter it. I have come with no weapon but my little lamp of sunshine; and behold! in its flash the base is discredited and the truth acknowledged. It is all so easy, Christ guard me! There is a Providence in what men call chance. Only, my father, pray that thy child be not misled by flattery to usurp its prerogatives. Men, in this dim world, are all too prone to worship the visible symbols of Immortality—to accept the prophet for the Master. I am already fêted and caressed as if I were a god. The Duke hath impropriated to me an income of a thousand ducatos, with free residence in the castello, and a retinue to befit a prince. At all this I cavil not, sith it affords me the sinews to a crusade. But what shall I say to his delegating me to the chief magistracy of Milan during his forthcoming absence? for he is on the eve of an expedition into Piedmont, touching the lordship of Vercelli, which he claims through his wife Bona of Savoy. Carlo, it is true, warns me against this perilous exaltation. "Seek'st thou," says he, "to depose the devil? Well, the devil, on his return, will treat thee like any other palace revolutionist." "Nay," says I, "the devil was never the devil from choice. Restore him to a converted dukedom, and he will aspire to be the saint of all." "Yes," he said, "I can imagine Galeazzo endowing a hospital for Magdalenes and washing the poor's feet. But I will stick to thee." A dear worldling he is, and only less uncertain than his master in these first infant steps towards godliness. For vice is very childlike in its self-plumings upon a little knowledge. Desiring beauty, it tears the rose-bush or clutches the moth, and so sickens on disillusionment. Forbearance is the wisdom of the great.

'The more destructive is a man, the simpler is he. Now, my father, this destroying Duke covets nothing so much as the applause of the world for gifts with which, in truth, he is ill-endowed. He cannot sing, or rhyme, or improvise but with the worst, yet, thinks he, they shall call me poet and musician, or burn. Well, he might fiddle over the holocaust, like Nero, and still be first cousin to a peacock. I told him so, but in gentler words, when he asked me to teach him my method. "To every soul its capacities," says I, "and mine are not in ruling a great duchy greatly." "So we are neither of us omnipotent," says he, with a smile. "Well, I will take the lesson to heart." Now, could so simple a creature be all corrupt?

'Of more complicated fibre is his brother, the Signior Ludovico. Very politic and abiding, he rushes at nothing; yet in the end, I think, most things come to him. He is gracious to thy child, as indeed are all; yet, God forgive me, I find something more inhuman in his gentleness than in Galeazzo's passion. These inexplicable antipathies are surely the weapons of Satan; whereby it behoves us to overcome them. That same Lascaris attributes them to an accidental re-fusion of particles, opposed to other chance re-combinations, in a present body, of particles similarly antipathetic to us in a former existence—a long "short cut" over the way again.

'Now, as for my days in this poignant city—where even the benches and clothes-chests, not to speak of most walls and ceilings, yea, and the very stair-posts themselves, are painted with crowded devices of scrolls and figures in loveliest gold and azure and vermilion—thou mayest believe they are strange to me. Amidst this wealth I, thy simple acolyte, am glorified, I say, and courted beyond measure. Yet fear nothing for me. I appraise this distinction at its right market value. The higher the Duke's favour, the greater my presumptive influence. Believe me, dear, my urbanity towards his attentions is an investment for my Master. I am an honest factor.

'In a week the Duke sets out. In the meantime, like an ambassador that must suffer present festival for the sake of future credit, I sit at feasts and plays; or, perchance, rise to denounce the latter for no better than whores' saturnalia. (O my father! to see fair ladies, the Duchess herself, smile on such shameless bawdry!) Whereon the Duke thunders all to stop, with threats of fury on the actors to mend their ways, making the poor fools gasp bewildered. For how had *they* presumed upon custom? Bad habit is like the moth in fur, so easily shaken out when first detected; so hardly when established. Once, more to my liking, we have a mummers' dance, with clowns in rams' heads butting; and again a harvest ballet, with all the seasons pictured very pretty. Another day comes a Mantuan who plays on three lutes at once, more curious than tuneful; and after him one who walks on a rope in the court, a steel cuirass about his body. Now happens their festival of the *Bacchidæ*, a pagan survival, but certes sweet and graceful, with its songs and vines and dances. Maybe for my sake they purge it of some licence. Well, Heaven witness to them what loss or gain thereby to beauty.

'Often the court goes hunting the wolf or deer—I care not; or a-picnicking by the river, which I like, and where we catch trouts and lampreys to cook and eat on the green; then run we races, perchance, or play at ball. So merry and light-hearted—how can wickedness be other than an accident with these children of good-nature? To mark the jokes they play on one another— mischievous sometimes—suggests to one a romping nursery, which yet I know not. Father, who was my mother? I trow we romped somewhere in heaven. Once some gallants of them, being in collusion with the watch, enter, in the guise of robbers, Messer Secretary Simonetta's house at midnight, and bind and blindfold that great man, and placing him on an ass in his night-gear (which is an excuse for nothing), carry him through the streets as if to their quarters. Which, having gained, they unbind; and lo! he is in the inner ward of the castello, the Duke and a great company about him and shouts of laughter; in which I could not help but join, though it was shameful. Next day the Duchess herself does not disdain a wrestling match with the lady Catherine, her adoptive daughter; when the lithe little serpent, enwreathing that stately Queen, doth pull her sitting on her lap, whereby she conquers. For all improvising and stories they have as great a passion as ingenuity; and therein, my gifts by Christ's ensample lying, comes my opportunity. Dear Father, am I presumptuous in my feeble might, like the boy Phæton when he coaxed the Sun's reins from Ph[oe]bus, and scorched the wry road since called the Milky Way? That is such an old tale as we tell by moonlight under trees—such as Christ Himself, the child-God, hath recounted to us, sitting shoulder-deep in meadow-grass, or by the pretty falling streams. Is He that exacting, that exotic Deity, lusting only for adoration, eternally gluttonous of praise and never surfeited, whom squeamish indoor men, making Him the fetish of their closets, have reared for heaven's type? O, find Him in the blown trees and running water; in the carol of sweet birds; in the mines from whose entrails are drawn our ploughshares; yea, in the pursuit of maid by man! So, in these long walks and rests of life, shall He be no less our Prince because He is our joyous comrade. For this I know: Not to a pastor, a lord, a parent himself, doth the soul of the youth go out as to the companion of his own age and freedom.

'Christ comes again as He journeyed with His Apostles, the bright wise comrade, fitting earth to heaven in the puzzle of the spheres. We know Him Human, my father, feeling the joy of weariness for repose' sake; not disdaining the cool inn's sanctuary; expounding love by forbearance. He beareth Beauty redeemed on His brow. Before the clear gaze of His eyes all heaped sophistries melt away like April snow. He calleth us to the woods and meadows. *Quasimodo geniti infantes rationabile sine dolo lac concupiscete.* O, mine eyelids droop! We are seldom at rest here before two o' the morning. The beds have trellised gratings by day, to keep the dogs from smirching their coverlets. *Ora pro me!'*

CHAPTER VIII

The castle at the Porta Giovia had its glooms as well as its pleasances. Indeed, it may be questioned if the latter were not rather in proportion to the former as a tiger's gay hide is to the strength and ferocity it clothes. Built originally for a great keep, or, as it were, breakwater, to stem the rush of barbarian seas which were wont to come storming down from the north-west, its constructors had aimed at nothing less than its everlastingness. So thick were its bastioned walls, so thick the curtains which divided its inner and outer wards, a whole warren of human 'runs' could honeycomb without appreciably weakening them. Hidden within its screens and massy towers, like the gnawings of a foul and intricate cancer, ran dark passages which discharged themselves here and there into dreadful dungeons, or secret-places not guessed at in the common tally of its rooms. These oubliettes were hideous with blotched and spotted memories; rotten with the dew of suffering; eloquent in their terror and corruption and darkness, of that same self-sick, self-blinded tyranny which, in place of Love and Justice, the trusty bodyguards, must turn always to cruelty and thick walls for its security. The hiss and purr of subterranean fire, the grinding of low-down grated jaws, the flop and echo of stagnant water, oozed from a stagnant moat into vermin-swarming, human-haunted cellars,—these were sounds that spoke even less of grief to others than of the hellish ferment in the soul of him who had raised them for his soul's pacifying. Himself is for ever the last and maddest victim of a despot's oppression.

There had been stories to tell, could the coulter of Time once have cut into those far-down vaults, and his share laid open. Now this was so far from promising, that their history and mystery were in process of being still further overlaid and stifled under accumulations of superstructure. Francesco, the great Condottiere, the present Duke's father, had been the first to realise dimly how a tyrant, by converting his self-prison into a shrine for his æstheticism, might enjoy a certain amelioration of his condition. It was he who, yielding an older palace and its grounds to the builders of the cathedral, had transferred the ducal quarters to the great fortress, which henceforth was to be the main seat of the Sforzas. Here the first additions and rebuildings had been his, the first decorations and beautifyings—tentative at the best, for he was always more a soldier than a connoisseur. The real movement was inaugurated by his successor, and continued, as cultivation was impressed on him, on a scale of magnificence which was presently to make the splendour of Milan a proverb. Galeazzo, an indifferent warrior, to whose rule but a tithe of the territory once gathered to the Visconti owned allegiance, contented his ambitions by rallying an army of painters and sculptors and decorators to the glorification of his houses at Milan, Cremona, and his ancestral petted Pavia,—after all a worthier rôle than the conqueror's for a good man; but then, this man was so bad that he blighted everything he touched. It is true that the disuse of secret torture would have been considered, and by men more enlightened than he, so little expedient a part of any ethical or æsthetical 'improvement' of an existing house, as that a premium would be put thereby on assassination. Yet Galeazzo's death-pits were never so much a politic necessity as a resource for cruelty in idleness. He would descend into them with as much relish as he would reclimb from, to his halls above, swelling and bourgeoning with growth of loveliness. The scream of torture was as grateful to his ears as was the love-throb of a viol; the scum bubbling from his living graves as poignant to his nostrils as was the scent of floating lilies. He continued to make his house beautiful, yet never once dreamt, as a first principle of its reclamation to sweetness, of cutting out of its foundations those old cesspools of disease and death.

One night he sat in his closet of the Rocca, a little four-square room dug out of the armourer's tower, and having a small oratory adjoining. This eyrie was so high up as to give a comfortable sense of security against surprise. There was but one window to it—just a deep wedge in the wall, piercing to the sheer flank of the tower. Sweet rushes carpeted the floor; the arras was pictured with dim, sacred subjects—Ambrosius in his cradle, with the swarm of bees settling on his honeyed lips; Ambrosius elected Bishop of Milan by the people; Ambrosius imposing penance on Theodosius for his massacre of the Thessalonicans—and the drowsy odours of a pastile, burning in the little purple shrine-lamp, robbed the air of its last freshness.

Another lamp shone on a table, at which the Duke was seated somewhat preoccupied with a lute, and his tablets propped before him; while, motionless in the shadows opposite, stood the figure of the provost marshal, its fixed, unregarding eyes glinting in the flame.

Intermittently Galeazzo strummed and murmured, self-communing, or addressing himself, between playfulness and abstraction, to the ear of Messer Jacopo:—

'The lowliest of all Franciscans was St. Francis, meek mate of beasts and birds, boasting himself no peer of belted stars.... Ha! a good line, Jacopo, a full significant line; I dare say it, our Parablist despite. Listen.' (He chaunted the words in a harsh, uncertain voice, to an accompaniment as sorry.) 'Hear'st? Belted stars—those moon-ringed spheres the aristocracy of the night. Could Messer Bembo himself have better improvised? What think'st? Be frank.'

'I think of improvising by book,' said Jacopo, short and gruff.

Galeazzo said 'Ha!' again, like a snarl, and his brow contracted.

'Why, thou unconscionable old surly dog!' he said—'why?'

Jacopo pointed to the tablets.

'Your saint asks no notes to *his* piping. A' sings like the birds.'

'Now,' answered his master, in a deep, offended tone, 'I'm in a mind to make *thee* sing on a grill,—ay, and dance too. What, dolt! are not first thoughts first thoughts, however they may be pricked down? Look at this, I say; flatten thy bull nose on it. Is it not clean, untouched, unrevised? Spotless as when issued from Helicon? Beast! thou shalt call me, too, an improvisatore.'

The statue was silent. Galeazzo sat glaring and gnawing his fingers.

'Answer!' he screeched suddenly.

'I will call thee one,' said Jacopo obstinately, 'but not the best.'

The Duke fell back in his chair, then presently was muttering and strumming with his disengaged fingers on the table.

'No—not the best, not the best—not to rival heaven! Yet, perhaps, it should be the Duke's privilege.'

The executioner laughed a little.

'The Duke should know how to take it.'

Galeazzo stopped short, quite vacant, staring at him.

'I've heard tell,' said Jacopo, 'how one Nero, a fiddling emperor, came to be acknowledged first fiddle of all.'

He paused, then answered, it seemed, an unspoken invitation: 'He just silenced the better ones.'

Galeazzo got hurriedly to his feet.

'Blasphemer! thou shalt die for the word. What! this Lord's anointed! A natural songster! no art, no culture in his voice—sweet and wild, above human understanding. I said nothing. Be damned, and damned alone! Go hang thyself like Judas!'

'Well, name my successor first,' said Jacopo.

The Duke leapt, and with one furious blow shattered his lute to splinters on the other's steel headpiece, then stamped upon the fragments, his arms flapping like wing stumps, his teeth sputtering a foam of inarticulate words. Jacopo, erect under the avalanche, stood perfectly silent and impassive. Then, as suddenly as it had burst, the storm ended. Galeazzo sank back on his seat, panting and nerveless.

'Well, I am no poet—curse thy block head, and mine for trusting to it—the Muses shall decide—Apollo or Marsyas—the Christian Muses and a Christian penance—flaying only for heretics. I am no poet nor musician, say'st? Calf! what know'st thou about such things?' He roared again: 'What brings thee here, with thy damned butcher's face, scaring my pretty lambs of song?'

'Thine order.'

'Mine?'

'This astrologer monk, this Fra Capello was it not? I neither know nor care.'

'Dost thou not? A faithful dog!'

'Faithful enough.'

'O! art thou? By what token?'

'By the token of the quarry run to earth.'

'To earth? Thou hast him? Good Jacopo!'

'This three days past. Had I not told thee so already? Let thine improvising damn thyself, not me.'

'The villain! to call himself a Franciscan, a lowly Franciscan, and pretend to read the stars! How about his prophecy now?'

'Why, he holds to it.'

'What! that I have but eleven years in all to reign—less than one to live?'

'Just that—no more.'

'Now, is it not a wicked schism from the plain humility of his founder? A curse on their spirituals and conventuals! *This* fellow to claim kinship with the stars—profess to be in their confidence, to share heaven's secrets? Dear Jacopo, sweet Jacopo! is it not well to cleanse this earth of such lying prophets, that truth may have standing-room?'

'Ask truth, not me.'

'Nay, not to grieve truth's heart—the onus shall be ours. This same Franciscan—this soothsaying monk—where hast lodged him?'

'In the "Hermit's Cell."'

'Ah, old jester! He shall prove his asceticism thereby. Let practised abstinence save him in such pass. He shall eat his words—an everlasting banquet. A fat astrologer, by the token, as I hear.'

'He went in, fat.'

'Wretch! wouldst thou starve him? Remember the worms, thy cousins. Hath he foretold his end?'

'Ay, by starvation.'

'He lies, then. Thou shalt take him *in extremis*, and, with thy knife in his throat, give him the lie. An impostor proved. What sort of night is it?'

'Why, it rains and thunders.'

'Hush! Why should we fear rain and thunder? God put His bow in the sky. Jacopo, it is a sweet and fearful thing to be chosen minister of one of His purifications—Noah, and Lot, and now thy prince.'

'Purification?' said the executioner: 'by what?'

'By love, thou fool!' whispered Galeazzo, half ecstatic, half furious, with a nervous glance about him. 'There were the purifications by water one, one by fire, and a third by blood, to the last of which His servants yet testify in the spirit of their Redeemer. Blood, Jacopo, thou little monster—blood flowing, streams of it, the visible token of the sacrifice. That was our task till yesterday. Now in the end comes Love, and calleth for a cleansed and fruitful soil. Let us hasten with the last tares—to cut them down, and let their blood consummate the fertilising. Quick: we have no time to lose.'

He flung himself from the statue, and tiptoed, in a sort of gloating rapture, to the door.

'Show me this tare, I say.'

He went down the tower a few paces, with assured steps, then, bethinking himself, beckoned the other to lead. The flight conducted them to a private postern, well secured and guarded inside and out. As they issued from this, the howl of blown rain met and staggered them. Looking up at the blackened sky from the depths of that well of masonry, it seemed to crack and split in a rush of fusing stars. The mad soul of the tyrant leapt to speed the chase. He was one with this mighty demonstration—as like a chosen instrument of the divine retribution. His brain danced and flickered with exquisite visions of power. He was an angel, a destroying angel, commissioned to purge the world of lies. 'Bring me to this monk!' he screamed through the thunder.

Deep in the foundations of the north-eastern tower the miserable creature was embedded, in a stone chamber as utterly void and empty as despair. The walls, the floor, the roof, were all chiselled as smooth as glass. There was not anywhere foothold for a cat—nor door, nor trap, nor egress, nor window of any kind, save where, just under the ceiling, the grated opening by which he had been lowered let in by day a haggard ghost of light. And even that wretched solace was withdrawn as night fell—became a phantom, a diluted whisp of memory, sank like water into the blackness, and left the fancy suddenly naked in self-consciousness of hell. Then Capello screamed, and threw himself towards the last flitting of that spectre. He fell and bruised his limbs horribly: the very pain was a saving occupation. He struck his skull, and revelled in the agonised dance of lights the blow procured him. But one by one they blew out; and in a moment dead negation had him by the throat again, rolling him over and over, choking him under enormous slabs of darkness. Now, gasping, he cursed his improvidence in not having glued his vision to the place of the light's going. It would have been something gained from madness to hold and gloat upon it, to watch hour by hour for its feeble re-dawn. Among all the spawning monstrosities of that pit, with only the assured prospect of a lingering death before him, the prodigy of eternal darkness quite overcrowed that other of thirst and famine.

Yet the dawn broke, it would seem, before its due. Had he annihilated time, and was this death? He rose rapturously to his feet, and stood staring at the grating, the tears gushing down his fallen cheeks. The bars were withdrawn; and in their place was a lamp intruded, and a face looked down.

'Capello, dost thou hunger and thirst?'

The voice awoke him to life, and to the knowledge of who out of all the world could be thus addressing him. He answered, quaveringly: 'I hunger and thirst, Galeazzo.'

'It is a beatitude, monk,' said the voice. 'Thou shalt have thy fill of justice.'

'Alas!' cried the prisoner: 'justice is with thee, I fear, an empty phrase.'

'Comfort thyself,' said the other: 'I shall make a full measure of it. It shall bubble and sparkle to the brim like a great goblet of Malmsey. Dost know the wine Malmsey, monk?—a cool, heady, fragrant liquid, that gurgles down the arid throat, making one o' hot days think of gushing weirs, and the green of grass under naked feet.'

The monk fell on his knees, stretching out his arms.

'I ask no mercy of thee, but to end me without torture.'

'Torture, quotha!' cried the fiend above—'what torture in the vision of a wine-cup crushed, or, for the matter of that, a feast on white tables under trees. Picture it, Capello: the quails in cold jelly; the melting pasties; the salmon-trout tucked under blankets of whipped cream; the luscious peaches, and apricots like maiden's cheeks. Why, art not a Conventual, man, and rich in such experiences of the belly? And to call 'em torture—fie!'

'Mercy!' gasped the monk. His swollen throat could hardly shape the word. Galeazzo laughed, and bent over.

'Answer, then: how long am I to live?'

'By justice, for ever.'

'What! live for ever on an empty phrase? Then art thou, too, provisioned for eternity.'

He held out his hand:—

'Art humbled at last, monk, or monkey? How much for a nut?'

Leaping at the mad thought of some relenting in the voice and question, the prisoner ran under the outstretched hand, and held up his own, abjectly, fulsomely.

'Master, give it me—one—one only, to dull this living agony!'

'A sop to thee, then,' cried Galeazzo, and dropped a chestnut. The monk caught it, and, cracking it between his teeth, roared out and fell spitting and sputtering. He had crunched upon nothing more savoury than a shell filled up with river slime. The Duke screamed and hopped with laughter.

'Is not that richer than quail, more refreshing than Malmsey?'

The monk fell on his knees:—

'Now hear me, God!' he gabbled awry: 'Let not this man ever again know surcease from torment, in bed, at board, in his body, or in his mind. Let his lust consummate in frostbite; let the worm burrow in his entrails, and the maggot in his brain. May his drink be salt, and his meat bitter as aloes. May his short lease of wicked life be cancelled, and death seize him, and damnation wither in the moment of his supreme impenitence. Darken his vision, so that for evermore it shall see despair and the mockery of fruitless hope. Let him walk a self-conscious leper in the sunshine, and strive vainly to propitiate the loathing in eyes in which he sees himself reflected an abhorred and filthy ape. May the curse of Assisi——'

Galeazzo screamed him down:—

'Quote him not—beast—vile apostate from his teaching!'

For a moment the two battled in a war of screeching blasphemy: the next, the grate was flung into place, the light whisked and vanished, a door slammed, and the blackness of the cell closed once more upon the moaning heap in its midst.

Quaking and ashen, babbling oaths and prayers, Galeazzo flung back to his closet.

'Bring wine!' he shook out between his teeth to Jacopo.

When it came, he tasted, and flung it from him.

'Salt!' he shrieked. His fancy quite overcrowed his reason. 'O God, I am poisoned!'

He rose, staggering, and entered his oratory, and cast himself on his knees before the little shrine.

'Not from this man,' he protested, whimpering and writhing; 'Lord, not from this man—I know him better than Thou—a recusant, a sorcerer! Be not deceived because of his calling. To curse Thine anointed! kill him, Lord—kill the blasphemer—I hold him ready to Thy hand! Good sweet St. Francis, I but weed thy pastures—a wicked false brother, tainting the fold. How shall love prevail, this poison at its root?—Poison! O my God, to be stricken for evermore! life's fruit to change to choking ashes in my mouth! It cannot be—I, Galeazzo the Duke—yet I taunted him with visions: what if I have caught the infection of mine own imagination—too fearful, spare me this once. Lord God, consider—as I put it to Thee—now—like this—listen. To starve with him should be but a fast enlarged. What then? Some, honest ascetics, no Conventuals, so push abstinence to ecstasy as that they may cross the lines of death in a dream, and wake without a pang to heaven gained. If he does not, should he suffer, he is properly condemned for a gross pampered brother, false to his vows, unworthy Thine advocacy. Now, call the test a fair one. Chain back this dog that ravens to tear me. How, so stricken, made corrupt, could I work Thy will but through corruption? Hush! Thou mean'st it not—only as a jest? Give me some sign, then. Ah! Thou laugh'st—very quietly, but I hear Thee. Canst not deceive Galeazzo— ha-ha! between me and You, Lord, between me and You! Silence, thou dog monk! What dost thou here? Escaped! by God, get back—the first word was mine—thou art too late. What! damnation seize thee! Lord! he scorns Thy judgment—catch him, hold him—he is there by the door!'

He sprang to his feet, glaring and gesticulating.

'Galeazzo!' exclaimed Bembo. The boy had mounted to the closet unheard. It was his privilege to come unannounced. He stood a moment regarding the madman in amazement and pity, then hurried softly to his side.

'What is it? The face again?'

His tone, his entreaty, dispelled the other's delirium. The tyrant gazed at him a minute, slow recognition dawning in his eyes; then, of a sudden, broke into a thick fast flurry of sobs, and cast himself upon his shoulder.

'My saint,' he wept adoringly—'my Conscience, my little angel! and I had thought thee—nay, but the sign for which I prayed art thou given.'

His emotion gushed inwardly, filling all his channels to gasping. Presently he looked up, with a passionate murmur and caress.

'Love, with thy red lips like a girl's! Would that my own were worthy to marry with them.'

Bembo withdrew a little:—

'What wild words are these? Yet, peradventure, the giddy babble of a conqueror. O Galeazzo! hast triumphed o'er thyself indeed—casting that old familiar? chasing him hereout? Why, then, I whom thou hast appointed to be thy conscience, interpreting thy rule through truth and love, am the more emboldened to beseech the favour for which I came.'

'Ask it only, sweet.' His chest still heaved spasmodically to the catching of his breath.

'It is,' said the boy steadily, 'that thou wouldst give me, thy conscience's delegate, a last justification by the sacraments.'

The Duke smiled faintly, and nodded, and murmured: 'I will confess ere midnight, and, fasting, receive the Holy Communion before I go to-morrow. Does it please thee? Come, then.'

He re-entered his cabinet, reeling a little, and sat himself down, as if exhausted, by the table.

'Bernardo,' he said weakly, half apologetically, 'I am overwrought: there is wine in that jug: I prithee give it me to drink.'

The boy, unhesitating, handed him the flagon.

'It is the symbol of joy redeemed,' he said. 'Put thy lips to the chalice, Galeazzo, and take what thy soul needest—no more.'

The Duke lifted the cup shakily, stumbled at its brim, steadied himself, and sipped. His eyes dilated and grew wolfish—'I am vindicated,' he stuttered: 'O sweet little saint!'—and he drank greedily, ecstatically, and, smacking his lips, put down the vessel.

He was himself again from that draught.

'Bernardo,' he said, in a reassured, half-maudlin confidence, 'canst thou read the stars?'

'Nay,' said the other gravely, 'they are the Sibyls' books.'

'True. Yet some essay.'

'Ay: then flies a comet, cancelling all their sums.'

'An impious vanity, is it not?'

'Truly, I think so.'

'And deserving of the last chastisement.'

'Poor fools, they make their own.'

'What?'

'Why, taking colds instead of rest—cramps, chills, and agues—immense pains, and all for nothing; the dead moon for the living sun; nursing all day that they may starve by night. God gave us level eyes. The star's best resting place for them is on a hill. We need no more knowledge than to read beauty through the wise lens Nature hath proportioned us. Not God Himself can foretell a future.'

'Not God?'

'No, for there is no Future, nor ever will be. The Past but eternally prolongs itself to the Present. Heaven or hell is the road we tread, and must retrace when we come to the brink of the abyss where Time drops sheer into nothingness. Joy or woe, then, to him the returning wanderer, according as he hath provisioned his way. So shall he starve, or travel in content, or meet with weary retributions. O, in providence, hold thy hand, thinking on this, whenever thy hand is tempted!'

Galeazzo was amazed, discomfited. This unorthodoxy was the last to accommodate itself to his principles of conduct. The Future to him was always an unmortgaged reversion, sufficient to pay off all debts to conscience and leave a handsome residue for income. He could only exclaim, again, like one aghast: '*No Future?*'

'Nay,' said Bembo, smiling, 'what is the heresy to reason or religion? To foresee the issues of to-day were, for Omniscience, to suppress all strains but the angels'. What irony to accept worship from the foredoomed! What insensate folly wantonly to multiply the devil's recruits! O Galeazzo, there is no Future for God or Men? Hope shudders at the inexorable word: Evil presumes on it: it is the lodestone to all dogmatism; the bogey, the weapon of the unversed Churchman; the very bait to acquisition and self-greed. Be what, returning, ye would find yourselves—no lovelier ambition. See, we walk with Christ, the human God and comrade, I have but this hour left him bathing his tired feet in the brook. He will follow anon; and all the pretty birds and insects and wildflowers he watched while resting will have suggested to him a thousand tales and reflections gathered of an ancient lore. He can be full of wonder too, but wiser by many moons than we. There is no Future. God possesses the Past.'

The Duke sprang to his feet, and went up and down once or twice. This view of a self-retaliatory entity—of a returning body condemned by natural laws to retraverse every point of its upward flight—disturbed him horribly. He desired no responsibility in things done and gone. Eternity, timely propitiated, was his golden chance. He stopped and looked at Bembo, at once inexpressibly cringing and crafty.

'Bernardino,' murmured he: 'I can never get it out of my head that whenever thou sayest God thou meanest gods. *The gods possess the past?*— why, one would fancy somehow it ran glibber than the other.'

Bembo sighed.

'Well, why not? Nature, and Love, and the Holy Ghost—*Tria juncta in Uno*—why not gods?'

The Duke pressed his hand to his forehead; then ran and clasped the boy about the shoulders.

'Adorable little wisdom,' he cried: 'take my conscience, and record on it what thou wilt!'

'To-morrow,' said Bembo, with a happy smile: 'when its tablets are sponged and clean.'

Galeazzo fawned, showing his teeth. There was something in him infinitely suggestive of the cat that, in alternate spasms of animalism, licks and bites the hand that caresses it. This strange new heresy of a limited omniscience oddly affected him. Could it be possible, after all, that the soul's responsibility was to itself alone? In any case so pure a spirit as this could represent him only to his advantage. Still, at the same time, if God were no more than relatively wiser and stronger than himself—why, it was not *his* theory—let the Parablist answer for it—on Messer Bembo's saintly head fall the onus, if any, of leaving Capello where he was. For his own part, he told himself, the God of Moses remaining in his old place in the heavens, he, Galeazzo, would have been inclined to consider the virtuous policy of releasing the Monk.

And so he prepared himself to confess and communicate.

CHAPTER IX

The Duke of Milan, confessed, absolved, and his conscience pawned to a saint, had, on the virtue of that pledge, started in a humour of unbridled self-righteousness for the territory of Vercelli. With him went some four thousand troops, horse and footmen, a drain of bristling splendour from the city; yet the roaring hum of that city's life, and the flash and sting thereof, were not appreciably lessened in the flying of its hornet swarm. Rather waxed they poignant in the general sense of a periodic emancipation from a hideous thralldom. The tyrant was gone, and for a time the intolerable incubus of him was lifted.

But, for the moment, there was something more—a consciousness, within the precincts of the palace and beyond them, of a substituted atmosphere, in which the spirit experienced a strange self-expansion— other than mere relief from strain—which was foreign to its knowledge. Men felt it, and pondered, or laughed, or were sceptical according as their temperaments induced them. So, in droughty days, the little errant winds that blow from nowhere, rising and falling on a thought, affect us with a sense of the unaccountable. There was such a sweet odd zephyr abroad in Milan. The queer question was, Was the little gale a little mountebank gale, tumbling ephemerally for its living, or did it represent a permanent atmospheric change?

A few days before Galeazzo's departure, Bernardo—by special appointment *custos conscientiae ducalis*—had, while walking in the outer ward of the Castello with Cicada, happened upon the vision of a Franciscan monk, plump and rosy, but with inflammatory eyes, entering with Messer Jacopo through a private postern in the walls. He had saluted the jocund figure reverentially, as one necessarily sacred through its calling, and was standing aside with doffed bonnet, when the other, halting with an expression of good-humoured curiosity on his face, had greeted him, puffed and asthmatic, in his turn:—

'Peace to thee, my son! Can this be he of whom it might be said, *"Puer natus est nobis: et vocabitur nomen ejus, Magni Consilii Angelus"*?'

The Franciscan had rumbled the query at Jacopo, who had shrugged, and answered shortly: 'Well; 'tis Messer Bembo.'

'So?' had responded the monk, gratified; 'the David of our later generation?' and instantly and ingratiatory he had waddled up, and, putting a prosperous hand on Bernardo's shoulder, had bent to whisper hoarsely, and quite audibly to Cicada, into the boy's ear:—

'Child—I know—I am to thank *thee* for this summons.' Then, before Bembo, wondering, could respond: 'Ay, ay; Saul's ears are opened to the truth. The stars cannot lie. You sent for me, yourself their sainted emissary, to confirm the verdict. What! I might have failed to answer else. We know the Duke, eh? But, mum!'

And with these enigmatic words, and a roguish wink and squeeze, he had hurried away again, following the impatient summons of Jacopo, who was beckoning him towards a flight of open stairs niched in the north curtain, up which the two had thereon gone, and so disappeared among the battlements.

Then had Bernardo turned, humour battling with reverence in his sensorium, and 'Cicca!' had exclaimed, with a little click of laughter.

The Fool's answer had been prompt and emphatic.

'Cracked!' he had snapped, like a dog at a fly.

'Who was he?'

'Nay, curtail not his short lease. He is yet, and, being, is the Fra Capello—may I die else.'

'Well, if he is, *what* is he?'

'Why, a short-of-breath monk; yet soon destined, if I read him aright, to be a breathless monk.'

'Nay, thou wilt only new-knot a riddle. I will follow and ask the Provost-Marshal, though I love him not.'

'Nor he thee, methinks. Hold back. The butcher looks askance at the pet lamb. Well, what wouldst thou? Of this same monkish rotundity, this hemisphere of fat, this moon-paunch, this great blob of star-jelly, this planet-counterfeiting frog, this astronomic globe stuffed out with pasties and ortolans? Well, 'tis Fra Capello, I tell thee, an astrologer, a diviner by the stars—do I not aver it, though I have never set eyes on the man before?'

'How know'st, then?'

'Why, true, my perspicacity is only this and that, a poor matter of inferences. As, for example, the inference of the fingers, that when I burn them, fire is near; or the inference of the nose, that when I smell cooking fish, it is a fast day; or the inference of the palate, that when I drink water, I am a fool.'

'A dear wise fool.'

'Ay, a wise fool, to know what one and one make. Dost thou?'

'Two, to be sure.'

'Well, God fit thy perspicacity with twins, when thy time comes. One out of one and one is enough for me.'

'Peace! How know'st this holy father is an astrologer?'

'Inference, sir—merely inference. As, for example again, the inference of the ears, that when I mark the substance of his whisper to thee, I seem to remember talk of a certain Franciscan, who, having predicted by the stars short shrift for Galeazzo, and been invited to come and discuss his reasons, did prove unaccountably coy, though certainly seer to his own nativity. Imprimis, the astrologer was reported a Conventual and fat; whereby comes in the inference of the eye. Now, "Ho-ho!" thinks I, "this same swag-bellied monk who babbles of stars! Surely it is our Fra Capello? And hooked at last? By what killing bait?"'

Here he had touched the boy's shoulder swiftly, and as swiftly had withdrawn his hand, an ineffable expression, shrewd and caustic, puckering his face. Bembo had looked serious.

'Cicca! I do believe thou art madder than any astrologer—unless——'

'No!' had cried the Fool; 'I am sober; wrong me not.'

Then Bembo had repented lovingly:—

'Pardon, dear Cicca. But, indeed, I understand thee not.'

'Why,' I said, 'what killing bait had tempted the monk's shyness at length?'

'What, then?'

'Thyself.'

'I?'

'Art thou not a star-child and Galeazzo's protégé? O, pretty, sweet decoy, to draw the astrologer from his cloister!'

'Dost mean that the Duke would use me to question the truth of these predictions? Alas! not I, nor any man, can interpret nothingness into a text.'

'Wilt thou tell him so?'

'Who?'

'The Duke.'

'I have told him so.'

'Thou hast? Then God keep the Franciscan in breath!'

'Amen!' had said Bembo, in all fervour and innocence. He had thought the other to mean nothing more than that the Duke was designing, on *his* authority, to win a faulty brother from the heresy—as he construed it—of divination.

As *he* construed it. Young and inexperienced as he was, he had yet a prophet's purpose and vision—the vision which, in despite of all traditional beliefs, looks backwards. His soft eyes were steadfast to that end which was the beginning. No sophistries could beguile him from the essential truth of his kind creed. *He* was an atavism of something vastly remoter than Caligula—than any tyranny. He 'threw back' to the stock of those first angels who knew the daughters of men—to the first fruits of an amazed and incredible sorrow. By so great a step was he close to the God his sires had offended; was close to the parting of the ways between earth and heaven, and with all the lore of the since-accumulated ages to instruct him in his choice of roads. O, believe little Bernardo that his was the true insight, the true wisdom! There is no Future, nor ever will be. The past but prolongs itself to the present; and all enterprise, all yearning, are but to recover the ground we have lost. That truth once recognised, the horror of Futurity shall close its gates; its timeless wastes shall be no more to us; and we—we shall be wandering back, by æons of pathetic memories, to trace to its source the love that gushed in Paradise.

Three days later the boy—the Duke being gone—was strolling, again with Cicada his shadow, on the ramparts. It had become something his habit to take the air, after hearing the morning causes, on these outer walls, whence the tired vision could stretch itself luxuriantly on leagues of peaceful plain. He liked then to be left alone, or at the most to the sole company of his dogged henchman, the erst Fool. Cicada's gruff but jealous sympathy was an emollient to lacerated sensibilities; his wit was a tonic; his tact the fruit of long necessity. No one would have guessed, not gentle Bernardo himself, how the little, ugly, caustic creature was, when most wilful or eccentric in seeming, watching over and medicining his moods of inevitable weariness or depression.

Perhaps he was in such a mood now—induced by that passion of the irremediable which occasionally must overtake every just judge—as he leaned upon the battlements, his cheek propped on his palm, and gazed out dreamily over the shining campagna.

'Cicca,' he said suddenly, 'what made thee a Fool?'

'Circumstance,' answered the other promptly.

'Ah!' sighed Bembo—'that blind brute force of Nature, wavering out of chaos. No agent of God—His foe, rather, to be anticipated and circumvented. Providence is the true wise name for our Master. He *provideth*, of the immensity of His love, for and against. He can do no further, nor foretell but by analogy the blundering spites of Circumstance. But always He persuades the monster of his interest lying more and more in sweet order—dreams of him sleeping caged, a lazy, satiated chimera, in the mid-gardens of love.'

'Che allegria!' said Cicada; 'I will go then, and poke him in the ribs, and ask him why he made a Fool of me.'

Bembo smiled and sighed.

'There is a proof of his blindness. What, in truth, was thy origin, dear Cicca?'

The Fool came and leaned beside him.

'Canst look on me and ask? I was born in this dark age of tyranny, and of it; I shall die in it and of it. I have never known liberty. Sobriety and reason are empty terms to me. Ask of me no fruit but the fruit of mine inheritance. A drunken woman in labour will bring forth a drunken child. I am Cicada the Fool, lower than a slave, curst pimp to Folly.'

Soft as a butterfly, Bernardo's hand fluttered to his shoulder and rested there. The creature's dim eyes were fixed upon the crawling plain; his face worked with emotion.

'There was a time,' he said, 'I understand, when governments were loyal at once to the individual and the state—when they wrought for the common weal. In those days, it would seem certain, riches—anything above a specified income—must have disqualified a man for office. It is the ideal constitution. Corruption will enter else. Wealth, and the emulation of wealth, are the moth in stored states. That was the age of the republics and all the virtues. I am born, alack, after my time. I have held Esau the first saint in the calendar. I am not sure I do not do so now, Messer Bembo despite.'

'And I, too, love Esau,' said Bernardo quietly.

Cicada, amazed, whipped upon him; then suddenly seized him in his arms.

'Thou dearest, most loving of babes!' he cried rapturously; 'sweet saint of all to me! What! did I twit thee, mine emancipator, with my curse to thralldom? Loves Esau, quotha! No cant his creed. Child, thou art asphodel to that cactus. Put thy foot on this mouth that could so slander thee!'

'Poor Cicca!' said Bembo, gently disengaging himself. 'Thou rebukest sweetly my idle curiosity.'

'Curiosity!' cried the other. 'Would the angels always showed as much! Thou art welcome to all of me I can tell:—as, for example, that my mother—*exitus acta probat*—was a fool, a sweet, pretty, vicious fool; and yet, after all, not such a fool as, having borne, to acknowledge me.'

'Poor wretch! Why not?'

'Why not? Why, for the reason Pasiphae concealed her share in the Minotaur. Motley is the labyrinth of Milan. My father was a bull.'

'Well, I am answered.'

'Ah! thou think'st I jest. Relatively—relatively only, sir, I assure thee. Hast ever heard speak of Filippo Maria, the last of the Visconti?'

'Little, alas! to his credit.'

'I will answer in my person to that. He was uglier than any bull—a monster so hideous as to be attractive to a certain order of frailty. I inclined his way. Perhaps that was my salvation. The child most interests the parent whose features it reflects. It is bad-luck to break a mirror; and so I was spared—for the labyrinth.'

'O infamous! He made thee his jester?'

'And fed me. Let that be remembered to him. When the reckoning comes, the bull, not Pasiphae, shall have my voice.'

'Hideous! Thy mother?'

'Let it pass on that. I need say no more, if a word can damn.'

'Cicca!'

'He was meat and drink to me, I say.'

'Drink, alas!'

'He meant it kindly. When I sparkled, 'twas his own wit he felt himself applauding. That was my easy time. He died in '47, and my majesty's Fooldom was appropriated incontinent to the titillation of these peasants of Cotignola their hairy ears.'

'Hush, and thou wilt be wise!'

'In my grave, not sooner. Francesco, our Magnificent's father, was so-so for humour—a good, blunt soldier, who'd take his cue of laughter from some quicker wit, then roar it out despotically. No sniggerer, like his son, who qualifies all praise with envy. Shall I tell thee how I lost Galeazzo's favour? He wrote a sonnet. 'Twas an achievement. A Roman triumph has been ceded to less—hardly to worse. Lord, sir! there was that applause and hand-clapping at Court! But Wisdom looked sour. "What, fool!" demanded the Duke: "dost question its merit?" "Nay," quoth Wisdom; "but only the sincerity of the praise. Sign thy next with my name, and mark its fate." He did—actually. Poor Wisdom! as if it had been truth the sonneteer desired! Never was poor doxy of a Muse worse treated. This was exalted like the other; but in a pillory. It made a day's sport for the mob, at my expense. Was not that pain and humiliation enough? But Galeazzo must visit upon me the rage of his mortification. Well, when he was done with me, Messer Lanti, high in favour, begged the remnant of my folly, and it was thrown to him. The story leaked out; I had had so many holes cut in me. It had been wiser to seal my lips with kindness. But the Duke, as you may suppose, loves me to this day.'

As he spoke, they turned an angle of the battlements, and saw advancing towards them, smiling and insinuative, the figure of Tassino. Bernardo started, in some wonder. He had not set eyes on this dandiprat since his public condemnation of him, and, if he thought of him at all, had believed him gone to make the restitution ordered. Now he gazed at him with an expression in which pity and an instinctive abhorrence fought for precedence.

The young man was brilliantly, even what a later generation would have called 'loudly,' dressed. He had emerged from his temporary pupation a very tiger-moth; but the soul of the ignoble larva yet obtained between the gorgeous wings. Truckling, insinuative, and wicked throughout, he accosted his judge with a servile bow, as he stood cringing before him. Bembo mastered his antipathy.

'What! Messer cavalier,' he said, struggling to be gay. 'Art returned?'—for he guessed nothing of the truth. Then a kind thought struck him. 'Perchance thou comest as a bridegroom, *bene meritus.*'

Tassino glanced up an instant, and lowered his eyes. How he coveted the frank audacity of the Patrician swashbuckler, with which he had been made acquainted, but which he found impossible to the craven meanness of his nature. To dare by instinct—how splendid! No doubt there is that fox of self-conscious pusillanimity gnawing at the ribs of many a seeming-brazen upstart. He twined and untwined his fingers, and shook his head, and sobbed out a sigh, with craft and hatred at his heart. Bernardo looked grave.

'Alas, Messer Tassino!' said he: 'think how every minute of a delayed atonement is a peril to thy soul.'

This sufficed the other for cue.

'Atone?' he whined: 'wretch that I am! How could a hunted creature do aught but hide and shake?'

'Hunted!'

'O Messer Bembo! 'twas so simple for you to let loose the mad dog, and blink the consequences for others.'

'Mad dog!'

'Now don't, for pity's sake, go quoting my rash simile. Hast not ruined me enough already?'

'Alas, good sir! What worth was thine estate so pledged? I had no thought but to save thee for heaven.'

'And so let loose the Duke, that Cerberus? O, I am well saved, indeed, but not for heaven! Had it not been for the good Jacopo taking me in and hiding me, I had been roasting unhousel'd by now.'

'Tassino, thou dost the Duke a wrong. 'Twas thy fear distorted thy peril. He is a changed man, and most inclined to charity and justice.'

Tassino let his jaw drop, affecting astonishment.

'Since when?'

'Since the day of thy disgrace.'

The other shook his head, with a smile of growing effrontery.

'Why, look you, Messer Bembo,' he said: 'you represent his conscience, they tell me, and should know. Yet may not a man and his conscience, like ill-mated consorts, be on something less than speaking terms?'

He laughed, half insolent, half nervous, as Bernardo regarded him in silence with earnest eyes.

'Supposing,' said he, 'you were to represent, of your holy innocence and credulity, a little more and a little sweeter than the truth? Think'st thou I should have dared reissue from my hiding, were Galeazzo still here to represent his own? If I had ever thought to, there was that buried a week ago in the walls yonder would have stopped me effectively.'

'Buried—in the walls! What?'

'Dost not know? Then 'tis patent he is not all-confiding in his conscience. And yet thou shouldst know. 'Tis said thou lead'st him by the nose, as St. Mark the lion. Well, I am a sinner, properly persecuted; yet, to my erring perceptives, 'tis hard to reconcile thy saintship with thy subscribing to his sentence on a poor Franciscan monk, a crazy dreamer, who came to him with some story of the stars.'

'O, I cry you mercy! I quote Messer Jacopo, who was present. "Deserving of the last chastisement"—were not those thy words? And Omniscience dethroned—a bewildered mortal like ourselves? Anyhow, he held thy saintship to justify his sentence on the monk.'

'What sentence?'

'Wilt thou come and see? I have my host's pass.'

He staggered under the shock of a sudden leap and clutch. Young strenuous hands mauled his pretty doublet; sweet glaring eyes devoured his soul.

'I see it in thy face! O, inhuman dogs are ye all! Show me, take me to him!'

Tassino struggled feebly, and whimpered.

'Let go: I will take thee: I am not to blame.'

Shaking, but exultant in his evil little heart, he broke loose and led the way to a remote angle of the battlements, where the trunk of a great tower, like the drum of a hinge, connected the northern and eastern curtains. This was that same massy pile in whose bowels was situate the dreadful oubliette known as the 'Hermit's Cell': a grim, ironic title signifying deadness to the world, living entombment, utter abandonment and self-obliteration. It was delved fathoms deep; quarried out of the bed-rock; walled in further by a mountain of masonry. Tyranny sees an Enceladus in the least of its victims. On so exaggerated a scale of fear must the sum of its deeds be calculated.

Here the Provost-Marshal had his impregnable quarters. Looking down, one might see the huge blank bulge of the tower enter the pavement below unpierced but by an occasional loop or eyelet hole. Its only entrance, indeed, was from the rampart-walk; its direct approach by way of the flying stair-way, up which Bembo had seen the monk disappear. His heart burned in his breast as he thought of him. There was a fury in his blood, a sickness in his throat.

A sentry, lounging by the door, offered, as if by preconcert with Tassino, no bar to his entrance. But, when Cicada would have followed, he stayed him.

'Back, Fool!' he said shortly, opposing his halberd.

Cicada struggled a moment, and desisted.

'A murrain on thy tongue,' snapped he, 'that calls me one!'

The sentry laughed, and, having gained his point, produced a flask leisurely from his belt.

'What! art thou not a fool?' said he, unstoppering it, and preparing to drink.

'Understand, I have forsworn all liquor,' said Cicada, with a wry twinkle.

'So art thou certainly a fool,' said the sentry, eye and body guarding the doorway, as he raised the horn.

'Hist!' whispered Cicada, staying him: 'this remoteness—that damning gurgle—come! a ducat for a mouthful! Be quick, before he returns!'

The soldier, between cupidity and good-nature, laughed and handed over the flask. 'Done on that!' said he. But on the instant he roared out, as the other snatched and bolted with his property.

'How, thou bloody filcher! Give me back my wine!'

Cicada crowed and capered, dangling his spoil.

'Judas! for a dirty piece of silver to betray temperance!'

The sentry, with a furious oath, made at him. He dodged; eluded; finally, under the very hands of his pursuer, threw the flask into a corner, and, as the other dived for it, slipped by and disappeared into the tower. The soldier, cursing and panting in his wake, ran into the arms of an impassive figure—staggered, fell back, and saluted.

Messer Jacopo eyed the delinquent a long minute without a word. He had been silent witness, within the guard-room, of all the little scene, and was considering the penalty meet to such a breach of orders and discipline.

There had been something of pre-arrangement in this matter between him and Messer Tassino. The two were in a common accord as to the loss and inconvenience to be entailed upon themselves by any reform of existing institutions—comprehensively, as to the menace this stranger was to their interests. It would be well to demonstrate to him the unreality of his influence with Galeazzo. Let him see the starving monk, in evidence of his power's short limits. It was possible the sight might kill his presumption for ever: return him disillusioned to obscurity.

So his presence here had been procured, with orders to the sentry to debar the Fool. Jacopo wanted no shrewd cricket at the boy's side, to leaven the horror for him with his song of cheer. The full impressiveness of the awful scene must be allowed to overbear his soul in silence. This sentry had erred rather foolishly.

It abated nothing of the terror of the man that no sign of passion ever crossed his face, nor word his lips. He turned away, not having uttered a sound; and left the delinquent collapsed as under a heat-stroke.

'Now, let it be no worse than the strappado!' prayed the poor wretch to himself.

In the meanwhile, Cicada, swift, quivering, alert, was descending, like a gulped Jonah, into the bowels of the tower. He had no need to pick his path: the well-stairway, like a screw pinning the upper to the underworld, transmitted to him every whisper and shuffle of the footsteps he was pursuing. Sometimes, so deceptive were the echoes in that winding shaft, he fancied himself treading close upon the heels of the chase; yet each little loop-lighted landing found him, as he reached it, audibly no nearer. His mocking mouth was set grim; he dreaded, not for himself but for his darling, some nameless entrapping wickedness. 'If they design it,' he thought—'if they design it! Hell shall not hide them from me.'

Suddenly the sounds below died away and ceased. He listened an instant; then went down again, turning and turning in a nightmare of blind horror. The walls grew dank and viscous to his palm. A stumble, and all might end for him hideously. Then, at the same moment, weak light and a weaker cry greeted him. He descended, still without pause—and shot into the glowing mouth of a tiny tunnel, where were the figures he sought.

They stood at a low grating in the wall, which was pierced into a subterranean chamber. The bars were thrown open, and through the aperture Tassino directed the light of a flaring torch he held upon a figure lying prostrate on the stones below. Cicada crept, and peered over his master's shoulder. The thing on the floor was grotesque, unnatural—a human skeleton emitting noises, heaving in its midst. That great bulk had become in its shrinkage a monstrous travesty of life. But existence still preyed upon its indissoluble vestments of flesh.

'He clings to life, for a monk,' whispered the Fool.

With the sound of his voice, Bernardo was sprung into a Fury. He lashed upon Cicada, tooth and claw:—

'Thou knew'st, and hid it from me in parables!'

'Inference, inference!' cried the Fool. 'I would have spared thee.'

'Spared *me*? Thus?'

'Ah! thy shame through wicked sophistries! He was foredoomed. Had I interfered, I had been lying myself there now, and you a loving servant the less.'

Bembo flung his arms abroad, as if sweeping all away from him.

'Love! Let pass!' he shrieked: 'Fiends are ye all, with whom to breathe is poison!' and he broke by them, and went flying and crying up into the daylight. He ran, without pause, by the walls, down the notched stairway, across the ward, and came with flaming colour into the buttery.

'Give me wine and bread!' he screamed of the steward there; and the man, in a flurry of wonder, obeyed him. Then away he raced again, his hands full, and never stopped until the sentry, a new one, at the tower door barred his progress. The way was private, quoth the man. He could let none past but by order.

'Of whom?' panted Bembo.

'Why, the Provost-Marshal.'

Then the boy tried wheedling.

'Dear soldier: thou art well cared for. There is one within perishes for a little bread.'

But the man was adamant.

'Where, then, is the Provost-Marshal?' cried the other in desperation.

Within or without—the sentry professed not to know. In any case, it was death to him to leave his post.

Bernardo put down his load on the battlements, and, turning, fled away again.

CHAPTER X

Bona sat amongst her maidens. They were all busy as spiders upon a loom of tapestry, spinning a symbolic web. The subject was as edifying as their talk over it was free. Their lips and fingers were perpetually at odds, weaving reputations and pulling them to pieces. Bona herself said little; but abstraction gave some indulgence to the smile with which she listened, or seemed to.

'Whither do her thoughts travel?' whispered one girl of another.

'Hush!' was the answer. 'Along the Piedmont Road with her lord, of course. What else would you?'

The first giggled.

'Nothing, indeed, if it left a chance for poor little me. But, alack! I fear her charity stops nearer home.'

'What then, insignificance? Would your presumption fly at an angel?'

'Yes, indeed, though it got a peck for its pains. (Mark the Caprona's ear pricked our way! She knows we are on the eternal subject.) Heigho! it will be something to share in this promised commonwealth of love, at least.'

She spoke loud enough for the little Catherine Sforza, sitting by her adopted mother, to hear her.

'Ehi, Carlina,' cried that pert youngster: 'What share do you expect for your small part?'

'I thought of Messer Bembo, Madonna,' answered Carlina demurely.

They crowed her down with enormous laughter.

'Nay, child,' said Catherine: 'there is to be no talk of exclusiveness in this Commonwealth. We are all to take alike—Mamma, and I, and the Countess of Casa Caprona, and whoever else subscribes to the Purification. For my part I shall be content with becoming very good; and I have hopes of myself. See the reformation in our dear Countess; and she was in his company but a day or two.'

'Peace, thou naughtiness!' cried Bona; while Beatrice's eyes burned dull fire; and a girl, one who worked near her, a soft and endearing little piety, looked up and choked in a panic, 'O Madonna!'

Catherine mimicked her:—

'O Biasia! Is the subject too tender for thy conscience? Alas, dear! but if thy only hope is in this Commonwealth? Angels are not monogamous.'

Biasia blushed like a poppy; yet managed to stammer amidst the laughter: 'It is only that he,—that the subject, seems to me too sacred. He preaches heavenly love—the brotherhood of souls—in all else, one man one maid.'

Catherine very gravely got upon a stool, and paraphrased Messer Bembo, voice and manner:—

'I kiss thee, kind Madonna, for thine exposition. A man must put a fence about his desires, would he be happy. A sweet mate, a cot, beehives and a garden—he shall find all love's epitome in these. None can possess the world but in the abstract—a plea for universal brotherhood. What doth it profit me to own a palace, and live for all my needs' content in one room of it? Go to and join, and leave superfluous woman to the preacher.'

Some tittered, some applauded; Biasia hung her head, and would say no more. Bona cried, 'Come down, thou wickedness!' but indulgently, as if she half-dreaded attracting to herself the flicker of the little forked tongue.

'O!' cried Catherine, 'I grant you that, with an angel, the manner spices the lesson. I will tell you, girls, how he rebuked me yesterday on this same legend of reciprocity. "How could you take sport," says he, "of witnessing that poor Montano's punishment?" "Why, very well," says I, "seeing he was a man, and therefore my natural enemy." "How is man so?" says he. "He makes me bear his children for him," says I. "But I suppose he will be made to suffer *his* share of the toil in this new Commonwealth of love." "You talk like a child," he says. "Then," says I, "I will sing like a woman," and I extemporised—very clever, you will admit.'

She pinched up her skirts, and put out a little foot, and chirruped, in no voice at all, but with a sauce of impudence:—

'"Love is give and take," says he,
"Every gander knows—
Wear the prickle for my sake;
For thine, I'll wear the rose."'

"*Grazie*, kind and true," says I,
"For that noble dower—
Only, between me and you,
I should like the flower."

"And hast thou not it?" cries St. Bernardo, interrupting me; and, would you believe it, swinging round his lute, his lips and his finger-tips join issue in the prettiest nonsense ever conceived for a poor wife's fooling. Wait, and I will recall it.'

She had the quickest wit and memory, and in a moment was chaunting:—

'"Whence did our bird-soft baby come?
How learned to prattle of this for home?

Some sleepy nurse-angel let her stray,
And she found herself in the world one day.

She heard nurse calling, and further fled:
She hid herself in our cabbage bed.

There we came on her fast asleep,
What could we do but take and keep,

Carry her in and up the stair?
She would have died of cold out there.

She woke at once in a little fright;
But Love beckoned her from the light.

Lure we had lit, for dear love fain;
She had seen it shine through the window pane.

Lure we had kindled of flame and bliss,
To catch such a little ghost-moth as this.

Ah, me! it shrivelled her pretty wing.
Here she must stay, poor thing, poor thing!"'

She ended: 'Faith, St. Charming's lips make that daintiest setting to his fancies, that I could have kissed 'em while he improved his song with a homily' (she mimicked again the boy's manner, comically emphasised).

'"Why," saith he, "would you grudge yourself that poignant privilege of your sex? would ye share the agony and halve the gain? What gift so careless in all the world makes such sweet possession? Furs, gowns, and trinkets pall; perishable things grow less by use; the diamond suffers by its larger peer. Only the gift of love, the wee babe, takes new delight of time; renews woman's best through herself; is a perpetual novelty, spring all the year round, flowers fresh burgeoning through faded blooms. To be sole warden of the quickening soul ye bore—you, you! to see the lamb-like heaven of its eyes cuddling to your bosom's fold—all thine, save the spent heat that cast it! O, rather be the mould than the turbulent metal it shapes! Go to, and thank God for labours yielding such reward. Go to, and be the mother of saints." Whereat I curtsied, and "Thank you, sir," says I, "for the offer, but my bed's already laid for me in Rome," and then——'

What more she might have quoted or invented none might say, for at the moment a wild figure burst into the chamber, and ran to its mistress, and entreated her with lips and hands.

'Give me thy gage—quick! There is one starves in the "Hermit's Cell," and they will not let me pass to him without. Thou art the Duke, thou art the Duke now. Give it me, in mercy, and avert God's vengeance from this wicked house!'

Bona had arisen, pale as death, pity and anguish pleading in her eyes.

'Alas! What say'st thou? Thou, not I, art the Duke.'

'Give it me,' demanded Bembo feverishly. 'Nay, quibble not, while he gasps out his agony—a monk—hear'st thou? A monk!'

She temporised a moment in her pain.

'There are black sheep in those flocks.'

'God forgive thee!'

'Alas! *thou* wilt not. Indeed I have no talisman will open doors that my lord has shut.'

Beatrice, intent, with veiled eyes, from her place, bestirred herself with an indolent smile.

'Madonna forgets. Love laughs at locksmiths.'

The two women faced one another a minute. Some subtle emotion of antagonism, already born, waxed into a larger consciousness between them.

'How, Countess?' said Bona quietly.

'Madonna wears her bethrothal ring—a very *passepartout*. It is the talisman will serve her with monks and saints alike.'

A little flush mantled to the Duchess's brow. Standing erect a moment she slipped the ring from her finger, and held it out to Bernardo.

'It should be the pledge through love of Charity. Take it, in my lord's good name, whose jealous representative I remain. And when thou return'st it, may it be sanctified of new justice, child, against the prick of envy and slander and the spite of venomous tongues.'

She turned away stately and resumed her needle as Bernardo, with a cry of thanks, ran from the room. A minute or two later he appeared before the sentry on the ramparts and flourished his token. To his surprise the man hardly glanced at it as he stepped aside to let him pass. He thought on this with some shapeless foreboding, as he leapt like a chamois down the steeps of the tower, the food, which he had snatched up, in his hands. God pity him and his awakening! There are emotions too sacred for minuting. Let it suffice that Jacopo had proved too faithful a prophylactic to superstition. The wretched monk had not been allowed to justify his own prediction by dying of starvation. In that last interval, between the Parablist's going and coming, his throat had been cut.

A minute later Bernardo leapt like a madman from the tower. His face was ashy, his hands trembling. At the foot of the curtain he stumbled over a poor patch, prostrate and moaning.

'*I am thy Fool, and I shall never make thee smile again.*'

All quivering and unstrung, he threw himself on his knees by Cicada's side.

'Up!' he screamed, 'up! Get you out of this Sodom ere the Lord destroy it!'

The Fool bestirred himself, raising eyes full of a sombre, eager questioning.

'I am forgiven?' he gasped; but Bernardo only cried frenziedly, 'Up! up!'

CHAPTER XI

There was consternation in the castello, for its angel visitant had disappeared. The evening following upon the episode of the ring saw his quarters void of him, his household retinue troubled and anxious, and some others in the palace at least as perturbed. It was not alone that the individual sense of stewardship towards so rare a possession filled each and all with forebodings as to the penalty likely to be exacted should Galeazzo return to a knowledge of his loss; the loss itself of so sweet and cleansing a personality was blighting. Now, for the first time, perhaps, people recognised the real political significance of that creed which they had been inclined hitherto merely to pet and humour as the whimsey of a very engaging little propagandist. How sweet and expansive it was! how progressive by the right blossoming road of freedom! Where was their silver-tongued guide? And they flew and buzzed, agitated like a bee-swarm that has lost its queen.

But, while they scurried aimless, a rumour of the truth rose like a foul emanation, and, circulating among them, darkened men's brows and drove women to a whispering gossip of terror. So yet another of the Duke's inhumanities was at the root of this secession! By degrees the secret leaked out—of that living entombment, of the boy's interference, of his bloody forestalling by the executioner, of his flight, accompanied by his Fool, from the gates. And now he was gone, whither none knew; but of a certainty leaving the curse of his outraged suit on the house he had tried to woo from wickedness.

The story gained nothing in relief as it grew. Whispers of that free feminine bandying with their Parablist's name, of Catherine's childish mockery of a sacred sentiment, deepened the common gloom. It mattered nothing to the general opinion that this little vivacious Sforza had but echoed its own bantering mood. Every popular joke that spells disaster must have its scapegoat. And she was not liked. In the absence of her father there were even venturings of frowning looks her way, which, when she observed, the shrewd elfin creature did not forget.

And Bernardo returned not that night, nor during all the following day was he heard of. Inquiries were set on foot, scouts unleashed, the sbirri warned: he remained undiscovered.

Messer Carlo Lanti went about his business with a brow of thunder. Once, on the second day, traversing, dark in cogitation, a lonely corner of the castle enceinte, he came upon a figure which, as it were some apparition of his thoughts suddenly materialised, shocked him to a stand. The walls in this place met in a sunless, abysmal wedge; and, gathered into the hollow between, the waters of the canal, welling through subterranean conduits, made a deep head for the moat. And here, gazing down at her reflection, it seemed, in that black stone-framed mirror, stood Beatrice.

She was plainly conscious, for all her deep abstraction of the moment before, of his approach, yet neither spoke nor so much as turned her head as he came and stood beside her. It must have been some startle more than human that had found her nerves responsive to its shock. Her languor and indolence seemed impregnable, insensate, revealing no token of the passion within. Like the warm, rich pastures which sleep over swelling fires, the placid glow of her cheek and bosom appeared never so fruitful in desire as when most threatening an outburst. Carlo, for all his rage of suspicion, could not but be conscious of that appeal to his senses. He frowned, and shifted, and grunted, while she stood tranquilly facing him and fanning herself without a word. At length he broke silence:—

'I had wished to see thee alone'—he stared fixedly and significantly at the water, struggling to bully himself into brutality—'Nay, by God and St. Ambrose,' he burst out, 'I believe we are well met in this place!'

Not a tremor shook her.

'Alone?' she murmured sleepily. 'Why not? there was not used to be this ceremony between us.'

'I have done with all that,' he cried fiercely. 'I see thee now—myself, at least, in the true light. Harlot! wouldst have turned my hand against the angel that revealed thee! Where is he? Hast struck surer the second time? I know thee—and if——'

He seized her wrist and turned her to the water. She did not resist or cry out, though her cheek flushed in the pain of his cruel clutch.

'Know me!' she said. 'Didst thou ever know me? Only as the bull knows the soft heifer—the nearest to his needs. *Thou* hast done with me—*thou*! I tell thee, if Fate had made a sacrament of thy passion, yielding the visible sign, I had brought hither the monstrous pledge and drowned it like a dog. Do we so treat what we love? I am not guilty of Bernardo's death, if that is what you mean.'

He let her go, and retreated a step, glaring at her. Her blood ebbed and flowed as tranquilly as her low voice had stabbed.

'This—to my face!' he gasped. Then he broke into furious laughter. 'Art well requited, if it is the truth. Love him! But, dead or alive, he will not love thee—that saint—a wife dishonoured.'

'O noble bull—thou king of beasts!' she murmured.

'Why should I be generous?' he snarled. 'Have I reason to spare thee? Yet I will be generous, an thou art guiltless of this, Beatrice. I have loved thee, after my fashion.'

'Thou hast. Ah! If I might sponge away that memory!'

'Well, I would fain do the same for his sake.'

'Dog!'

'What!'

'Barest thou talk of love?—thou, who hast rolled me in thine arms, and waked from sated ecstasy to call me murderess!'

'Had I not provocation, then? Faith, you bewilder me!'

'Poor, stupid brute!'

'Stupid I may be, yet not so blind as woman's folly. Hast borne me once, Beatrice. Well, it is past: I ask nothing of it but thy trust.'

'*My trust!*'

'Ay, when I warn thee. This saint is not for thee. O, I am wide awake! Stupid? like enough; but when a wife, the queenliest, parts with her betrothal ring——'

She made a quick, involuntary gesture, stepping forward; then as suddenly checked herself, with a soft, mocking laugh.

'O this bull!' she cried huskily—'this precisian of the new cult! Not for me, quotha, but for another—a saint to all but the highest bidder!'

'Not for you nor any one,' he said savagely.

'What! not Bona either?' she said. 'Be warned by me, rather. Yours is no wit for this encounter. Love is a coil, dear chuck; no battering-ram. Not for me nor any? Maybe; but the game is in the strife. Go, find your saint: I know nothing of him.'

'No, nor shall. Be warned, I say.'

'Well, you have said it, and more than once.'

He hesitated, ground his teeth, clapped his hands together, and turning, left her.

Glooming and mumbling, he went back to the palace. A page met him with the message that the Duchess of Milan desired his attendance. He frowned, and went, as directed, to her private closet. He found Bona alone, busy, or affecting to be busy, over a strip of embroidery. She greeted him chilly; but it was evident that nervousness rather than hauteur kept her seated. He saluted her coldly and silently, awaiting her pleasure. She glanced once or twice at the closed portière; then braced herself to the ordeal with a rather quivering smile.

'This is a sad coil, Messer Carlo.'

He answered gruffly:—

'If I understand your Grace.'

She put the quibble by.

'We, you and I, are in a manner his guardians—accountable to the Duke.'

'I can understand your Grace's anxiety,' he said shortly.

'Nevertheless, it was not I introduced him to the court,' she said.

'But only to some of its secrets,' he responded.

'I do not understand you.'

'It is very plain, Madonna. You gave him the key to that discovery.'

She rose at once, breathing quickly, her cheeks white.

'Ah, Messer! in heaven's name procure me the return of my ring!'

Her voice was quite pitiful, entreating. He looked at her gloomily, gnawing his upper lip.

'Madonna commands? I will do my best to find and take it from him, alive or dead.'

She fell back with a little crying gasp.

'Find him—yes.'

'No more?' he demanded grimly.

'I thought you loved him?' she gulped.

'Too well,' he answered, 'to be your go-between.'

She uttered a fierce exclamation, and clenched her hands.

'Go, sir!' she said.

He turned at once. She came after him, fawning.

'Good Messer Carlo, dear lord,' she breathed weepingly; 'nay, thou art a loyal and honest friend. Forgive me. We are all in need of forgiveness.'

He faced about again.

'Penitence is blasphemy without reform,' he said.

'Ah me! it is. How well thou hast caught the sweet preacher's style. Hast *thou* reformed?'

'Ay, in the worst.'

'Thou hast made an enemy of thy mistress? Poor Bembo, poor child! He will need a mother.'

'Wouldst thou be that to him?'

'What else? Get me my ring.'

'Beatrice hates him — —'

'She would, the wretch, for his parting you and her.'

'Or loves him—I don't know which.'

'Wanton! how dare she?'

'Well, if you will play the mother to him — —'

'Is he not a child to adore? Ah me! to be foster-parent to that boon-comrade of the Christ!'

Carlo looked at her with some satisfaction darkling out of gloom. His honest hot brain was no Machiavellian possession; his temper was the travail of a warm heart. He believed this woman meant honestly; and so, no doubt, she did in her loss, not considering, or choosing not to consider, the emotionalism of regain.

'Ay, Madonna,' said he, kindling, ''tis the most covetable relation. Who but a Potiphar's wife would associate what we call love with this Joseph? God! a look of him will make me blush as I were a brat caught stealing sugar. There is that in him, we blurt out the truth in the very act of hiding it. A child to adore? Is he not, now, the dear put? and to hearken to and imitate what we can. Ay, and more—to shield with this arm—let men beware. Only the women harass me, this way and that. Their loves and hates be like twin babes. None but their dam can tell each from the other. Therefore, would ye mother him—'

'Yes—'

'And cherish and protect—'

'Yes—'

'And of your woman's wisdom keep skirts at a distance—'

'I will promise that most.'

'Why, I will bring him back to thee, ring and all, though I turn Milan upside down first.'

He bowed and was going; but she detained him, with sycophant velvet eyes.

'Dear lord, so kind and loyal. Tell him that without him we find ourselves astray.'

'Ay.'

'Tell him that from this moment his Duchess will aid and abet him in all his reforms.'

'I will tell him.'

'Ask him—' she hesitated, and turned away her sweet head—'doth he seek to retaliate on his mistress's innocent confidence, that, by absenting himself, he would turn it to her undoing?'

Carlo grunted.

'By your Grace's leave, an I find him, I will put it my way.'

She acquiesced with a meek, lovely smile, and the words of the Mass: '*Ite, missa est!*'

And when he was gone, she sighed, and looked in a mirror and murmured to herself in a semi-comedy of grief: 'Alas! too weak to be Messalina! I must be good if he asks me.'

And, being weak, she let her thoughts drift.

CHAPTER XII

In a street of the quarter Giovia the armourer Lupo had his smithy. He had been a notable artisan in a town famous for its steel and niello work; but in his age, as in any, a plethora of fine production must cheapen the value of the individual producer. Therefore when a vengeful caprice blinded him, and his door remained shut and his chimney ceased to smoke, patronage transferred its custom to the next house or street without a qualm; and his achievements in his particular business were forgotten, or confounded with those of fellow-craftsmen, deriving, perhaps, in their art from him. It was a sample of that banal heartlessness of society, which in a moral age breeds collectivists, and desperadoes in an age of lawlessness. And of the two one may pronounce the latter the more logical.

In Milan men came quickly to maturity, whether in the art of forging a blade or using it. Life flamed up and out on swift ideals of passion. Parental love, high education, the intricate cults of beauty and chivalry, were all gambling investments in a speculative market. The odds were always in favour of that old broker Death. Yet the knowledge abated nothing of the zeal. It was strange to be so fastidious of the terms of so hazardous a lease. One might be saving, just, virtuous—one's life-tenancy was not made thereby a whit securer. The ten commandments lay at the mercy of a dagger-point; wherefore men hurried to realise themselves timely, and to cram the stores of years into a rich banquet or two.

Master Lupo, a sincere workman and a conscientious, was flicked in one moment off his green leaf into the dust. There, maimed and helpless, the tears for ever welling in his empty sockets, he cogitated tremulously, fiercely, the one sentiment left to him, revenge—revenge not so primarily on the instrument of his ruin, as on Tassino *through* the system which had made such a creature possible. He lent his darkened abode to be the nest to one of those conspiracies, which are never far to gather in despotic governments, and which opportunity in his case showed him actually at hand.

Cola Montano, it has been said, had been borne away after his scourging by some women of the people. Grace, or pity, or fear was in their hearts, and they nursed him. Scarcely for his own sake; for, democracy being impersonal, he was at no trouble to be a grateful patient. He took their ministries as conceded to a principle, and individually was as surly and impatient with them as any ill-conditioned cur.

Recovering betimes (the dog had a tough hide), he learned of neighbour Lupo's condition, and walked incontinently into that wretched artificer's existence. He found a blind and hopeless wreck, shelves of rusting armour, a forge of dead embers, and, brooding sullen beside it, a girl too plainly witnessing to her own dishonour. He heard the rain on the roof; he saw the set grey mother creeping about her work; and he sat himself down by the sightless armourer, and peered hungrily into his swathed face.

'Dost know me, Lupo? I am Montano.'

The miserable man groaned.

'Master Collegian? Stands yet thy school of philosophy? A' God's name, lay something of that on this hot bandage!'

'The school stands in its old place, armourer; but its doors, like thine, are shut. What then? Its principles remain open to all.'

The poor wretch put out a hand, feeling.

'Where art thou? Have thy wounds healed so quickly? Mine are incurable.'

'What!' croaked Montano jeeringly, 'with such a salve to allay them! I heard of it—logic meet to an angel—to renew thine image through her yonder. Marry, sir! conception runs before the law. Hast chased thy likeness down and taken it to church? Mistress Lucia there would seem a sullen bride. Hath her popinjay come and gone again? Well, you must be content with the legitimising.'

The armourer writhed in answering.

'What think you? There has been none. Mock not our misery. Is it the concern of angels to see their sentences enforced?'

'No, but to be called angels. Heaven is not easy surfeited with adulation.'

'He was glorified in his judgment; and there, for us, the matter ended.'

'Not quite.'

The pedagogue bent his evil head to look again into that woful face.

'Lupo, my school is closed; alumnus loiters in the streets. Shall he come in here?'

There was something so significant in his tone that the broken man he addressed started, as if a hand had been laid on his eyes.

'For what? Who is he?' he muttered.

'I will tell you anon,' answered Montano. 'No prelector but hath his favourite pupils. He, alumnus, is in this case threefold—three dear homeless scholars of mine, Lupo, needing a rallying-place in which to meet and mature some long-discussed theory of social cure. I have heard from them since—since my illness. They chafe to resume their studies and their mentor—honest, good fellows, confessing, perhaps, to a heresy or so.'

'Master,' muttered the armourer, 'you will do no harm to be explicit.'

'Shall I not? Well, if you will, and by grace of an example, such a heresy, say, as that, when the devil rules by divine right, the God who nominated him is best deposed.'

'Yes, yes, to be sure. That is blasphemy as well as heresy. But I think of Messer Bembo, who is still His minister, and I believe your pupils go too far.'

'Why, what hath this minister done for you?'

'Very much, in intention.'

'Well, I thought that was said to pave the other place; but, in truth, the issues of all things are confounded, since we have an angel for the Lord's minister and a devil for His vicegerent.'

'Pity of God! are they not? And ye would resolve them by deposing the Christ—by knocking out the very keystone of hope?'

'Nay, by substituting a rock for a crumbling brick.'

'What rock?'

'The people.'

'Might they not, too, elect a tyrant to be their representative?'

'How could tyranny represent a commonwealth?'

'A commonwealth! It is out, then! It is not God ye would depose, but Galeazzo. Commonwealth! Is that a name for keeping all men under a certain height? But the giant will dictate the standard, and any one may reach to him who can. Messer Montano, I seem to have heard of a republican called Cæsar.'

'Then you must have heard of another called Brutus?'

'Ay, to be sure; and of a third called Octavian.'

'Those were distracted times, my friend.'

'And what are these? Have you ever heard of the times when a man's interest was one with his neighbour's? Besides, the flame of art burns never so sprightly as under a despot. It finds no fuel in uniformity—each man equal to his neighbour.' He put out groping hands pitifully. 'I loved my art,' he quavered. 'They might have spared me to it!'

Montano bit his lip scornfully. It was on his tongue to spurn this spiritless creature. But he suppressed himself.

'What would you, then?' he demanded; 'you, the wretched victim of the system you commend?'

'Ah!' sighed Lupo, 'ideally, Messer, an autocracy, with an angel at its head.'

The philosopher laughed harshly.

'Why,' he sneered, 'there is your ideal come to hand. Be plain. Shall we depose a tyrant, and elect in his place this new-arrived, this divine boy, as ye all title him?'

'Why not?'

Montano started and stared at the speaker. There was suggestion here—of a standard for innovation; of a rallying-point for reform. A republic, like a despotism, might find its telling battle-cry in a saint. The boy, as representing the liberty of conscience, was already a subject of popular adoration. Why should they not use him as a fulcrum to the lever of revolution, and, having done with, return him to the cloisters from which he drew? There was suggestion here.

He mused a little, then broke out suddenly:—

'Brutus is none the less indispensable.'

'I do not gainsay it, master.'

'What! you do not? Then there, at least, we are agreed. Wilt have him come here?'

'Who is he, this Brutus? I grope in the dark—O my God, in the dark!'

During all this time the two women had remained passive and apparently apathetic listeners. Now, suddenly, the girl rose from her place by the chimney and came heavily forward, her eyes glaring, her hands clenched in woe, like some incarnated, fallen pythoness.

'Tell *me*,' she said hoarsely. 'I haven't *his* patience for my wrongs, nor caution neither. What's gained by caution when one stands on an earthquake? Let me make sure of *him*, my fine lover, and the world may fall in, for all I care.'

The pale mother hurried to her husband's side. He put out helpless, irresolute hands, with a groan. Montano stooping, elbow on knee, and rubbing his bristly chin, conned the speaker with sinister approval.

'Spoken like a Roman,' said he. 'Thou art the better vessel. If all were as you! Tyranny is hatched of the gross corpse of manliness—a beastly fly. Wilt tell thee my Brutus's name, girl, if thou wilt answer for these.'

He pointed peremptorily at her parents.

'Ay, will I,' she answered scornfully; 'though I have to wrench out their tongues first.'

He applauded shrilly, with a triumphant, contemptuous glance at the cowering couple.

'That is the right way with cowards. I commit my Brutus to thee. 'Tis a threefold dog, as I have said—a fanged Cerberus. Noble, too—as Roman as thou; and, in one part at least, like wounded. He, this third part, this Carlo Visconti, had a sister. Well, she was a flower which Galeazzo plucked; and, not content therewith threw into the common road. Another head is Lampugnani, beggared by the Sforzas; and Girolamo Olgiati is my third, a dear beardless boy, and instigated only by the noblest love of liberty.'

The girl nodded.

'And are these all?'

'All, save a fellow called Narcisso—a mere instrument to use and break—no principles but hate and gain. Was servant to that bully Lanti and dismissed—hum! for excess of loyalty. Fear him not.'

'Alas!' broke in the armourer: 'why should we fear him or anybody? There is no harm in this letting my shop to be thy school's succedaneum.'

Lucia laughed like a fury.

'No harm at all,' sniggered Montano, 'save in these heresies I spoke of. And what are they?—to reorganise society on a basis of political and social freedom. No harm in these young Catalines discussing their drastic remedies, perhaps in the vanity of a hope that some Sallust may be found to record them.'

'Nay, have done with all this,' cried the girl witheringly. 'I know nothing of your Catalines and Sallusts. Ye meet to kill—own it, or ye meet elsewhere.'

Her mother cried out: 'O Lucia! per pieta.'

She made no answer, only fixing Montano with her glittering eyes. He rose from his stool stiffly, with a snarl for his aching wounds. But his face brightened towards her like a spark of wintry sun.

'We meet to kill, Madonna,' he said, 'ruined, crippled, debauched—the victims of a monster and his system. And thou shalt have thy share, never fear, when the feast comes to follow the sacrifice.'

Bembo had fled, like one distracted, from the walls, his faithful shadow jumping in his wake. The two, running and following, never slackened in their pace until a half-mile separated them from the city; and then, in a gloomy thicket, under a falling sky, the boy threw himself down on the grass, and buried his face from heaven. Pitiful and distraught, the Fool stood over, silently regarding him. At length he spoke, panting and reproachful.

'Nay, in pity, master, wert thou not advised?'

The boy writhed.

'So lying, so wicked cunning, to make me his decoy and seeming abettor! O, I am punished for my faith! Is Christ dead?'

The Fool sighed.

'By thy showing, He lingers behind in the wood.'

'Tell Him I have gone on to my father.'

'Thou wilt?'

Bernardo sat up, a towzled angel. In the interval the tears had come fast, and his face was wet.

'God help you all!' he sobbed. 'You, even you, prevaricated to me. Whither shall I turn? I see everywhere a death-dealing wilderness, lies and lust and inhumanity.'

'I prevaricated,' said Cicada mournfully. 'I admit it. You once claimed my wit and experience to your tutoring. Well, do I not know the tyrant—the persistent devil in him? He had his teeth in that monk. Not Christ Himself would have loosened them.'

'Ah! what shall I do?'

'What, but go forward steadfast. This is but a jog by the way. Judge life on the broad lines of action, the ruts which mark the progress of the wheels. 'Tis a morbid sentiment that wastes itself on the quarrel between the wheels and the road.'

'Ah, me! if I could but foresee the end of that bloody mire—the sweet, crisp path again! I can advance no further. My weak heart fails. I will go back to the wood.'

'Then back, a' God's name, so I come too.'

Bernardo rose and seized the Fool's hand, the tears streaming down his cheeks.

'This dreadful race—monsters all!' he cried. 'Is there one kind deed recorded to its credit—one, one only, one little deed? Tell me, and if there is, by its memory I will persevere.'

'Humph! Should I wish thee to? Think again of that wood.'

'Tell me, kind, good Cicca, my nurse and friend.'

'Go to! Shalt not put a bone in my throat. Well, they are monsters, but made by that same brute Circumstance thou decriest. "Wavering out of chaos," says you? Very like, sir; but, after all, Circumstance is our head artist in a tuneless world. What a dull sing-song 'twould be without him—league-long choirs of saints praising God—a universe of chirping crickets! With respect, sir, I, though his Fool, would not have him caged in my time.'

'Alas, dear, for thine understanding! Love, that I would have depose him, is ten thousand times his superior in art—ay, and in humour. But go on.'

'I doubt the humour. However, as things are, I owe to him, as do you, and Galeazzo—the Fool, the Saint, and the Monster. Could love conceive such a trio? But to the point. Hast ever heard speak of our Duke's grand-dad?'

'Muzio?'

'So he called himself, or was called, pretending to trace his descent from Mutius Scævola the Roman. Flattery, you see, will make a braying ass of honesty. He was Giacommuzzo—just that; one of a family of fighting yeomen. But he had points. Hast been told how he began?'

'No.'

'Why, he was digging turnips by the evening star in his father's farm at Cotignola, when the sound of pipes and drums disturbed him. 'Twas some band of Boldrino of Panicale come to recruit from the fields; and they halted by the big man. "Be a soldier of fortune like us," says they; and he tossed his dusty hair from his eyes, and saw the glint of gold in baldricks. He looked at the evening star, and 'twas pale beside. Borrowers glean the real heaven of credit in this topsy-turvy world. Look at any pool of water: what a glittering prospectus it makes of the moon! Muzzo flung his spade into an oak hard by, leaving the decision to Circumstance. If it fell, he would resume it; if it stayed, a soldier he would be. It stuck in the branches.'

'Cicca!'

'Peace! I will tell thee. He fought up and down, but never back to Cotignola. He put his ploughing shoulder to his work, and dug a furrow to fame. Popes and kings engaged for and against this Condottieri. He took them all to market like his beans. He knew the values of fear and money and discipline—bought over honour; wrenched treason by the joints; flogged slackness for a rusty hinge in its armour; made warriors of his rabble. Sought letters, too, to spur them on by legend.'

'All this is nothing.'

'He went to Mass every day— —'

'Alas!'

'Cast his true plain wife, and took to bed the widow of Naples— —'

'Alas! Alas!'

'And lost his life at Pescara, trying to save another.'

'Ah! How was that?'

'He had crossed the river on a blown tide, when he saw his page a-drowning in the stream. "Poor lad," quoth he, "will none help thee?" And he dashed back, was overwhelmed himself, and sank. They saw his mailed hands twice rise and clutch the air. A' was never seen again. The waters were his tomb.'

Bernardo was silent.

'Was not that a creditable deed?' quoth the Fool.

The boy, pressing the tangled hair from his eyes, feverishly seized his comrade's hands in his own.

'God forgive me!' he cried; 'am I one to judge him, who have let my father's friend go under, and never reached a hand?'

The Fool looked frankly amazed.

'Montano,' cried Bembo, 'whom, in my pride of place, I have forgotten! I will go down among the people where he lies, and seek to heal his wounds, and sing Christ's parables to simple hearts. Love lies not in palaces. I will seek Montano.'

'Come, then,' said Cicada.

'Nay, in a little,' said the boy. 'Let the kind night find us first. I will flaunt my creed no longer in the sun.'

From behind the barred door of Lupo's shop came the sound of muffled laughter. The tragic incongruity of it in that house of ruin was at least arresting enough to halt a pedestrian here and there on his passage along the dark, wet-blown street outside. The mirth broke gustily, with little snarls at intervals, bestial and worrying; hearing which, the lingerer would perhaps hurry on his way with a shudder, crossing himself against, or spitting out like a bad odour, the influence of the fiend who had evidently got hold of the master armourer. *Libera nos à malo!*

The fiend, in fact, in possession was no other than Messer Montano's Cerberus, and its orgy, had the listener known it, had more than justified his apprehensions. The mirth which terrified his heart was perhaps even a degree more deadly in its evocation than anything he could imagine. It was really laughter so dreadful that, had he guessed its import, he had rushed, in an agony of self-vindication, to summon the watch. But guessing nothing, unless it might be Lupo's madness under the shock of his misfortunes, he simply crossed himself and hurried away.

Blood conspiracies are rarely successful. Perhaps a too scrupulous forethought against contingencies tends to clog the issues. If that is so, the recklessness of these men may, in a measure, have spelt their present security. A laugh, after all, is less open to suspicion than a whisper. Who could imagine a fatal thrust in a guffaw? Nevertheless, every chuckle uttered here punctuated a stab.

In rehearsal only at present, it is true; but practice, good practice, sirs. The victim of the attack was a dummy, contrived suggestively to represent Galeazzo. At least the habit made the man; and hate and a stinging imagination supplied the rest.

It stood in a dusky corner by the dead forge. Not so much light as would certainly guide a hand was allowed to fall upon it; for deeds of darkness, to be successful, must be prepared against darkness. Its stuffed, daubed face, staring from out this gloom, was like nothing human. To catch sudden sight, within a vista of dim lamp-shine, of its motionless eyes and features warped with stabs, was to gasp and shrink, as if one had looked into a glass and seen Death reflected back. Its suggestion of reality (and it possessed it) was to seek rather in velvet and satin; in a cunning, familiar disposition of its dress; in the sombre but profuse sparkle of artificial gems with which it was looped and hung. Thence came a grotesque and wicked semblance to a doomed figure. For the rest, in the bloodless slashes, gaping, rag-exuding, which had taken it cunningly in weak places—through the neck, under the gorget, between joints of the mail with which Lupo's craft had fitted it— there was a suggestiveness almost more horrible than truth.

It was in actual fact a sop to Cerberus, was this grisly-ludicrous doll, fruit of the decision (which had followed much discussion of ways and means) to postpone its prototype's murder to some occasion of public festivity, when the sympathies of the mob might be kindled and a revolution accomplished at a stroke. Politic Cerberus must nevertheless have something to stay the gnawing and craving of a delayed revenge which had otherwise corroded him. He took a ferociously boyish delight in fashioning this lay-figure, and, having made, in whetting his teeth on it; in clothing it in purple and fine linen; in addressing it wheedlingly, or ironically, or brutally, as the mood swayed him. And to-night his mood, stung by the tempest, perhaps, was unearthly in its wildness. It rose in fiendish laughter; it mocked the anguish of the blast, a threefold litany, now blended, now a trifurcating blasphemy. There were the roaring bass of Visconti, Lampugnani's smooth treble, the deadly considered baritone of Olgiati. And, punctuating all, like the tap of a baton, flew the interjections of Messer Montano, the conductor:—

'Su! Gia-gia! Bravo, Carlo! That was a Brutus stroke! Uh-uh, Andrea! hast bled him there for arrears of wages! a scrap of gold-cloth, by Socrates! A brave sign, a bright token, Andrea!'

He chuckled and hugged himself, involuntarily embracing in the action the long pendant which hung from his roundlet or turban, and half-pulling the cap from his skull-like forehead.

'Death!' he screeched in an ecstasy, and Lampugnani, glancing at him, went off into husky laughter, and sank back, breathed, upon a bench.

'Cometh in a doctor's gown,' he panted. 'Nay, sir, bonnet! bonnet! or the dummy will suspect you.'

He might have, himself, and with a better advantage to his fortunes, could he have penetrated the vestments of that drear philosophic heart. There was a secret there would have astounded *his* self-assurance. Montano wore his doctor's robe, meetly as a master of rhetoric, not the least of whose contemplated flights was one timely away from that political arena, whose gladiators in the meanwhile he was bent only on inflaming to a contest in which he had no intention of personally participating. He had a fixed idea, his back and his principles being still painfully at odds, that the cause would be best served by his absence, when once the long train to the explosion he was engineering had been fired at his hand. And so he hugged himself, and Lampugnani laughed.

'Look at Master Lupo, with the sound of thy screech in his ears! As if he thought we contemplated anything but to bring slashed Venetian doublets into vogue!'

He was a large, fleshly creature, was this Lampugnani, needing some fastidious lust to stir him to action, and then suddenly violent. His face was big and vealy, with a mouth in its midst like a rabbit's, showing prominently a couple, no more, of sleek teeth. His eyes drooped under lids so languid as to give him an affectation of fatigue in lifting them. His voice was soft, but compelling: he never lent it to platitudes. An intellectual sybarite, a voluptuary by deliberation, he had tested God and Belial, and pronounced for the less Philistine lordship of the beast. Quite consistent with his principles, he not hated, but highly disapproved of Galeazzo, who, as consistently, had pardoned him some abominable crime which, under Francesco the father, had procured him the death sentence. But Messer Andrea had looked for a more sympathetic recognition of his merits at the hands of his deliverer than was implied in an ill-paid lieutenancy of Guards; and his exclusion from a share in the central flesh-pots was a conclusive proof to him of the æsthetic worthlessness of the master it was his humility to serve.

The Visconti, at whom he breathed his little laugh, was a contrast to him in every way—a bluff, stout-built man, with fat red chaps flushing through a skin of red hair, a braggadocio manner, and small eyes red with daring. There was nothing of his house's emblematic adder about him, save a readiness with poisons; and after all, that gave him no particular distinction. He took a great, stertorous pull at a flagon of wine, and smacked his lips bullyingly, before he answered with a roar:—

'Wounds! scarlet scotched on a ground of flesh-tint—a fashion will please our saint.'

Montano chuckled again, and more shrilly.

'Good, good!' he cried: 'scarlet on flesh!' and he squinted roguishly at the blind smith, who sat beside him on a bench, nervously kneading together his wasted hands.

'Messers,' muttered the poor fellow; 'but will this holy boy approve the means to such a fashion? For Love to exalt himself by blood!'

He turned his sightless eyes instinctively towards Olgiati, where the boy stood, a dark, fatalistic young figure, breathing himself by the forge. He, he guessed, or perhaps knew, was alone of the company actuated by impersonal motives in this dread conspiracy. But he did not guess that, by so much as the young man was a pure fanatic of liberty, his hand and purpose were the most of all to be dreaded.

Olgiati gave a melancholy smile, and, stirring a little, looked down. He was habited, as were his two companions, for the occasion—a recurrent dress-rehearsal—in a coat and hose of mail, and a jerkin of crimson satin. It was not the least significant part of his undertaking that he, like the others, was court-bred and court-employed. The fact, at its smallest, implied in them a certain anatomic-cum-sartorial acquaintance with their present business.

'*Offerimus tibi, Domine, Calicem salutaris!*' he quoted from the Mass, in his sweet, strong voice. 'Hast thou not a first example of that exaltation, Lupo, in the oblation of the chalice?'

Revolution knows no blasphemy.

'Bah!' grumbled Visconti.

'He died for men: we worship the sacrifice of Himself,' protested the armourer.

'And shall not Messer Bembo sacrifice himself, his scruples and his reluctances, that love may be exalted over hate, mercy over tyranny?' asked Olgiati.

'I know not, Messer,' muttered the suffering armourer. 'I cannot trace the saint in these sophistries, that is all.'

'True, he is a saint,' conceded Lampugnani, yawning as he lolled. 'Now, what is a saint, Lupo?'

'O, Messer! look on his mother's son, and ask!'

'Why, that is the true squirrel's round. We are all born of women'—he yawned again.

'They bear us, and we endure them,' he murmured smilingly, the water in his eyes. 'It is so we retaliate on their officiousness.'

Montano tittered.

'Lupo,' Lampugnani went on, lazily stirring himself, 'you suggest to me two-thirds of a syllogism: *I* am my mother's son; therefore I am a saint.'

'Ho! ho!' hooted Visconti.

'Messer,' entreated the bewildered armourer, 'with respect, it turns upon the question of the mother.'

'The mother? O dog, to question the repute of mine!'

'I did not—no, never.'

'Well, who was his?'

'None knows. A star, 'tis said.'

'Venus, of course. And his father?'

'Some son of God, perchance.'

'Ay, Mars. He was that twain's by-blow, and fell upon an altar. I know now how saints are made. Yet shall we, coveting sanctity, wish our parents bawds? 'Tis a confusing world!'

He sank back as if exhausted, while Montano chirped, and Visconti roared with laughter.

'Saints should be many in it, Andrea,' he applauded. 'Knows how they are made, quotha!' and he stamped about, holding his sides till, reeling near to the dummy, he paused, and made a savage lunge at it with his dagger. His mood changed on the instant.

'Death!' he snarled, 'I warrant here's one hath propagated some saints to his undoing!' and he went muttering a rosary of curses under his breath.

Lampugnani, smilingly languid, continued:—

'Well, Lupo, so Messer Bembo is the son of his mother? It seems like enough—what with his wheedling and his love-locks. He shall be Saint Cupid on promotion. I think he will regard scarlet or pink as no objectionable fashion, does it come to make a god of him.'

The armourer uttered an exclamation:—

'Some think him that already. It is the question of his coming to be Duke that hips me. I can't see him there.'

'Nor I,' said Visconti, with a sarcastic laugh.

Olgiati interposed quietly:—

'Have comfort, Lupo. We are all good republicans. The exaltation of Messer Bembo is to be provisional only, preceding the consummation. He is to be lifted like the Host, to bring the people to their knees, and then lowered, and——'

'Put away,' said Lampugnani blandly.

The armourer started to his feet in agitation.

'Messers!' he cried, 'he poured oil into my wounds; I will consent to no such wickedness.'

'*You* won't?' roared Visconti; but Lampugnani soothed him down.

'When I said "put away," I meant in a tabernacle, like that sacred bread. I assure you, Lupo, he is the rose of our adoration also; he shall cultivate his thorn in peace; he shall wax fat like Jeshurun, and kick.'

'And in the meantime,' grumbled Visconti, 'we are measuring our fish before we've hooked him.'

Lampugnani's face took on a very odd expression.

'What the devil's behind that?' hectored the bully.

'O, little!' purred the other. 'I fancy I feel him nibble, that's all. Perhaps you don't happen to know how he hath cut his connection with the palace?'

'What! When?'

They all jumped to stare at him.

'This day,' he said, 'in offence of some carrion of Galeazzo's which he had nosed out. The poor boy is particular in his tastes, for a shambles—ran like a sheep from the slaughter-house door, taking his Patch with him, and a ring her Grace had loaned him for a safe-conduct. I heard it said she would have been ravished of anything rather—by him. 'Twas her lord's troth-gift. The castle is one fume of lamentation.'

Montano, rubbing his lean hands between his knees, went into a rejoicing chatter:—

'We have him, we have him! Gods! who's here?'

Their intentness had deafened them some minutes earlier to a more mouthing note in the thunder of the rain, as if the swell of the tempest had been opened an instant and shut. The moment, in fact, and a master-key, had let in a new comer. He had closed the latch behind him, and now, seeing himself observed, stood ducking and lowering in the blinking light. The philosopher heaved a tremulous sigh of relief.

'Narcisso!'

The hulking creature grinned, and stabbed a thumb over his shoulder.

'Hist! him you speak of's out there, a-seeking your worship.'

'Seeking *me*? Messer Bembo?'

'Why not? A' met him at the town gate half-drowned, with his Patch to heel. The report of his running was got abroad, and, thinks I to myself, here's luck to my masters. To take him on the hop of grievance like——'

Montano seemed to sip the phrase:—

'Exactly: on the hop of grievance. Well?'

'Why, I spoke him fair: "Whither away, master?" A' spat a saintly word—'twere a curse in a sinner—and sprang back, a' did, glaring at me. But the great Fool pushed him by. "You're the man," says he. "Desperation knows its fellows. Where's Montano?" "Why, what would you with him?" says I, taken off my guard. "A salve for his wounds," he answered. And so I considered a bit, and brought 'em on, and there they wait.'

Visconti uttered a furious oath, but Lampugnani hushed him down.

'Didst well, pretty innocence,' he said to Narcisso. 'The hop of grievance?—never a riper moment. Show in your friends.'

He was serenely confident of his policy—waved all protest aside.

'I see my way: the hook is baited: let him bite.'

'Bite?' growled Visconti. 'And what about our occupation here?'

'Why, 'tis testing mail, nothing more. Is a lay-figure in an armoury so strange?'

'Ay, when 'tis a portrait-model.'

'O glowing tribute to my art! I designed the doll, true. You make me look down, sir, and simper and bite my finger. Yet my mind misgives me thou flatterest. A portrait-model, yes; but will he recognise of whom?'

'The knave may—the shrewder fool of the pair.'

'The greater fool will testify to me? O happy artist! Well, if he do, I will still account him naught. He will take the bait also. The shadow swims and bites with the fish. Besides, should this befall, 'twill save mayhap a world of preliminaries. Remember that "hop of grievance." He comes, it seems, in a mood to jump with ours. Let them in.'

Like souls salvaged from a wreck they came—the Fool propping the Saint—staggering in by the door. Grief and storm and weariness had robbed the boy of speculation, almost of his senses. His drenched hair hung in ropes, his wild eyes stared beneath like a frightened doe's, his clothes slopped on his limbs.

Narcisso struggled with the door and closed it.

Suddenly Bernardo, lifting his dazed lids, caught sight of the shadowed lay-figure, recoiled, and shrieking out hoarsely:—'Galeazzo! Thou! O God, doomed soul!' tottered and slid through Cicada's limp arms upon the floor. Instantly Narcisso was down by his side, and fumbling with his hands.

'A's in a swound,' he was beginning, when, with a rush and heave, the Fool sent him wallowing.

'Darest thou, hog! darest thou! Go rub thy filthy hoofs in ambergris first!' and he squatted, snarling and showing his teeth.

Narcisso rose, to a chorus of laughter, and stood grinning and rubbing his head.

'Well, I never!' he said.

CHAPTER XIII

The Countess of Casa Caprona was a widow. The news was waiting to overwhelm, or transport, her upon her return to the castello after her interview with Lanti. On the one hand it committed her to dowagery, that last infirmity of imperious minds; on the other to the freedom of a glorified spinsterhood. Though she recognised that, on the whole, the blow was destructive of the real zest of intrigue, she behaved very handsomely by the memory of the deceased, who had died, like a soldier, in harness. She caused a solemn requiem mass to be sung for him in the Duomo; she commissioned a monody, extolling his marital virtues, from an expensive poet; she distributed liberal alms to the poor of the city. There is no trollop so righteous in her matronhood as she made timely a widow. Besides, to this one, the zest of all zests for the moment was revenge. She withdrew to mature it, and to lament orthodoxly her lord, to her dower-house in the Via Sforza.

It was a very pretty spot for melancholy and meditation—cool, large, secluded, and its smooth, silent walks and bubbling fountains cloistered in foliage. From its gardens one had glimpses of the castello and of the candied, biscuit-like pinnacles of the cathedral. Cypresses and little marble fauns broke between them the flowering intervals, and peacocks on the gravel made wandering parterres of colour. Sometimes, musing in the shades, with a lock of her long hair between her lips, she would pet her frowning fancy with the figure of a youthful Adam, golden and glorious, approaching her down an avenue of this smiling paradise, making its mazes something less than scentless; and then, behold! a lizard, perhaps, would wink on the terrace, and she would snatch and crush the little palpitating life under her heel, cursing it for a symbol of the serpent desolating her Eden, and transforming it all into a mirage of warmth and passion. Not Adam he, that lusted-for, but the angel at the gate, menacing and awful. She must be more and worse than Eve to seek to corrupt an angel.

Perhaps she was, in her most tortured, most animal moods. The sensuous, by training and heredity, had quite over-swollen and embedded in her beautiful trunk the small spike of conscience, which as a child had tormented, and which yet, at odd moments, would gall and tease her like an ancient wound. She might even have been stung by it into some devotional self-sacrifice in her present phase of passion, could she have been assured of, or believed in, its object's inaccessibility to a higher grace of solicitation. But jealousy kept her ravening.

On a languorous noon of this week of losses she was lying, a conventionally social exile, having her hair combed and perfumed, in a little green pavilion pitched in her grounds, when a heavy step on the gravel outside aroused her from a dream of voluptuous rumination. The tread she recognised, yet, though moved by it to a little flutter of curiosity, would not so far alloy a drowsy ecstasy as to bid the visitor enter while it lasted. Hypnotised by the soft burrowing of the comb, she closed her eyes until the perfect moment was passed, when, with a sigh, she bade the intruder enter, and Narcisso came slouching in by the opening.

Beatrice dismissed her attendants with a look. She never spoke to her servants where a gesture would serve, and could draw hour-long silent enjoyment from the weary hands of tire-woman or slave, hairdresser or fanner, without a sign of embarrassment, or indeed understanding. Now she lay back, restful, impassive—indifferent utterly to any impression her will for a solitary interview with this gross creature might make upon them. And, indeed, there was little need for such concern. Hired assassination, a recognised institution, explained many otherwise strange conjunctions between the beauties and beasts of Milan.

The beast, in the present instance, behaved as was habitual with him in the presence of this Circe. That is to say, he was awkward, deprecating, and, of stranger significance, devoted to truthfulness. He adored her, as Caliban Miranda, but more fearfully: was her slave, the genii of the lamp of her loveliness, with which to be on any familiar terms, even of debasement, was enough. What did it matter that she paid him with offence and disdain? Her use of him was as her use of some necessary organic part of herself. And she might deprecate the necessity; but the secret of it was, nevertheless, their common property. Her beauty and his devotion were as near akin as blood and complexion. Perhaps some day, in the resurrection of the flesh, he would be able to substantiate that kinship.

The thought may have been there in him, instinctive, unilluminated, as he stood fumbling with his cap, and raising and lowering his hang-dog eyes, and waiting for her to open. Physically, at least, she showed no shame in implying his close right to her confidence. The noon was a noon of slumbering fires, and her mood a responsive one. A long white camisole, of the frailest tissue, rounded on her lower limbs, and, splitting at the waist, straddled her shoulders clingingly, leaving a warm breathing-space between. Round her full neck clung one loop of emeralds; and to the picture her black falling hair made a tenderest frame, while the sun, penetrating the tilt above, finished all with a mist of green translucence. A Circe, indeed, to this coarse and animal rogue, and alive with awful and covetable lusts, to which, nevertheless, he was an admitted procurer. He had not ceased to be in her pay and confidence, cursed and repudiated though he had been by his master, her erst protector. He had not even resented that episode of his betrayal at her hands, though it had condemned him for a living to the rôle of the hired bravo. She might always do with him as she liked; overbid with one imperious word his fast pledges to others; convert his craft wheresoever she wished to her own profit. The more she condescended to him, the more was he claimed a necessary part of her passions' functions. She discharged through him her hates and desires, and he was beatified in the choice of himself as their medium. There was a suggestion of understanding, of a conscious partnership between them, in the very fulsomeness with which he abased himself before her.

'Well,' she murmured at last, 'hast drunk thy senses to such surfeit that they drown in me?'

'Ay,' he mumbled, 'I could die looking.'

'A true Narcissus,' she scoffed; 'but I could wish a sweeter. Stand away, fellow. Your clothes offend me.'

He backed at once.

'Now,' she said, 'I can breathe. Deliver yourself!'

He heaved up his chest, and looked above her, concentrating his wits on an open loop of the tent, behind which a bird was flickering and chirping.

'I come, by Madonna's secret instructions, from privately informing Messer Lanti where Messer Bembo lies hidden,' he said, speaking as if by rote.

She nodded imperiously.

'What questions did he ask?'

'How I knew; and I answered, that I knew.'

'Good. That least was enough. Art a right rogue. Now will he go seek him, and be drawn by his devotion into this net.'

Narcisso was silent.

'Will he not?' she demanded sharply.

The fellow dropped his eyes to her an instant.

'Madonna knows. He loves the Messer Saint. No doubt a' will hold by him.'

'What then, fool?'

'They have not caught Messer Bembo yet, they at the forge—that is all.'

'How!' she cried angrily, 'when thou told'st me——'

'With humility, Madonna,' he submitted, 'I told thee naught but that he and this Montano were agreed on the State's disease.'

'Well?'

'But I never said on its cure.'

She frowned, leaning forward and again biting a strand of her hair—a sullen trick with her in anger.

'A doctor of rhetoric, and so feeble in persuasion!' she muttered scornfully.

'A' starts at a shadow, this saint,' pleaded Narcisso. 'A' must be coaxed, little by little, like a shy foal. We will have him in the halter anon. Yet a' be only one out of five, when all's said.'

'Dolt!' she hissed. 'What are the other four, or their purpose, to me, save as a lever to my revenge? I foresee it all. Why telled'st me not before I sent thee? Now this gross lord, instead of himself tangling in the meshes, will persuade the other back to court and reason and forgiveness, and I shall be worse than damned. Dolt, I could kill thee!'

She rose to her height, furious, and he shrunk cowering before her.

'Listen, Madonna,' he said, trembling: 'Canst net them all yet at one swoop. Go tell Messer Ludovico, and certes a' will jump to destroy the nest and all in it, before a' inquires their degrees of guilt.'

She stared at him, still threatening.

'Why?'

'Why, says Madonna? Listen again, then. Does the Ser Simonetta trust Messer Ludovico, or Messer Ludovico love the Ser Simonetta? The secretary clings to the Duchess. If she falls, a' falls with her.'

'Again, thou tedious rogue, why should the Saint's destruction bring Bona down?'

'A' would have his mouth shut from explaining.'

'Explaining what? I lose patience.'

'How a' came, a conspirator against the Duke, to be found wi' his wife's troth ring in his possession. Here it be. I've filched it for thee at last.'

She sprang to seize the token, glowing triumphant in a moment, and putting it on her own finger, pressed the clinched hand that enclosed it into her bosom.

She laughed low and rejoicingly, shameless in the quick transition of her mood.

'Good Narcisso! It is the Key at last! Let Lanti persuade him back now—I am content. I hold them, and Bona too, in the hollow of this hand.'

She held it out, her right one, palm upwards, and, smiling, bade him kiss it.

'Rogue,' she said, 'to tease and vex me, and all the time this talisman in thy sleeve. Ay, make the most of it: snuffle and root. My dog has deserved of me.'

He wiped his lips with the back of his hand, as if he had drunk.

'Now,' she said, 'how wert successful? how won'st it, sweet put?'

'Took it from him, that was all.'

'How?'

'When a' came tumbling in and staggered in a swound. Had heard Messer Andrea relating of how 'twas on him as I entered. Ho, ho! thinks I, here's that, maybe, will pay the filching! and I dropped and got it, all in a moment like.'

'You never told me.'

'You never asked till yesterday. Then I had it not with me. But to-day, thinks I, I'll bring it up my sleeve for a win-favour—a good last card.'

'No matter, since I have got it.'

She held it out, and gloated on its device and sparkle. She knew it well: indeed it was a famous gem, the Sforza lion cut in cameo on a deep pure emerald, and known as the Lion ring.

'Hath he not missed it?' she murmured.

'Not by any sign a' gives. The sickness of that night still holds him half-amazed. A' thinks our fine doll, even, but a bug of it—fancies a' saw it in a dream like. They'd locked it away when he came to.'

'Poor worldling! Poor little new-born worldling! He shall cut his pretty teeth anon. Well—for Messer Lanti? Did he leap to the trail, or what?'

'That same moment. Belike they are together now.'

She stood musing a little: then heaved a sudden sigh.

'Poor boy,' she murmured, 'poor boy! is it I must seek to destroy thee!'

Her mood had veered again in a breath. Her eyes were full of a brooding love and pity.

'Not for the first time,' muttered Narcisso.

She seemed not to hear him—to have grown oblivious of his presence.

'The song he sang to me!' she murmured: 'Ah, me, if that hour could be mine! A saint in heaven?—not Bona's! she hath a lord—no saint, did he love her. He looked at me: it came from his heart. If that hour could be mine! Not then—'twere a sin—but now! That one hour—cherished—unspent—the seed of the unquickened pledge between us to all eternity. I could be content, knowing him a saint through that abstinence. My hour—*mine*—to passion to my breast—the shadow of the child that would not be born to me. He looked at me—no spectre of a dead lost love in his eyes—only a hopeless quest—bonds never to be riven. But now—Ah! I cannot kill him!'

She hid her eyes, shuddering. Narcisso, vaguely troubled, gloomed at her.

'You will not go to Messer Ludovico?' he said.

She returned to knowledge of him, as to a sense of pain out of oblivion.

'Go,' she said coldly. 'Leave all to me. You have done well, and been paid your wages.'

And he did not demur. It was not in her nature to gild her favours unnecessarily. Gold came less lavishly from her than kisses. Her pounds of flesh were her most profitable assets. She was a spendthrift in everything but money.

CHAPTER XIV

'Messer Bembo,' said Montano, between meditative and caustic, 'you do not agree that our poor Lupo's definition of a perfect government, an autocracy with an angel at its head, is a practicable definition?'

He was sitting, as often during the last few days, at talk with the boy, on subjects civic, political, and theological. They had discussed at odd times the whole ethics of government, from the constitution of Lycurgus to the code of Thomas Aquinas: they had expounded, each in his way, a scheme or a dream of socialism: they had agreed, without prejudice, to liken the evolution of the simple Church of Peter into the complicated fabric of the fourth Sixtus to a woodland cottage, bought by some great princely family, and improved into a summer palace, which was grown out of harmony with its environments. Somewhat to his amazement, Montano discovered that the boy was the opposite to a dogmatic Christian; that his was a religion, which, while conforming or adapting itself to the orthodox, was in its essence a religion of mysticism. No doubt the traditions of his origin were, to some extent, to seek for this. A pledge, so to speak, of spontaneous generation, Bernardo accounted for himself on a theory of reincarnation from another sphere. He believed in the possibility of the resurrection of the body, which, though destroyed, and many times destroyed, could be, in its character of mere soul-envelope or soul expression, as regularly reconstructed at the will of its informing spirit. Death, he declared, was just the beginning of the return of that divested spirit to the spring of life—to the river welling in the central Eden from the loins of the Father, the spouse of Nature, the secret, the unspeakable God, of whom was Christ, his own dear brother and comrade.

He would tell Messer Montano, with his sweet, frank eyes arraigning that crabbed philosopher's soul, how this unstained first-born of Nature, this sinless heir of love, this wise and pitying Christ, moved by an infinite compassion to see the wounded souls of his brothers—those few who had not made their backward flight too difficult—come, soiled and earth-cloyed, to seek their reincarnation in the spring, had descended, himself, upon earth at last, sacrificing his birthright of divinity, that he might teach men how to live. And the men his brothers had slain him, in jealousy, even as Cain slew Abel; yet had his spirit, imperishably great, continued to dwell in their midst, knowing that, did it once leave the earth, it must be for ever, and to mankind's eternal unregeneracy. For, so Bernardo insisted, there was an immutable law in Nature that no soul reincarnated could re-enter the sphere from which it was last returned, but must seek new fields of action. Wherefore all earth-loving spirits, which we call apparitions, were such as after death clung about the ways of men, in a yearning hopefulness to redeem them by touching their hearts with sympathy and their eyes with a mist of sorrow. And, of such gentle ghosts, Christ was but the first in faith and tenderness.

A wild, dim theory, peopling woods, and fields, and cities with a mystic company—phantoms, yet capable of revealing themselves in fitful glimpses to the sinless and the sympathetic among men—ghosts, weaving impalpable webs of love across populous ways to catch men's souls in their meshes. Montano called it all transcendental fustian. It aroused his most virulent scorn. What had this cloud-moulding, moon-paring stuff to do with the practical issues of life, with freedom, and government by popular representation? He even professed to prefer to it Lascaris, with his metaphysical jargon and apostolic succession of atoms.

'He gives you at least something to take hold of,' he snarled. 'Listen to this'—and he condescended to read an excerpt from a recent treatise by his hated rival:—

'"Life,"' he read, '"is put out at compound interest. We represent, each in himself, a fraction of the principal, having a direct pedigree *ab initio*. As a spider will gather the hundred strands of his web into a little ball which he will swallow, so might we each absorb and claim the whole vast web of life. Rolled up to include each radiating thread, the web becomes I; the spider is I; I am the principal of life—not the principle: that is Prometheus' secret."'

'"I am a fraction of life's compound interest. The sum of the mental impressions of all my thread of tendency (which gathers back, taking up cross threads by the way, to the central origin) is invested in my paltry being, and lieth there, together with mine own interest on the vast accumulation, in tail for my next of kin. What can I do in my tiny span but touch the surface of this huge estate: pluck here and there a flower of its fields, whose roots are in immemorial time? Imagination founders in those fathomless depths. Tenuous, dim-forgotten ghosts rise from them. Who shall say that my dreams, however seeming mad and grotesque, are not faithful reflexes of states and conditions which were once realities; memories of forms long extinct; echoes of times when I flew, or spun, or was gaseous, or vast, or little; when I mingled intimate with shapes which are chimerical to my present understanding——"'

The reader broke off, with an impatient grunt.

'There!' he said, 'dreams mad and grotesque enough, in good sooth; yet not so mad as thine.'

'Well,' said Bernardo, 'well,' with perfect sweetness and good temper.

'Christ in the world? Fah!' snarled the philosopher. 'I know him. He sits at Rome under a triple tiara. Quit all this sugared dreaming, boy, and face the future like a man.'

'Does the sun shine out of yesterday or to-morrow? It is enough for the moment to take thought for itself. The future is not.'

'Pooh! a mere Jesuitry, justifying the moment's abomination.'

'Nay: for we shall have to retraverse our deeds, and carry back their burden to our first account—with most, a toilful journey.'

'They would do better to stop with your Christ, then; and, judged by the preponderance of evil spirits here, I think most do. No future, say'st? But how about that heir of the compound interest? Is there not one waiting to succeed to him? Where? Why, in the future, as surely and inevitably as this date, which I am going to swallow in a moment, will be blood and tissue in me to-morrow.'

He held the fruit up—with a swift movement Bernardo whipped it out of his hand and ate it himself.

'How for your future now?' he chuckled, pinking all over.

Cicada laughed loudly, and Montano swore. His philosophy was not proof against such practical jokes. But, seeing his fury, the boy put out all his sweetness to propitiate him. He was his father's friend; he was a man of learning; he had suffered grievous wrong. The dog was coaxed presently into opening again upon the angelic principles. It was by such virulent irony that he thought—so warped was his mental vision—to corrode the candour of this saint, and bend him to his own views and uses—a diseased vanity, even had he not reckoned, as will now appear, without the consideration of another possible factor.

And 'So,' said he upon a later occasion, in the sentence which opens this chapter, 'you do not agree with our poor Lupo's practicable definition of a perfect government?'

The Saint's steadfast eyes canvassed the speaker's soul, as if in some shadowy suspicion of an integrity which they were being led, not for the first time, to probe.

'Why, Messer,' said he, 'practicable in so far as, by the dear Christ's influence, grace may come to make an angel even of our Duke.'

Montano tried to return his steady gaze, but failed meanly.

'With submission, Messer Bernardo,' he sniggered, 'I can only follow, in my mind's eye, one certain road to that great man's apotheosis.'

Bembo was silent.

''Tis the road,' continued the other, 'taken before by the Emperor Nero.'

'He stabbed himself, the most wretched pagan, in fear of a worser retribution than heaven's,' said Bembo. 'Alas! do you call that an apotheosis?'

'There are gods and gods,' said Montano,—'Hades and Olympus. Belike Nero was welcomed of his kind, as Galeazzo would be. I can scarce see in the Duke the raw material of your fashion of angel. There's more of the harpy about him than the harp.'

It was a heavenly day. Bernardo, still a little hectic and languid from his fever, sat in the embrasure of a window which gave upon the back court of the smithy. A muffled tinkling of armourers' hammers reached his ears pleasantly from the rear of neighbouring premises. There was a certain happy suggestiveness to him in the sound, evoked, as he hoped it might be, at his host Lupo's instigation. For his endearing optimism had so wrought upon that stricken artificer, during the week he had dwelt in hiding with him, as to persuade the poor man to quit his self-despairing, and hire out his skill—not practically; that was no longer possible; but theoretically— to a deserving fellow-craftsman. Already the sense of touch was curiously refining in the sightless creature, and the glimmer of a new dawn of interest penetrating him. And he was at work again elsewhere.

On the floor at Bembo's feet squatted Cicada, acrid, speaking little, and spending his long intervals of silence in staring at the girl Lucia, who, crouching at a distance away by the fireless forge, in the gloom of the shuttered smithy, seemed given over to an eternal reverie of hate. She, alone of the household, had remained impervious to all the sweet influences of sorrow and pity. Her wrong was such as no angel could remedy.

Cicada spoke now, with a scowl of significance for Montano:—

'Speak plain, master philosopher. Innuendo is the weapon of Fools, and wisdom shall prevail in candour. Thou canst not picture to thyself this evangelised Duke?'

Montano shot a lowering glance at him.

'No, I confess, master Patch,' said he—'unless,' he added grinning, 'by Nero's road.'

'Two whispers do not make one outspokenness,' answered the Fool. 'Hast hinted Nero once, and once again, and still we lack the application. Nero was driven to the road, quotha; well, by whom?—one Galba, an my learning's not a'rust. What then? Is Galba going to drive Galeazzo?'

'Nay, Love, dear Cicca,' put in Bernardo, but half hearing and half understanding.

'Love!' cried the Fool. 'Thou hast hit it. Hear wisdom from the mouths of babes. Love in the hands of rascals—a tool, a catspaw, to pull them their chestnuts from the fire, and then be cast burnt aside.'

He addressed himself, with infinite irony, to Montano.

'Good master philosopher,' said he, 'there is one fable for you: listen while I relate another. A certain rogue was stripped and beaten by a greater, who going on his way, there came a stranger, a mere child, and marked the fellow groaning. "Poor soul!" quoth he in pity; and knelt and bound his hurts and gave him wine, and by kind arts restored him. When shortly the aggressor returning and whistling by that place, his erst-victim, stung to revenge, yet having no weapon left him, did leap and incontinent seize up by his heels the ministering angel, and using his body for flail, knock down his enemy with him, killing both together. Which having done, and picked their pockets, on his way goes he rejoicing, "Now do I succeed to mine enemy's purse and roguery!"'

He ended. Montano, glancing stealthily at Bernardo, wriggled and tittered uneasily.

'Patch hath spoken,' he said; 'great is Patch!'

'I have spoken,' quoth the Fool. 'Dost gather the moral?'

'Not I, indeed.'

'Why, sir, 'tis of roguery making himself master of Love's estate; and yet that is not the full moral neither. For I mind me of a correction; how, before the blow was struck, Folly stepped between, and snatched Love from such a fate, and left the rogues to their conclusions.'

'Well, Folly and Love were well mated. Have you done? I am going to my books.'

He yawned, and stretched himself, and rose.

'I will show you to the door, says Folly,' chirped Cicada, and skipped about the other as he went, with a mincing affectation of ceremonial. But when they were got out of immediate sight and hearing of Bernardo into the front chamber, like a wolf the Fool snapped upon the philosopher, and pinned him into a corner.

'Understood'st my fable well enough,' he grated, in a rapid whisper. 'What! I have waited this opportunity a day or two. Now the stopper is out, let us flow.'

Montano, taken by surprise, was seized with a tremor of irresolution. He returned the Fool's gaze with a frown uncertain, sullen, eager all in one.

'Flow, then,' he muttered, after a little.

'I flow,' went on the other, 'oil and verjuice combined. Imprimis, think not that because I read I would betray thee. Ay, ay—no need to start, sir. Thou shalt not quit playing with thy doll for me; nay, nor dressing and goring it, if thou wilt, with triangles of steel. O, I saw!—the face and the slashes in it, too. I have not since been so ill, like him there, as to read a phantasy out of fact. What then? Would ye silence me?'

'Go on,' whispered Montano hoarsely.

'Well, I flow,' returned the Fool. 'Did I not tell thee candour was the best part of wisdom? Learn by it, then. I have marked thee of late; O, trust me, I have marked thee, thy hints and insinuations. And hereby by folly I swear, could once I think my master wax to such impressions, I would kill him where he stands, and damn my soul to send his uncorrupt to heaven. You sneer? Sneer on. Why, I could have laughed just now to see you, tortuous, sound his sweet candid shallows, where every pebble's plain. Do your own work, I'll not speak or care. You shall not have him to it, that's all. Sooner shall the heavens fall, than he be led by you to poison Galeazzo. Is that plain?'

It was so plain, that the philosopher gasped vainly for a retort.

'Who—who spoke of poison?' he stammered. 'Not I. Dear Messer Fool, you wrong me. This boy—the protégé of della Grande—mine old friend—I would not so misuse him. Why, he succoured me—an ill requital. If I sounded him, 'twas in self-justification only. We seek the same end by different roads—the ancient Gods restored—the return to Nature. Is it not so? Christ or Hyperion—I will not quarrel with the terms. "Knowledge," saith he, "is the fool that left his Eden." Well, he harks back, and so do I.'

'No further, thou, than to Rome and Regillus; but he to Paradise. Halt him not, I say. He shall not be thy catspaw. On these terms only is my silence bought.'

'Then is it bought. Why, Fool, I could think thee a fool indeed. He hath forsworn the court: how could we think to employ him there?'

'You know, as I know, sir, that this secession is a parenthesis, no more. He came to cure the State—not your way. A little repentance will win him back. The disease is in the head—he sees it; not in these warped limbs that the brain governs. He will go back anon.'

'And reign again by love?'

'I hope so, as first ministers reign.'

'No more? Well, we will back him there.'

'Again, be warned; not your way. Make him no text for the reform which builds on murder. I have spoken.'

'Well, we will not. *Vale!*'—and the philosopher, bowing his head, slunk out by the door which the other opened for him.

A little later, creeping into a narrow court which was the 'run' to his burrow, at the entrance he crossed the path of two cavaliers, whom, upon their exclaiming over the encounter, he drew under an archway.

They were come from playing pall-mall on the ramparts, and carried over their shoulders the tools of their sport—thin boxwood mallets, painted with emblematic devices in scarlet and blue, and having handle-butts of chased silver. Each gentleman wore red full-hose ending in short-peaked shoes, a plain red biretta, and a little green bodice coat, tight at the waist and open at the bosom to leave the arms and shoulders free play. Montano squinted approval of their flushed faces and strong-breathed lungs.

'Well exercised,' quoth he, in his high-pitched whisper; 'well exercised, and betimes belike.'

'News?' drawled Lampugnani. 'O, construe thyself!'

'The Fool,' answered Montano, 'sees through us, that is all.'

'What!' Visconti's brows came down.

'Hush! He hath warned me—not finally; only he pledges his silence on the discontinuance of my practices on his cub.'

'Well,' said Lampugnani serenely; 'discontinue.'

'Messer, he looks, with certainty, to the boy being won back to court anon. How, then! shall we let him go?'

'No!' rapped out Visconti.

'Yes,' said Lampugnani. 'I trow his good way is after all our best. Let him go back, and make the State so fast in love with Love as to prove Galeazzo impossible. He will sanctify our holocaust for us.'

'But the Fool, Messer—the Fool!'

'Will never conspire against his adored master's exaltation.'

'Exaltation? Would ye let this saint, then, to become the people's idol?'

'Ay, that we may discredit him presently for an adulterous idol. No saint so scorned as he whose sanctity trips on woman.'

'What! You think— —?'

'Exactly—yes—the Duchess. *Vale*, Messer Montano!'—and he lifted his cap mockingly, and moved off.

In the meanwhile Cicada, having watched, through a slit of the unclosed door, the retreat and disappearance of the philosopher, was about to shut himself in again, with a muttered objurgation or two, when a rapid step sounded without, and on the instant the door was flung back against him, and Messer Lanti strode in. There was no opportunity given him to temporise: the great creature was there in a moment, and had recognised him with a 'pouf!' of relief. He just accepted the situation, and closed the door upon them both.

'Well,' he said acridly, 'here you be, and whether for good or ill let the gods answer!'

Lanti stretched his great chest.

'It is well, Fool; and I am well if he is well. Where is he?'

Cicada pointed. The girl by the forge crouched and glared unwinkingly. The next moment Carlo was in his loved one's arms.

'Why hast hidden thyself, boy?—ah! it is a long while, boy—good to see thee again—stand off—I cannot see thee after all—a curse on these blinking eyes!'

'Dear Carlo, I have been a little ill; my joints ached.'

He wept himself, and fondled and clung to his friend.

'Thou great soft bully! For shame! Why, I love thee, dear. Wert thou so hurt? O Carlo! I have been most ill in spirit.'

'Come back, and we will nurse thee.'

'Alas! What nurses!'

'The tenderest and most penitent—Bona, first of all.'

The arms slid from his neck. Sweet angel eyes glowered at him.

'Bona to heal my spirit? To pour fire into its wounds rather! O, I had thought her pure till yesterday!'

And, indeed, Montano, in the furtherance of his corroding policy, had spared him no evidences of court scandal.

Carlo hung his bullet head.

'Lucia!' cried the boy suddenly and sternly.

The girl, at the word, came slinking to him like a dog, setting her teeth by the way at the stranger. Bernardo put his hand on her lowered head.

'Dost know who this is?' he asked of Carlo.

'Why, I can guess.'

'Canst thou, and still talk of Bona's penitence? Here's proof of it—in this foul deed unexpiated. Was it ever meant it should be?'

He raised his arm denunciatory.

'They have used me to justify their abominations; they have made mine innocence a pander to their lusts. Beware! God's patience nears exhaustion. We wait for Tassino. Will he come? Not while lewd arms imprison and protect him. Talk to me of Bona! Go, child.'

The girl crept back to her former seat. Carlo burst out, low and urgent:—

'Nay, boy, you do the Duchess wrong; now, by Saint Ambrose, I swear you do! She hath not set eyes on Jackanapes since that day—believe it—nor knows, more than another, what's become of him.'

'I could enlighten her. Can she be so fickle?'

'What! Don't you want her fickle? You make my brain turn.'

'O Carlo! What can such a woman see in such a man?'

'God! You have me there. She's just woman, conforming to the fashions.'

'Ah, me! the fashions!'

'Woman's religion.'

'She was taught a better. The fashions! Her wedding-gown should suffice her for all.'

'What! Night and day? But, there, I don't defend her!'

'No, indeed. Art thyself a fashion.'

'I don't defend her, I say. I'm worn and cast aside too.'

'Poor fashion! You'll grace your mistress' tire-woman next; and after her a kitchen-maid; and last some draggled scarecrow of the streets. O, for shame, for shame!'

'Go on. Compare me to Tassino next.'

'Indeed, I see no difference.'

'A low-born Ferrarese! A greasy upstart! Was carver to the Duke, no better; and oiled his fingers in the dish, and sleeked his hair!'

'Well, he was made first fashion. The Duchess sets them.'

'Now, by Saint Ambrose! First fashion! this veal-faced scullion, this fat turnspit promoted to a lap-dog! His fashion was to nurse lusty babies in his eyes!'

'What nursed thou in thine?'

'Go to! I'm a numskull, that I know; but to see no more in me!'

'I speak not for myself.'

'Why, these women, true, whom we hold so delicate—coarser feeders than ourselves—their tastes a fable. There, you're right; I've no right to talk.'

'Not yet.'

'Then, you're wrong. We've parted, I and Beatrice.'

'Carlo!'

'Didst think I 'd risk a quarrel with my saint on so small a matter?'

'Carlo!'

He flew upon the great creature and hugged him.

'My dear, my love! O, I went on so! Why did you let me? O, you give me hope again!'

'There,' growled the honest fellow, still a little sulkily. ''Twas to please myself, not you.'

'Not me!'

'Well, if I did, please me by returning.'

Bernardo shook his head.

'And seem to acquiesce in this?' He signified the girl.

'No seeming,' said Lanti. 'The Duchess promises to abet you in everything. I was to say so, an I could find thee.'

'How did you find me?'

'Let that pass. Will you come?'

'Will she hold Tassino to his bond?'

'She'll try to—I'll answer for it.'

'Will she excuse the Countess of Casa Caprona from her duties to her—for your sake, dear?'

'No need. The lady's a widow, and already self-dismissed.'

'Alas, a widow! O Carlo, that heavy witness gone before!'

'I must stand it. Will you come?'

'Why is this sudden change? I sore misdoubt it for a fashion.'

'Not sudden. I have her word the court goes all astray without thee. She pines to mother thee.'

'Mother!—an adulteress for mother! Alack, I am humbled!'

'Not so low as she. That touches the last matter. She wants the ring back she lent thee.'

'The ring?'

'Ay, the ring.'

'Carlo!'

He searched his clothes and hands in amaze.

'My God! It's gone!'

'Gone? Look again.'

'I had it on my finger. Till this moment I had forgot it clean—my brain so ached. Cicca!'

He turned in trouble on his servant.

'I know nought of it,' growled the Fool. 'If you had but chose to tell me. I am no gossip. Bona's ring was it, and leased to thee? Mayhap the rain that night washed it from thy finger.'

'If it were so—so great a trust abused! O Carlo! What shall I do?'

'Come back and make thy peace with her.'

Yet his brow gloomed, and he shook his head.

'O, O!' choked Bernardo, noting him with anguish.

'She sent a message—I can't help myself,' grunted Carlo. 'Did you seek to retaliate on her innocent confidence by ruining her? She meant the ring—your withholding it—'twas her troth-token from the Duke. Well, this is like getting a woman into trouble.'

Bernardo cast himself with a cry upon him.

'I will go back! I have no longer choice. I must hold myself a hostage to that loss!'

Carlo let out his satisfaction in a growl. But Cicada, squinting at the two, and rasping thoughtfully on his chin, pondered a speculation into a conviction.

'Narcisso!' he mused, 'was it he took it? As sure as he is a villain, it was Narcisso took it!'

CHAPTER XV

The astutest of all the six Sforza brothers was, without question, Messer Ludovico, at present sojourning in the castello of Milan. No higher than fourth in point of age, policy or premonition had never ceased to present him to himself for the first in succession. The uncertainty of life's tenure, unless ameliorated a little by qualities of tact and conciliation like his own, made him some excuse for this secret conviction. His eldest brother was a monster of the order which, in every age, invites tyrannicide; the Lord of Bari, the second, an ease-loving, good-humoured monster of another kind (he was to die shortly, in fact, of his own obesity), he valued only as so much gross bulk of supineness to be surmounted; Filippo, the third, was an imbecile, whose very existence was already slipping into the obscurity which was presently to spell obliteration. There remained only, junior to himself, Ascanio, a nonentity, and Ottaviano, a headstrong, irresponsible boy, whose possible destiny concerned him as little as though he foresaw his drowning, within the year, in the Adda river.

It was true that one other, more shrilly self-assertive, stood between himself and the light—the Duke's little son, Gian-Galeazzo. Here, most people would have thought, was his real insuperable barrier.

He did not regard matters from these popular points of view. He was very patient and far-seeing. At the outset of his career he had adopted for his device the mulberry-tree, because he had observed it to be cautious of putting forth its leaves until the last of winter was assured. He could picture the fatherless child as the most opportune of all steps to his exaltation. To climb presently those little shoulders to the regency! It would go hard with him but they sank gradually crushed under his weight. This was the wise policy, to get his seat as proxy, and through merciful and enlightened rule secure its permanency. There was infinite scope in the reaction he would make from a coarse and bloody despotism. His nature hated violence; his reason recognised the eternal insecurity of power built on it. Otherwise there was little doubt he might, in that first emergency, strike with good chance the straight usurper's stroke. His name, for graciousness and refinement, already shone like a star in the gross bog of Milan, revealing to it its foulness. Men, in the shame of their fulsome bondage to tyranny, looked up to him for hope and sympathy. He was even *persona grata* with the people.

But he abhorred, and disbelieved in, violence. He would rule, if at all, in the popular recognition of great qualities: he would prevail through bounty and tolerance. Bona was his crux—Bona, and the secretary Simonetta, a fellow incorruptibly devoted to the reigning family. While these two lived in credit with the duchy, the regency was secure from him, and the State, he told himself, from progress. For what woman-regent had ever mothered an era of enlightenment? Good for Milan, good for Lombardy, could he once discredit and ruin Bona and Simonetta. They would fall together. The uses of Tassino as an instrument to this end had occurred to him—only to be rejected. How could he hope so to disgrace corruption in corruption's eyes? Such puppyish intrigue was not worth even the Duke's interference. He rated that curly perfumed head in Bona's lap at exactly the value of a puppy's.

But, with the advent of the stranger, the little pseudo-oracle, the child Tiresias, sweet and blind as Cupid, a sounder opportunity offered. To involve Bona in the defilement of this purity, in the violating of this holy trust, adored by the people and bequeathed to her by her lord—that was, in the vernacular, another pair of shoes. He had noted, with secret gratification, her first coquetting with the pretty toils. He had heard, with plenteous dismay, of the boy's untimely secession. But he possessed, almost alone in his tumultuous time, the faculty of patience; and he was well served by his well-paid spies and agents. Almost before he could order their reports, almost before he could gauge the significance of one especial piece of information they gave him, the boy, won to forgiveness, was back at court again. Thenceforth he saw his way smoothly, if any term so bland could be applied to such a devious course of policy.

That was a matter of cross-roads, leading from, or to, himself, the mute signpost of direction. One, for instance, pointed to Bona's disgrace through Bembo; another to Simonetta's disgrace through Bona's disgrace; a third, to Bembo's downfall; a fourth, and last, to his nephew's orphaned minority. And the meeting-place, the nucleus, of all these tendencies was—where he himself stood, on a grave. For did they not bury suicides at cross-roads, and was not Galeazzo's policy suicidal? Of all these birds he might kill three, at least, with one stone; and that stone, he believed, was already in his hand, or nearly.

Let it not be supposed that Ludovico was a wicked man. He was destined to bear one of the greatest of the renaissance reputations; but that reputation was to draw no less from munificence than from magnificence, from tolerance than from power. He stood, at this time, on the forehead of an epoch, feeling the promise of his wings, poising and waiting only for their maturity. His sympathies were all with progress, with moral emancipation.

He was even now, in Milan (if it can be said without blasphemy), comparable to Christ in Hades. In a filthy age he was fastidious; precise and delicate in his speech; one of those men before whom the insolence of moral offences is instinctively silent. Guicciardini, a grudging Florentine, nevertheless pronounced him when he came to rule, 'milde and mercifull'; Arluno credited him with a sublimity of justice and benevolence. Others, less interested, testified to his wisdom and sagacity, about which there was certainly no disputing. If at any period the wrong that is ready to perpetrate itself in order to procure good is justifiable, it was to be justified in these corrupt years, when conformity with usage spelt putrefaction. He could foresee no health for the State in patching its disease. He was the operator predestined by Providence to remove, stock and block, the cancer.

Yet, though loving truth, he lied; yet, though hating the sight of blood, he procured its shedding; yet, though admiring virtue, he did not hesitate to prostitute it to his ends. There were crimes attributed to him of which he was no doubt innocent; there were lesser, or worse, unrecorded, of which he was no doubt guilty. Feeling himself, by temperament and intellect, the inevitable instrument of a vast emancipation, recognising his call to be as peremptory as it was unconsidered, he had no choice, in obeying it, but to cast scruples to the winds. With him, as with his contemporary the English Richard, a deep fervour of patriotism was at once the goad and the destruction. Judgment on the means both took to vindicate their commissions rests with the gods, who first inspired, then repudiated them. But there is no logic in Olympus.

Ludovico was sitting one evening in his private cabinet in the castello, when a lady was announced to him by the soft-voiced page. Every one instinctively subdued his speech in the presence of Messer Ludovico, even the rough venderaccios who occasionally came to make him their reports or receive his instructions.

The lady came in, and stood silent as a statue by the heavy portière, which, closed, cut off all eavesdropping as effectively as a mattress. Nevertheless Messer Ludovico waited for full assurance of the page's withdrawal before he rose, and courteously greeted his visitor.

'Ave, Madonna Beatrice!' he said. 'You are welcome as the moonlight in my poor apartment.'

It was so far from being that, as to make the compliment an extravagance. Yet the beauty of the woman in her long black robe and mantle, and little black silk cap dropping wings of muslin, sorted gravely enough with the slumberous gold of picture frames under the lamplight, and all the sombre sparkle of gems and glass and silver with which the chamber was strewed in a considered disorder.

'You sent for me, Messer, and I have come,' she said. Her low, untroubled voice was quite in keeping with the rest.

'Fie, fie!' he answered smoothly. 'I begged a privilege, I begged an honour—with diffidence, of one so lately stricken. Will you be seated while I stand?'

As her subject, he meant to imply. She accepted the condescension for what it was worth. He bent his heavy eyebrows on her pleasantly. They were full and shaggy for so young a man. Presently she found the silence intolerable.

'You sent for me, Messer,' she repeated coldly. 'Will you say on account of which of your interests?'

'See the dangerous intuition of your sex!' he retorted smilingly—'a weapon wont to cut its wielder's hand. On account of *your* interest, purely.'

She glanced up at him with insolent incredulity.

'True,' he said. 'I desired only to save you the consequences of an imprudence. That troth-ring, Madonna, our Duchess's: is it not rather a perilous toy to play with?'

She was startled, for all her immobility—so startled, that he could see the breath jump in her bosom. But, in the very gasp of her fear, she caught herself to recollection, and stiffened, silent, to the ordeal she felt was coming.

'How did I know it was in your possession?' he said, with a little whisper of a laugh. 'Your beauty is ever more speaking than your lips, Madonna; but I am an oracle: I can read the unspoken question. There is a creature, Narcisso his name, once fellow to a loved servant of our court. You know Messer Lanti? an honest, bluff gentleman. He did well to part with such a dangerous rogue. Why, the times are complicate: we should be choice in our confidants. This Narcisso is very well to slit a throat; but to negotiate a delicate theft— —'

He paused. 'Go on,' she whispered.

'I will be frank as day,' he purred. ''Twas seen on this rogue's finger, when making for your house. It was not there when he left.'

'The gloating fool!' She stabbed out the words. 'Seen! By whom?'

'By one,' he answered, 'whose business it was to look for it.'

'Who, I say?'

'Most high lady, the very predestined man—no other. Would you still ask who? I had thought you more accomplished. Intrigue, like a statue, is not carved out with a single tool. The eyes, the ears, the lips, each demand their separate instrument. Dost thou seek to shape all with one? O, fie, fie!'

He shook his finger gaily at her. She sat, frowning, with her hands clenched before her; but she gave no answer.

'Why, I am but a tyro,' said the prince; 'yet could I teach thee, it seems, some first precepts in our craft—as thus: Use things most useful for their uses; employ not your dagger as a shoe-horn, or it may chance to cut your heel; an instrument hath its purpose and design; think not one password will unlock all camps; selection is the cream of policy—and so on.'

She started to her feet, in an instant resolution.

'I have the ring,' she said.

He bowed suavely. She stared at him.

'What then, Messer?'

'Why,' he said, 'only that, do you not think, it were safer in my hands than in yours?'

'Safer!' she cried in a suppressed voice; 'for whom?'

'Yourself,' he answered serenely.

'Ah!' she cried, 'you would threaten, if I refuse, to destroy me with it?'

He made a deprecating motion with his hands.

'Beware,' she said fiercely; 'I can retort. Where is Tassino?'

He looked at her kindly.

'Madonna, do you not know? Nay, do I not know that you know? He lies hidden in the burrow of this same Narcisso.'

'At whose instigation? Not yours, Messer—O no, of course, not yours!'

His lips never changed from their expression of smiling good-humour.

'Entirely at mine,' he said.

She gave a little gasp. His subtlety was too chill a thing for her fire; but she struggled against her quenching by it.

'Why do you not produce him, then? Do you not know that he is cried for high and low? that he is wanted to complete his contract with the armourer's drab? It is an ill thing to cross, this present ecstasy of conversion. We are all Bernardines now—lunatics—latter-day Cistercians—raging neophytes of love.'

'While the ecstasy lasts,' he murmured, unruffled.

'Ah!' she cried violently, 'yet may it last your time. Fanaticism is no respecter of rank or service. Standest thou so well with Bona? She would have racked the racker himself in the first fury of her contrition—torn confession from Jacopo's sullen throat with iron hooks, had not her saint rebuked her. Tassino had been last seen by him in the man's company, but, when they went to look for him, he was gone. When or whither, the fellow swore he knew not. It was like enough, thou being the lure. Will you not produce him now, and save your peace?'

Ludovico, regarding her vehemence from under half-closed lids, exhibited not the slightest tremor.

'Madonna,' he said, 'thy mourning beauty becometh thee like Cassandra's. Hast thou, too, so angered Apollo with thy continence as to make him nullify in thee his own gift of prophecy? Alas, that lips so moving must be so discounted in their warnings!'

She drew back, chilled and baffled.

'Thou wilt not?' she muttered. 'Well, then, thou wilt not. Take thou thine own course; I may not know thy purpose.'

For a moment the cold of him deepened to deadliness, and his voice to an iron hardness:—

'Nor any like thee—self-seekers—dominated by some single lust. My purpose is a labyrinth of Cnossus. Beware, rash fools, who would seek to unravel it!'

Her lips were a little parted; the fine wings of her nostrils quivered. For all her bravery she felt her heart constricting as in the frost of some terror which she could neither gauge nor compass. But, in the very instant of her fear, Ludovico was his own bland self again.

'Tools, tools!' he said smiling—'for the eyes, the ears, the lips. I shall take up this one when I need it, not before. Meanwhile it lies ready to my hand.'

'I do not doubt thy cunning,' she said faintly.

'What then, Madonna?' he asked.

She struggled with herself, swallowing with difficulty.

'Its adequacy for its purpose—that is all.'

'What purpose?'

She looked up, and dared him:—

'To destroy the Duchess.'

He laughed out, tolerantly.

'Intuition! Intuition! O thou self-wounding impulse! To destroy the Duchess? Well! What is thy ring for? To destroy Monna Beatrice, belike. And Monna Beatrice had her instrument too, they will say afterwards—a blunt, coarse blade, but hers, hers only—as she thought. Yet, it seems, one Ludovic used something of him, this Narcisso, also—played him for his ends—marked him down, even, for landlord to a fribble called Tassino. What, Carissima! He hath not told thee so much?'

She shook her head dully.

'No?' mocked the Prince. 'And ye such sworn allies! O sweet, you shall learn policy betimes! You will not yield the ring? Well, there is Tassino, as you say. Play him against it.'

She knew she dared not. The vague implication of forces and understandings behind all this banter quite cowed her. She had defied the serpent, and been struck and overcome. Hate was no match for this craft. But emotion remained. She dwelt a long minute on his smooth, impenetrable face; then, all in an instant, yielded up her sex, and stole towards him, arms and moist eyes entreating.

'I dared thee; I was wrong. Only——'

Her palms trembled on his shoulders; her bosom heaved against his hand.

'I have suffered, what only a woman can. O, Messer, let me keep the ring!'

Her voice possessed him like an embrace; the soft pleading of it made any concession to his kindness possible. He was very sensitive to all emotions of loveliness, but with the rare gift of reasoning in temptation. He shook his head.

'Ah!' she murmured, 'let me. Thou shalt find jealousy a hot ally.'

She pressed closer to him. He neither resisted nor invited.

'Most excellent sweetness,' he said gently. 'I melt upon this confidence. Henceforth we'll bury misunderstanding, and kiss upon his grave. But truth with sugar is still a drug. A jealous woman is bad in policy. Trust her always to destroy her betrayer, though through whatever betrayal of her friends. Besides, forgive me, Messer Bembo may yet prove accommodating.'

At that she dropped her hands and stepped back.

'Is this to bury misunderstanding?' she cried low. 'O, I would *I* were Duchess of Milan.'

'More impossible things might happen,' he said thickly, for all his self-control.

She stared at him fascinated a moment; then swiftly advanced again.

'Let me keep the ring,' she urged hoarsely. 'I could set something against it—some knowledge—some information.'

He had mastered himself in the interval; and now stood pondering upon her and fondling his chin.

'Yes?' he murmured. 'But it must be something to be worth.'

She hesitated; then spoke out:—

'A plot to kill the Duke—no more.'

The two stared at one another. She could see a pulse moving in his throat; but when at last he spoke, it was without emotion.

'Indeed, Madonna? They are so many. When is this particular one to be?'

'Do you not know?' she answered as derisively as she dared. 'I thought you had a tool for everything. Well, it is to be in Milan.'

'In Milan—as before,' he repeated ironically. 'And the heads of this conspiracy, Madonna?'

'Ah!' she cried, with a sigh of triumph; 'they are yours at the price of the ring.'

He canvassed her a little, but profoundly.

'After all,' he murmured, 'why should I seek to know?'

'Why?' she said, with a laugh of recovering scorn, 'why but to nip it in its bud, Messer?'

He was quick to grasp this implied menace of retaliation.

'Tell me,' he said, 'why are you so hot to retain this same ring?'

'For only a woman's reason,' she answered. 'Wouldst thou understand it? Not though I spoke an hour by St. Ambrose' clock. I would deal the blow myself, in my own way—that is all.'

'Thou wouldst ruin Bona?'

'Ay, and her saint, who robbed me of my love.'

'By her connivance? Marry, be honest, sweet lady. Was it not rather Messer Bembo who denied you Messer Bembo?'

'Will you have the names?'

'Hold a little. Here's matter black enough, but unsupported. I must have some proof. Tell me who's your informant?'

'And have you go and bleed him? Nay, I am learning my tools.'

'Bravo!' he said, and kissed his hand to her. 'Well, I see, we must call a truce awhile.'

'And I will keep the ring,' she said.

He beamed thoughtfully on her. No doubt he was considering the possibility of improving the interval by rooting out, on his own account, details of the secret she held from him.

'Provisionally,' he said pleasantly—'provisionally, Madonna; so long as you undertake to make no use of it until you hear from me my decision.'

'The longer that is delayed, the better for your purpose, Messer,' she dared to say.

He smiled blankly at her a little; then courteously advancing, and raising her hand, imprinted a fervent kiss on it.

'Though I fail to gather your meaning,' he said, 'it is nevertheless certain that you would make a very imposing Duchess, Monna Beatrice.'

CHAPTER XVI

'Father Abbot, we thank you for your trust. We were less than human to abuse it. O, it flew with white wings to shelter in our bosom! Shall we be hawks to such a dove! Take comfort. It hath ruffled its feathers on our heart; it hath settled itself thereon, and hatched out a winged love. Pure spirit of the Holy Ghost, whence came it? From a star, they say, born of some wedlock between earth and sky. I marvel you could part with it. I could never.... The pretty chuck! What angel heresies it dares! "Marry," saith the dove, "I have been discussing with Christ the subtleties of dogmatic definition, and I find he is no Christian." This for intolerance! He finds honesty in schism—speaks with assurance of our Saviour, his discourses with Him by the brook, in the garden, under the trees—but doubtless you know. How can we refute such evidence, or need to? Alas! we are not on speaking terms with divinity. But we listen and observe; and we woo our winsome dove with pretty scarves and tabbards embroidered by our fingers; and some day we too hope to hear the voices. Not yet; the earth clings to us; but he dusts it off. "Make not beauty a passion, but passion a beauty," says he. "Learn that temperance is the true epicurism of life. The palate cloys on surfeit." O, we believe him, trust me! and never his pretty head is turned by our adoring.... "By love to make law unnecessary,"—there runs his creed: the love of Nature's truths—continence, sobriety, mate bound to mate like birds. Only our season's life. He convinces us apace. Already Milan sweetens in the sun. We curb all licence, yield heat to reason, clean out many vanities; have our choirs of pure maidens in place of the Bacchidæ—hymns, too, meet to woo Pan to Christ, of which I could serve thee an example.... All in all, we prepare for a great Feast of the Purification which, at the New Year's beginning, is to symbolise our re-conversion to Nature's straight religion. Then will be a rare market in doves—let us pray there be at least—which all, conscious of the true virgin heart, are to bring. Doves! Alack! which of us would not wish to be worthy to carry one that we know?'

So wrote the Duchess of Milan to the Abbot of San Zeno, and he answered:—

'Cherish my lamb. The fold yearns for him. He would leave it, despite us all. My daughter, be gracious to our little dreamer, for of such is the Kingdom of Heaven.'

For years after it was become the dimmest of odd memories, men and women would recall, between laughter and tears, the strange little moral fantasia which, during a month or two of that glowing autumn of 1476, all Milan had been tickled into dancing to the pipe of a small shepherd of a New Arcadia. The measure had certainly seemed inspiring enough at the time—potential, original, weaving an earnest purpose with joy, revealing novel raptures of sensation in the seemliness of postures, which claimed to interpret Nature out of the very centre of her spiritual heart. David dancing before the ark must have exhibited just such an orderly abandonment as was displayed by these sober-rollicking Pantheists of the new cult. Crossness with them was sunk to an impossible discount. There was no market for gallantry, *épanchements*, or any billing and cooing whatever but of doves. Instead, there came into vogue intercourses between Dioneus and Flammetta of sweet unbashful reasonableness; high-junkettings on chestnut-meal and honey; the most engaging attentions, in the matter of grapes and sweet biscuits and infinite bon-bons, towards the little furred and feathered innocents of the countryside. That temperance really was, according to the angelic propagandist, the true epicurism, experience no less astonishing than agreeable came to prove. Then was the festival of beans and bacon instituted by some jaded palates. Charity and consideration rose on all sides in a night, like edible and nutritious funguses. From Hallowmas to Christmas there was scarce a sword whipped from its scabbard but reflection returned it. It was no longer, with Gregory and Balthazar, 'Sir, do you bite your thumb at me? Sir, the wall to you,' but 'Sir, I see your jostling of me was unavoidable; Sir, your courtesy turns my asps to roses.' Nature and the natural decencies were on all tongues; the licences of eye and ear and lip were rejected for abominations unpalatable to any taste more refined than yesterday's. Modesty ruled the fashions and made of Imola an Ippolita, and of Aurelio an Augustine. The women, as a present result, were all on the side of Nature. Impudicity with them is never a cause but a consequence. They found an amazing attractiveness in the pretty dogma which rather encouraged than denounced in them the graceful arts of self-adornment. 'Naked, like the birds,' attested their little priest, 'do we come to inherit our Kingdom. Shall we be more blamed than they for adapting to ourselves the plumages of that bright succession?' Only he pleaded for a perfect adaptation to conditions—to form, climate, environments, constitution. The lines of all true beauty, he declared, were such as both suggested and defended. Could monstrosities of head furniture, for instance, appeal to any but a monster? Locks, thereat, were delivered from their fantastic convolutions, from their ropes of pearls, from their gold-dust and iris-powder, and were heaped or coiled *di sua natura*, as any girl, according to circumstances, might naturally dispose of them. There was a general holocaust of extravagances, with some talk of feeding the sacrifice with fuel of useless confessional boxes; and, in the meanwhile, the church took snuff and smiled, and the devil hid his tail in a reasonable pair of breeches, and endured all the inconveniences of sitting on it without a murmur.

Alas! 'How quick bright things come to confusion!' But the moment while it held gathered the force of an epoch; and no doubt much moral amendment was to derive from it. Intellect in a sweet presence makes a positive of an abstract argument; and when little Bembo asserted, in refutation of the agnostics, that man's dual personality was proved by the fact of his abhorring in others the viciousnesses which his flesh condoned in himself, the statement was accepted for the dictum of an inspired saint. But his strength of the moment lay chiefly in his undeviating consistency with his own queer creed. He never swerved from his belief in the soul's responsibility to its past, or of its commitment to a retrogressive movement after death. 'We drop, fainting, out of the ranks in a desolate place,' he said. 'We come to, alone and abandoned. Shall we, poor mercenaries, repudiating a selfish cause, not turn our faces to the loved home, far back, from which false hopes beguiled us? Be, then, our way as we have made it, whether by forbearance or rapine.' Again he would say: 'Take, so thy to-day be clean, no fearful thought for thy to-morrow, any more than for thy possible estrangement from thy friend. There is nothing to concern thee now (which is all that *is*) but thy reason, love, and justice of this moment. They are the faculty, devotion, and quality to which, blended, thy soul may trust itself for its fair continuance.'

There was a little song of his, very popular with the court gentlemen in these days of their regeneracy, which, as exemplifying the strengths and weaknesses of his propaganda, is here given:—

> 'Here's a comrade blithe
> To the wild wood hieth—
> Follow and find!
> Loving both least and best,
> His love takes still a zest
> From the song-time of the wind.
>
> The chuckling birds they greet him,
> The does run forth to meet him—
> Follow and find!
> Strange visions shall thou see;

Learn lessons new to thee
In the song-time of the wind.

Couldst, then, the dear bird kill
That kiss'd thee with her bill?
Follow and find
How great, having strength, to spare
That trusting Soft-and-fair
In the song-time of the wind.

He is both God and Man;
He is both Christ and Pan—
Follow and find
How, in the lovely sense,
All flesh being grass, wakes thence
The song-time of the wind.

It was, I say, popular with the Lotharios. The novelty of this sort of renunciation tickled their sensoriums famously. It suggested a quite new and captivating form of self-indulgence, in the rapture to be gathered from an indefinite postponement of consummations. The sense of gallantry lies most in contemplation. I do not think it amounted to much more. Teresa and Elisabetta enjoyed their part in the serio-comic sport immensely, and were the most cuddlesome lambs, frisking unconscious under the faltering knife of the butcher. Madonna Caterina laughed immoderately to see their great mercy-pleading eyes coquetting with the greatly-withheld blade. But then she had no bump of reverence. The little wretch disliked sanctity in any form; loved aggressiveness better than meekness; was always in her heart a little Amazonian terrier-bitch, full of fight and impudence. It might have gone crossly with Messer Bembo had she been in her adoptive mother's position of trustee for him.

But luckily, or most unluckily for the boy, he was in more accommodating hands. This was the acute period of his proselytising. He had been persuaded back to court, and Bona had received him with moist eyes and open arms, and indeed a very yearning pathos of emotionalism, which had gathered a fataler influence from the contrition which in the first instance must be his. He had stood before her not so much rebuking as rebuked. Knowing her no longer saint, but only erring woman, it added a poignancy to his remorse that he had led her into further error by his abuse of her trust. She had answered his confession with a lovely absolution:—

'What is lost is lost. Thou art the faithfullest warrant of my true observance of my lord's wishes. Only if thou abandon'st me am I betrayed.'

Could he do aught after this but love her, accept her, her fervour and her penitence, for a first factor in the crusade he had made his own? And, while the soft enchantment held, no general could have wished a loyaler adjutant, or one more ready to first-example in herself the sacrifices he demanded. She abetted him, as she had promised, in all his tactics; lent the full force of an authority, which his sweetness and modesty could by no means arrogate to himself, to compel the reforms he sang. She gave, amongst other gifts, her whole present soul to the righting of the wrong done to the girl Lucia and her father; and when all her efforts to discover the vanished Tassino had failed, and she, having sent on her own initiative a compensatory purse of gold to the blind armourer, had learned how Lucia had banged the gift and the door in the messenger's face, was readily mollified by Bernardo's tender remonstrance: 'Ah, sweet Madonna! what gold can give her father eyes, or her child a name!'

'What! it is born?' she murmured.

'I saw it yesterday,' said Bembo. 'It lay in her lap, like the billet that kills a woman's heart.'

And, indeed, he had not, because of his re-exaltation, ceased to visit his friends, or to go to occasional discussion with the crabbed Montano; whose moroseness, nevertheless, was petrifying. Yet had he even sought to interest the Duchess there; though, for once, without avail; for she dared not seem to lend her countenance to that banned, if injured, misanthrope.

So she led the chorus to his soloing, and helped and mothered him with an infatuation beyond a mother's. Like the Emperor's jewelled nightingale, he was the sweetest bird to pet while his tricks were new. His voice entranced the echoes of those sombre chambers and blood-stained corridors. The castello was reconsecrated in his breath, and the miasma from its fearful pits dispelled. His lute was his psalter and psaltery in one: it interpreted him to others, and himself to himself. Its sob was his sorrow, and its joy his jubilance. He could coax from it wings to expression inexpressible by speech alone. Here is one of his latest parables, or apologues, baldly running, as it appears, on the familiar theme, which, through that vehicle, he translated for his hearers into rapture:—

'Down by a stream that muttered under ice—
Winter's thin wasted voice, straining for air—
Lo! Antique Pan, gnawing his grizzled beard.

Chill was the earth, and all the sky one stone,
The shrunk sedge shook with ague; the wild duck,
Squattering in snow, sent out a feeble cry.
Like a stark root the black swan's twisted neck
Writhed in the bank. The hawk shook by the finch;
The stoat and rabbit shivered in one hole;
And Nature, moaning on a bedded drift,
Cried for delivery from her travail:—

"O Pan! what dost thou? Long the Spring's delayed!
O Pan! hope sickens. Son, where art thou gone?"

Thereat he heaved his brows; saw the starved fields,
The waste and horror of a world's eclipse;
And all the wrong and all the pity of it
Rushed from him in a roar:—
"I'm passed, deposed: call on another Pan!
Call Christ—the ates foretel him—he'll respond.
I'm old; grown impotent; a toothless dog.
New times, new blood: the world forgets my voice.
This Christ supplants me: call on him, I say.
Whence comes he? Whence, if not from off the streets?
Some coxcomb of the Schools, belike—some green,
Anæmic, theoretic verderer,
Shaping his wood-lore from the Herbary,
And Nature from his brazen window-pots.
The Fates these days have gone to live in town—
Grown doctrinaires—forgot their rustic loves.
Call on their latest nominee—call, call!
He'll ease thee of thy produce, bear it home,
And in alembics test and recompose it.
Call, in thine agony—loud—call on Christ:
He'll hear maybe, and maybe understand!"

"No Pan," she wailed: "No other Pan than thou!"

"What!" roared he, mocking: "Christ not understand?

Your loves, your lores, your secrets—will he not?
Not by his books be master of your heart?
Gods! I am old. I speak but by the woods;
And often nowadays to rebel ears.
He'll do you better: fold your fogs in bales;
Redeem your swamps; sweep up your glowing leaves;
People his straight pastures with your broods;
Shape you for man, to be his plain helpmeet;
No toys, no tricks, no mysteries, no sports—
But sense and science, scorning smiles and tears."

Raging, he rose: A light broke on the snow:
The ice upon the river cracked and spun:
Long milky-ways of green and starry flowers
Grew from the thaw: the trees nipped forth in bud:
The falcon sleeked the wren; the stoat the hare;
And Nature with a cry delivered was.

Pan stared: A naked child stood there before him,
Warming a frozen robin in his hands.
Shameless the boy was, fearless, white as milk;
No guile or harm; a sweet rogue in his eyes.
And he looked up and smiled, and lisped a word:—

"Brother, *thou* take and cure him, make him well.
Or teach *me* of thy lore his present needs."

"*Brother!*" choked Pan. "*My* father was a God.
Who art thou?" "Nature's baby," said the child.
"Man was *my* father; and my name is Christ."

He slid his hand within the woodman's palm:—
"Dear elder brother, guide me in my steps.
I bring no gift but love, no tricks but love's—
To make sweet flowers of frost—locked hearts unfold—
The coney pledge the weasel in a kiss.
Canst thou do these?" "No, by my beard," said Pan.

Gaily the child laughed: "Clever brother thou art;
Yet can I teach thee something." "All," said Pan.

He groaned; the child looked up; flew to his arms:—
"O, by the womb that bore us both, do love me!"

A minute sped: the river hushed its song:
The linnet eyed the falcon on its branch:
The bursting bud hung motionless—And Pan
Gave out a cry: "New-rooted, not deposed!
Come, little Christ!" So hand in hand they passed,
Nature's two children reconciled at last.'

And what about Messer Lanti and the Fool Cicada during this period of their loved little saint's apotheosis? Were *they* more *advocati diaboli* than Bona? Alas! they were perhaps the only two, in all that volatile city, to accept him, with a steadfast and indomitable faith, at his true worth. There was no angelic attribute, which Carlo, the honest blaspheming neophyte, would not have claimed for him—with blows, by choice; no rebuke, nor suggestion, nor ordinance issuing from his lips, which he would not accept and act upon, after the necessary little show of self-easing bluster. It was as comical as pathetic to observe the dear blunderhead's blushing assumptions of offence, when naughtiness claimed his intimacy; his exaggerated relish of spring water; his stout upholding, on an empty stomach, of the æsthetic values of abstinence. But he made a practical virtue of his conversion, and was become frequent in evidence, with his strong arm and voice and influence, as a Paladin on behalf of the oppressed. He and Cicada were the boy's bristling watch-dogs, mastiff and lurcher; and were even drawn, by that mutual sympathy, into a sort of scolding partnership, defensive and aggressive, which had for its aim the vindication of their common love. There, at least, was some odd rough fruit of the reconciliation preached by little Bembo between the God-man and the man-Nature. Such a relationship had been impossible in the old days of taskmaster and clown. Now it was understood between them, without superfluous words, that each held the other responsible to him for his incorruptible fidelity to his trust, and himself for a sleepless attention to the duty tacitly and by implication assigned to be his. That is to say, Messer Carlo's strength and long sword, and the other's shrewd wit, were assumed, as it were, for the right and left bucklers to the little charioteer as he drove upon his foes.

Carlo had a modest conception of his own abilities; yet once he made the mistake of appropriating to himself a duty—or he thought it one—rather appertaining to his fellow buckler. They had been, the Fool and himself, somewhat savagely making merry on the subject of Bona's conversion—in the singleness of which, to be candid, they had not much faith—when his honest brain conceived the sudden necessity of bluntly warning the little Bernardino of the danger he was courting in playing with such fire. His charge, no sooner realised than acted upon, took the boy, so to speak, in the wind. Bembo gasped; and then counter-buffed with angelic fury:—

'Who sleeps with a taper in his bed invites his own destruction? Then wert thou sevenfold consumed, my Carlo. O, shame! she is my mother!'

'Nay, but by adoption,' stammered the other abashed.

'Her assumption of the name should suffice to spare her. O, thou pagan irreclaimable—right offspring of Vesta and the incestuous Saturn! Is this my ultimate profit of thee? Go hide thy face from innocence.'

Lanti, thus bullied, turned dogged.

'I will hide nothing. Abuse my candour; spit on my love if thou wilt, it will endure for its own sake,' and he flung away in a rage.

But he had better have deputed the Fool to a task needing diplomacy. Cicada laughed over his grievance when it was exploded upon him.

'Shouldst have warned Bona herself, rather,' he said.

'How!' growled the other: 'and been cashiered, or worse, for my pains?'

'Not while her lost ring stands against her; and thou, her private agent for its recovery.'

'True; from the mud.'

'Well, if thou think'st so.'

'Dost thou not?'

'Ay; for as mud is mud, Narcisso is Narcisso.'

'Narcisso!'

He roared, and stared.

'Has *he* got it?'

'I do not say so.'

'I will go carve the truth out of him.'

'Or Monna Beatrice.'

'What!'

The great creature fairly gasped; then muttered, in a strangled voice: 'Why should she want it? What profit to her?'

'What, indeed?' whined the Fool. 'She fancies Messer Bembo too well to wish to injure him, or through him, Bona—does she not?'

Carlo's brow slowly blackened.

'I will go to her,' he said suddenly. The Fool leapt to bar his way.

'You would do a foolish thing,' he said—'with deference, always with deference, Messer. This is my part. Leave it to me.'

Carlo choked, and stood breathing.

'Why,' said the Fool, 'these are the days of circumspection. God, says Propriety, made out hands and faces, and whatever else that is not visible was the devil's work. You would be shown, by Monna Beatrice, for all her self-acknowledged parts, just clean hands and a smiling face. She conforms to fashion. For the rest, the devil will attend to his own secrets.'

The other groaned:—

'I would I could fathom thee. I would I had the ring.'

'I would thou hadst,' answered Cicada. ''Twould be a good ring to set in our Duchess's little nose, to persuade her from routling in consecrated ground: a juster weapon in thy hands than in some other's. Well, be patient; I may obtain it for thee yet.'

He meant, at least, to set his last wits to the task. Somehow, he was darkly and unshakably convinced, this same Lion ring was the pivot upon which all his darling's fortunes turned. That it was not really lost, but was being held concealed, by some jealous spirit or spirits, against the time most opportune for procuring the boy's, and perhaps others', destruction by its means, he felt sure. All Milan was not in one mind as to the disinterested motives of its Nathan. Tassino, Narcisso, the dowager of Casa Caprona, even the urbane Messer Ludovico himself, to name no others, could hardly be shown their personal profits in the movement. They might all, as the world's ambitions went, be excused from coveting the stranger's promotion. And there was no doubt that, at present, he was paramount in the eyes of the highest. That, in itself, was enough to make his sweet office the subject of much scepticism and blaspheming. Tough, wary work for the watch-dogs, Cicada pondered. That same evening he was walking in the streets, when a voice, Visconti's, muttered alongside him:—

'Good Patch, hast been loyal so far to thy bargain. Hold to it for thy soul's sake. There are adders in Milan.' Then he bent closer, and whispered: 'A word in thy ear: is the ring found yet?'

The Fool's hard features did not twitch. He shook his head.

'Marry, sir,' answered he, as low, 'the mud is as close a confidant as I. I have not heard of its blabbing.'

'So much the better,' murmured the other, and glided away. But he left Cicada thinking.

'It was not for them, then, the conspirators, that Narcisso stole it. And yet he stole it—that I'll be sworn. For whom? Why, for Monna Beatrice. For why? Why, for a purpose that I'll circumvent—when I guess it. A passenger going by cursed him under his breath. The oath, profound and heartfelt, was really a psychologic note in the context of this history. Cicada heard it, and, looking round, saw, to his amazement, the form of the very monster of his present deliberations.

Narcisso, the rancorous mongrel, having snarled his hatred of an old associate, who, he verily believed, had once betrayed him, slouched, with a heavier vindictiveness, on his way. The Fool, inspired, skipped into cover, and peeped. He knew that the coward creature, once secure of his distance, would turn round to sputter and glower. He was not wrong there, nor in his surmise that, finding him vanished, Narcisso would continue his road in reassurance of his fancied security. He saw him actually turn and glare; distinguished, as plainly as though he heard it, the villainous oath with which the monster flounced again to his gait. And then, very cautiously, he came out of his hiding, and slunk in pursuit.

It could serve, at least, no bad purpose, he thought, to track the beast to his lair; and, with infinite circumspection, he set himself to the task.

It proved a simple one, after all—the more so as the animal, it appeared, was tenant in a very swarming warren, where concealment was easy. It was into a frowzy hole that, in the end, he saw him disappear—a tunnel, with a grating over it, like a sewer-trap.

And so, satisfied and not satisfied, he was turning away, when he was conscious in a moment of a face looking from the grating.

A minute later, threading his path along a by-alley, he emerged upon a sweeter province of the town, and stood to disburden himself of a mighty breath.

'So!' he muttered: 'He is there, is he! Well, the plot grows complicate.'

CHAPTER XVII

There was a quarter of Milan into which the new light penetrated with some odd uncalculated effects. It was called, picturesquely enough, 'The Vineyard,' and as such certainly produced a great quantity of full-blooded fruit. Vines that batten on carrion grow fat; and here was the mature product of a soil so enriched. There was no disputing its appetising quality. That derived from the procreant old days of paganism, before the germ of the first headache had flown out of Pandora's box into a bung-hole. 'The Vineyard's' body yet owed to tradition, if centuries of adulteration had demoralised its spirit. Still, altogether, it was faithfuller of the soil, self-consciously nearer to the old Nature, than was ever the extrinsic Guelph or Ghibelline that had usurped its kingdom. Wherefore, it seemed, it had elected to construe this new reactionism, this *redintegratio amoris*, this sudden much-acclaiming of Nature, into a special vindication of itself, its tastes, methods and appetites, as representing the fundamental truth of things; and, *ex consequenti*, to appropriate Messer Bembo for its own particular champion and apologist.

Alas, poor Parablist! There is always that awakening for an enlightened agitator in any democratic mission. Does he look for some comprehension by the Demos of the necessity of *radical* reform, his eyes will be painfully opened. The pruning, by its leave, shall never be among the suckers down by the root, but always among the lordly blossoms. Shall Spartacus once venture openly to stoop with his knife, he shall lose at a blow the popular suffrage. At a later date, Robespierre, who was not enlightened, had to subscribe to the misapplication of his own reforms, or be crushed by the demon he had raised. Here in Milan, 'The Vineyard' was the first to renounce its champion, when once it found itself to be intimately included in that champion's neo-Christianising scheme.

Alas, poor Parablist! Not Reason but Fanaticism is the convincing reformer! the bigot, not the saint, the effective drover of men.

In the meanwhile 'The Vineyard' swaggered and held itself a thought more brazenly than heretofore, on the strength of its visionary election. Always a clamorous rookery, one might have fancied at this time a certain increase in the boisterous obscenity of its note, as that might presage the fulfilment of some plan for its breaking out, and planting itself in new black colonies all over the city. But as certainly, if this were so, its illusionment was a very may-fly's dance.

Now as, on a noon of this late Autumn, we are brought to penetrate its intricacies, a certain symbolic fitness in its title may or may not occur to us. Supposing that it does, we will accept this Via Maladizione where we stand, this gorge of narrow high-flung tenements, looped between with festoons of glowing rags, for the supports and dead trailers of a gathered vintage. Below, the vats are full to brimming, and the merchants of life and death forgathered in the markets. Half-way down the street a little degraded church suddenly spouts a friar, who, punch-like, hammers out on the steps his rendering of the new nature, which is to remember its cash obligations to Christ, and so vanishes again in a clap of the door. A barber, shaving a customer in the open street, gapes and misses his stroke, thereby adding a trickle to the sum of the red harvest. Mendicants pause and grin; oaths rise and buzz on all sides, like dung-flies momentarily disturbed. And predominant throughout, the vintagers, the true natives of the soil, swarm and lounge and discuss, under a rent canopy, the chances of the season and its likely profits.

Ivory and nut-brown are they all, these vintagers, with cheeks like burning leaves, and hair blue-black as grape-clusters, and eloquent animal eyes, and, in the women, copious bosoms half-veiled in tatters, like gourds swelling under dead foliage. But the milk that plumps these gourds is still of the primeval quality. Tessa's passions are of the ancient dimensions, if her religion is of to-day. Her assault and surrender borrow nothing from convention. No billing and rhyming for her, with canzonarists and madrigalists under the lemon trees, in the days when the awnings are hung over to keep the young fruit from scorching; but rough pursuit, rather, and capture and fulfilment—all uncompromising. She is here to eat and drink and love, to enjoy and still propagate the fruits of her natural appetites. She does not, like Rosamonda, brush her teeth with crushed pearls; she whets and whitens them on a bone. She does not powder her hair with gold dust; the sun bronzes it for her to the scalp. No spikenard and ambergris make her rags, or perfumed water her body, fragrant for her master's mouthing. Yet is she desirable, and to know her is to taste something of the sweetness of the apple that wrought the first discord. She is still a child of Nature, though Messer Bembo's creed surpasses her best understanding. She loves burnt almonds and barley-sugar, and crunches them joyously whenever some public festival gives her the chance; but the instincts of order and self-control are long vanished from the category of her qualities, and she survives as she is more by virtue of her enforced than her voluntary abstinences.

For the rest, civilisation—the civilisation that always encompasses without touching, without even understanding her—has made her morals a terror, and the morals of most of her comrades, male or female, of 'The Vineyard.'

It is, in fact, the sink of Milan, is this vineyard—a very low quarter indeed; and, it is to be feared, other red juice than grapes' swells the profits from its vats. Here are to be found, and engaged, a rich selection of the tagliacantoni, the hired bravos who kill on a sliding scale of absolution, with fancy terms for the murder which allows no time for an act of contrition. Here the soldier of fortune, who has gambled away, with his sword and body-armour, the chances of an engagement to cut throats honestly, festers for a midnight job, and countersigns with every vein he opens his own compact with the devil. Here the oligarchy of beggars has its headquarters, and composes its budgets of social taxation; and here, finally, in the particular den of one Narcisso, desperado and ladrone, hides and shivers Messer Tassino, once a Duchess's favourite.

He does not know why he is hidden here, or for what purpose Messer Ludovico beguiled and threatened him from the more sympathetic custody of his friend Jacopo, to deposit him in this foul burrow. But he feels himself in the grip of unknown forces, and he fears and shivers greatly. He is always shivering and snuffling is Messer Tassino; whining out, too, in rebellious moods, his pitiful resentments and hatreds. His little garish orbit is in its winter, and he cries vainly for the sun that had seemed once to claim him to her own warmth and greatness. He has heard of himself as renounced by her, condemned, and committed, on his detested rival's warrant, to judgment by default. Yet, though it be to save his mean skin, he cannot muster the moral courage to come forth and right the wrong he has done. That, he knows, would spell his last divorce from privilege; and he has not yet learned to despair. He had been so petted and caressed, and—and there are no lusty babies to be gathered from Messer Bembo's eyes. At least, he believes and hopes not; and, in the meanwhile, he will lie close, and await developments a little longer.

Perhaps, after all, there is knowledge if little choice in his decision. He may be justified, of his experience, in being sceptical of the disinterestedness of spiritual emotionalism, or at least of the feminine capacity for accepting its appeal disinterestedly. But of this he is quite sure—that sanctity itself shall not propitiate, by mere virtue of its incorruptibility, the woman it has scorned; and, in that certainty, and by reason of that experience, he nurses the hope of still profiting by the revulsion of feeling which he foresees will occur in a certain high lady as a consequence of her rebuff.

Still, however that may chance, he finds his present state intolerable. It is not so much its dull and filthy circumstance that appals him, though that is noxious enough to a boudoir exquisite; it is the shadow of Messer Ludovico's purpose, shapeless, indistinct, eternally conning him from the dark corners of his imagination, which takes the knees out of his soul. Is he really his friend and patron, as he professes to be? He recalls, with a sick shudder, how once, when in the full-flood of his arrogance, he had dared to keep that smooth and accommodating prince waiting in an ante-room while he had his hair dressed. He, Tassino, the fungus of a night, had ventured to do this! What a fool he had been; yet how worse than his own folly is the dissimulation which can ignore for present profit so unforgettable an insult! It is not forgotten; it cannot be; yet, to all appearances, Ludovico now visits him, on the rare occasions when he does so, with the sole object of informing him, sympathetically, of the progress of Bona's new infatuation. Why? He has not the wit to fathom. Only he has not so much faith in this disinterestedness as in the probability of its being a blind to some deadly policy.

How he hates them all—the Duchess, the Prince, the whole world of courtly rascals who have flattered him out of his obscurity only to play with and destroy him! If he can once escape from this trap, he will show them he can bite their heels yet. But what hope is there of escaping while Ludovico holds the secret of the spring? Day after day finds him gnawing the bars, and whimpering out his spite and impotence.

He has not failed, of course, to question his landlord Narcisso, or to weep over the futile result. Even if the little wretch's tact and wit were less negligible quantities, there is that of crafty doggedness in his gaoler to baffle the shrewdest questioner. Deciding that the man is in the paid confidence of the 'forces,' Tassino soon desists from attempting to draw him, and vents on him instead his whole soul of vengeful and disappointed spite.

Narcisso, for his part, offers himself quite submissively to the comedy; waits on him with a sniggering deference; stands while he eats; brings water, none the most fragrant, for him to dip his fingers in afterwards; dresses his hair with a broken comb, and takes his own dressing for pulling it with a grinning impassivity; lends, in short, his huge carcass in every way to be the other's butt and footstool. This exercise in overbearance is a certain relief to the prisoner; but, for all the rest, his time hangs deadlily on his hands. There are no restrictions placed upon him. He is free to come and go—as he dares. His terror is held his sufficient gaoler, and it suffices. He never, in fact, puts his nose outside the door, but contents himself, like the waspish little eremite he has become, with criticising and cursing from his solitary grille the limbs and lungs and life of the f[oe]tid world in which his later fortunes seem cast. So much for Messer Tassino!

One particular night saw him cowering before the caldano, or little domestic brazier, which must serve his present need in lieu of hotter memories; for the season was chilling rapidly, and what freshness had ever been in him was long since starved out. He was grown a little grimy and unkempt in these days, and his clothes were stale. The room in which he sat was, in its meanness and squalor, quite typically Vineyardish. Its furniture was of the least and rudest; it had not so much as a solitary cupboard to hold a skeleton; it was as naked to inspection as honesty. That was its owner's way. Narcisso was a very Dacoit in carrying all his simple harness on and about him. He cut his throats and his meat impartially with the same knife; or toasted, as he was doing now, slices of Bologna sausage on its point. His abortive scrap of a face puckered humorously, as the other, drawing his cloak tighter about him, damned the pitiful dimensions of their hearth.

'I would not curse the fire for its smallness, Messer,' he said. 'Wilt need all thy breath some day for blowing out a furnace.'

Tassino wriggled and snarled:—

'May'st think so, beast; but I know myself damned as an unbaptized one, to no lower than the first circle of our Father Dante.'

'Wert thou not baptized?'

'Do I not say so? And, therefore, lacking that grace, exonerated.'

'What's that?'

'Not responsible for my acts, pig.'

'Who says so?'

'Dante.'

'Who's he? Has a' been there? I would not believe him. What doth a' say o' me?'

'*You*? That you shall choke for all eternity in a river of blood.'

'Anan!' said Narcisso, and blew, scowling, on his sausage, which had become ignited. 'That's neither sense nor justice, master. I kill by the decalogue, I do. Did I ever put out a man's eyes for sport?'

'It's no matter,' answered Tassino. 'Thou wert baptized.'

'What will they do to thee?'

'I shall be forbidden the Almighty's countenance, no more—punishment enough, of course, for a person of taste; but I must e'en make shift to do without.'

'It's not fair,' growled Narcisso. 'I had no hand in my own christening. Do without? Narry penalty in doing without what you've never asked nor wanted.'

A figure that had stolen noiselessly into the room as they spoke, and was standing watching, with its cloak caught to its face, sniggered, literally, in its sleeve.

Tassino snapped rebelliously at the knife point, and began to eat without ceremony.

'Punishment enough,' he whined, 'if it means such a life in death as this.'

He sobbed and munched, quarrelling with his meat.

'How canst thou understand! The foul fiend betray him who condemned me to it! That saint; O, that saint! If I could only once trip *his* soul by the heels!'

'No need, my poor Tassino,' murmured a sympathetic voice; 'indeed, I think, there is no need.'

The prisoner staggered from his stool, and stood shaking and gulping.

'Messer Ludovico!' he gasped. 'How——'

'By the door, my child—plainly, by the door,' interrupted the Prince smoothly. And then he smiled: 'Alas! thou hast no ante-room here for the scotching of undesirable suitors.'

The terrified creature had not a word to say. One could almost hear his fat heart thumping.

Ludovico, lowering his cloak a little, made an acrid face. The room offended his particular nostrils: its atmosphere was nothing less than sticky. But, reflecting on the choice moral of it, he looked at the little tarnished clinquant before him, and was content to endure. He even affected a pleasant envy.

'This is worth all the glamour of courts,' he said, waving his hand comprehensively. 'To eat, or lie down; to go in or out as thou will'st. Never to know that suspicion of thine own shadow on the wall. To waste no words in empty phrases, nor need the wealth to waste on empty show. What a rich atmosphere hath this untroubled, irresponsible freedom; it is a very meal of itself! I would I could say, For ever rest and grow fat thereon; but, alas! I bring discomforting news. My poor Tassino. I fear the fortress at last shows signs of yielding.'

The little wretch opposite him whimpered as if at a whip-cut.

'Is it so indeed? Then, Messer Ludovico, it is a foul shame of her. She hath betrayed me—may God requite her!' He snivelled like a grieved child; then, on a sudden thought, looked up, with a child's cunning. 'At least in that case I shall be forgotten. There can be no object in my hiding here longer.'

The Prince lifted his eyebrows, with an inward-drawn whistle.

'Object? Object?' he protested, acting amazement. 'But more than ever, my poor simpleton. Thy case is double-damned thereby. Think you the other would rest on the thought of a rival, and such a rival, at large? Thy very existence would be a menace to his guilty peace. I come, indeed, as a friend to warn thee. Lie close; stir not out; the very air hath knives. Be cautious, even of thy shadow on the wall, of thy hand in the dish.'

He said it calmly and distinctly, looking towards Narcisso, who all this time had stood hunched in the background, his dull brain struggling bewildered in a maze. But the urgency of this innuendo penetrated even him; the more so when he saw Tassino leap and fling himself on his knees at the Prince's feet.

'What do you mean?' shrieked the young man. 'Is *he* in their pay? O Messer, save me! don't let me be poisoned.'

He pawed and grovelled, looking madly over his shoulder. Ludovico laughed gently, disregarding him.

'Nay, I know not,' he cooed. 'It is a dog that serves more masters than one.'

Narcisso slouched forward, and ducked a sort of obeisance between sullen and deferential.

'What's to-do?' he growled. 'I serve my patron, Messer Duke's son, like an honest man. What call, I say, to warn 'en of me? Do I not earn my wages fairly?'

'Scarcely, fellow,' murmured Ludovico—'unless to betray thine employer be fair.'

Narcisso scowled and lowered.

'Betray!' he protested, but uneasily. 'That is a charge to be proved, Messer.'

Ludovico suddenly leapt to a blaze.

'Dog! Wouldst bandy with me, dog? Beware, I say! Who blabbed my secrets to the lady of Casa Caprona?'

He was himself again with the cry. His faculty of instant self-control was a thing quite fearful. Narcisso cowered before him; shrunk under the playful wagging of his finger.

'Messer—in the Lord's name!' he could only stammer—'Messer!'

'O thou fond knave!' complained the Prince, showing his teeth in a smile; 'to think to play that double game, one patron against another, and stake thine empty wits against the reckoning! Well, thou art confessed and damned.' He drew back a pace. 'But one word more,' he said, raising his voice. 'What hast thou to plead that I call not up those that will silence for ever thy false, treacherous tongue?'

He stood by the door. It was a very reasonable inference that he had not ventured into such a quarter unattended. Narcisso stood gasping and intertwining his thick fingers, but he could find no words.

'What!' smiled Ludovico; 'no excuse, no explanation? No answer of any kind? Shall I call, then?' He seemed to hesitate. 'Yet perhaps one loop-hole, though undeserved, I'll lease thee on condition.' He moved again forward a little, and spoke in a lower tone: 'There's news wanted of a certain stolen ring. Dog! do I not know who thieved it, and for whom? Now shalt thou undertake to go yet once again, and, robbing the receiver, bring the spoil to me—or be damned here and now for thy villainy.'

He thought he had netted at last the quarry of his long, patient stalking; but for once his confidence was at fault. Watching intently for the effect of his words, he grew conscious of some change transfiguring, out of terror and astonishment, the face of his victim. Foul, ignoble, animal beyond redemption as that was in all its features, its swinish eyes could yet extract and emit, it seemed, from the thin, dead ashes of some ancient fire, a stubborn spark of self-renunciation. He could read it in them unmistakably. The man stood straight before him, for the first and only time in his life, a hero.

Ludovico gazed in silence. He found, to do him the right justice, this psychic revelation of acuter interest to him than his own defeat foreseen in the light of it. But Tassino's subdued whimpering jarred him out of his abstraction.

'Well, is it agreed?' he asked with a sigh. For the moment he almost shrunk in the apprehension of an affirmative reply.

The rogue drew himself suddenly together.

'Call, Messer,' he said. 'That is my answer.'

His chin dropped on his breast. Tassino uttered a cry, and hid his face in his hands. Not a word or apparent movement followed; but when, goaded by the fearful stillness, the two dared to look up once more, they found themselves alone.

Then, at that, Tassino shrieked and sprang to the grille.

'My God!' he sobbed; 'he has gone, and left me to my fate!'

He moved to escape by the door, but Narcisso caught and wrenched him back.

'What ails the fool!' he protested in his teeth. 'My orders be to keep, not kill thee, man!'

Messer Ludovico, walking enveloped within a little cloud of his adherents, smiled to himself on his way back to the palace.

'The fascination of the serpent,' mused he, shaking his head—'the fascination of the serpent! How could that crude organism be expected to resist the arts of our Lamia, when I myself could fall near swooning to them? Hath he betrayed me to others? I think not; yet it were well to have him silenced betimes. The weakness was to threaten where I dared not yet perform. Yet it may chance, after all, he shall come to be prevailed on for the ring.'

'The ring!' he muttered, as he climbed presently to his chamber—'the ring! I think it comes to zone the world in my imagination!'

As he was passing through the ante-room to his private closet, a draped and voiceless figure moved suddenly out of the shadows to accost him. He gave the faintest start, then offered his hand, and, without a word, ushered this strange ghost into his sanctum. The portière swung back, the door clanged upon them, and there on the threshold he dwelt, looking with a silent, smiling inquisition into the eyes of his visitor.

Hast thou ever seen the dead, leafy surface of a woodland pool stir, scarce perceptibly, to the movement of some secret thing below? So, as Beatrice stood like a statue before the Prince, did the soul of her reveal itself to him, writhing somewhere under the surface of that still mask.

Then suddenly, swiftly, passionately, she thrust out a hand.

'There is the ring,' she said. 'Do what you will with it.'

CHAPTER XVIII

That same evening had witnessed, in the dower Casa Caprona, the abortive finish to a venture long contemplated by its mistress, and at length, in a moment of desperation, dared. She had wrought herself, or been wrought at this last, into privately communicating to the little Saint Magistrate of Milan, how she had certain information where the ring lay, which if he would learn, he must follow the messenger to her house. She had claimed his utmost confidence and secrecy, and, on that understanding alone, had procured herself an interview. And Bernardo had come, and he had gone—how, her tumbled hair, her self-bruised bosom, her abandonment to the utter shame and fury of her defeat, were eloquent witnesses.

She had not been able to realise her own impotence to disarm an antagonist already half-demoralised, as she believed this one to be. For, before ever she had precipitated this end, gossip had been busy whispering to her how the saint was beginning to melt in the sun of adulation, to confess the man in the angel, to inform with a more than filial devotion his attitude towards Bona. To have to cherish yet hate that thought had been her torture; to anticipate its consummation her frenzy. She had known him first; he was hers by right. Long wasting in the passion of her desire, she had conceived of its fruition a savour out of all proportion with her experiences. She must conquer him or die. He was hers, not Bona's.

She had disciplined herself, in order to propitiate his prejudices, into the enduring of a decent period of retirement. It must end at last. She never knew when Ludovico might exact from her that security, held by her conditionally only, against her ruin by him. For the present indeed she retained the ring, but any moment might see it claimed from her. Now, if she could only once lure, and overcome by its means, the object of her passion, the question of its restoration to, or use by another against, its owner, must necessarily cease of being an acute one with either her or Bernardo.

With him, at least—with him, at least. And as for herself?

Turning where she lay, she had seen her own insolent smile reflected from a mirror.

'He said,' she had whispered, pondering some words of Ludovico's, *'More impossible things might happen.'*

Then, taking the ring from her bosom, and apostrophising its green sparkle softly:—

'A little star—a little bribe, to win me both love and a throne!' she had said, and so had sunk back, closing her eyes, and murmuring:—

'Let it only prove its power here, and it and the heads of that conspiracy shall be all Ludovico's. He will not claim the latter, I think, until their purpose is accomplished. And then——'

And then Messer Ludovico himself had been announced. He visited her not infrequently in these days, though never, it seemed, with any purpose of foreclosing on that little mortgage of the ring. He came in the fashion of a confidential gossip, to enlighten her as to the doings of the world outside. They were very pleasant and intimate together, with a hint, no more, of closer relations to come. The lion rolled in a silken net, and affected his subjugation, as the lady affected not to notice the stealthy claws of her capture. It was a pretty little comedy, which engaged the sympathies of both, each according to its temperament. But it ended in tragedy.

Ludovico had, indeed, no interest in dissuading his beautiful gossip's mind from its tormenting suspicions as to the Messer Saint's gradual corruption by Bona; a scandal to which, no doubt—the wish in him being father to the thought—he himself gave ready credence. The report suited him in every way, both as to his policy and its instruments; and he only awaited its certain substantiation to let fly the bolt which was to involve three fortunes in one ruin—under warrant of the ring, if possible, but timely in any event.

And in the meanwhile it afforded him, whether from jealousy or pure love of mischief, some wicked gratification to nip and sting this already tormented lady in sensitive places, and to do it all under an affectation of the softest sympathy.

Yet, while for his own purpose he hugged and fostered the slander, whose growth and justification he most desired, the slander itself, for some inexplicable reason, did not grow, but even began to exhibit signs, for a time almost imperceptible, of attenuating. Ludovico could not acknowledge this fact to himself, or even consider it. It is difficult, no doubt, while we are calculating our probable gains, to admit the possibility of a blight in the harvest of our hopes. A fervid prospect blinds us to the road between; and this prince, for all his far-seeing, because of it rather, may have been less open to immediate impressions than some others about him.

Yet to souls less acute, there *were* the signs: the first little shadow of a smut on the ear—a hitch, just the faintest, in the ecstatic programme of Nature. Was it that Tassino, the mean worldling, was a true prophet of his parts, and that the reaction from a starved continence was already actually threatening? Whispers there certainly were of a growing impatience of restrictions in the castello; of schisms from the pure creed of its little priest; of hankerings, even on the part of the highest, after the old fleshpots. They rose, and died down, and rose again. There was no melting a certain snow-child, it was said, into anything but ice water. The Duchess, who had somehow expected to gather flowers from frost, went about white and smiling, and chafing her hands as if they were numb. She had once stopped before a new young courtier, who bore some resemblance to a past favourite, and, while speaking to him kindly, had been seen to flush as though her cheeks had caught the sudden warmth of a distant fire. Madam Caterina, it was certain, waxing bold in impishness, had commiserated her mother on the bad cold she had caught. 'Madre mia,' she had said, 'you have wandered too much in the chill woods, and would be the better for a hot brick to your bed.'

For such tittle-tattle was this after season of the sowing responsible, when, against all expectations, tares began to appear amidst the crops. Messer Ludovico, for his part, would recognise no sinister note in the laughter. It was just the rocking and babbling of empty vessels. Its justification in fact would not have suited his book at all; and so he continued in confidence to plant his little shafts in madam's raw places.

Monna Cat'rina, he had told her on the occasion of this particular visit, had been very saucy to her mother the evening before, advising her, this cold weather, to make herself a coverlet of angel down. 'Whereat,' said he, 'Madam our Duchess slapped the chit's pink knuckles, answering, "Shall I wish him, then, to die of cold for me?" to which Catherine replied: "No; for to die of love is not to die of cold"'; and the other had blushed and laughed, and turned away.

And it had been this sting, thrust into the place of a long inflammation, which had finally goaded Beatrice into writing and sending her letter.

VENUS AND ADONIS

The days were beginning to darken early. It was the season when exotic flowers of passion luxuriate under glass, in that close coverture which is the very opposite to the law's understanding of the term.

Beatrice, like all tropical things, loved this time; basked in the glow of tapers; hugged her own warm sweetness in the confidence of a sanctuary for ever besieged by, and for ever impervious to, the forces of cold and gloom. To fancy herself the desired of night, unattainable through all its storming, was a commanding ecstasy. She liked to hear the hail on the roof, trampling and threshing for an opening, and flinging away baffled. The muffled slam of the thunder was her lullaby; while the candles shivered in it, she closed her eyes and dreamed. The thought of wrenched clouds, of crying human shapes, of torn beasts and birds sobbing and circling without the closed curtains of her shrine, served her imagination like a hymn. She measured her content against the strength of such hopeless appeals, like a very nun of incontinence, shut from the rigour of the world within the scented oratory of her own worship. She was Venus Anno Domini, the Paphian goddess yet undethroned, and yet justified of her influence over man and Nature.

> *'About her carven palace walls a thousand blossoming lilies brake;*
> *Within, a thousand years of love had wrought, for utter beauty's*
> *sake, Triumphs of art for her blue eyes, and for her feet rich*
> *stainèd floors, And ever in her ears sweet moan of music down*
> *dim corridors?*

Agapemone was her temple, and its inmost chamber her shrine. Here, under stained glass windows, ran a frieze in relievo of warm terra-cotta, thronged with little goat-faced satyrs pursuing nymphs through groves of pregnant vines. Here, supporting the frieze, were pilasters of blood-red porphyry, which burst high up into fronds of gold; while, screening the interspaces on the walls, were panels of glowing tapestry relating the legend of Adonis, from his first budding on the enchanted tree to his final shrouding under the winter of love's grief. Here, also, the faces of dead Capronas, past lords of this House Beautiful, winked and gloated out of shadowy corners, whenever a log, toppling over on the hearth, sent up a shower of sparks. Prominent in one place was a tall massive clock, copper and brass, a *chef-d'[oe]uvre* of Dondi the horologist, which thudded the hours melodiously, like a chime of distant bells, and made the swooning senses in love with time. Couches there were everywhere, soft and wooing to the soul of languor; thick rugs and skins upon the marble floor; tables with clawed legs, of chalcedony or jasper, on which were scattered in lovely wantonness a hundred toys of Elysium. Lutes, sweets, and goblets of rich repoussé; wine in green flasks, and delicate long-stemmed glasses; an ivory and silver crucifix, half-hidden under a pile of raisins; two love-birds in a gilded cage, and a golden salver containing an aspic of larks' tongues, tilted upon a volume of some French Romaunt touching the knightly adventures of Messer Roland a troubadour—these and their like, varied or repeated, returned, in a thousandfold interest of colour and sparkle, the soft investment of the tapers—enough, but not too many—in their beauty.

One velvet cloth had been swept from its place, spilling upon a rug, where it sprawled unregarded, its costly burden of a begemmed chalice, a pair of perfumed gloves, and an illuminated volume of sonnets in a jewelled cover, dedicated to the goddess herself, and celebrating, in letters of gold and silver on vellum, her incomparable seductions. She had pulled them over, no doubt, when she reached for the orange which now, untasted, filled her hand, soft and covetous as a child's.

The warmth and drowsy stillness of the room penetrated her as she lay holding it. Gradually her lids closed, her bare arm drooped from its sleeve, and the orange rolled on the floor. Her thoughts and expectations had been already busy for an hour with, 'Will he come? Will he come? Will he come?' It had been like counting sheep trotting through a hedge — one, two, three, four — up to a hundred — and now her drugged brain confused the tally, and she seemed to herself to swerve all in a moment into a luminous mist.

He entered like a pale scented flower into her dream — a soft and shapely thing, melting into its ecstasy, fulfilling its enchantment. She held him, and whispered to him: 'The hour, sweet love! Is it mine at last?' — and, so murmuring, stirred and opened her eyes.

He was there, close by her, looking down upon her as she lay. How pale was his face, and how wistful. His walk through the icy dark had but just tinted it, as when November flaws blow the snow from the rose's dead cheek. He looked dispirited and tired. The childlike pathos of his eyes moved her heart-strings no less than did the red, combative swelling of his lips. She longed to master him in order to be mastered. Her hedonism's highest moral attainment was always in pleasing herself by surrendering herself to the pleasure of another; and how, knowing herself, could she doubt the irresistible persuasiveness of her faith?

She did not speak for a little, the wine of slumber in her brain emboldening her in the meanwhile to dare this vision with her beauty, to seek her response in its eyes. Her cheeks, her half-closed lids, were, like a baby's, flushed with sleep. Suddenly she stirred, and, smiling and murmuring, held out white arms to it: —

'The hour thou sang'st to me! Bernardo, hast thou come to make that mine?'

He stood as if stricken — white, dumfoundered. She stretched her shoulders a little, and, raising her hands, put their rosy knuckles to her eyes; and so relaxed all, and drooped.

'I was dreaming,' she murmured. 'I thought thou camest to me and said: "Beatrice, I will forego that heaven for thy sake. Give me the hour, to kiss and shame." She stole a glance at him, and dropped her clasped hands to her lap, and hung her head. 'And I answered,' she whispered, '"Take it, and make one woman happy."'

He gave a little cry. And then, suddenly, before he could move or speak, she had sat up swiftly, and whipped her arms about his neck, and pulled him to the couch beside her.

'Listen,' she urged—'nay, thou shalt not go. I hold thy weakness in a vice. Struggle, and I will tighten it. Listen, child, while I tell thee a child's tale. It is about a huntsman that followed a voice; and he pushed into a thicket, and lo! enchantment seized him beyond. And he whispered amazed, "What is this?" and the voice answered, "Love—the end to all thy hunting." O! little huntsman of Nature, be content. Thou hast traced the voice of thy long longing to its home.'

She repaid his struggles with kisses, his wild protests with honeyed words. He set his pretty teeth at her, and she pouted her mouth to them; he hurled insult at her head, and she bore the sweet ache of it for the sake of the lips that bruised. When he desisted, exhausted, she would get in her soft pleas, rebuking him with a tearful meekness:—

'Ay, scourge me, set thy teeth in me, only hate me not. Shalt find me but the tenderer, being whipped. Talk on of Nature. Is it not natural to want to be loved; and, for a woman, in a woman's way?'

'Forbear!—O, wicked! O, thou harlot!' he panted, still fighting with her.

'Lie still! So a sick infant quarrels with its food,' she answered. 'O love—dear love, will you not hear reason?'

'Reason!' he stormed. 'O, thou siren! to beguile me here on that lying pretext, and thus shame me for my trust!'

'No lie,' she pleaded. 'Thou shalt have the ring indeed.'

'At thy price? I will die first.'

'Bernardo!'

'*Thou* to talk of natural love! False to it; false to thy lord; false even to thy stained bed! Unhand me! Why, I loathe thee.'

'Not yet.'

Her eyes were hot waters, all misted over with passion. 'Thou canst not indeed, so pitiful to the worst. I cry to thee in my need. I knew thee first. Bernardo! will you forsake your friend?'

'Friend!'

'Ay. Only tell me what you would do with the ring?'

'What but return it to her that trusted me with it,'

'And for what reward?—Nay, strive not.'

'My conscience's peace—just that. Unclasp thy hands.'

'See there! Her gratitude would kill it in thee for ever. As would be hers to thee, so be thine to me. Art thou for a fall? Fall soft, then, on my love. She will not let thee down so kindly, who hath a lord and duchy to consider.'

He made a supreme effort—her robe tore in his hand—and, breaking from her, stood panting and disordered. She made no effort to recapture him, but, flinging herself to abandonment, sobbed and sighed.

'O, I am undone! Wilt thou forsake me? Kill me first! Nay, I will not let thee go!'

She sprang to her feet. He leapt away from her.

'Beast!' he cried, 'that foulest our garden! I will have thee whipped out of Milan with a bow-string.'

Scorn and hatred flashed into her face. She was no longer Venus, but Ashtoreth, the goddess of unclean frenzy.

'Thou wilt?' she hissed. 'I thank thee for that warning. Go, sir, and claim thy doxy to thy vengeance. She will leap, I promise thee, to that chance. Only, wouldst thou view the sport'—she struck her naked bosom relentlessly—'by this I advise thee—O, I advise thee like a lover!—hide well in her skirts—hide well. They will need to be thick and close to screen thee from a woman scorned. Wilt thou not go? I have the ring, I tell thee—*I*, myself, no other. Let her know. She'll bid thee pay the price perchance—too late. A fatal ring to thee. Why art thou lingering? I would not spare thee now, though thou knelt'st and prayed to me with tears of blood.'

She stood up rigid, her hands clenched, as, without another word, Bernardo turned, and, stalking with high head and glittering eyes, passed out of the room.

But, the moment the door had closed upon him, she flung herself face downwards on the couch, writhing and choking and clutching at her throat.

'I must kill him,' she moaned; 'I must kill my love!'

CHAPTER XIX

The hitch in the progress of the harvest came ever a little and a little more into evidence: the smut darkened on the ear; the whisper of a threatened blight grew from vague to articulate—grew clearer, grew bolder—until, lo!—all in a moment it was a definite voice.

This happened on the morning succeeding Bernardo's visit to the Casa Caprona—a visit of which, it would appear, the Duchess of Milan had been made somehow cognisant.

Bona, on this morning, came into the hall of council, her white hand laid, as she walked, upon the shoulder of Messer Cecco Simonetta, the State Secretary. That light, caressing touch was an arresting one to some eyes observing it—Ludovico's among the number. Its like, in that particular context of confidence and affection, had not been seen for many weeks—never, indeed, since the secretary had taken it upon himself to caution his mistress on the subject of a perilous fancy. He would have had no wish to balk any whim of hers that turned on self-indulgence. It was this whim of self-renunciation which had alarmed him. There was a mood which might conceivably vindicate itself in the sacrifice of a kingdom to a sentiment. Such things had happened; and saints were men. He would put it to her with all humility.

And she had listened and answered icily: 'I thank thee, Messer Secretary. But our faith is commensurate with our purpose, which is to sweep out our house, not pull it down. What then? Dread'st thou to be included in the scourings? Fear not. It is no part of our faith to forget our obligations.'

Which was a cruel response; but its hauteur silenced Mr. Secretary. And thenceforth he served in silence, watching, anxiously enough, the progress of his lady's infatuation, and feeling at last immensely relieved when on this day, her warm palm settled on his shoulder, melting the long frost between them.

She looked rather wistfully into his worn eyes, and smiled a little tale without words of confidence restored. And he, for his part, spoke of no matters less commonplace than the State's welfare.

'The Duke will make Christmas with us, Madonna,' he said; 'I have advices from him.'

'He will be most welcome,' she answered, and her face coloured with real pleasure. But the next moment it was like snow, and its vision hard crystals of frost. She had seen the Saint Magistrate advancing to accost her.

There was a strange look in the boy's eyes as they gazed, unflinchingly nevertheless, into hers—a look mingled of pain and doubt and fortitude. She had said no unkind word to him; yet a frost can nip without wind; and surely here was a plant very sensitive to the human atmosphere. He questioned her face a little; then spoke out bold, though low—while Messer Ludovico, turning papers at the table, was very busy—watching.

'Madonna, wilt thou walk apart? I am fain to crave thy private ear a moment.'

She stood like ice.

'Touching whose shortcomings now?' she asked aloud, and with a little cold laugh which disdained that implied confidence.

He gazed at her steadily, though in trouble.

'Nay, I spoke of none. It is of moment. Madonna, I entreat thee.'

For an instant the milk of her sweetened to him. He was such a baby after all. And then she remembered whence he had lately come, and gall flooded her veins—gall not so much of jealousy, perhaps, as of contempt. Doubtless, she thought, he could have ventured himself into that hothouse in the Via Sforza with impunity, since, though spirit he might be, he was of that uninflammability that his virtue amounted to little better than the virtue of sexlessness. She felt almost glad, at last, to have this excuse for dissociating herself from a cause which had always chilled, and had ceased now for some time even to amuse her.

Feel no surprise over the seeming suddenness of her revolt. Apart from her position, this Duchess of Milan was never anything but a typical woman, common-souled, lacking spiritual sensitiveness, leaning to her masculine peers. Breeding was her business, and motherhood her passion. She took no more jar of offence from the intimate custody of babies, than does a cat in licking open the eyes of its seven-days born. Her refinements were adventitious, an accident of her condition. She had felt it no outrage to her stately loveliness to yield it to Tassino's usings. She had that Madonna-like serenity of face which is the expression of an inviolable mindlessness; and no impressions other than physical could long pervade her. Stupidity is the rarest beauty-preserver; and it is to be feared that Bona was stupid.

Now, it is to be remembered that Bernardo had not mentioned shortcomings at all; but her object being to snub rather than answer him, she chose to take refuge in her sex's prerogative of intuition. Dwelling a moment in a rising temper, she suddenly flounced on him.

'If you will seek doubtful company, Messer, you must not cry out to have your fervour misread by it.'

He was about to answer; but she stopped him peremptorily.

'Women will be women, good or bad. We cannot promote a civil war in Milan to avenge some pin-prick to thy conscience. Indeed, sir, we weary a little of this precisianism. Is it come to be a sin to laugh, to warm our hands at a fire, to prefer a fried collop to a wafer? You must forgive us, like the angel that you are. We are human, after all, and pledged to human policies. Our State's before the magistracy. There are things weightier to discuss than a mischief's naughty word. We cannot hear you now.'

She turned away, relenting but a little, though flushed and trembling.

'Come, brother,' she said. 'Shall we not pass to the order of the day?'

Ludovico responded with smooth and smiling alacrity. One could never have guessed by his face the consternation which had seized his soul. Yet, so cleverly had he hoodwinked himself, this sudden leap of light was near staggering him. Merriment and warmth and fried collops? The charge in its utter, its laughable irrelevancy, was, he thought, a little hard on the saint, seeing how the gist of the new creed lay all in a natural enjoyment of life's bounties. What powder had winged such a startling shot?—weariness?— disenchantment?—remorseful hankerings, perhaps, after a discarded suet pudding, which, after all, had been infinitely more native to this woman's taste than the ethereal soufflé, whose frothy prettiness had for the moment appealed to her meat-fed satiety?

The last, most probably. And, in that case— —

His brain, through all the mazes of council, went tracing out a busy thread of self-policy. If this were really the end, he must hurry to foreclose on it ere the split widened into a gulf—before ever the first whisper of its opening reached Tassino's ears. The time for temporising was closed.

'It touches, your Grace,' he purred, 'upon the reception to be accorded the envoys of Ferrara and Mantua.'

The wind of a fall, like the wind of an avalanche, runs before the body of it. Messer Bembo, passing out, amazed, from his rebuff, found in himself an illustration of this inevitable human truism. All the envies, spites, and jealousies which his sweetness, under favour, had kept at bay, seemed now gathered in his path to hustle and insult him.

'Good Master Nature,' mocked one, 'hast ever a collop in thy pocket for a starved woodman?'

'See how he stumbles, missing his leading-strings!' cackled another.

A third knocked off his bonnet.

'Prophesy, who is he that smote thee!' he cried, and ducking, came up elsewhere.

'Ay, prophesy!' thundered a fourth voice; and a fist like a rammer crashed upon the assailant's face, spread-eagling it. The man went down in a welter. Bembo fled to Lanti's arms, feebly imprisoning them.

'Thou thing of bloody passions!' he shrieked. 'Wouldst thou so vindicate me?'

Carlo roared over his shoulder:—

'Help his prophecy, ye vermin, when he's ears to hear; and tell him I wait to carve them from his head.'

He bore Bembo with him from the hall, as he might carry a moth fluttering on his sleeve. Murmurs rose in his wake, seething and furious; but he heeded them not. In a deserted court beyond, he shook the pretty spoil from his arm, not roughly but with an air of madness, and stood breathing like a driven ox.

'What now?' he groaned at last—'what now?'

Then all in a moment the boy was sobbing before him.

'O Carlo! dear Carlo! I would the Duke were returned!'

His grief and helplessness moved the other to a frenzy. His chest heaved, he caught at his throat, struggling vainly for utterance of the fears which had of late been tormenting him without definite reason. Seeing his state, Bernardo sought to propitiate it with a smile that trembled out of tears.

'Nay, mind me not—a child to cry at a shadow.'

Lanti choked, and found voice at length.

'The Duke? Monstrous! Call'st thou for him? Forget'st Capello? Art changed indeed.'

'Alas!' cried the boy, 'no change in me. I think only of a more ruling tyranny than mine. Pitiless himself, he made pity sweet in others. I've converted 'em from deeds to words, that's all.'

'The Duke!'

'I begin to see. Thou warned'st me, I remember. The fashion of me passes, like thy shoe's long beaks. Yesterday they were a span; to-day they're shrunk by half; to-morrow, mayhap, ye'll trim them from your feet and run on goat's hooves.'

'Thou ravest. 'Tis for thee, being Duke-deputy, to trim *us*.'

'Into what? Cherubs or satyrs? Be quick, lest the fashion change while you talk.'

'Go to! Thou art the Duke, I say.'

'Well, a fine puppet, and great at righting wrongs. There's Lucia to witness.'

'She's provided for.'

'With bread. O, I am a very Mahomet. If I but nod my head, the city shall crack and crumble to it.'

'God! What ails thee, boy?'

'Something mortal, I think. A breath withered me just now!'

'A breath? Whose breath?'

'Whose? O Carlo, forgive me! What have I said or done? Look, I'm myself again. It just fell like a frost in June, killing my young olives. I had so hung upon it, too—its help and promise. The harvest seemed so certain.'

'Ah! She's thrown you over?'

'Dreams, dreams!' sighed poor little Nathan; 'to live on dreams—a deaf man's voices, a blind man's vision. I have seen such things, built such kingdoms out of dreams. Carlo! what have I done?'

Lanti ground his teeth.

'Done? Proved woman's constancy a dream—that's all.'

He clapped his chest, and looked earnestly at Bembo, and cried in a broken voice:—

'Boy—before God—tell me—thou hast not learned to desire her?'

The child looked up at him, with a pitiful mouth.

'Ah! I know not what you mean; unless it be that pain with which I see her melt from out my dream when most possessing it.'

'Most? She? She to possess thy dream, thy purpose?' cried Lanti, and drew back in great emotion.

'She *is* my purpose,' said the boy—'or *was*, alack!'

'Is and was,' growled the other. 'Well, 'tis true that for the purpose of thy purpose *I* remain; but then I don't count. What am *I* to thee?'

'My love, beyond all women.'

'I am? That's much. Now will we do without the Duchess.'

'Alas!'

'Shall we not?'

'She hath so nursed my flock to pasture—the kind ewe-mother. The bell was about her neck. Now, it seems, she will have neither bell nor shepherd, and the flock must stray.'

'Hath she in truth cast thee? On what pretext?'

'Nay, I know not. It seemed the twin-brother of him that once she used for loving me.'

'Ay, it is their way. But scorn, for your part, to show caloric as she cools.'

'Alas!'

'Trust me there. What had you said to chill her?'

'Nothing that I know, but to crave her ear a moment.'

'It is the sink of slander in a woman—a pink shell with a dead fish inside. Yet thy whisper might have sweetened it.'

'Stung it rather. Carlo, I know not what to do.'

'Tell me.'

'Shall I, indeed? I fear thee. Wilt thou be gentle?'

'As a lamb.'

'Well, then, I'll tell thee—I am so lost. Carlo, dear, I know where the ring is.'

'You do? Do you see how calm I am? Where is it?'

'Beatrice hath it—thy Beatrice.'

'You know that?'

'She sent to tell me—last night. God help me, Carlo, for a credulous fool!'

'You went to her? Well?'

'She would give it me, Carlo—O Carlo! on such a condition!'

'Which if you refused ——?'

'It shall be a fatal ring to me, she ended.'

'Shall it?—or to her? Well, that's said. And now, wilt thou go rest a little, sweetheart, while I think? I cannot think in company.'

'I will go, but not to rest.'

'Pooh! thy Fool shall drug thy folly with his greater.'

'Alas! he's gone.'

'Gone?'

'He too. Nay, blaspheme not. He had his reasons.'

'For what?'

'For leaving me awhile. "My folly starves on thine ambrosia," he said. "I would fain feed it a little on human flesh."'

'How long's he gone?'

'Some days.'

'Let him keep out of my way when he returns.'

'I'll not love you if you hurt him.'

'Then I'll not hurt him. Thy love is mine, and thy confidence, look you. This ring—speak not a word on it, to Bona or another, till I bid you.'

'Then I will not.'

'That's good. God rest you, sweetling.'

He watched him go, with frowning eyes; then, no message coming to him from the hall, strode off to his own quarters in the palace, and bided there all day.

'These women,' was the burden of his fury—'these women—soulless beasts! To aim at winning heaven by debauching its angel!—there's their morality in a nutshell! But I'll send him back there first. So Beatrice hath the ring! What will she do with it? What shall I with the knowledge? God! if my wits could run with my rage! To forestall her, else ——'

His fingers worked, as he tramped, on the jewelled hilt of his poniard.

It was Messer Lanti's misfortune that, in knocking down Bernardo's assailant, he had defaced, literally as well as symbolically, the escutcheon of a powerful family. The fact was brought to the Duchess's notice when, shortly after the event, she passed through the hall in company with her brother-in-law. Hoarse clamour of kinsmen and partisans greeted her, backed, by way of red evidence, by the condition of the victim himself.

Her wrath and emotion knew no bounds. She flushed, and stamped, and wept, and in the midst collapsed. It was outrageous that her authority should be so defied (though, indeed, it had not been) by the brute creature of a creature of her lord's. The Duke had never foreseen or intended such an arrogation of his prerogatives by his deputy. She would teach this swashbuckler a lesson.

Then she broke down and turned, tearful, almost wringing her hands, to her brother-in-law. Sure never woman was cursed in such a false position—impotent and responsible in one. What should she do?

He took her aside.

'These two,' he said, 'are as yet *persona gratæ* with Galeazzo. At the same time thou canst not with decency or safety ignore the outrage. Seize and confine Messer Lanti out of harm's way until the Duke's return—just a formal and considerate detention, pending his decision. There's thy wise compromise, sister.'

And so indeed it seemed. But undoubtedly the best wisdom lay in his own adroit seizure of a fortuitous situation. He had wanted this Lanti out of the way; had foreseen him, as it were, lurking in the thickets far ahead through which his policy sought a road. Here was the fine opportunity, and without risk to himself, to ambush the ambuscado, and have it laid by the heels.

Bona sobbed and fretted, nursing her grievance.

'Why did this angel come to vex us with his heaven? The world, I think, would be very well but for its schooling by saints and prophets. Children grow naughty under inquisition. There, have it as you will, brother; use or abuse me—it is all one. It is my fate to be persecuted through my best intentions.'

Ludovico put force on himself to linger a little and soothe her. His soul leapt with anxiety to be gone. To instruct Jacopo; to commission Tassino—to loose his long-straining bolt in fact—here was the moment sprung inevitable upon him. He had no choice but to seize it; and then—

'Your Grace must excuse me,' he said at length, smiling. 'I have to go prepare against a journey.'

'A journey!' she exclaimed, aghast.

'Surely,' he answered mildly. 'The matter is insignificant enough to have escaped your burdened memory; but smaller souls must hold to their engagements. My brother Bari and I are to Christmas with the King of France in Tours. We sail from Genoa, whither, in a day or two, I must ride to join him. It is unfortunate, at this pass; but— —'

'Go, sir,' she broke in—'go. I see I am to be the scapegoat of all your policies,' and she hurried from him, weeping.

CHAPTER XX

More and more drearily the burden of his long days pressed upon Tassino. He was not built for heroic endurance; and to have to suffer Damocles' fate without the feast was a very death-in-life to him. Here, in this dingy cabin, was no solace of wine to string his nerves; no charm of lights to scare away bogies; no outlook but upon beastliness and squalor. He seemed stranded on a mud-bank amidst the ebbing life of the city, and he despaired that the tide would ever turn and release him.

Listening at his grille, he would often curse to hear the name of his hated rival—'Bembo! Bembe, Bambino!' sing out upon the swarming air. It was the rallying-cry of the new socialism, the popular catchword of the moment; and he hugged himself in the thought of what it would spell to Galeazzo on his return, and by what racking and rending and stretching of necks he would mark his appreciation of its utterers' enthusiasm. If the Duke would only come back! Here was the last of three who desired, it appeared, each for a very different reason, the re-installation of an ogre in his kingdom.

But, in the meanwhile, he cowered in an endless apprehension as to his own safety, which Ludovico's last visit had certainly done nothing to reassure. On the contrary, it had but served to intensify the gloom of mystery in which he dwelt. He had since made sundry feeble-artful attempts to discover from Narcisso what secret attached to the ring, which, it appeared, that amiable peculator was accused of having filched, and why Messer Ludovico was so set on possessing it. Needless to say, his efforts met with no success whatever; and the corrosion of a new suspicion was all that they added to his already palsied nerves. The sick flabbiness and demoralisation of him grew positively pitiful, as he stood day after day at his grille, watching and moping and snivelling, and sometimes wishing he were dead.

Well, the thicker the mud, the more productive the tide when it comes; but he was fairly sunk to his neck before it floated him out.

One day, gazing down, his attention was attracted to a figure which had halted near below his coign of espial. As things went, there was nothing so remarkable in this figure, in its alien speech or apparel, as to make it arresting otherwise than by reason of its contiguity to himself. It was simply that of a crinkled hag, swart, snake-locked, cowled, her dress jingling with sequins, her right hand clawed upon a crutch. She appeared, in fact, just an old Levantine hoodie-crow, of the breed which was familiar enough to Milan in these cataclysmic days, when all sorts of queer, tragic fowl were being driven northwards from overseas before a tidal wave of Islamism. For half Christendom was writhing at this time under the embroidered slipper of the Turk, while other half was fighting and scratching and backing within its own ranks, in a *sauve qui peut* from Sultan Mahomet's ever nearer-resounding tread.

From Bosnia and Servia and Hungary; from Negropont and the islands of the Greek Archipelago; from new Rome itself, whose desolated houses and markets weeping Amastris had been emptied to repeople; from Trebizond and the Crimea, it came endlessly floating, this waste drift of palaces and temples and antique civilisations, which had been wrecked and scattered by that ruthless hate. Ruined merchants and traders; unfrocked satraps; priests of outlandish garb; girl derelicts blooded and defiled by janissaries; childless mothers and motherless children—scared immigrants all, they wailed and wandered in the towns, denouncing in their despair the creed whose jealousies and corruptions had delivered them to this pass.

In the first of their coming, a certain indignant sympathy had helped to the practical amelioration of their bitter lot. Men scowled and muttered over the histories of their wrongs; took warning for a possible overthrow of the entire Christian Church; talked big of sinking all differences in a kingdom-wide crusade; and, finally, fell to fisticuffs upon the question of a common commander for this problematic host. After which the immigrants, always flocking in thicker, and making civil difficulties, fell gradually subject to an indifference, not to say intolerance, which was at least half as great as that from which they had fled. Fashion, moreover, began to find in the Ser Mahomet a figure more and more attractive, in proportion as he approached it, issuing from the mists of the Orient. It was ravished with, if it did not want to be ravished by, those adorable Spahis, with their tinkling jackets and sashes and melancholy, wicked faces. It adapted prettily to itself the caftan, and the curdee, and the turban; re-read Messer Boccaccio's most Eastern fables; acted them, too, in drawers of rose-coloured damask, and little talpoes, which were tiny jewelled caps of velvet, cocked, and falling over one ear in a tassel. But by that time the cult of immigrancy was discredited *du haut en das*.

Many of the unhappy wretches were drawn by natural process into such sinks as 'The Vineyard.' The poor are good to the poor, and pitiful—which is strange—towards any fall from prosperity. In the instance of this old woman, it was notable how she was humoured of the drifting populace. The very ladroni, who, outside their own rookery, might have tormented and soused her in the kennel, were content here to rally and banter her a little, showing their white teeth to one another in jokes whose bent she was none the worse for misapprehending. For she had not much Italian, it appeared; though what was hers she was turning to the best possible advantage in the matter of fortune-telling.

Tassino saw many brawny palms thrust out for her shrewd conning; echoed from his eyrie many of the *Eccomi perdútos* and *O mè beátos* which greeted her broken sallies. She got a mite here and there, and buzzed and mumbled over it, clutching it to her lean bosom. Presently some distraction, of rape or murder, carried her audience elsewhere, and she was left temporarily alone. Then Tassino, moved by a sudden impulse, reached down his arm through the grate and tapped her reverend crown. She started, and ducked, and peered up. He whispered out to her:—

'Zitto, old mother! Come up here, and tell me my fortune for money.'

She seemed to hesitate; he signified the way; and lo! on a thought she came. He met her at the door, and dragged her in.

'Tell me my fortune,' he said, and thrust out a dirty palm.

She pored over it, chuckling and pattering her little incomprehensible shibboleth. Presently she seemed to pounce triumphantly on a knot. She leered up, her hand still clutching his, her hair falling over her eyes.

'Ah-yah!' she muttered. 'Ringa, ringa!' and shook her head.

He shrugged peevishly:—

'What do you mean, old hag?'

'Ringa!' she repeated: 'no ringa, no fortuna.'

He snatched his hand away.

'What ring, thou cursed harridan?'

She shook her head again.

'No know. Ringa—I see it—green cat-stone—hold off Fortuna. Get, and she change.'

He gnawed his lip, frowning and wondering. There was a ring in question, certainly. Could it be possible its possession was connected somehow with his personal fortunes? If that were so, here was a veritable Pythoness.

Her eyes stared dæmonic: she thrust out a finger, pointing:—

'I see, there: green cat-stone: get, and Fortuna change.'

Superstition mastered him. He trembled before her, quavering:—

'How can I? O mother! how can I?'

A voice in the street startled him. He leapt to the window and back again.

'Narcisso!' he gasped, and ran to bundle out his visitor.

'To-morrow—come again to-morrow—after dark,' he whispered hurriedly. 'I shall be alone—I will pay you—' and he drove her forth. Narcisso met her, issuing from the court below. He growled out a malediction, and came growling into the room.

'You keep nice company, Messer.'

'That is not my fault, beast,' answered Tassino pertly. 'When I choose my own, it is to amuse myself.'

'Well, I hope she amused you?'

'Not so much as I expected. I saw her telling fortunes down below, and called her up to read me mine. Acquaint me of the mystery of a certain ring I asked her; but, oimè! she could enlighten me nothing.'

Narcisso leered at him cunningly, and spat.

'It was as well, perhaps. I see th' art set upon that impertinence; and I'll only say again, "beware!"'

'You may say what you like, old yard-dog,' answered the youth. 'It's your business, chained up here, to snarl.'

But his fat brain was busy all night with the weird Hecate and her necromancy. What did this same ring portend to him, and how was his fate involved in its possession? There *was* a ring in question, doubtless; but whose? Then, all in an amazed moment inspiration flashed upon him. A green cat-stone! Had he not often seen such a ring on Bona's finger? It might indeed be the Duchess's own troth-ring!

He shrunk and cowered at first in the thought of the issues involved in such a possibility. Was it credible that it had been stolen from her? How could he tell, who had been imprisoned here so long? Only, if it were true that it had been, and he, Tassino, could secure it from whatever ravisher, what a weapon indeed it might be made to prove in his hand!

He exulted in that dream of retribution; had almost convinced himself by morning that its realisation lay within his near grasp. She, that old soothsayer, could surely show him the way to possess himself of what her art had so easily revealed to him for his fortune's talisman. This Eastern magic was a strange and terrible thing. He would pay her all he had for the secret!—make crawling love to her, if necessary.

All day he was in a simmer of agitated expectancy; and when dusk at last gathered and swelled he welcomed it as he had never done before. Fortunately Narcisso went out early, and need not be expected back betimes. He was engaged, the morrow being the feast of the Conception, to confess and prepare to communicate himself fasting from midnight; and it was a matter of religion with him on such occasions to take in an especial cargo against the ordeal. Before the streets were dark, Tassino was sitting alone; and so he sat, shuddering and listening, for another hour.

A step at last on the shallow stair! He held his breath. No, he was deceived. Sweating, on tiptoe, he stole to the door and peered out. All was silent, and dark as pitch. Then suddenly, while he looked, there came a muffled tramp and shuffle in the street, and on the instant a figure rose from the well of blackness below, mounting swiftly towards his door. He had barely time to retreat into the unlighted room before he felt his visitor upon him.

'My God!' he quavered; 'who is it? Keep away!' and he backed in ghastly fear to the wall.

'Hush!' (Ludovico's voice.) 'Are you alone?'

The frightened wretch stole forward a step.

'Messer! I thought you— —'

'Never mind,' interrupted the other impatiently. 'Answer me.'

'Quite alone.'

'Humph! I thought you loved the dark less.'

'I—I was about to light the tapers; I swear I was. Wait only one moment, Messer.'

'Stop. No need. The night's the better confidant. Come here.'

Trembling all through, Tassino obeyed. A smooth hand groped, and fastening on his wrist, pressed a hard, round object into his palm. He had much ado not to shriek out.

'What's this?' he gasped.

'Be silent. Have you got it? Put it where it's secure. Well?'

''Tis in the scabbard of my knife, Messer—' (the blade clicked home).

'A good place; keep it there. Now, listen. There's no other here?'

'On my oath, no.'

'Nor on the stair?'

'How can there be between us and Messer's gentlemen?'

'Hark well, then. Thy life depends on it. They 've wind of thee, Tassino.'

'O, O! God pity me!'

'He helps those—you know the saw. 'Tis touch and go—come to this at last; either they destroy you, or you—them.'

'How? O, I shall die!'

'Wilt thou, then? Well, then, if thou wilt. Yet not so much as thy ear-lobe's spark of nerve were needed to forestall and turn the tables on them. They are very fond together, Tassino.'

'Curse them! If I could stab him in the back!'

'Well, why not? Thy scabbard holds the means.'

'My dagger?'

'Better.'

'What?'

'The Duchess's troth-ring.'

'Messer! My God!'

He leapt as if a trigger had clicked at him. Here was to have the gipsy's prophecy, his own fulsome hope, realised at a flash; but with what fearful significances for himself. So this had actually been the ring of contention, and secured at last—he might have known it would be—by Ludovico.

He gave an absurd little shaky laugh, desperately playful.

'How am I to stab with a ring, Messer?'

'Fool! answer for thyself.'

He was crushed immediately.

'By carrying it to the Duke?' he whispered fearfully.

'It is thy suggestion,' said Ludovico—'not for me to traverse. Well?'

'Ah! help me, Messer, for the Lord's sake. I turn in a maze.'

The Prince's thin mouth creased in the dark.

'Nay, 'tis no affair of mine,' he said. 'I am but friendship's deputy.'

Tassino almost whimpered, writhing about in helpless protest.

'He will thunder at me, "Whence reaches me this?"'

'Likely.'

'What shall I reply then?'

'Do you put the case hypothetically? I should answer broadly, on its merits, somehow as follows: "By the right round of intrigue, O Duke, completing love's cycle."'

'O Messer! How am I to understand you?'

'Why, easily—(I speak as one disinterested). Call it the cycle of the ring, and thus it runs: *From the husband to the wife; from the wife to her paramour; from the paramour to his doxy; from the doxy back to the husband.*'

'His doxy? O beast! Hath he a second?'

'Or had. I go by report, which says—but then I 'm no scandalmonger— that a certain lady, Caprona's widow, finds herself scorned of late.'

'And it comes from her—to me? For what? To destroy them both?'

'A shrewd suggestion. In that case your moods run together.'

'Monna Beatrice! She sends it?'

'Does she? Quote me not for it. It were ill so to requite my over-fond friendship. Thou hast the ring. I wish thee well with it. Dost mark?'

'I mark, Messer.'

'Why, so. Thou shouldst suffer after-remorse, having dragged in my name; and there is hellbane, so they tell me, in remorse.'

'I will die before I mention thee in it.'

'Well, I can trust the grave. That's to know a friend. So might I add something to thy credentials.'

'If it please you, Messer.'

'Why, look you, child, love may very well have its procurer—say a State Secretary, where love is of high standing. And thence may follow the subversion of a State. There's a pretender in Milan, they tell me, something an idol of the people—I know not. Only this I ponder: What if there be, and he that same idol which the Duchess is reported to have raised? Would Simonetta, in such case, join in the hymn of praise? One might foresee, if he did, a trinity very strong in the public worship. His Grace, I can't help thinking, would find himself *de trop* here at present. You might put it to him—your own way. When will you set out?'

'When?'

'This moment, I'd advise. To-morrow might mean never. The Duke's at Vigevano—less than six leagues away. A good horse might carry thee there by morning. I've such a one in my stables. He'll honour thee for this service, trust me.'

Tassino's little soul spirted into flame.

'*Viva il duca!*' he piped, and ran to the door.

He drove it before him—it opened outwards—and, descending the dark stairs with his patron, passed into the night.

An hour later he was spurring for Vigevano, while the Prince was engaged in preparing against his own journey to Genoa on the morrow.

.

CHAPTER XXI

Carlo kept his room all day, gnawing and tramping out his problem, and extracting nothing from it. Not till it was deep dark did he call for lights, and then he cursed his page, Ercole, who brought them, because they dazzled his brain from thinking. Swerving on his heel, he was in the act of bidding the boy let no one enter, unless it might be Messer Bembo, when, the door being ajar, there hurried into the chamber the figure of a fantastic hag, who, upon noting his company, stopped suddenly, and stood mumbling and sawing the air.

'Begone!' he roared, astounded, and took a furious step towards her.

She laughed harshly. His clenched fists dropped to his sides. There was no mistaking that bitter cackle. He flung his arm to the page, dismissing him.

The moment the door was shut upon them, off went the cloak and sequins, off went the hood and snaky locks, and the Fool Cicada, clean and lithe in a tight suit of jarnsey, stood revealed.

Carlo leapt upon him, mouthing.

'What mummery, beast, and at such a time? Wait while I choke thee.'

In the tumult of his fury he remembered his promise to Bernardo, and fell back, breathing.

'Hast finished?' said Cicada, acrid and unmoved. 'I could retort upon a fool but for lacking time. Where's the boy?'

'Renegade! What concerns it thee to know?'

'I say, where's the boy?'

'If I might trounce thee! Safe, at present, no thanks to thee.'

'Have I asked any? You must take horse and ride after the ring.'

'The ring!'

'I warn thee, lose not a moment. It may be even now upon the road.'

'The road!'

'That echo's a scrivener. Say after me thus, word for word, so thy skull shall keep the record: *The ring goes this moment to the Duke at Vigevano, in false witness against our Saint. Narcisso gave it to Beatrice, Beatrice to Ludovic, Ludovic to Tassino—and Tassino carries it, wrapped round with fifty damning lies.* Can you fill in the rest?'

'My God! How know you this?'

'I know. Why have I been mumming else?'

'O, thou good Fool!'

'So beatified in a moment? But stay not. To horse, and after, or by luck in front of, this ill-omened popinjay. He must be anticipated, overreached, despoiled, poniarded—anything. I've had my ear to his door—it smarts yet—Ludovic was with him. I was before the Prince and heard him coming—"trapped!" I thought. But the fool looked out—door opens to the stairs—and shut me into its angle against the wall. So again when they left together, and I slipped away behind their worships, and presently ran before. There you've the tale. And so, a' God's name mount and spur, for a minute's delay may kill all. But sith even now it be too late, why, run after to traverse that foul evidence, and the Lord speed thee. Remember—Tassino and the Vigevano road.'

Stunning, bewildering as was the nature of this blast, it served to clear Carlo's brain as a southerly wind clears stagnant water. It meant action, and in action lay his *métier*. Prompt and comprehensive instantly, now that the sum of things had been worked out for him, he dwelt but on the utterance of a single curse—so black and monstrous that the candle-flames seemed to duck to it—before he turned and strode heavily from the room.

'Mercy!' muttered Cicada, tingling where he stood; 'if Monna Beatrice isn't blinking smut out of her eyes at this very moment, there's no virtue in Hell.'

Ten minutes later, Carlo, booted, spurred, and cloaked, issued hurriedly from his quarters, and made for a postern in the north wall, on t' other side of which Ercole, so he had sped his errand well, should be already in waiting with the cavalier's horse, 'l'Inferno,' saddled and bridled for the hunt.

A thin muffle of snow lay on the pavements, choking echo; a thin, still fog, wreathing upwards from it, made everything loom fantastic—curtains, towers, the high battlemented spectres of the sentries.

He clapped his hand to his hip, in assurance of the firm hilt there, and was clearing his throat to answer the guard's challenge, when, on the moment, a whisk of sudden light seemed to overtake and pass him, and he whipped about, with a catch in his breath, to face an expected onset.

Nothing was there. Only the ghosts of mist and snow peopled the ward he had traversed; but, across it, licking and leaping from a high window in the Armourer's Tower, spat a tongue of flame.

He dwelt a moment, fascinated. Faint cries and hurried warnings reached him. The flame shrunk, broke from its curb, and writhed out again.

'Galeazzo's room!' he muttered; 'a red portent to greet him!' and, turning to pursue his way—ran into a vice of arms and was in a moment a prisoner.

The shock was so stunning, that he found himself bound and helpless before he could realise its import. And then he roared out like a lassoed bull:—

'Dogs! What's this?'

The Provost Marshal answered him, waving aside his capturing sbirri.

'Her Grace's warrant, Messer.'

Lanterns seemed to have sprung like funguses from the ground, grossly multiplying the strong company which surrounded him. He stared about him bewildered; then, all in an instant, drove forward like a battering-ram. There was a clash of pikes and mail; an arquebus exploded, luckily without disaster; and Carlo was down in a writhe of men, pounding with his heels.

It brought him nothing but a full interest of bruises. Shortly he was on his feet again, torn and dishevelled; but this time with a thong about his ankles.

He found wisdom of his helplessness to temporise.

'Save thee, Provost Marshal, I have an important errand toward. Spare me to it, and I'll give my parole to deliver up my person to thee on my return.'

The dummy wagged aside the appeal, woodenly.

'I've my orders.'

Carlo lost his brief command of temper.

'Swine! To truss me like a thief?'

'To hold thy person secure, Messer.'

'With ropes, dog?'

'I'll unbind them, on that same parole.'

For all answer, Carlo dropped and rolled on the ground, bellowing curses and defiance. It was childish; but then, what was the great creature but a child? Despair divorced from reason finds its last resource in kicking; and strength of body was always this poor fellow's convincing argument. The presumption that, by his own impulsive retort on Bernardo's assailant, he had brought this cowardly retaliation on himself, made not the least of his anguish. Why could his thick head never learn the craftier ways of diplomacy? And here, in consequence, was he himself scotched, when most required for killing! He bounded like a madman.

It took a dozen of them, hauling and swaying and tottering, to convey him up, and into, and so down again within, the tower of the dungeons. Jacopo had no orders other than for his safe durance and considerate keep; but no doubt that 'swine' weighed a little on the human balance side of the incorruptible blockhead's decision. There was a cell—one adjoining the 'Hermit's'—very profound and safe indeed, though far less deadly in its appointments (so to speak, for the other had none) than its neighbour. And into this cell, by the Provost Marshal's directions, they carried Master Carlo, still struggling and roaring; and, having despoiled him of his weapons, and—with some apprehension—uncorded him, there locked him in incontinent to the enjoyment of his own clamour, which, it may be said, he made the most of up to midnight.

And then, quite suddenly, he broke into tears—a thing horrible in such a man; and casting himself down by the wall, let the flood of despair pass over his head—literally, it almost seemed, in the near cluck and rustle of waters moving in the moat outside.

CHAPTER XXII

In the fortress of Vigevano the Duke of Milan sat at wine with his gentlemen, his dark face a core of gloom, blighting the revel. Flushed cheeks; sparkling cups; hot dyes of silk and velvet, and the starry splintering of gems; sconces of flaming tapers, and, between, banners of purple and crimson, like great moths, hanging on the walls above the heads of shining, motionless men-at-arms, whose staves and helmets trickled light—all this, the whole rich damasked picture, seemed, while the sullen eye commanded it, to poise upon its own fall and change, like the pieces in a kaleidoscope,— the Duke rose and passed out; and already, with a leap and clatter, it had tumbled into a frolic of whirling colours.

This company, in short, conscious of its deserts, had felt any cold-watering of its spirits at the present pass intolerable. There were captains in it, raw from the icy plains of Piedmont, whence they had come after rallying their troops into winter quarters, against a resumption of hostilities in the spring. Tried men of war, and seasoned toss-pots all, they claimed to spend after their mood the wages of valour, vindicated in many a hard-wrung victory. They had stood, Charles the Bold of Burgundy opposing, for the integrity of Savoy, and had trounced its invaders well over the border. The sense of triumph was in them, and, consequently, of grievance that it should be so discounted by a royal mumps, who till yesterday had been their strutting and crowing cock of conquest. What had happened in the interval, so to return him upon his old damned familiar self?

Something beyond their rude guessing—something which, at a breath, had re-enveloped him in that cloud of constitutional gloom, which action and the rush of arms had for a little dispelled. The change had taken him earlier in the day, when, about the hour of Mass, a little white, cake-fed Milanese had come whipping into Vigevano on a foam-dropping jade, and, crying as he clattered over the drawbridge to the castle, 'Ho there, ho there! Despatches for the Duke!' had been snapped up by the portcullis, and gulped and disposed of; and was now, no doubt—since no man had set eyes on him since—in process of being digested.

It may have been he that was disagreeing with their lord, and sending the black bile to his cheek; or it may have been that second tale-bearer who, riding in about midday from the capital, had brought news of the fire which, the evening before, had gutted his Grace's private closet. Small matters in any case; and in any case, the death's-head having withdrawn itself from the feast, hail the bright reaction from that malign, oppressive gloom! A fresh breeze blows through the hall; the candle-flames are jigging to the rafters; away with mumps and glumps! *Via-via*! See the arras blossom into a garden; the sentries, leaning to it, relax into smiling Gabriels of Paradise; the wine froth and sparkle at the cup rim! 'Way, way for the Duke's Grace!' the seneschal had cried at the door; and Galeazzo, clumsily ushered by Messer Castellan, that blunt old one-eyed Cyclops, had slouched heavily out, and the curtain had dropped and blotted him from the record.

He turned sharply to the sound of its thud, and gave a quick little stoop and start, as if he were dodging something. The face—that haunting, indefinable ghost—was it behind him again, unlayed, in spite of all the hope and promise? Why not, since its exorcist had proved himself a Judas?

He ground his teeth, and moved on, muttering and maddening. Only yesterday he had been flattering himself with the thought of returning to his capital wreathed in all the glamour of conquest. And now! False fire—false, damning fire. What victor was he, who could not command himself? What vicegerent of the All-seeing, who could nominate a traitor and hypocrite to be his proxy? And he had so believed in the accursed boy!

The prophecy of the monk Capello stuck like a poisonous burr in his soul. He could not shake it off. Now, he remembered, was the near season for its maturing—a superstition aggravated tenfold by the thought that its ripening had been let to prosper in the sun of his own credulous trust. And he could not temporise while the moment struck and passed, for his fate turned upon the moment. Moreover, Christmas was at hand, a time dear to the traditions of his house; and, rightly or mistakenly, he believed that upon a maintenance of those traditions depended his house's prevalence. His acts must continue to compare royally, in seasonable largesse and bounty, with those of Francesco, its yet adored founder; and he could not afford to ignore those obligations. He felt himself trapped, and turning, turning, between the devil and the deep sea.

But he was not without a sort of desperado courage; and fury lent him nerve.

'Lead on, lead on, Castellano,' he snarled, grinning like a wolf. 'The calf by now should be in train for his blooding.'

They found him stalled deep among the foundations of the fortress, in a stone chamber whose kiln-like conformation shaped itself horribly to the needs and privacies of the 'question.' He might, this Tassino, have been a calf indeed, by the deadly pallor of his flesh. From the moment when, still in the glow of his send-off, he had dared, producing his *pièce de conviction* before the Duke, to incriminate Bona on its evidence, and had been gripped by the neck for his pains, and flung, squealing like a rat, into this sewer, it had never warmed by a degree from this livid hue. Sickened, rather, since here, dreadfully interned throughout the day, like a schoolboy locked in with an impossible imposition, he had been left to writhe and moan, in awful anticipation of the coming inquisition and its likely consequences to himself. They were prefigured for him, in order to the sharp-setting of his wits, in a score or so instruments, all slack and somnolent and unstrung for the time being, but suggestive of hideous potentialities in their tautening. The rack riveted to the floor; the pulley pendent from the ceiling; the stocks in the corner, with the chafing-dish, primed with knobs of charcoal, ready at its foot-holes; the escalero or chevalet, which was a trough for strangling recalcitrant hogs in, limb by limb; the iron dice for forcing into the heels, and the canes for twisting and breaking the fingers; the water-bag and the thumbscrew and the fanged pincers—such, and such in twenty variations of hook and stirrup and dangling monstrosities of block and steel, but all pointing a common moral of terrific human pain, where the inducements to a calmly thought-out self-exculpation which had been offered to Tassino's solitary consideration. No wonder that, when at last the key turned and the harsh door creaked to admit his inquisitors, he should have screamed out with the mortal scream of a creature that finds itself cut off from escape in a burning house.

The Castellan struck him, judicially, across the mouth, and he was silent immediately, falling on his knees and softly chattering bloody teeth. Galeazzo, rubbing his chin, conned him at his smiling leisure; while, motionless and apathetic in the opening of the door, stood a couple of dark, aproned figures, one a Nubian.

'Ebbéne, Messer Tassino,' purred the Duke at length; 'has reconsideration found your indictment open to some revision? Rise, sir—rise.'

He waved his hand loftily. The wretch, after a vain attempt or two, succeeded in getting to his feet, on which he stood like a man palsied. He essayed the while to answer; but somehow his tongue was at odds with his palate.

The Duke, watching him, stealthily lifted his left hand, showing a green stone on one of its fingers.

'Mark ye that?' said he, smiling.

The other's lips moved inaudibly; his glittering eyes were fixed upon the token.

'Say again,' said Galeazzo, 'who charged ye with it to this errand?'

The poor animal mumbled.

'Now hist, now hist, my lord's Grace,' put in the Castellan, the light in his solitary eye travelling like a spark in dead tinder: 'there's an emetic or so here would assist the creature's delivery.'

Tassino gulped and found his voice—or a mockery of it:—

'My lord—spare me—'twas Caprona's widow.'

'And for what purpose?'

The fool, lost in terror, garbled his lesson.

'To destroy the Duchess, whom she hates. I know not: 'twas Messer Ludovic made himself her agent to me.'

'Ho!' cried the Duke, and the monosyllable rolled up and round under the roof, and was returned upon him. 'Here's addition, not subtraction. What more?'

Advancing, with set grinning lips, he thumbed the victim's arm, as he might be a market-wife testing a fowl.

'Plump, plump,' he said, turning his head about. 'Shall we not singe the fat capon, Messer Castellan, before trussing him for the spit?'

At a sign, the two butchers at the door advanced and seized their victim. He struggled desperately in their grasp. Shriek upon shriek issued from his lips. Galeazzo thundered down his cries:—

'Lay him out,' he roared, 'and bare his ribs.'

In a moment Tassino was stretched in the rack, an operator, head and heel, gripping at the spokes of the drums. The Duke came and stood above, contemplative again now, and ingratiatory.

'So!' he said; 'we are in train, at last, for the truth. Tassino, my poor boy, who indeed sent you with this ring to me?'

'O Messer! before God! It was your brother.'

'And acting for whom?'

'The lady, Beatrice.'

'Who had been given it by?'

'Messer Bembo.'

'Ay: and he had received it from — —?'

The poor wretch choked, and was silent. Galeazzo glanced aside: the winches creaked.

'Mercy, in God's name! Mercy!' shrieked the miserable creature. 'I will swear that it was won from her Grace by fraud—that she never knowingly parted with it to—to——'

'Ha!' struck in the Duke; and drew himself up, and pondered awhile blackly.

'My brother—my brother,' ran his thought. 'It may be; it may well be. To ruin her in mine eyes—yes: a fond fool. But a loyal fool. She'd not conspire—not she; nor Simonetta, loyal too—who mistrusts him, and whom he 'd drag down with her. What, Ludovic!—too crafty, too overreaching. Yet, conspiracy there may be, and she its unconscious tool.'

He looked down again, glooming, grating his chin.

'Here's some revision, then. Thou whelp, so to have bitten the hand that stroked thee! Shall I not draw thy teeth for it?'

'Pity, pity!' moaned Tassino. 'I spoke under compulsion.'

'And so shall,' snarled the other. 'What! To mend a slander on compulsion! More physic may bring more cure. Perchance hast made this Countess too thy cats-paw?'

'My lord! No! On my soul!'

'She hates the Duchess?'

'Yes, poisonously.'

'Why?'

'My lord!'

'Why, I say?'

'Alas! she covets for herself what the Duchess claims to heaven.'

'Riddles, swine! Covets! What or whom?'

'O, O! Your Grace's false deputy, Messer Bembo.'

'What! false? You'll stick to it?'

'How can I help?—O! dread my lord, how can I help the truth, unless you 'd wrench from me a travesty of it?'

His breast heaved and sobbed. The tyrant gloomed upon him.

'Is it true, then, he's a traitor?'

'O, the blackest—the most subtle! There can I utter without prompting.'

It was true that he believed he could. Remember how, mongrel though he was, his mind had been fed on slander of our saint.

Galeazzo dropped into a moody reverie. A long quivering sigh thereat broke from his prostrate victim. Mean wits are cunning for themselves; and, looking up into the dark eyes bent above him, Tassino thought he saw reflected there a first faint ghost of hope. O, to hold, to materialise it! He must be infinitely cautious.

He moaned, and wagged his head. The Duke broke out again:—

'False! is he false to me? And yet my wife is true, thou sayest? and yet this woman of Caprona's jealous, thou sayest? Of whom?—O, dog, beware!'

'Master, of a shadow. She reads the woman's baseness in the man's.'

'Ho! Not like thou: what, puppy?'

'Before God, no. 'Tis Madonna's very innocence helps his designs.'

'How?'

'By trusting in, and exalting them for heaven's. She'll wake when it's too late, and weep and curse herself for having betrayed thee.'

'She will? Betray? Too late? These be terms meeter to a rebellion than a schism.'

'Yet must I speak them, weeping, though I die.'

The despot gnawed his lip.

'Hast venom in thee, and with reason, to sting the boy?'

'Alas! to warn thee rather from his fang.'

'Ha!'

'It will lie flat against his palate, till the time when with his subtle eyes he shall invite thy hand to stroke his head. No rebellion, lord; no python rearing on his crushing folds. Yet may the little snake be deadlier.'

He was gathering confidence hair by hair. There were glints of coming tempest, well known to him, blooding the corners of Galeazzo's eyes. He believed, by them, that he should presently ride this storm of his own evoking.

'Ah!' he moaned, 'I'm sick. Mercy, lord! Truth 's not itself unless upright.'

The tyrant tossed his hand:—

'Set the dog on his legs.'

The dog so far justified his title that, being released, he crawled abject on all fours to his master's feet, and crouched there ready to lick them.

'Bah!' cried the Duke, and spurned him. 'Get on thy hind legs, ape! The rope's but slackened from thy hanging; the noose yet cuddles to thy neck. Stand'st there to justify thyself, or answer with a separate rack and screw for every lie thou 'st uttered.'

He strode a pace or two like one demented; turned, snarled out a sudden shocking laugh, and came close up again to the trembling, but still confident wretch.

'See, we'll be reasonable,' he said, mockingly insinuative; 'a twin amity of dialecticians, ardent for the truth, cooing like love-birds. "Well, on my faith, he's a traitor," says you; and "your faith shall be mine on vindication, sweet brother," says I. Now, what proves him traitor? I ask.'

'He rules the palace.'

'Why, I set him in my place.'

'You did indeed; but—ah! dare I say what's whispered?'

'You 'd better.'

'Why—O, mercy! Bid me not.'

'I'll not ask again.'

'You force me to it—that, being there, he designs to stay.'

'He'll be Duke?'

'No, no.'

'You shall wince with better reason. Dog, you dog my patience. I'll turn. What then?'

'Only that he sits for Christ. Let them depose him that are devils' men.'

'My men?'

'O! he's subtle. No word against your Grace; only the dumb pleas of love and pity courting comparison.'

'With what?'

'Your Grace's sharper methods.'

'Beast! Did I not waive them for his sake? Did I not leave my conscience in his keeping?'

'Alas! if thou didst, he's used it, like a false friend, in damning evidence against thee.'

'O Judas!'

'Used it to point the moral of his own large tolerance. The people rise to him—cry him in the streets: "Down with Galeazzo! Nature's our God!"'

'Ha! He's Nature?'

'As they read him—lord of the slums.'

'Lord of filthy swine. I'll ring their snouts. Well, goon. God of the slums, is he?'

'God of thy palace, too; mends and amends thy laws—sugars them for sweet palates—gains the women—O, a prince of confectioners! There's the ring to prove.'

'What!'

'I can guess when he wheedled it.'

'Thou canst?'

'The moment thy back was turned. So quick he sped to discredit thee—to reverse thy judgments. The monk thou'd left to starve, a dog well-served— he'd release him, a fine text to open on. But Jacopo was obdurate—would not let him pass, neither him nor Cicada——'

'What! the Fool?'

'O, they're in one conspiracy—inseparable. He's to be Vizier some day.'

'I'll remember that.'

'So he ran off, and presently returned with a pass-token. I guessed not what at the time; now I guess. It was the ring he'd coaxed from Madonna.'

'And saved the monk thereby?'

'Ah-ha! Jacopo had forestalled him; the monk was dead.'

'What did he then?'

'Cursed thy lord's Grace, and ran; ran and hid himself away among the people, he and his Fool, and spat his poison in that sewer, to fester and bear fruit. 'Twas only presently the Duchess heard of him, and persuaded him on sweet promise of amendment back to the Court. He's made the most of that concession since, using it to——'

He checked himself, and whimpered and sprang back. On the instant the storm which he had dreaded while provoking was burst upon him. Credulous and irrational like all tyrants, Galeazzo never thought to analyse interests and motives in any indictment whose pretext was devotion to himself and his safety. Wrapped in eternal unbelief in all men, no man was so easily arrested as he by the first hint of a plausible rogue professing to serve him, or so quick, being inoculated, to develop the very confluent scab of suspicion. It were well only for Autolycus to make the most of his fees during his little spell of favour, and to disappear on the earliest threat of himself falling victim to the disease he had promoted.

Now, for this dumb-struck quartette of knaves and butchers, was enacted one of those little *danses-diaboliques* in which this fearful man was wont to vent his periodic frenzies. He shrieked and leapt and foamed, racing and twisting to and fro within the narrow confines of the dungeon. Ravings and blasphemies tore and sputtered from his lips; mad destruction issued at his hands. He spurned whatever blocked his path, things living or inanimate; nor seemed to feel or recognise how he bruised himself, but stumbled over, and snatched at, and hurled aside, all that crossed the red vision of his rage. Struggling for coherence, he could force his imprecations but by fits and snatches to rise articulate:—

'Subtle!—I'll be subtler—devil unmasked—no Future?—a specious dog—hell gapes in front—master of my own—to vindicate the monk?— treason against his lord—ha, ha! Jacopo! good servant! good refuter of a sacrilegious hound!'

Then all at once, quite suddenly as it had risen, the tempest passed. Slack, dribbling, hoarse, unashamed, he stopped beside his death-white informer and pawed and mouthed upon him:—

'Why, Tassino! Why—my little honest carver o' joints! Thou mean'st me well, I do believe.'

'O my lord!' cried the trembling rogue, 'if you would but trust me!'

'Why, so I do, Tassino,' urged the Duke, nervously handling and stroking the young man's arm. 'So I do, little pretty varlet. I believe thy story—fie! an impious tale. Deserv'st well of me for that boldness—good courage—the truth needs it. Wilt serve me yet?'

'My lord, to the death.'

'Fie, fie! Not so far, I hope. Yet, listen; 'twere meet this viper were not let to crawl himself within our laurels, and crown our triumph with a poisonous bite. Hey?'

'I understand your Grace.'

'A hint's enough, then. 'Tis no great matter; but these worms will sting.'

'I'll jog Jacopo.'

'You will? He's true to me?'

'O yes!'

'No convert to the other?'

'He hates him well.'

'Does he? A viper has no friends but his kind. This one—hark! a word in your ear. He 'd loose Capello, who damned me, and was damned? Were it not right then the false prophet should take the false prophet's place?'

'Most right.'

'The word's with thee, little chuck. How about the Fool?'

'As bad, or worse, my lord.'

'Hush! Two vipers, do you say?'

'My lord!'

'Be circumspect, that's all. 'Tis our will to give great largesse this Christmastide.'

'The very sound will jingle out his memory—bury the golden calf under gold.'

'Good, little rogue. We'll linger on the Mount meanwhile—just a day or so, to let the promise work. 'Twere a sleeveless triumph through a grudging city. Let these thorns be plucked first from our road.'

'I'll ride at once, saving your Grace.'

'Do so, and tell Jacopo, "Quietly, mind—without fuss."'

'Trust me.'

The Duke flicked his arm and turned, smiling, to the Castellan.

'You shall provide Messer Tassino,' said he smoothly, 'with his liberty, and a swift horse.'

A week later, Sforza the second of Milan set out for his Capital, in all the pomp and circumstance of state which befitted a mighty prince greatly homing after conquest. His path, by all the rules of glory, should have been a bright one; yet his laurels might have been Death's own, from the gloom they cast upon his brow. Last night, looking from his chamber window, he had seen a misty comet cast athwart that track: to-day, scarce had he started, when three ravens, rising from the rice-swamps, had come flapping with hoarse crow to cross it. He had thundered for an arbalest—loosed the quarrel—shot wide—spun the weapon to the ground. An inexplicable horror had seized him. Thenceforth he rode with bent head and glassy eyes fixed upon the crupper. The road of death ran before; behind sat the shadow of his fear, cutting him from retreat. So he reached the Porta Giovia, passed over the drawbridge, in silence dismounted, and for the first time looked up vaguely.

'Black, black!' he muttered to the page who held his horse. 'Let Mass be sung in it to-morrow, and for the chaunts be dirges. See to it.'

Did he hope so to hoodwink heaven, by abasing himself in the vestments of remorse? Likely enough. He had always been cunning to hold from it the worst of his confidence.

But in the thick of the night a voice came to him, blown upon the wind of dreams:—

'No Future, O, no Future! Look to thy Past!'

And he started up in terror, quavering aloud:—

'Who's that that being dead yet speaketh!'

CHAPTER XXIII

It is remarkable how quickly the brute genii will adapt himself to his pint bottle when once the cork is in. Elastic, it must be remembered, has the two properties of expansion and retraction, the latter being in corresponding proportion with the former. Wherefore, the greater its stretching capacity the more compact its compass unstretched.

So it is with life, which is elastic, and mostly lived at a tension. Relax that tension, and behold the buoyant temperament rinding roomier quarters in a straitened confinement than would ever a flaccid one in the same; and this in defiance of Bonnivard, that fettered Nimrod of the mountains, whose heart broke early in captivity, and who, nevertheless, as a matter of fact, did not exist.

The truth is, a pint pot is over-enough to contain the mind of many an honest vigorous fellow; and it is the mind, rather than the body, which struggles for elbow-room. Carlo, in his prison, suffered little from that mere mental horror of circumscription which, to a more sensitive soul, had been the infinite worst of his doom. He champed, and stamped, and raged, sure enough; cursed his fate, his impotence, his restrictions; but all from a cleaner standpoint than the nerves—from one (no credit to him for that) less constitutionally personal. That he should be shut from the possibility of helping in a sore pass the little friend of his love, of his faith, of his adoration—the pretty child who had needed, never so much as at this moment, the help and protection of his strong arm—here was the true madness of his condition. And he bore it hardly, while the fit possessed him, and until physical exhaustion made room for the little reserves of reason which all the time had been waiting on its collapse.

Then, suddenly, he became very quiet; an amenable, wicked, dangerous thing; fed greedily; nursed his muscles; spake his gaolers softly when they visited him; refrained from asking useless questions to elicit evasive answers; brooded by the hour together when alone. They treated him with every consideration; answered practically his demands for books, paper, pens and ink, wine—for all bodily ameliorations of his lot which he chose to suggest, short of the means to escape it. There, only, was there no concession—no response to the request of an insulted cavalier to be returned the weapons of his honour of which he had been basely mulcted. His fingers must serve his mouth, he was told, and his teeth his meat—they were sharp enough. At which he would grin, and click those white knives together, and return to his brooding.

But not, at last, for long. Very soon he was engaged in exploring his dungeon, a gloomy cellar, two-thirds of it below the level of the moat, and lit by a single window, deep-shafted under the massive ceiling. His search, at first, yielded him no returns but of impenetrable induracy—no variations, knock where he might, in the echoless irresponsiveness of dumb-thick walls. Only, with that incessant tap-tapping of his, the trouble in his brain fell into rhythm, chiming out eternally, monotonously, the inevitable answer to a fruitless question with which, from the outset, he had been tormenting himself, and from which, for all his sickness of its vanity, he could not escape.

'What hath Cicada done? Concluded me safely sped? Done nothing, therefore. What hath Cicada done? Concluded me safely sped? Done nothing, therefore.'

So, the villainy was working, and he in his dungeon powerless to counteract it.

He lived vividly through all these phases—of despair, of self-concentration, of resourceful hope—during the opening twenty-four hours of his confinement. And then, once upon a time, very suddenly, very softly, very remotely, there was borne in upon him the strange impression that he was not alone in his underworld.

The first shadow of this conviction came to haunt him during the second night of his imprisonment, when, having fallen asleep, there presently stole into his brain, out of a deep sub-consciousness of consciousness, the knowledge that some voice, extraneous to himself, was moaning and throbbing into his ear.

At the outset this voice appealed to him for nothing more than the emotional soft babble of a dream. It seemed to reach to him from a vast distance, breathing very faint, and thin, and sweet through æons of pathetic memories. He could not identify or interpret it, save in so far as its burden always hinted of a wistful sadness. But, gradually, as the spell of it enwrapped and claimed him, out of its inarticulateness grew form, and out of that form recognition.

It was Bernardo singing to his lute. How could he not have known it, when here was the boy actually walking by his side? They trod a smiling meadow, sweet with narcissus and musical with runnels. The voice made ecstasy of the Spring; frisked in the blood of little goats; unlocked the sap of trees, so that they leapt into a spangled spray of blossoms.

A step—and the turf was dry beneath their feet. The sun smote down upon the plain; the grasshopper shrieked like a jet of fire; the full-uddered cattle lowed for evening and the shadowed stall.

Again, a step—and the leaves of the forest blew abroad like flakes of burning paper; the vines shed fruit like heavy drops of blood; the sky grew dark in front, rolling towards them a dun wall of fog—the music wailed and ceased.

He turned upon his comrade; and saw the lute swung aside, the pale lips yet trembling with their song. He knew the truth at once.

'We part here,' he murmured. 'Is it not? So swiftly run thy seasons. And you return to Spring; and I—O, I, go on! Whither, sweet angel? O, wilt thou not linger a little, that, reaching mine allotted end, I may hurry back to overtake thee?'

Then, clasping his hands in agony, the tears running down his cheeks, he saw how the boy bent to whisper in his ear—words of divine solace— nay, not words, but music—music, music all, of an unutterable pathos.

And he awoke, to hear the shrunk, inarticulate murmur of it still whispering to his heart.

He sat up, panting, in the deep blackness. His hands trembled; his face was actually wet. But the music had not ended with his dream. Grown very soft and far and remote, it yet went sounding on in fact—or was it only in fancy?

His still-drugged brain surged back into slumber on the thought. Instantly the voice began to take shape and reality: he caught himself from the mist—as instantly it fell again into a phantom of itself.

And thus it always happened. So surely as he listened wakeful, straining his hearing, the voice would reach him as a far plaintive murmur, a vague intolerable sweetness, without identity or suggestion save of some woful loss. So surely did his brain swerve and his aching eyes seal down, it would begin to gather form, and words out of form, and expression out of words— expression, of a sorrow so wildly sad and moving, that his dreaming heart near broke beneath the burden of its grief.

A strange experience; yet none so strange but that we must all have known it, what time our errant soul has leapt back into our waking consciousness, carrying with it, on the wind of its return, some echo of the spirit world with which it had been consorting. Who has not known what it is to wake, in a dumb sleeping house, to the certain knowledge of a cry just uttered, a sentence just spoken, of a laugh or whisper stricken silent on the instant, nor felt the darkness of his room vibrate and settle into blankness as he listened, and, listening, lost the substance of that phantom utterance?

But at length for Carlo dream and reality were blended in one forgetfulness.

Morning weakened, if it could not altogether dissipate, his superstitions. Though one be buried in a vault, there's that in the mere texture of daylight, even if the thinnest and frowziest, to muffle the fine sense of hearing. If, in truth, those mystic harmonics still throbbed and sighed, his mind had ceased to be attuned to them. He lent it to the more practical business of resuming his examination of his prison.

At midday, while he was sitting at his dinner, a visitor came and introduced himself to him, leaping, very bold and impudent, to the table itself, where he sat up, trimming his whiskers anticipatory. It was a monstrous brown rat; and self-possessed—Lord! Carlo dropped his fists on the cloth, and stared, and then fell to grinning.

'O, you've arrived, have you!' said he. 'Your servant, Messer Topo!'

It was obviously the gentleman's name. At the sound of it, he lowered his fore-paws, flopped a step or two nearer, and sat up again. Carlo considered him delightedly. He was one of those men between whom and animals is always a sympathetic confidence.

'Is it, Messer Topo,' said he, 'that you desire to honour me with the reversion of a former friendship? What! You flip your whiskers in protest? No friend, you imply, who could educate your palate to cooked meats, and then betray it, returning you to old husks? Has he deserted you, then? Alas, Messer! We who frequent these cellars are not masters of our exits and our entrances. How passed he from your ken, that same unknown? Feet-first? Face-first? Tell me, and I'll answer for his faith or faithlessness.'

The visitor showed some signs of impatience.

'What!' cried Carlo. 'My grace is overlong? Shall we fall to? Yet, soft. Fain would I know first the value of this proffered love, which, to my base mind, seems to smack a little of the cupboard.'

His hand went into the dish. Messer Topo ceased from preening his moustache, and stiffened expectant, his paws erect.

'Ha-ha!' cried Carlo. 'You are there, are you? O, Messer Topo, Messer Topo! Even prisoners, I find, possess their parasites.'

He held out a morsel of meat. The big rat took it confidently in his paws; tested, and approved it; sat up for more.

'What manners!' admired Carlo. 'Art the very pink of Topos. Come, then; we'll dine together.'

Messer Topo acquitted himself with perfect correctness. When satisfied, he sat down and cleaned himself. Carlo ventured to scratch his head. He paused, to submit politely to the attention—which, though undesired, he accepted on its merits—then, the hand being withdrawn, waited a moment for courtesy's sake, and returned to his scouring. In the midst, the key grated in the door, and like a flash he was gone.

'Ehi!' pondered Carlo; 'it is very evident he has been trained to shy at authority.'

It seemed so, indeed, and that authority knew nothing of him. Otherwise, probably, authority would have resented his interference with its theories of solitary confinement to the extent of trapping and killing him.

The prisoner saw no more of his little sedate visitor that evening; but, with night and sleep, the voice again took up the tale of his haunting; and this time, somehow, to his dreaming senses, Messer Topo seemed to be the medium of its piteous conveyance to him. Once more he woke, and slept, and woke again; and always to hear the faint music gaining or losing body in opposite ratio with his consciousness. He was troubled and perplexed; awake by dawn, and harking for confirmation of his dreams. But daylight plugged his hearing.

He had expected Messer Topo to breakfast. He did not come. He called— and there he was. They exchanged confidences and discussed biscuits. The key grated, and Messer Topo was gone.

This day Carlo set himself to solve the mystery of his visitor's lightning disappearances—*Anglicè*, to find a rat-hole. Fingering, in the gloom, along the joint of floor and wall, he presently discovered a jagged hole which he thought might explain. Without removing his hand, he called softly: 'Topo! Messer Topo!' Instantly a little sharp snout, tipped with a chilly nose, touched him and withdrew. He stood up, as the key turned in the lock once more.

This time it was Messer Jacopo himself who entered, while his bulldogs watched at the door. He came to bring the prisoner a volume of Martial, which Carlo had once had recommended to him, and of which he had since bethought himself as a possible solace in his gloom. The Provost Marshal advanced, with the book in his hand, and seeing his captive's occupation, as he thought, paused, with a dry smile on his lips. Then, with his free palm, he caressed the wall thereabouts.

'Strong masonry, Messer,' he said; 'good four feet thick. And what beyond? A dungeon, deadlier than thine own.'

Carlo laughed.

'A heavy task for nails, old hold-fast, sith you have left me nothing else. *Lasciate ogni speranza*, hey, and all the rest? I know, I know. Yet, look you, there should have been coming and going here once, to judge by the tokens.'

He signified, with a sweep of his hand, a square patch on the stones, roughly suggestive of a blocked doorway, wherein the mortar certainly appeared of a date more recent than the rest.

The other made a grim mouth.

'Coming, Messer,' he said; 'but little going. Half-way he sticks who entered, waiting for the last trump. He'll not move until.'

Carlo recoiled.

'There's one immured there?'

'Ay, these ten years——'

And the wooden creature, laying the book on the table, stalked out like an automaton.

He left the prisoner gulping and staring. Here, in sooth, was food for his fancy, luckily no great possession. But the horror bit him, nevertheless. Presently he took up the book—tried to forget himself in it. He found it certainly very funny, and laughed: found it very gross, and laughed—and then thought of Bernardo, and frowned, and threw the thing into a corner. Then he started to his feet and went up and down, nervously, with stealthy glances to the wall. Haunted! No wonder he was haunted. Did it sob and moan in there o' nights, beating with its poor blind hands on the stone? Did it——

A thought stung him, and he stopped. The rat! Its run broke into that newer mortar, penetrated, perhaps, as far as the buried horror itself. Was *there* the secret of the music? Was it wont, that hapless spectre, putting its pallid lips to the hole, to sigh nightly through it its melodious tale of griefs?

He stood gnawing his thumb-nail.

What might it be—man or woman? There was that legend of a nun with child by—Nay, horrible! What might it be? Nothing at this last, surely—sexless—just a spongy chalk of bones, a soft rubble for rats to nest in. O, Messer Topo, Messer Topo! on what dust of human tragedy did you make your bed! Perhaps——

No! perish the thought! Messer Topo was a gentleman—descendant of a long line of gentlemen—no hereditary cannibal. He preferred meats cooked to raw. An hereditary guardian, rather, of that flagrant tomb. And yet—

He lay down to rest that night, lay rigid for a long while, battling with a monstrous soul-terror. A burst of perspiration relieved him at last, and he sank into oblivion.

Then, lo! swift and instant, it seemed, the unearthly music caught him in its spell. It was more poignant than he had known it yet—loud, piercing, leaping like the flame of a blown candle. He awoke, sweating and trembling. The vibration of that gale of sorrow seemed yet ringing in his ears—from the walls, from the ceiling, from the glass rim of his drinking-vessel on the table, which repeated it in a thousand tinkling chimes. But again the voice itself had attenuated to a ghost of sound—a mere Æolian thread of sweetness.

But it was a voice.

Carlo sat up on his litter. He was a man of obdurate will, of a conquering resolution; and the moment, unnerving as it seized him out of sleep, found him nevertheless decided. A shaft of green moonlight struck down from the high grate into his dungeon, spreading like oil where it fell; floating over floor and table; leaving little dark objects stranded in its midst. Its upper part, reflecting the moving waters of the moat outside, seemed to boil and curdle in a frantic dance of atoms, as though the spirit music were rising thither in soundless bubbles.

He listened a minute, scarce breathing; then dropped softly to the floor, and stole across his chamber, and stooped and listened at the wall.

The next moment he had risen and staggered back, panting, glaring with dilated eyes into the dark. There was no longer doubt. It was by way of Messer Topo's pierced channel that the music had come welling to him.

But whence?

Commanding himself by a tense effort, he bent once more, and listened. Long now—so long, that one might have heard the passion in his heart conceive, and writhe, and grow big, and at length deliver itself in a fierce and woful cry: 'Bernardo! my little, little brother!'

With the words, he leapt up and away—tore hither and thither like a madman—mouthed broken imprecations, fought for articulate speech and self-control. The truth—all the wicked, damnable truth—had burst upon him in a flash. No ghostly voice was this of a ten years immured; but one, now recognised, sweet and human beyond compare, the piteous solution of all his hauntings. The run pierced further than to that middle tragedy—

pierced to a tragedy more intimate and dreadful—pierced through into the adjoining cell, where lay his child, his little love, perishing of cold and hunger. He read it all in an instant—the disastrous consequences of his own disaster. And he could not comfort or intervene while this, his pretty swan, was singing himself to death hard by.

Pity him in that minute. I think, poor wretch, his state was near the worse—so strong, and yet so helpless. He shrieked, he struck himself, he blasphemed. Monstrous? it was monstrous beyond all human limits of malignity. So the ring had sped and wrought! What had this angel done, but been an angel? What had Cicada, so hide-bound in his own conceit of folly? Curst watchdogs both, to let themselves be fooled and chained away while the wolf was ravening their lamb!

He sobbed, fighting for breath:—

'Messer Topo, Messer Topo! Thou art the only gentleman! I crave thy forgiveness, O, I crave thy forgiveness for that slander! A rat! I'll love them always—a better gentleman, a better friend, bringing us together!'

With the thought, he flung himself down on the floor, and put his ear to the hole. Still, very faint and remote, the music came leaking by it—a voice; the throb of a lute.

He changed his ear for his lips:—

'Bernardo!' he screamed; 'Bernardo! Bernardo!' and listened anew.

The music had ceased—that was certain. It was succeeded by a confused, indistinguishable murmur, which in its turn died away.

'Bernardo!' he screeched again, and lay hungering for an answer.

It came to him, suddenly, in one rapturous soft cry:—

'Carlo!'

No more. The sweet heart seemed to break, the broken spirit to wing on it. Thereafter was silence, awful and eternal.

He called again and again—no response. He rose, and resumed his maddened race, to and fro, praying, weeping, clutching at his throat. At length worn out, he threw himself once more by the wall, his ear to the hole, and lying there, sank into a sort of swoon.

Messer Topo, sniffing sympathetically at his face, awoke him. He sat up; remembered; stooped down; sought to cry the dear name again, and found his voice a mere whisper. That crowned his misery. But he could still listen.

No sound, however, rewarded him. He spent the day in a dreadful tension between hope and despair—snarled over the periodic visits of his gaolers—snarled them from his presence—was for ever crouching and listening. They fancied his wits going, and nudged one another and grinned. He never thought to question them; was always one of those strong souls who find, not ask, the way to their own ends. He knew they would lie to him, and was only impatient of their company. Seeing his state, they were at the trouble to take some extra precautions, always posting a guard on the stairs before entering his cell. Messer Lanti, normal, was sufficiently formidable; possessed, there was no foretelling his possibilities.

But they might have reassured themselves. Escape, at the moment, was farthest from his thoughts or wishes. He would have stood for his dungeon against the world; he clung to his wall, like a frozen ragamuffin to the outside of a baker's oven.

Presently he bethought himself of an occupation, at once suggestive and time-killing. He had been wearing his spurs when captured—weapons, of a sort, overlooked in the removal of deadlier—and these, in view of vague contingencies, he had taken off and hidden in his bed. His precaution was justified; he saw a certain use for them now; and so, procuring them, set to work to enlarge with their rowels the opening of the rat hole. He wrought busily and energetically. Messer Topo sat by him a good deal, watching, with courteous and even curious forbearance, this really insolent desecration of his front door. They dined together as usual; and then Carlo returned to his work. His plan was to enlarge the opening into a funnel-like mouth, meeter for receiving and conveying sounds. It had occurred to him that the point of the tiny passage's issue into the next cell might be difficult of localisation by one imprisoned there, especially if the search—as he writhed to picture it—was to be made in a blinding gloom. If he could only have continued to help by his voice—to cry 'Here! Here!' in this tragic game of hide-and-seek! He wrought dumbly, savagely, nursing his lungs against that moment. But still by night it had not come to be his.

Then, all in an instant, an inspiration came to him. He sat down, and wrote upon a slip of paper: 'From Carlo Lanti, prisoner and neighbour. Mark who brings thee this—whence he issues, and whither returns. Speak, then, by that road—' and having summoned Messer Topo, fastened the billet by a thread about his neck, and, carrying him to his run, dismissed him into it. Wonder of wonders! the great little beast disappeared upon his errand. Henceforth kill them for vermin that called the rat by such a name!

Messer Topo did not return. What matter, if he had sped his mission? Only, had he? There was the torture. Hour after hour went by, and still no sign.

Carlo fell asleep, with his ear to the funnel. That night the music did not visit him. He awoke—to daylight, and the knowledge of a sudden cry in his brain. Tremulous, he turned, and found his voice had come back to him, and cleared it, and quavered hoarsely into the hole, 'Who speaks? Who's there?'

He dwelt in agony on the answer—thin, exhausted, a croaking gasp, it reached him at length:—

'Cicca—the Fool—near sped.'

'The Fool! Thou—thou and none other?' His cry was like a wolf's at night; 'none other? Bernardo!' he screeched.

A pause—then: 'Dead, dead, dead!' came wheezing and pouring from the hole.

'Ah!'

He fell back; swayed in a mortal vertigo; rallied. He was quite calm on the instant—calm?—a rigid, bloodless devil. He set his mouth and spoke, picking his words:—

'So? Is it so? All trapped together, then? When did he die?'

'Quick!' clucked the voice; 'quick, and let me pass. When, say'st? Time's dead and rotten here. I know not. A' heard thee call—and roused—and shrieked thy name. His heart broke on it. A' spoke never again. All's said and done. What more? I could not find the hole—till thy rat came. Speak quick.'

What more? What more to mend or mar? Nothing, now. Hope was as dead as Time—a poxed and filthy corpse. Love, Faith, and Charity—dead and putrid. Only two things remained—two things to hug and fondle: revenge and Messer Topo. He bent and spoke again:—

'Starved to death?'

'Starved——'

The queer, far little mutter seemed to reel and swerve into a tinkle—an echo—was gone. Carlo called, and called again—no answer. Then he set himself to ruminate—a cud of gall and poison.

On the eighth morning of his confinement, Jacopo, in person and alone, suddenly showed himself at the door, which he threw wide open.

'Free, Messer,' he said; 'and summoned under urgency to the palace.'

Carlo nodded, and asked not a single question, receiving even his weapons back in silence. He had had a certain presentiment that this moment would arrive. He begged only that the Provost Marshal would leave him to himself a minute. He had some thanks to offer up, he said, with a smile, which had been better understood and dreaded by a gentler soul.

The master gaoler was a religious man, and acquiesced willingly, going forward a little up the stairway, that the other might be private. Carlo, thereupon, stepped across to the wall, and whispered for Messer Topo.

The big rat responded at once, coming out and sitting up at attention. Carlo put his hands under his shoulders, and lifting him (the two were by now on the closest terms of intimacy), apostrophised him face to face:—

'My true, mine only friend at last,' he said (his voice was thick and choking). 'I must go, leaving him to thee. Be reverent with him for my sake—ah! if I return not anon, to carry out and plant that sweet corse in the daisied grass he loved—not dust to dust, but flower to the dear flowers. Look to it. Shall I never see him more—nor thee? I know not. I've that to do first may part us to eternity—yet must I do it. Come, kiss me God-be-with-ye. Nay, that's a false word. How can He, and this bloody ensign on my brow? My brain in me doth knell already like a leper's bell. Canst hear it, red-eyes? No God for me. Why should I need Him—tell me that? Christ could not save His friend. I must go alone—quite alone at last. Only remember I loved thee—always remember that. And so, thou fond and pretty thing, farewell.'

He put his lips to the little furry head; put the animal gently down; longed to it a moment; then, as it disappeared into its run, turned with a wet and burdened sigh.

But, even with the sound, a black and gripping frost seemed to fall upon him. He drew himself up, set his face to the door, and passed out and on to freedom and the woful deed he contemplated.

CHAPTER XXIV

A despotism (Messer Bembo invitus) is the only absolute expression of automatic government. The fly-wheel moves, and every detail of the machinery, saw, knife, or punch, however distant, responds instantly to its initiative. Galeazzo, for example, had but to make, in Vigevano, the tenth part of a revolution, and behold, in Milan! Messer Jacopo—saw, knife, and punch in one—had 'come down,' automatically, upon the objectives of that movement. Within a few minutes of Tassino's return, Bernardo and his Fool, seized quietly and without resistance as they were taking the air on the battlements, were being lowered with cords into the 'Hermit's Cell.'

Sic itur ad astra.

The Duke of Milan re-entered his capital on the 20th of December. His Duchess met him with happy smiles and tears, loving complaints over his long absence, a sweet tongue ready with vindication of her trust, should that be demanded of her. The last week had done much to reassure her, in the near return to familiar conditions which it had witnessed; and she felt herself almost in a position to restore to her Bluebeard the key, unviolated, of the forbidden chamber. If only he would accept that earnest of her loyalty without too close a questioning!

And, to her joy, he did; inasmuch, you see, as he had his own reasons for a diplomatic silence. It would appear, indeed, that recent great events had altogether banished from his memory the pious circumstances of his departure to them. He had returned to find his duchy as to all moral intents he had left and could have wished to recover it. The fashion of Nature had shed its petals with the summer brocades, and Milan was itself again.

For the exquisite, who had set it, was vanished now some seven days gone; and that is a long time for the straining out of a popular fashion. He had departed, carrying his Fool with him, none—save one or two in the secret—knew whither; but surmise was plentiful, and for the most part rabid. That he had fallen out of home favour latterly was obvious and flagrant; now, the report grew that this alienation had received its first impetus from Piedmont. That whisper in itself was Nature's very quietus. Eleven out of a dozen presumed upon it, and themselves, to propitiate tyranny with a very debauch of reactionism to old licence. Moreover, scandal, in mere self-justification, must run intolerable riot. Nothing was too gross for it in its accounting for this secession. The pure love which had striven to redeem it, it tortured into a text for filthy slanders. The Countess of Caprona had her windows stoned in retaliation one day by a resentful crowd; the wretched girl Lucia was dragged from her bed and suffocated in a muddy ditch. The logic of the mob.

The most merciful of these tales represented Bembo as having run back to San Zeno, there to hide in terror and trembling his diminished head. It was the solution of things most comforting to Bona—one on which her conscience found repose. She wished the boy no evil; had acted as she did merely in the interests of the State, she told herself. If, for a moment, her thoughts ever swerved to Tassino—now returned, as it was whispered, to his old quarters with the Provost Marshal, and abiding there a readjustment of affairs—she hid the treason under a lovely blush, and vowed herself for ever more true wife and incorruptible.

So for the most part all was satisfactory again; and there remained only to alienate the popular sympathy from its idol. And that the Church undertook to do. The moment the false prophet was exposed and deposed, it rose, shook the crumbs from its lap, and gave him his *coup de grâce* in the public estimation.

'He but sought,' it thundered, 'to turn ye over, clods; to cleanse your gross soil for the fairer growing of his roses.' A parable: but so far comprehensible to the demos in that it implied its narrow escape from some cleaning process, a vindication of its prescriptive rights to go unwashed, and therefore convincing. Down sank the threatening swine-monster thereon; and, being further played upon with comfits of a festal Christmas-tide, did yield up incontinent its last breath of revivalism, and kick in joyful reassurance of its sty.

So the whole city absolved itself of redemption, and set to making enthusiastic provision for the devil's entertainment against the season of peace and goodwill.

Si finis bonus est, totum bonum erit: nor less *Bona bona erit*. Only there was a rift within the happy wife's lute, which somehow put the whole orchestra out of tune. She saw, for all her sweet chastened sense of relief, that the Duke was darkly troubled. The oppression of his mood communicated itself to hers; and she began to dream—horrible visions of cloyed fingers, and clinging shrouds, and ropey cobwebs that would drop and lace her mouth and nostrils, the while she could not fight free a hand to clear them.

Then, double-damned in his own depression, by reason of its reacting through his partner on himself, the Duke one day sent for the Provost Marshal.

'The season claims its mercies,' gloomed he. 'Take the boy out and send him home to his father.'

'His father!' jeered Jacopo brusquely, grunting in his beard. 'A's been safe in his bosom these three days.'

'What!' gasped the tyrant.

'Dead, Messer, dead, that's all,' said the other impassively; 'passed in a moment, like a summer shower.'

There was nothing more to be said, then. As for poor Patch, he was too cheap a mend-conscience for the ducal mind even to consider. It took instead to brooding more and more on the drawn whiteness of its Duchess's face, hating and sickened by it, yet fascinated. The air seemed full of portents in its ghostly glimmer. His fingers were always itching to strike the hot blood into it. A loathly suspicion seized him that perhaps here, after all, was revealed the illusive face of his long haunting. Constantly he fancied he saw reflected in other faces about him some shadow of its menacing woe. Once he came near stabbing a lieutenant of his guards, one Lampugnani, for no better reason than that he had caught the fellow's eyes fixed upon him.

So the jovial season sped, and Christmas day was come and gone, bringing with it and leaving, out of conviviality, some surcease of his self-torment.

But, on that holy night, Madonna Bona was visited by a dream, more ugly and more definite than any that had terrified her hitherto. Groping in a vast cathedral gloom, she had come suddenly upon a murdered body prostrate on the stones. Dim, shadowy shapes were thronged around; the organ thundered, and at its every peal the corpse from a hundred hideous wounds spouted jets of blood. She turned to run; the gloating stream pursued her—rose to her hips, her lips—she awoke choking and screaming.

That morning—it was St. Stephen's Day—the Duke was to hear Mass in the private chapel of the castello. He rose to attend it, only to find that, by some misunderstanding, the court chaplain had already departed, with the sacred vessels, for the church dedicated to the Saint. The Bishop of Como, summoned to take his place, declined on the score of illness. Galeazzo decided to follow his chaplain.

Bona strove frantically to dissuade him from going. He read some confirmation of his shapeless suspicions in her urgency, and was the more determined. She persisted; he came near striking her in his fury, and finally drove her from his presence, weeping and clamorous.

She was in despair, turning hither and thither, trusting no one. At length she bethought herself of an honest fellow, always a loyal friend and soldier of her lord, of whom, in this distracting pass, she might make use. She had spoken nothing to the Duke of her disposal of his favourite, Messer Lanti, leaving the explanation of her conduct to an auspicious moment. Now, in her emergency, she sent a message for Carlo's instant release, bidding him repair without delay to the palace. She had no reason, nor logic, nor any particular morality. She was in need, and lusting for help—that was enough.

The messenger sped, and returned, but so did not the prisoner with him. Bona, sobbing, feverish, at the wit's end of her resources, went from member to member of her lord's suite, imploring each to intervene. As well ask the jackalls to reprove the lion for his arrogance.

At eleven the Duke set out. His valet and chronicler, Bernardino Corio, relates how, at this pass, his master's behaviour seemed fraught with indecision and melancholy; how he put on, and then off, his coat of mail, because it made him look too stout; how he feared, yet was anxious to go, because 'some of his mistresses' would be expecting him in the church (the true explanation of his unharnessing, perhaps); how he halted before descending the stairs; how he called for his children, and appeared hardly able to tear himself away from them; how Madonna Catherine rallied him with a kiss and a quip; how at length, reluctantly, he left the castle on foot, but, finding snow on the ground, decided upon mounting his horse.

Viva! Viva! See the fine portly gentleman come forth—tall, handsome, they called him—in his petti-cote of crimson brocade, costly-furred and opened in front to reveal the doublet beneath, a blaze of gold-cloth torrid with rubies; see the flash and glitter that break out all over him, surface coruscations, as it were, of an inner fire; see his face, already chilling to ashes, livid beneath the sparkle of its jewelled berretino! Is it that his glory consumes himself? Viva! Viva!—if much shouting can frighten away the shadow that lies in the hollow of his cheek. It is thrown by one, invisible, that mounted behind him when he mounted, and now sits between his greatness and the sun. Viva! Viva! So, with the roar of life in his ears, he passes on to the eternal silence.

As he rides he whips his head hither and thither, each glance of his eyes a quick furtive stab, a veritable *coup d'[oe]il*. He is gnawed and corroded with suspicion, mortally *nervous*—his manner lacks repose. It shall soon find it. He will make a stately recumbent figure on a tomb.

The valet, after releasing his master's bridle, has run on by a short cut to the church, where, at the door, he comes across Messers Lampugnani and Olgiati lolling arm in arm. They wear *coats and stockings of mail, and short capes of red satin.* Corio wonders to see them there, instead of in their right places among the Duke's escort. But it is no matter of his. There are some gentlemen will risk a good deal to assert their independence—or insolence.

In the meanwhile, the motley crowd gathering, the Duke's progress is slow. All the better for discussing him and his accompanying magnificence. He rides between the envoys of Ferrara and Mantua, a gorgeous nucleus to a brilliant nebula. This, after all, is more 'filling' than Nature. Some one likens him, audibly, to the head of a comet, trailing glory in his wake. He turns sharply, with a scowl. 'Uh! Come sta duro!' mutters the delinquent. 'Like a thunderbolt, rather!'

At length he reaches the church door and dismounts. He throws his reins to a huge Moor, standing ready, and sets his lips.

From within burst forth the strains of the choir—

'*Sic transit gloria mundi,*'

Bowing his head, he passes on to his doom.

CHAPTER XXV

'That being dead yet speaketh'

Through the chiming stars, the romp of wind in woods, the gush of spring freshets, the cheery drone of bees; through all happy gales—of innocent frolic, of children's laughter, of sighing, unharmful passion, of joy and gaiety ungrudging; through the associations of his gentle spirit with these, the things it had loved, whereby, by those who had listened and could not altogether forget, came gradually to be vindicated the truth of his kind religion, Bernardo's voice, though grown a phantom voice, spoke on and echoed down the ages. Sweet babble at the hill-head, it was yet the progenitor of the booming flood which came to take the world with knowledge—knowledge of its own second redemption through the humanity which is born of Nature. Already Art, life's nurse and tutor, was, unknown to itself, quickening from the embrace of clouds and sunlight and tender foliage; while, unconscious of the strange destinies in its womb, it was scorning and reviling the little priest who had brought about that union.

And, alas! it is always so. Nor profit nor credit are ever to the pioneer who opens out the countries which are to yield his followers both.

He perished very soon. Its third night of darkness and starvation saw the passing of that fragile spirit, gentle, innocuous, uncomplaining as it had lived. Frail as a bird that dies of the shock of capture, he broke his heart upon a song.

I would have no gloomy obsequies attend his fate. In tears, and strewing of flowers, and pretty plaintive dirges of the fields—in sighs and lutes of love, such as waited on the sweet Fidele, would I have ye honour him. Not because I would belittle that piercing tragedy, but because he would. It was none to him. He but turned his face for home, sorrowing only for his failure to win to his Christ, his comrade, a kingdom he should never have the chance to influence again. What had he else to fear? The star that had mothered, the road that had sped him? All grass and flowers was the latter; of the first, a fore-ray seemed already to have pierced the darkness of his cell, linking it to heaven.

'"Let's sing him to the ground."

"I cannot sing; I'll weep, and word it with thee;
For notes of sorrow, out of tune, are worse
Than priests and fanes that lie."'

Bring hither, I say, no passion of a vengeful hate. It is the passing of a rose in winter.

At near the end, lying in his Fool's arms, he panted faintly:—

'My feet are weary for the turning. Pray ye, kind mother, that this road end soon.'

'What! shall I hurry mine own damnation?' gurgled the other (his tongue by then was clacking in his mouth). 'Trippingly, I warrant, shall ye take that path, unheeding of the poor wretch that lags a million miles behind lashed by a storm of scorpions.'

'Marry, sweet,' whispered the boy, smiling; 'I'll wait thee, never fear, when once I see my way. How could I forego such witness as thou to my brave intentions? We'll jog the road together, while I shield thy back.'

'Well, let be,' said Cicca. 'Better they stung that, than my heart through thine arm'—whereat Bernardo nipped him feebly in an ecstasy of tears.

In the first hours of their fearful doom he was more full of wonder than alarm—astounded, in the swooning sense. He had not come yet to realise the mortal nature of their punishment. How should he, innocent of harm? Attributing, as he did, this sudden blow to Bona, he marvelled only how so kind a mother could chastise so sharply for a little offence—or none. Indeed he was conscious of none; though conscious enough, latterly, poor child, of an atmosphere of grievance. Well, the provocation had been his, no doubt—somehow. He had learned enough of woman in these months to know that the measure of her resentment was not always the measure of the fault—how she would sometimes stab deeper for a disappointment than for a wrong. He had disappointed her in some way. No doubt, his favour being so high, he had presumed upon it. A useful rebuke, then. He would bear his imposition manly; but he hoped, he did hope, that not too much of it would be held to have purged his misconduct. The Duke was returning shortly. Perhaps he would plead for him.

So sweetly and so humbly he estimated his own insignificance. Could his foul slanderers have read his heart then, they had surely raved upon God, in their horror, to strike them, instant and for ever, from the rolls of self-conscious existence.

Cicada listened to him, and gnawed his knotted knuckles in the gloom, and wondered when and how he should dare to curse him with the truth. He might at least have spared himself that agony. The truth, to one so true, could not long fail of revealing itself. And when it came, lo! he welcomed it, as always, for a friend.

Small birds, small flowers, small wants perish of a little neglect. His sun, his sustenance, were scarce withheld a few hours from this sensitive plant before he began to droop. And ever, with the fading of his mortal tissues, the glow of the intelligence within seemed to grow brighter, until verily the veins upon his temples appeared to stand out, like mystic writing on a lighted porcelain lamp.

So it happened that, as he and his companion were sitting apart on the filthy stones late on the noon of the second day of their imprisonment, he ended a long silence by creeping suddenly to the Fool's knees, and, looking up into the Fool's face in the dim twilight, appealed to its despair with a tremulous smile.

'Cicca,' he whispered, 'my Cicca; wilt thou listen, and not be frightened?'

'To what?' muttered the other hoarsely.

'Hush, dear!' said the boy, fondling him, and whimpering—not for himself. 'I have been warned—some one hath warned me—that it were well if we fed not our hearts with delusive hopes of release herefrom.'

'Why not?' said the Fool. 'It is the only food we are like to have.'

'Ah!'

He clung suddenly to his friend in a convulsion of emotion.

'You have guessed? It is true. Capello. We might have known, being here; but—O Cicca! are you sorry? We have an angel with us—he spoke to me just now.'

'Christ?'

'Yes, Christ, dearest.'

The Fool, smitten to intolerable anguish, put him away, and, scrambling to his feet, went up and down, raving and sobbing:—

'The vengeance of God on this wicked race! May it fester in madness, living; and, dead, go down to torment so unspeakable, that——'

The boy, sprung erect, white and quivering, struck in:—

'Ah, no, no! Think who it is that hears thee!'

Cicada threw himself at his feet, pawing and lamenting:—

'Thou angel! O, woe is me! that ever I were born to see this thing!'

So they subsided in one grief, rocking and weeping together.

'O, sweet!' gasped the boy—'that ever I were born to bring this thing on thee!'

Then, at that, the Fool wrapped him in his arms, adoring and fondling him, to a hurry of sighs and broken exclamations.

'On me!—Child, that I am thought worthy!—too great a joy—mightst have been alone—yet did I try to save thee—heaven's mercy that, failing, I am involved!'

And so, easing himself for the first time, in an ecstasy of emotion he told all he knew about the fatal ring, and his efforts to recover it.

Bernardo listened in wonder.

'This ring!' he whispered at the end. 'Right judgment on me for my wicked negligence. Why, I deserve to die. Yet—' he clung a little closer—'Cicca,' he thrilled, 'it is the Duke, then, hath committed us to this?'

Cicada moaned, beating his forehead:—

'Ay, ay! it is the Duke. So I kill thy last hope!'

'Nay, thou reviv'st it.'

'How?' He stared, holding his breath.

'O, my dear!' murmured the boy rapturously; 'since thou acquittest *her* of this unkindness.'

'Her? Whom? *Unkindness!*' cried the Fool. 'Expect nothing of Bona but acquiescence in thy fate.'

'Yet is she guiltless of designing it.'

'Guiltless? Ay, guiltless as she who, raving, "that my shame should bear this voice and none to silence it!" accepts the hired midwife's word that her womb hath dropped dead fruit! O!' he mourned most bitterly, 'I loved thee, and I love; yet now, I swear I wish thee dead!'

'Then, indeed, thou lovest me.'

'Had it come to this, in truth?'

'Alas! I know not what you mean. My mother is my mother still.'

'Thy mother! I am thy mother.'

'Ah!' Laughing and weeping, he caught the gruff creature in his arms:—'Cicca, that sweet, fond comedy!'

The other put him away again, but very gently, and rose to his feet.

'Comedy?' he muttered; 'ay, a comedy—true—a masque of clowns. Yet I've played the woman for thy sake.'

Bernardo stared at him, his face twitching.

'Thou hast, dear—so tragically—and in that garb! I would I could have seen thee in it. O! a churl to laugh, dear Cicca; but——'

'But what?'

'*Thou*, a woman!'

He fell into a little irresistible chuckle. Strange wafts of tears and laughter seemed to sing in the drowsy chambers of his brain.

'*Thou* a woman!' he giggled hysterically.

The Fool gave a sudden cry.

'Why not? Have I betrayed my child?'

He turned, as if sore stricken, and went up and down, up and down, wringing his hands and moaning.

Suddenly he came and threw himself on his knees before the boy, but away from him, and knelt there, rocking and protesting, his face in his hands.

'Ah! let me be myself at last. That disguise—thou mockest—'twas none. Worn like a fool—mayhap—unpractised—yet could I have kissed its skirted hem. I am a woman, though a Fool—what's odd in that?—a woman, dear, a woman, a woman!'

He bowed himself, lower, lower, as if his shame were crushing him. In the deep silence that followed, Bernardo, trembling all through, crept a foot nearer, and paused.

'Mother?' cried the Fool, still crouching, his head deeper abased; 'no name for me. Cry on—cry scorn, in thy hunger, on this lying dam! No drop to cool thy drought in all her withered pastures.'

He writhed, and struck his chest, in pain intolerable.

'Mother!' thrilled the boy, loud and sudden.

The Fool gave a quick gasp, and started, and shrunk away.

'Not I. Keep off! I am as Filippo made me—after his own image. He was a God—could name me man or woman. 'Twas but a word; and lo! too hideous for my sex, I leapt, his male Fool. That, of all jests, was his first. He spared me for it. I had been strangled else.'

'Mother!'

Again that moving, rapturous cry,

'No, no!' cried the Fool. 'Barren—barren—no woman, even! Still as God wrought me, and human taste condemned. Let be. Forget what I said. Let me go on and serve thee—sexless—only to myself confessing, not thou awarding. I ask no more, nor sweeter—O my babe, my babe!'

'Mother!'

'Hush! break not my heart—not yet. This darkness? Speak it once more. Why, I might be beautiful. Will you think it—will you, letting me ply you with my conscious sweets? I could try. I've studied in the markets. Your starving rogue's the best connoisseur of savours. I'll not come near you— only sigh and soothe. I'll tune myself to speak so soft—school myself out of your knowledge. Perchance, God helping, you shall think me fair.'

'Mother!'

Once more—and he was in her arms.

Surely the loveliest miracle that could have blossomed in that grave—a breaking of roses from the pilgrim's dead staff!

Henceforth Bernardo's path was rapture—a song of love and jubilance— his spirit flamed and trembled out in song.

They had spared him his lute; and his fingers, strong in their instinct to the last, were seldom long parted from its strings. He lay much in his Fool mother's lap; and one had scarcely known when their converse melted into music, or out of music into speech, so melodious was their love, so rapt their soul-union, and so triumphant over pain and darkness, as to evoke of fell circumstance its own balm-breathing, illuminating spirits. What was this horror of bleak, black burial, when at a word, a struck chord, one could see it quiver and break into a garden of splendid fancies!

Once only was their dying exaltation recalled to earth—to consciousness of their near escape from all its hate and squalor. It happened in a moment; and so shall suffer but a moment's record.

There came a sudden laugh and flare—and there was Tassino, torch in hand, looking from the grate above.

'Ehi, Messer Bembo!' yapped the cur; 'art there? And I here? What does omnipotence in this reverse? Arise, and prove thyself. Lucia's dead; the Duke's returned; Milan is itself again. The memory of thee rots in the gutter; and stinks—fah! I go to the Duchess soon. What message to her, bastard of an Abbot?'

The boy raised his head.

'The season's, Tassino,' he whispered, smiling. 'Peace and goodwill.'

The filthy creature mouthed and snarled.

'Ay. Most sweet. I'll wait thine agony, though, before I give it. She'll cry, then; and I shall be by; and, look you, emotion is the mother of desire. I'll pillow her upon thy corpse, bastard, and quicken her with new lust of wickedness. She'll never have loved me more. God! what a use for a saint!'

Cicada crawled, and rose, from under her sweet burden.

'Wait,' she hissed; 'the grate's open. A strong leap, and I have him.'

An idle threat; but enough to make the whelp start, and clap to the bars, and fly screaming.

The Fool returned, panting, to her charge.

'Forget him,' she said.

'I have forgotten him, my mother. But his lie— —'

'Yes?'

'Was it a lie?'

'About Bona? I am a woman now. I'll answer nothing for my sex.'

'I'll answer for her. About my father, I meant?'

'As thou'lt answer for her, so will I for him.'

Bernardo sighed, and lay a long while silent. Suddenly he moaned in her arms, like a child over-tired, and spoke the words already quoted:—'My feet are weary for the turning.'

'Death is Love's seed—a sweet child quickened of ourselves. He comes to us, his pink hands full of flowers. "See, father, see, mother," says he, "the myrtles and the orange blooms which made fragrant your bridal bed. I am their fruit—the full maturity of Love's promise. Will you not kiss your little son, and come with him to the wise gardens where he ripened? 'Tis cold in this dark room!"'

So, in such rhapsodies, 'in love with tuneful death,' would he often murmur, or melt, through them, into song as strange.

> 'Love and Forever would wed
> Fearless in Heaven's sight.
> Life came to them and said,
> "Lease ye my house of light!"

He put them on earth to bed,
All in the noonday bright:
"Sooth," to Forever Love said,
"Here may we prosper right."

Sudden, day waned and fled:
Truth saw Forever in night.
"We are deceived," he said;
"Who shall pity our plight?"

Death, winging by o'erhead,
Heard them moan in affright.
"Hold by my hem," he said;
"I go the way to light."'

All the last day Cicada held him in her arms, so quiet, so motionless, that the gradual running down of his pulses was steadily perceptible to her. She felt Death stealing in, like a ghostly dawn—watched its growing glimmer with a fierce, hard-held agony. Once, before their scrap of daylight failed them, she stole her wrist to her mouth, and bit at it secretly, savagely, drawing a sluggish trickle of red. She had thought him sunk beyond notice of her; and started, and hid away the wound, as he put up a gentle, exhausted arm, detaining hers.

'Sting'st thyself, scorpion?'

Cicada gave a thick crow—merciful God! it was meant for a laugh—and began to screak and mumble some legend of a bird that, in difficult times, would bleed itself to feed its young—a most admirable lesson from Nature. The child laughed in his turn—poor little croupy mirth—and answered with a story: how the right and left hands once had a dispute as to which most loved and served the other, each asserting that he would cut himself off in proof of his devotion. Which being impracticable, it was decided that the right should sever the left, and the left the right; whereof the latter stood the test first without a wince. But, lo! when it came to the left's turn, there was no right hand to carve him.

'Anan?' croaked Cicada sourly.

'Why,' said Bernardo, 'we will exchange the wine of our veins, if you like, to prove our mutual devotion; but, if I suck all thine first, there will be no suck left in thy lips to return the compliment on me.'

'Need'st not take all; but enough to handicap thee, so that we start this backward journey on fair terms.'

'Nay, it were so sweet, I'd prove a glutton did I once begin. Cicca?'

'My babe?'

'Canst thou see Christ?'

'Ay, in the white mirror of thy face.'

'I see Him so plain. He stands behind thee now—a boy, mine own age. Nay, He puts His finger on His sweet lips, and smiles and goes. "Naughty," that means: "shall I stay to hear thee flatter me?" He blushes, like a boy, to be praised. He's gone no further than the wall. Cicca, thy disguise was deep. I never thought thee beautiful before. O, what an unkind mother, to hide her beauty from her boy!'

'Am I beautiful?'

'Dost not know it? As the moon that rises on the night. It was night just now, and my soul was groping in the dark; and, lo! of a sudden thou wert looking down.'

'Let it be night, I say!'

'What is that in thy voice? I am so happy—always; only not when I think of Carlo. My dear, dear Carlo! Alas! what have they done with him? He will often think of us, and wonder where we are, and frown and gnaw his lip. If I could but hear him speak once more—cry "Bernardo!" in that voice that made one's eyeballs crack like glass, and tickle in their veins. O, my sweet Carlo! Mother, have I failed in everything?'

'Let be! Thou'lt kill me with thy prattle. Thy Christ remains behind. He'll see thy seed is honoured in its fruits.'

'Well, wilt thou kiss me good-night? I'm sleepy.'

He seemed to doze a good deal after that. But, about midnight, it might be, he suddenly sat up, and was singing strongly to his lute—a sweet, unearthly song, of home-returning and farewell. Cicada clung and held him, held to him, pierced all through with the awful rapture of that moment.

'Leave me not: wait for me!' she whispered, sobbing.

Suddenly, in a vibrating pause, a faint far cry was wafted to their ears:—

'Bernardo! Bernardo!'

The fingers tumbled on the lute, plucking its music into a tangle of wild discords. A string snapped.

'Carlo!' he screamed—'it is Carlo!'

The cry leapt, and fell, and eddied away in a long rosary of echoes. The Fool fumbled for his lips with hers.

But who might draw death from that sweet frozen spring!

She feared nothing now but that they would come and take him from her—snarled, holding him, when her one sick glint of day stole in to cross her vigil—was in love with utter solitude and blind night. Once, after a little or a long time—it was all one to her—she saw a thread of ghostly whiteness moving on the floor; watched it with basilisk eyes; thought, perhaps, it was his soul, lingering for hers according to its promise. The moving spot came on—stole into the wan, diffused streak of light cast from the grating;—and it was a great rat, with something bound about its neck.

She understood on the instant. Long since, her instinctive wit had told her—though she had not cared or been concerned to listen to it—that that sudden voice in the darkness had signified that Carlo was imprisoned somewhere hard by. Well, he had found this means to communicate with her—near a miracle, it might be; but miracles interested her no longer. No harm to let him know at last. *He* could not rob her of her dead.

She coaxed the creature to her; found him tame; read the message; re-fastened on the paper, and, by its glimmer, marked the way of his return.

Then she rose, and spoke, and, speaking, choked and died.

In the dark all cats are grey, and all women beautiful. But I think the countenance of this one had no need to fear the dawn.

CHAPTER XXVI

Amongst all her costly possessions in the Casa Caprona, there had once been none so loved, so treasured, so often consulted by Beatrice as a certain portrait of the little Parablist of San Zeno, which she had bought straight from the studio of its limner, Messer Antonello da Messina, at that time temporarily sojourning in Milan. This was the artist, pupil of Jan Van Eyck, who had been the first to introduce oil-painting into Italy; and the portrait was executed in the new medium. It was a work perpetrated *con amore*—one of the many in which the exaltation of the moment had sought to express itself in pigments, or marble, or metal. For, indeed, during that short spring of his promise, Bernardo's flower-face had come to blossom in half the crafts of the town.

Technically, perhaps, a little wan and flat, the head owed something, nevertheless, to inspiration. Through the mere physical beauty of its features, one might read the sorrow of a spiritual incarnation—the wistfulness of a Christ-converted Eros of the ancient cosmogonies. Here were the right faun's eyes, brooding pity out of laughter; the rather square jaw, and girlish pointed chin; the baby lips that seemed to have kissed themselves, shape and tint, out of spindle-berries; the little strutting cap and quill even, so queerly contrasted with the staid sobriety of the brow beneath. It was the boy, and the soul of the boy, so far as enthusiasm, working through a strange medium, could interpret it.

Beatrice, having secured, had hung the picture in a dim alcove of her chamber; and had further, to ensure its jealous privacy from all inquisition but her own, looped a curtain before. Here, then, a dozen times a day, when alone, had she been wont to pray and confess herself; lust with her finger-tips to charm the barren contours of the face into life; lay her hot cheek to the painted flesh, and weep, and woo, and appeal to it; seek to soften by a hundred passionate artifices the inflexible continence of its gaze.

But that had been all before the shock and frenzy of her final repulse. Not once since had she looked on it, until...

Came upon her, still crouching self-absorbed, that white morning of the Duke's tragedy; and, on the vulture wings of it, Narcisso.

The beast crept to her, fulsome, hoarse, shaken with a heart-ague. She conned him with a contemptuous curiosity, as he stood unnerved, trembling all through, before her.

'Well?' she said at last.

He grinned and gobbled, gulping for articulation.

'It's come, Madonna.'

She half rose on her couch, frowning and impatient.

'What, thou sick fool?'

'Sick!' he echoed loudly; and then his voice fell again. 'Ay, sick to death, I think. The Duke——'

'What of him?'

'Rides to San Stefano.'

'Does he?'

'He'll not ride home again.'

She stared at him in silence a moment; then suddenly breathed out a little wintry laugh.

'So?' she whispered—'So? Well, thou art not the Duke.'

He struggled to clear, and could not clear, his throat. His low forehead, for all the cold, was beaded with sweat.

'All's one for that,' he muttered thickly. 'There's no class in carrion.'

She still conned him, with that frigid smile on her lips.

'Dost mean they'll seek to kill thee too?'

He clawed at his head in a frenzy.

'Ay, I mean it.'

'Why?'

'Why? quotha. Why, won't they have held me till this moment for one of themselves?'

'Till this moment?' she murmured. 'Ah! I see; this Judas who hath not the courage to play out his part.'

'My part!' He almost screamed it at last. 'Was death my part?' He writhed and snuffled. 'I tell thee, I've but now left them, on pretence of going before to the church. Shall I be there? God's death! Let but this stroke win through and gain the people, and my life's not worth a stinking sprat.'

She sank back with a sigh.

'Better, in that case, to have joined thy friends at San Stefano.'

The rogue, staring at her a moment, uttered a mortal cry:—

'Thou say'st it—*thou?*—Judas?—Who made me so?—Show me my thirty pieces—Judas? Ay; and what for wages?—Thy tool and catspaw—I see it all at last—thine and Ludovic's—bled, and my carcass thrown to swine!—Judas? Why, I might have been Judas to some purpose with the Duke—a made man by now. And all for thee foregone; and in the end by thee betrayed. I asked nothing—gave all for nothing—ass—goose—cried quack and quack, as told—decoy to these fine fowl, and, being used, my neck wrung with the rest. Now——'

She put up a hand peremptorily. The fury simmered down on his lips.

'You presume, fellow,' she said. '*I* betray *thee?*'

She raised her brows, amazed. Too stupendous an instance of condescension, indeed.

He slunk down on his knees before her, cringing and praying.

'No, Madonna, no! I spake out of my great madness.'

'Answer me,' she said disdainfully, 'out of thy little reason. What wouldst thou of me?'

He lifted his shaking hands.

'Sanctuary, sanctuary. Let me hide here.'

He crawled to her, pawing like a beaten dog.

'Sanctuary,' he reiterated brokenly. 'You owe it me—that at least. I've bided, bided—and ye made no sign—yielded all for guerdon of a sweet word, the whiles I thought thyself and Ludovic were stalking that conspiracy to cut it off betimes. God's death! Not you. And now I know the reason. Now comes the reckoning, and I'm left to face it as I will. God's death!' His panic mastered him again. 'What of my substance have I changed for nothing! There was Bona's ring—I might have lived ten year on't. And I parted with it—for what? O, you're a serpent, mistress! You worm your way—and get it too. What! Bona may bide a little, and Simonetta? They're but the bleeding trunk. The head's lopped while I talk.'

His voice rose to a screech—broke—and he grovelled before her.

'Mercy, Madonna. Spare me to be thy slave. All comes thy way—love, and revenge, and power. The boy's dead—the Duke's to die——'

He had roused her at last, and in a flash. She sprang to her feet, white, hardly breathing.

'The boy?' she hissed; 'what boy?'

He whimpered, sprawling:—

'God a' mercy! Lady, lady! the boy, the very boy you sped the ring to kill.'

'Dead!' she whispered.

'Ay,' he snivelled from the ground; 'what would you? dead as last Childermas—starved to death, in the "Hermit's Cell" they call it, by the Duke's orders.'

Her fingers battled softly with her throat.

'Dead!' she said again. 'Narcisso, good Narcisso, who hath gulled thee with this lie?'

'No lie,' he answered, squatting, reassured, on his hams. ''Twas Messer Tassino, no less, that carried thy token to Vigevano. 'Twas no later than yesternight I met our fine cockerel louping from the stews. A' was drunk as father Noah—babbled and blabbed, a' did—perked up a's comb, and cursed me for presuming fellowship with a duke's minion. I plied him further, e'en to tears and confidence—had it all out of him; how a'd carried the ring for Messer Ludovic, and brought back the deadly order. Jacopo nipped the Saint that noon. A's singing in paradise these days past.'

Beatrice stood and listened. A dreadful smile was on her lips. But, when she spoke, it was with wooing softness.

'Good trust—always the faithful trust. Why, Narcisso, what should I do betraying thee? We'll work and end together, and take our wages. Dead, do you say? Why, then, all's said. Now go, and tuck thyself within the roof till the storm pass. This lightning's all below. Go, comrade, do you hear?'

He dwelt a moment only to gasp and mumble out his thanks; then turned and slouched away.

For minutes she dwelt as he had left her, rigid, smiling, bloodless. Presently, still standing motionless, she moved her lips and was muttering:—

'Dead? So swift? Made sure against all chances? Starved? He said starved. Not to that I betrayed him. Inhuman hound! Thou mightst have spared him bread!—left sorrow and cold durance to work their lingering end. What then? Why, Bona then—Bona made widow; free to work her will. Should *I* be the better?—Dead? was he not always dead to me? Starved to death! O, hell heat Lampugnani's dagger scarlet, that it hiss and bubble in his flesh! Galeazzo! Galeazzo! I'll follow soon to nurse thy pains to ecstasy!'

She fell silent; presently began to sway; then, with a sudden shriek, had leapt upon the picture, and torn aside its curtain.

'Bernardo!' she moaned and sobbed—'Bernardo, I loved thee! O God! he eats me with his eyes. Here, here! fasten with thy starved lips. I'll not speak or cry, though they burrow to my heart. All thine—hold on—I'll smile and pet mine agony—Bernardo——!'

In the tumult of her passion she heard a sound at the door; caught her breath; caught herself to knowledge of herself, and, instinctively closing the curtain, stood panting, dishevelled, its hem in her hand.

Someone, something, had entered—a haggard, unshorn ghost of ancient days. It came very softly, closing the door behind; then, set and silent, moved upon her. Her pulses seemed to sink and wither.

'Carlo!' she shuddered softly.

It was fearful that the thing never spoke as it came on. Nor did she speak again. Love that has once joined keeps understanding without words. What has it bred but death? Here was the natural fruit of a sin matured—she saw it gleam suddenly in his clutch.

She watched fascinated. As he drew near, without a word she slowly raised her hands, and rent from her bosom its already desecrated veil. Then at last she spoke—or whispered:—

'I'm ready. Here's where you kissed and sighed. Bloody thy bed.'

He took her to his remorseless grasp. She had often thrilled to know her helplessness therein—wondered what it would be to feel it closed in hate. Now she had her knowledge—and instantly, in an ecstasy of terror, succumbed to it.

'No, no!' she gasped. 'Carlo, don't kill me!'

Voiceless still, he raised his hand. She gave a fearful scream.

'I never meant it. I'm innocent. Not without a word. Carlo! Carlo!—I loved him!'

Writhing in her agony, she tore herself free a moment, and sank at his feet, rending, as she fell, the curtain from its rings. His back was to the wall. In a mirror opposite he caught the sudden vision of his intent, and, looking down upon it, dim and spiritual, the sweet face of the Saint.

The dagger dropped from his hand.

The silence of a minute seemed to draw into an age.

Suddenly he was groping and stumbling like a drunken man. Words came to him in a babble:—

'Let be!—I'll go—spare her?—Where's thy Christ? He forgave too—I'm coming—answer for me—here!'

And he drove a staggering course from the room.

Tears began to gush from her as she lay prone. Then suddenly, in a quick impulse, she rose to her feet, and re-veiling the picture, turned with her back to it.

'Ludovic remains,' she whispered.

Reeling, dancing, to himself it seemed, Carlo passed down the streets. White was on the ground; his brain was thick with whirling flakes; the roar of coming waters tingled in his veins. Sometimes he would pause and look stupidly at his right hand, as if in puzzle of its emptiness. There should have been something there—what was it?—a knife—a stone for two birds—Beatrice—and then Galeazzo. What had he omitted? He must go back and pick up the thread from the beginning.

The waters came on as he stood, not close yet, but portentous, with a threatening roar. A crying shape, waving a bloody blade, sped towards and past him.

'Arm, arm, for liberty!' it yelled as it ran. 'Tyranny is dead!'

Carlo chuckled thickly to himself.

'That was Olgiati. What does he with my dagger? I'll go and take it from him.'

He turned, swaying, and in the act was swept upon, enveloped, and washed over by the torrent. It stranded him against a wall, where he stood blinking and giggling in the vortex of a multitudinous roar.

'Murdered! the Duke! Murdered! Close the gates!'

It thundered on and away. He looked at his hand once more; then turned for home.

CHAPTER XXVII

Murdered? Ay; struck down in a moment on the threshold of God's house, lest his bloody footsteps entering should desecrate its pavement; snatched away to perdition from under the very shadows of stone saints, the gleam of the golden doors fading out of the horror of his fading eyes. He had had but time for one cry—'O Mother of God!'—a soul-clutch as wild as when a drowning man grasps at a flowering reed. In vain; he is under; the fair blossom whisks erect again, dashing the tears from her eyes; the white face far below is a stone among the stones.

'*So passeth the world's glory!*'

The choir sang, the organ thundered on; and still their blended fervour, while the dead body was relaxing and settling into the pool itself had made, rose poignant, sharper, more unearthly, piercing with tragic utterance its own burden, until at length, flood crashing upon flood, the roar of human passion below burst and overwhelmed it.

What had happened?

This.

As the Duke entered the church by the west door, a full-bodied gentleman, dressed all in mail, with a jaque of crimson satin, had stepped from the crowd to make a way for him; which having affected to do, he had turned, and raising his velvet beret with his left hand, and dropping on one knee as if to crave some boon, had swiftly driven a dagger into Galeazzo's body, and again, as the Duke fell away from the stroke, freeing the blade, into his throat. Whereat, springing on the mortal cry that followed, flew other sparks of crimson from the body of the spectators, and pierced the doomed man with vicious stings, labouring out cries as they stabbed:—

'For my sister!'

'For liberty!'—until the hilts slipping in their fingers sent their aims wavering.

It was all the red act of a moment—the lancing of a ripened abscess—the gush, the scream, the silence.

And then, the sudden stun and stupefaction yielding to mad tumult.

None might know the gross body of this terror; only for the moment red coats and their partisans seemed paramount. But for the moment. The next, the scarlet clique seemed to break up and scatter, like a ball of red clay in a swirl of waters, and, flying on all sides, was caught and held in isolated particles among the throng. Whereat, for the first time, authority began to feel its paralysed wits, and to counter-shriek the desperate appeals of murder to rally and combine for liberty. A mighty equerry of the Duke, one da Ripa, fought, bellowing and struggling, to pull out his sword. Francione, a fellow of Visconti's, stabbed him under the armpit, and he wobbled and dropped amid the screaming crush, grinning horribly. Lampugnani, smiling and insinuative, slipped into a wailing group of women, and urged his soft passage through it, making for the door. He was almost out when, catching his foot in a skirt plucked sickly from his passing, he stumbled and rolled; and the spear of a giant Moor, who on the instant mounted the steps, passed through his throat.

His body was first-fruits to the frenzied people without. They seized and bowled it through the streets, whacking it into shreds; then returned, breathed and blooded, for more. They were in high feather, ripe for prey and plunder. Galeazzo was dead! Viv' Anarchia!

They pressed their way into the tumult; snatched gems and trinkets from the hair and bosoms of girls half mad with terror; took their brief toll of dainties, and only fell away, pushing and gabbling, before the onset of the ducal guard.

Order followed presently; and then the tally and reckoning. The last fell swift enough to crown an orgy of perfection: screams in the squares; dismembered limbs; mangled scarecrows tossing in file from the battlements. Only two principals, Olgiati and Visconti, escaping for the moment, were reserved for later torments. A conspiracy, like near all blood conspiracies, abortive; founded on the common error that slaves abhor their bonds. They do not, in this world of unequal gifts and taxes. Moreover, it is inconsistent to suppose one can inaugurate an era of tolerance with murder.

Olgiati, the last of that dark band to suffer, was also its only martyr. He had struck for a principle, straight in itself, oblique in its fanatic workings. Cursed by his father, abandoned by his friends and relatives, committed to unspeakable tortures, his courage never blenched or wavered. He gloried in his deed to the last; and, if a prayer escaped him, it was only that his executioners should vouchsafe him strength at the end to utter forth his soul in prayer. To Bona he sent a gentle message, deprecating his own instrumentality in the inevitable retributions of Providence. She answered, saintly vengeance, with a priest, urging him to save his soul by penitence.

He retorted that, by God's mercy, his final deed should serve his sins for all atonement; and, so insisting, was carried to his mortal mangling. At the last moment a cry escaped him: 'Mors acerba: fama perpetua!' and, with that, and the shriek of 'Courage, Girolamo!' on his lips, he passed to his account.

'The peace of Italy is dead!' cried Pope Sixtus on the day when news of the crime was brought to him. His prophecy found its first justification in a fervent appeal from the Duchess of Milan that he would posthumously absolve of his sins the man whom 'next to God she had loved above all else in the world.'

And no doubt, being left to the present mercy of factions, she believed it.

EPILOGUE

Long after the body of that tragedy had been committed to its eternal sleep, silently and by night, under the pavement of the vast cathedral; long after, in years so remote that the very bones of it, crumbling into ashes, might hardly be distinguished from the fibrous weeds of the golden shroud in which they had first been laid, fit moral to the deadly irony of human glory; long after, when the rise and fall of Ludovico Sforza, ripe achievement of his house and race, were already grown a tale for the wind to sob and whisper through lonely keyholes of a winter's night, there survived in Lombard legend the story of a marvellous boy, who, coming to earth and Milan once upon a time with some strange message of Christ in Arcady, had taken the winter in men's hearts with a brief St. Martin's summer of delight, and had so, in the bright morning of his promise, been snatched back to the heaven's nursery from which he had estrayed, leaving faint echoes of divinity in his wake. It whispered of a tomb, to which old tyranny had consigned this embodied angel, found emptied, like its sacred prototype's; and of the awe thereat which had fallen on its searchers. A fable, scared away at first in the strenuous roar of Time struggling for the mastery of great events; yet, in the later days of peace, still to be heard, very faint and far like a lark's song, dropping from the clouds.

Sweet music, but a fable; and therefore more potent than reality to move men's hearts. Beatitudes are pronounced on things less tangible. Had Bernardo preached a creed more orthodox, he had been at this day a calendared saint on the strength of it. But he had only interpreted the human Christ to a people his prince and comrade had wrought to redeem.

There had been those who—unless crushed under the fall of the tyranny which had sustained them—might have nipped the legend at its sprouting; telling how, on the night of that first dark and dire confusion, a cavalier, taking advantage of the brief anarchy that reigned, had appeared, with a force of his adherents, before the provost-marshal of that date, and had demanded of his hands the body of the martyred boy; how, kissing and wrapping the poor corpse in a costly cloak, this cavalier had lifted it with giant strength to his pommel, and, dismissing his silent followers, had ridden forth with his burden into the snowy darkness of the plains; how, in the ghostly dawn of a winter's morning, there had broken tears and wailing from a spectral throng gathered about the portal of an abbey in the distant hills; how, when presently the spring came with music of birds and gushing waters, there were no turves so green, no daisies so lush and fearless in all the monastic God's-acre, as those which the heart-stricken sorrow and tenderness of a newly received brother had brought to cover the grave of one, the youngest and most innocent of all the silent community gathered thereto.

God rest thee, Carlo! Peace to thy faithful, passionate heart.

An imperishable love, whose fruits, descended from that ancient stock, we eat to-day.

But the body of the Fool, flung into a pit, was the carrion which first enriched its roots.